WORLD
CULTURAL HERITAGE LIBRARY

MARK TWAIN
A DOG'S TALE
AND OTHER STORIES

PUBLISHED FIRST: 1904
REPRINT 2018 ISBN: 1-4330-9023-6

A DOG'S TALE
AND OTHER STORIES

TABLE OF CONTENTS

MARK TWAIN

Born	Samuel Langhorne Clemens November 30, 1835 Florida, Missouri, U.S.
Died	April 21, 1910 (aged 74) Redding, Connecticut, U.S.
Resting place	Woodlawn Cemetery, Elmira, New York, U.S.
Pen name	Mark Twain
Occupation	Writer, humorist, entrepreneur, publisher, lecturer
Notable works	Adventures of Huckleberry Finn The Adventures of Tom Sawyer
Spouse	Olivia Langdon Clemens (m. 1870; her death 1904)
Children	4 (including Susy, Clara, and Jean)
Relatives	John Marshall Clemens (father) Orion Clemens (brother)

BIOGRAPHIC INFORMATION

Samuel Langhorne Clemens (November 30, 1835 – April 21, 1910), better known by his pen name **Mark Twain**, was an American writer, humorist, entrepreneur, publisher, and lecturer. Among his novels are *The Adventures of Tom Sawyer* (1876) and its sequel, the *Adventures of Huckleberry Finn* (1885), the latter often called "The Great American Novel".

Twain was raised in Hannibal, Missouri, which later provided the setting for *Tom Sawyer* and *Huckleberry Finn*. He served an apprenticeship with a printer and then worked as a typesetter, contributing articles to the newspaper of his older brother Orion Clemens. He later became a riverboat pilot on the Mississippi River before heading west to join Orion in Nevada. He referred humorously to his lack of success at mining, turning to journalism for the Virginia City *Territorial Enterprise*. His humorous story, "The Celebrated Jumping Frog of Calaveras County", was published in 1865, based on a story that he heard at Angels Hotel in Angels Camp, California where he had spent some time as a miner. The short story brought international attention and was even translated into French. His wit and satire, in prose and in speech, earned praise from critics and peers, and he was a friend to presidents, artists, industrialists, and European royalty.

Twain earned a great deal of money from his writings and lectures, but he invested in ventures that lost most of it—notably the Paige Compositor, a mechanical typesetter that failed because of its complexity and imprecision. He filed for bankruptcy in the wake of these financial setbacks, but he eventually overcame his financial troubles with the help of Henry Huttleston Rogers. He chose to pay all his pre-bankruptcy creditors in full, even after he had no legal responsibility to do so.

Twain was born shortly after an appearance of Halley's Comet, and he predicted that he would "go out with it" as well; he died the day after the comet returned. He was lauded as the "greatest humorist this country has produced",and William Faulkner called him "the father of American literature"

Mark Twain was born Samuel Langhorne Clemens on November 30, 1835 in Florida, Missouri, the sixth of seven children born to Jane (*née* Lampton; 1803–1890), a native of Kentucky, and John Marshall Clemens (1798–1847), a native of Virginia. His parents met when his father moved to Missouri, and they were married in 1823. Twain was of Cornish, English, and Scots-Irish descent. Only three of his siblings survived childhood: Orion (1825–1897), Henry (1838–1858), and Pamela (1827–1904). His sister Margaret (1830–1839) died when Twain was three, and his brother Benjamin (1832–1842) died three years later. His brother Pleasant Hannibal (1828) died at three weeks of age.

When he was four, Twain's family moved to Hannibal, Missouri, a port town on the Mississippi River that inspired the fictional town of St. Petersburg in *The Adventures of Tom Sawyer* and the *Adventures of Huckleberry Finn*. Slavery was legal in Missouri at the time, and it became a theme in these writings. His father was an attorney and judge, who died of pneumonia in 1847, when Twain was 11. The next year, Twain left school after the fifth grade to become a printer's apprentice. In 1851 he began working as a typesetter, contributing articles and humorous sketches to the *Hannibal Journal*, a newspaper that Orion owned. When he was 18, he left Hannibal and worked as a printer in New York City, Philadelphia, St. Louis, and Cincinnati, joining the newly formed International Typographical Union, the printers trade union. He educated himself in public libraries in the evenings, finding wider information than at a conventional school.

Twain describes his boyhood in *Life on the Mississippi*, stating that "there was but one permanent ambition" among his comrades: to be a steamboatman.

> Pilot was the grandest position of all. The pilot, even in those days of
> trivial wages, had a princely salary – from a hundred and fifty to two
> hundred and fifty dollars a month, and no board to pay.

As Twain describes it, the pilot's prestige exceeded that of the captain. The pilot had to:

...get up a warm personal acquaintanceship with every old snag and one-limbed cottonwood and every obscure wood pile that ornaments the banks of this river for twelve hundred miles; and more than that, must... actually know where these things are in the dark

Steamboat pilot Horace E. Bixby took Twain on as a cub pilot to teach him the river between New Orleans and St. Louis for $500, payable out of Twain's first wages after graduating. Twain studied the Mississippi, learning its landmarks, how to navigate its currents effectively, and how to read the river and its constantly shifting channels, reefs, submerged snags, and rocks that would "tear the life out of the strongest vessel that ever floated".It was more than two years before he received his pilot's license. Piloting also gave him his pen name from "mark twain", the leadsman's cry for a measured river depth of two fathoms (12 feet), which was safe water for a steamboat.

While training, Samuel convinced his younger brother Henry to work with him. Henry was killed on June 21, 1858 when their steamboat *Pennsylvania* exploded. Twain claimed to have foreseen this death in a dream a month earlier, which inspired his interest in parapsychology; he was an early member of the Society for Psychical Research. Twain was guilt-stricken and held himself responsible for the rest of his life. He continued to work on the river and was a river pilot until the Civil War broke out in 1861, when traffic was curtailed along the Mississippi River. At the start of hostilities, he enlisted briefly in a local Confederate unit. He later wrote the sketch "The Private History of a Campaign That Failed", describing how he and his friends had been Confederate volunteers for two weeks before disbanding.

He then left for Nevada to work for Orion, who was Secretary of the Nevada Territory. Twain describes the episode in his book *Roughing It*

Orion became secretary to Nevada Territory governor James W. Nye in 1861, and Twain joined him when he moved west. The brothers traveled more than two weeks on a stagecoach across the Great Plains and the Rocky Mountains, visiting the Mormon community in Salt Lake City.

Twain's journey ended in the silver-mining town of Virginia City, Nevada where he became a miner on the Comstock Lode. He failed as a miner and went to work at the Virginia City newspaper *Territorial Enterprise*, working under a friend, the writer Dan DeQuille. He first used his pen name here on February 3, 1863, when he wrote a humorous travel account entitled "Letter From Carson – re: Joe Goodman; party at Gov. Johnson's; music" and signed it "Mark Twain".

His experiences in the American West inspired *Roughing It*, written during 1870–71 and published in 1872. His experiences in Angels Camp (in Calaveras County, California) provided material for "The Celebrated Jumping Frog of Calaveras County" (1865).

Twain moved to San Francisco in 1864, still as a journalist, and met writers such as Bret Harte and Artemus Ward. He may have been romantically involved with the poet Ina Coolbrith.

His first success as a writer came when his humorous tall tale "The Celebrated Jumping Frog of Calaveras County" was published on November 18, 1865 in the New York weekly *The Saturday Press*, bringing him national attention. A year later, he traveled to the Sandwich Islands (present day Hawaii) as a reporter for the *Sacramento Union*. His letters to the *Union* were popular and became the basis for his first lectures.

In 1867, a local newspaper funded his trip to the Mediterranean aboard the *Quaker City*, including a tour of Europe and the Middle East. He wrote a collection of travel letters which were later compiled as *The Innocents Abroad* (1869). It was on this trip that he met fellow passenger Charles Langdon, who showed him a picture of his sister Olivia. Twain later claimed to have fallen in love at first sight.

Upon returning to the United States, Twain was offered honorary membership in Yale University's secret society Scroll and Key in 1868. Its devotion to "fellowship, moral and literary self-improvement, and charity" suited him well.

MARRIAGE AND CHILDREN

Twain and Olivia Langdon corresponded throughout 1868. She rejected his first marriage proposal, but they were married in Elmira, New York in February 1870, where he courted her and managed to overcome her father's initial reluctance. She came from a "wealthy but liberal family"; through her, he met abolitionists, "socialists, principled atheists and activists for women's rights and social equality", including Harriet Beecher Stowe (his next-door neighbor in Hartford, Connecticut), Frederick Douglass, and writer and utopian socialist William Dean Howells, who became a long-time friend.

wallpaper, and a hand-carved mantel purchased in Scotland

The couple lived in Buffalo, New York, from 1869 to 1871. He owned a stake in the *Buffalo Express* newspaper and worked as an editor and writer. While they were living in Buffalo, their son Langdon died of diphtheria at the age of 19 months. They had three daughters: Susy (1872–1896), Clara (1874–1962), and Jean (1880–1909).

Twain moved his family to Hartford, Connecticut, where he arranged the building of a home starting in 1873. In the 1870s and 1880s, the family summered at Quarry Farm in Elmira, the home of Olivia's sister, Susan Crane.

In 1874, Susan had a study built apart from the main house so that Twain would have a quiet place in which to write. Also, he smoked cigars constantly, and Susan did not want him to do so in her house.

Twain wrote many of his classic novels during his 17 years in Hartford (1874–1891) and over 20 summers at Quarry Farm. They include *The Adventures of Tom Sawyer* (1876), *The Prince and the Pauper* (1881), *Life on the Mississippi* (1883), *Adventures of Huckleberry Finn* (1885), and *A Connecticut Yankee in King Arthur's Court* (1889).

The couple's marriage lasted 34 years until Olivia's death in 1904. All of the Clemens family are buried in Elmira's Woodlawn Cemetery.

LOVE OF SCIENCE AND TECHNOLOGY

Twain in the lab of Nikola Tesla, early 1894

Twain was fascinated with science and scientific inquiry. He developed a close and lasting friendship with Nikola Tesla, and the two spent much time together in Tesla's laboratory.

Twain patented three inventions, including an "Improvement in Adjustable and Detachable Straps for Garments" (to replace suspenders) and a history trivia game. Most commercially successful was a self-pasting scrapbook; a dried adhesive on the pages needed only to be moistened before use. Over 25,000 were sold.

Twain's novel *A Connecticut Yankee in King Arthur's Court* (1889) features a time traveler from the contemporary U.S., using his knowledge of science to introduce modern technology to Arthurian England. This type of storyline became a common feature of the science fiction subgenre alternate history.

In 1909, Thomas Edison visited Twain at his home in Redding, Connecticut and filmed him. Part of the footage was used in *The Prince and the Pauper* (1909), a two-reel short film. It is said to be the only known existing film footage of Twain

LATER LIFE AND DEATH

Twain lived in his later years at 14 West 10th Street in Manhattan.

Twain passed through a period of deep depression which began in 1896 when his daughter Susy died of meningitis. Olivia's death in 1904 and Jean's on December 24, 1909 deepened his gloom.

On May 20, 1909, his close friend Henry Rogers died suddenly. In 1906, Twain began his autobiography in the *North American Review*. In April, he heard that his friend Ina Coolbrith had lost nearly all that she owned in the 1906 San Francisco earthquake, and he volunteered a few autographed portrait photographs to be sold for her benefit. To further aid Coolbrith, George Wharton James visited Twain in New York and arranged for a new portrait session. He was resistant initially, but he eventually admitted that four of the reulting images were the finest ones ever taken of him.

Twain formed a club in 1906 for girls whom he viewed as surrogate granddaughters called the Angel Fish and Aquarium Club. The dozen or so members ranged in age from

10 to 16. He exchanged letters with his "Angel Fish" girls and invited them to concerts and the theatre and to play games. Twain wrote in 1908 that the club was his "life's chief delight".In 1907, he met Dorothy Quick (aged 11) on a transatlantic crossing, beginning "a friendship that was to last until the very day of his death".

Oxford University awarded Twain an honorary doctorate in letters in 1907.

Twain was born two weeks after Halley's Comet's closest approach in 1835; he said in 1909:

> I came in with Halley's Comet in 1835. It is coming again next year, and I expect to go out with it. It will be the greatest disappointment of my life if I don't go out with Halley's Comet. The Almighty has said, no doubt: "Now here are these two unaccountable freaks; they came in together, they must go out together".

Twain's prediction was accurate; he died of a heart attack on April 21, 1910 in Redding, Connecticut, one day after the comet's closest approach to Earth.

Upon hearing of Twain's death, President William Howard Taft said:

> Mark Twain gave pleasure – real intellectual enjoyment – to millions, and his works will continue to give such pleasure to millions yet to come …
> His humor was American, but he was nearly as much appreciated by Englishmen and people of other countries as by his own countrymen. He has made an enduring part of American literature.

Twain's funeral was at the "Old Brick" Presbyterian Church in New York. He is buried in his wife's family plot at Woodlawn Cemetery in Elmira, New York. The Langdon family plot is marked by a 12-foot monument (two fathoms, or "mark twain") placed there by his surviving daughter Clara. There is also a smaller headstone. He expressed a preference for cremation (for example, in *Life on the Mississippi*), but he acknowledged that his surviving family would have the last word.

Officials in Connecticut and New York estimated the value of Twain's estate at $471,000 ($12,000,000 today).

WRITING

Twain began his career writing light, humorous verse, but he became a chronicler of the vanities, hypocrisies, and murderous acts of mankind. At mid-career, he combined rich humor, sturdy narrative, and social criticism in *Huckleberry Finn*. He was a master of rendering colloquial speech and helped to create and popularize a distinctive American literature built on American themes and language.

Many of his works have been suppressed at times for various reasons. The *Adventures of Huckleberry Finn* has been repeatedly restricted in American high schools, not least for its frequent use of the word "nigger", which was in common usage in the pre-Civil War period in which the novel was set.

A complete bibliography of Twain's works is nearly impossible to compile because of the vast number of pieces he wrote (often in obscure newspapers) and his use of several different pen names. Additionally, a large portion of his speeches and lectures have been lost or were not recorded; thus, the compilation of Twain's works is an ongoing process. Researchers rediscovered published material as recently as 1995 and 2015.

EARLY JOURNALISM AND TRAVELOGUES

Twain was writing for the Virginia City newspaper the *Territorial Enterprise* in 1863 when he met lawyer Tom Fitch, editor of the competing newspaper *Virginia Daily Union* and known as the "silver-tongued orator of the Pacific".He credited Fitch with giving him his "first really profitable lesson" in writing. "When I first began to lecture, and in my earlier writings," Twain later commented, "my sole idea was to make comic capital out of everything I saw and heard." In 1866, he presented his lecture on the Sandwich Islands to a crowd in Washoe City, Nevada. Afterwards, Fitch told him:

> Clemens, your lecture was magnificent. It was eloquent, moving, sincere. Never in my entire life have I listened to such a magnificent piece of descriptive narration. But you committed one unpardonable sin – the unpardonable sin. It is a sin you must never commit again. You closed a most eloquent description, by which you had keyed your audience up to a pitch of the intensest interest, with a piece of atrocious anti-climax which nullified all the really fine effect you had produced

It was in these days that Twain became a writer of the Sagebrush School; he was known later as the most notable within the genre. His first important work was "The Celebrated Jumping Frog of Calaveras County," published in the *New York Saturday Press* on November 18, 1865. After a burst of popularity, the *Sacramento Union* commissioned him to write letters about his travel experiences. The first journey that he took for this job was to ride the steamer *Ajax* on its maiden voyage to the Sandwich Islands (Hawaii). All the while, he was writing letters to the newspaper that were meant for publishing, chronicling his experiences with humor. These letters proved to be the genesis to his work with the San Francisco *Alta California* newspaper, which designated him a traveling correspondent for a trip from San Francisco to New York City via the Panama isthmus.

On June 8, 1867, he set sail on the pleasure cruiser *Quaker City* for five months, and this trip resulted in *The Innocents Abroad or The New Pilgrims' Progress*. In 1872, he published his second piece of travel literature, *Roughing It*, as an account of his journey from Missouri to Nevada, his subsequent life in the American West, and his visit to Hawaii. The book lampoons American and Western society in the same way that *Innocents* critiqued the various countries of Europe and the Middle East. His next work was *The Gilded Age: A Tale of Today*, his first attempt at writing a novel. The book is also notable because it is his only collaboration, written with his neighbor Charles Dudley Warner.

Twain's next work drew on his experiences on the Mississippi River. *Old Times on the Mississippi* was a series of sketches published in the *Atlantic Monthly* in 1875 featuring his disillusionment with Romanticism. *Old Times* eventually became the starting point for *Life on the Mississippi*.

TOM SAWYER AND *HUCKLEBERRY FINN*

 This section **needs additional citations for verification**. Please help improve this article by adding citations to reliable sources. Unsourced material may be challenged and removed. *(March 2017) (Learn how and when to remove this template message)*

Twain's next major publication was *The Adventures of Tom Sawyer*, which draws on his youth in Hannibal. Tom Sawyer was modeled on Twain as a child, with traces of schoolmates John Briggs and Will Bowen. The book also introduces Huckleberry Finn in a supporting role, based on Twain's boyhood friend Tom Blankenship.

The Prince and the Pauper was not as well received, despite a storyline that is common in film and literature today. The book tells the story of two boys born on the same day who are physically identical, acting as a social commentary as the prince and pauper switch places. Twain had started *Adventures of Huckleberry Finn* (which he consistently had problems completing) and had completed his travel book *A Tramp Abroad*, which describes his travels through central and southern Europe.

Twain's next major published work was the *Adventures of Huckleberry Finn*, which confirmed him as a noteworthy American writer. Some have called it the first Great American Novel, and the book has become required reading in many schools throughout the United States. *Huckleberry Finn* was an offshoot from *Tom Sawyer* and had a more serious tone than its predecessor. Four hundred manuscript pages were written in mid-1876, right after the publication of *Tom Sawyer*. The last fifth of *Huckleberry Finn* is subject to much controversy. Some say that Twain experienced a "failure of nerve," as critic Leo Marx puts it. Ernest Hemingway once said of *Huckleberry Finn*:

> If you read it, you must stop where the Nigger Jim is stolen from the boys. That is the real end. The rest is just cheating.

Hemingway also wrote in the same essay:

> All modern American literature comes from one book by Mark Twain called *Huckleberry Finn*.

Near the completion of *Huckleberry Finn*, Twain wrote *Life on the Mississippi*, which is said to have heavily influenced the novel. The travel work recounts Twain's memories and new experiences after a 22-year absence from the Mississippi River. In it, he also explains that "Mark Twain" was the call made when the boat was in safe water, indicating a depth of two fathoms (12 feet or 3.7 metres).

LATER WRITING

Twain produced President Ulysses S. Grant's *Memoirs* through his fledgling publishing house, Charles L. Webster & Company, which he co-owned with Charles L. Webster, his nephew by marriage.

At this time he also wrote "The Private History of a Campaign That Failed" for *The Century Magazine*. This piece detailed his two-week stint in a Confederate militia during the Civil War. He next focused on *A Connecticut Yankee in King Arthur's Court*, written with the same historical fiction style as *The Prince and the Pauper*. *A Connecticut Yankee* showed the absurdities of political and social norms by setting them in the court of King Arthur. The book was started in December 1885, then shelved a few months later until the summer of 1887, and eventually finished in the spring of 1889.

His next large-scale work was *Pudd'nhead Wilson*, which he wrote rapidly, as he was desperately trying to stave off bankruptcy. From November 12 to December 14, 1893, Twain wrote 60,000 words for the novel. Critics have pointed to this rushed completion as the cause of the novel's rough organization and constant disruption of the plot. This novel also contains the tale of two boys born on the same day who switch positions in life, like *The Prince and the Pauper*. It was first published serially in *Century Magazine* and, when it was finally published in book form, *Pudd'nhead Wilson* appeared as the main title; however, the "subtitles" make the entire title read: *The Tragedy of Pudd'nhead Wilson and the Comedy of The Extraordinary Twins*.

Twain's next venture was a work of straight fiction that he called *Personal Recollections of Joan of Arc* and dedicated to his wife. He had long said that this was the work that he was most proud of, despite the criticism that he received for it. The book had been a dream of his since childhood, and he claimed that he had found a manuscript detailing the life of Joan of Arc when he was an adolescent. This was another piece that he was convinced would save his publishing company. His financial adviser Henry Huttleston Rogers quashed that idea and got Twain out of that business altogether, but the book was published nonetheless.

To pay the bills and keep his business projects afloat, Twain had begun to write articles and commentary furiously, with diminishing returns, but it was not enough. He filed for bankruptcy in 1894. During this time of dire financial straits, he published several literary reviews in newspapers to help make ends meet. He famously derided James Fenimore Cooper in his article detailing Cooper's "Literary Offenses". He became an extremely outspoken critic of other authors and other critics; he suggested that, before praising Cooper's work, Thomas Lounsbury, Brander Matthews, and Wilkie Collins "ought to have read some of it".

George Eliot, Jane Austen, and Robert Louis Stevenson also fell under Twain's attack during this time period, beginning around 1890 and continuing until his death. He outlines what he considers to be "quality writing" in several letters and essays, in addition to providing a source for the "tooth and claw" style of literary criticism. He places emphasis on concision, utility of word choice, and realism; he complains, for example, that Cooper's *Deerslayer* purports to be realistic but has several shortcomings. Ironically, several of his own works were later criticized for lack of continuity (*Adventures of Huckleberry Finn*) and organization (*Pudd'nhead Wilson*).

Twain's wife died in 1904 while the couple were staying at the Villa di Quarto in Florence. After some time had passed he published some works that his wife, his *de facto* editor and censor throughout her married life, had looked down upon. *The Mysterious Stranger* is perhaps the best known, depicting various visits of Satan to earth. This particular work was not published in Twain's lifetime. His manuscripts included three versions, written between 1897 and 1905: the so-called Hannibal, Eseldorf, and Print Shop versions. The resulting confusion led to extensive publication of a jumbled version, and only recently have the original versions become available as Twain wrote them.

Twain's last work was his autobiography, which he dictated and thought would be most entertaining if he went off on whims and tangents in non-chronological order. Some archivists and compilers have rearranged the biography into a more conventional form, thereby eliminating some of Twain's humor and the flow of the book. The first volume of the autobiography, over 736 pages, was published by the University of California in November 2010, 100 years after his death, as Twain wished. It soon became an unexpected best seller, making Twain one of a very few authors publishing new best-selling volumes in the 19th, 20th, and 21st centuries.

VIEWS

Twain's views became more radical as he grew older. In a letter to friend and fellow writer William Dean Howells in 1887 he acknowledged that his views had changed and developed over his lifetime, referring to one of his favorite works:

> When I finished Carlyle's *French Revolution* in 1871, I was a Girondin; every time I have read it since, I have read it differently – being influenced and changed, little by little, by life and environment ... and now I lay the book down once more, and recognize that I am a Sansculotte! And not a pale, characterless Sansculotte, but a Marat.

ANTI-IMPERIALIST

Before 1899, Twain was an ardent imperialist. In the late 1860s and early 1870s, he spoke out strongly in favor of American interests in the Hawaiian Islands. He said the war with Spain in 1898 was "the worthiest" war ever fought. In 1899, however, he reversed course. In the *New York Herald*, October 16, 1900, Twain describes his transformation and political awakening, in the context of the Philippine–American War, to anti-imperialism:

> I wanted the American eagle to go screaming into the Pacific ... Why not spread its wings over the Philippines, I asked myself? ... I said to myself, Here are a people who have suffered for three centuries. We can make them as free as ourselves, give them a government and country of their own, put a miniature of the American Constitution afloat in the Pacific, start a brand new republic to take its place among the free nations of the world. It seemed to me a great task to which we had addressed ourselves.

> But I have thought some more, since then, and I have read carefully the treaty of Paris [which ended the Spanish–American War], and I have seen that we do not intend to free, but to subjugate the people of the Philippines. We have gone there to conquer, not to redeem.

> It should, it seems to me, be our pleasure and duty to make those people free, and let them deal with their own domestic questions in their own

way. And so I am an anti-imperialist. I am opposed to having the eagle put its talons on any other land.

During the Boxer rebellion, Mark Twain said that "the Boxer is a patriot. He loves his country better than he does the countries of other people. I wish him success."

From 1901, soon after his return from Europe, until his death in 1910, Twain was vice-president of the American Anti-Imperialist League, which opposed the annexation of the Philippines by the United States and had "tens of thousands of members".He wrote many political pamphlets for the organization. The *Incident in the Philippines*, posthumously published in 1924, was in response to the Moro Crater Massacre, in which six hundred Moros were killed. Many of his neglected and previously uncollected writings on anti-imperialism appeared for the first time in book form in 1992.

Twain was critical of imperialism in other countries as well. In *Following the Equator*, Twain expresses "hatred and condemnation of imperialism of all stripes".

He was highly critical of European imperialists, notably Cecil Rhodes, who greatly expanded the British Empire, and Leopold II, King of the Belgians. *King Leopold's Soliloquy* is a stinging political satire about his private colony, the Congo Free State. Reports of outrageous exploitation and grotesque abuses led to widespread international protest in the early 1900s, arguably the first large-scale human rights movement. In the soliloquy, the King argues that bringing Christianity to the country outweighs a little starvation. Leopold's rubber gatherers were tortured, maimed and slaughtered until the movement forced Brussels to call a halt.

During the Philippine–American War, Twain wrote a short pacifist story titled *The War Prayer*, which makes the point that humanism and Christianity's preaching of love are incompatible with the conduct of war. It was submitted to *Harper's Bazaar* for publication, but on March 22, 1905, the magazine rejected the story as "not quite suited to a woman's magazine". Eight days later, Twain wrote to his friend Daniel Carter Beard, to whom he had read the story, "I don't think the prayer will be published in my time. None but the dead are permitted to tell the truth." Because he had an exclusive contract with Harper & Brothers, Twain could not publish *The War Prayer* elsewhere; it remained unpublished until 1923. It was republished as campaigning material by Vietnam War protesters.

Twain acknowledged that he had originally sympathized with the more moderate Girondins of the French Revolution and then shifted his sympathies to the more radical Sansculottes, indeed identifying himself as "a Marat". Twain supported the revolutionaries in Russia against the reformists, arguing that the Tsar must be got rid of by violent means, because peaceful ones would not work. He summed up his views of revolutions in the following statement:

> I am said to be a revolutionist in my sympathies, by birth, by breeding and by principle. I am always on the side of the revolutionists, because there never was a revolution unless there were some oppressive and intolerable conditions against which to revolute.

CIVIL RIGHTS

Twain was an adamant supporter of the abolition of slavery and the emancipation of slaves, even going so far as to say, "Lincoln's Proclamation ... not only set the black slaves free, but set the white man free also". He argued that non-whites did not receive justice in the United States, once saying, "I have seen Chinamen abused and maltreated in all the mean, cowardly ways possible to the invention of a degraded nature ... but I never saw a Chinaman righted in a court of justice for wrongs thus done to him".He paid for at least one black person to attend Yale Law School and for another black person to attend a southern university to become a minister.

Twain's sympathetic views on race were not reflected in his early writings on American Indians. Of them, Twain wrote in 1870:

> His heart is a cesspool of falsehood, of treachery, and of low and devilish instincts. With him, gratitude is an unknown emotion; and when one does him a kindness, it is safest to keep the face toward him, lest the reward be an arrow in the back. To accept of a favor from him is to assume a debt which you can never repay to his satisfaction, though you bankrupt yourself trying. The scum of the earth!

As counterpoint, Twain's essay on "The Literary Offenses of Fenimore Cooper" offers a much kinder view of Indians. "No, other Indians would have noticed these things, but Cooper's Indians never notice anything. Cooper thinks they are marvelous creatures for noticing, but he was almost always in error about his Indians. There was seldom a sane one among them."

In his later travelogue *Following the Equator* (1897), Twain observes that in colonized lands all over the world, "savages" have always been wronged by "whites" in the most merciless ways, such as "robbery, humiliation, and slow, slow murder, through poverty and the white man's whiskey"; his conclusion is that "there are many humorous things in this world; among them the white man's notion that he is less savage than the other savages".In an expression that captures his East Indian experiences, he wrote, "So far as I am able to judge nothing has been left undone, either by man or Nature, to make India the most extraordinary country that the sun visits on his rounds. Where every prospect pleases, and only man is vile."

Twain was also a staunch supporter of women's rights and an active campaigner for women's suffrage. His "Votes for Women" speech, in which he pressed for the granting of voting rights to women, is considered one of the most famous in history.

Helen Keller benefited from Twain's support as she pursued her college education and publishing despite her disabilities and financial limitations.

LABOR

Twain wrote glowingly about unions in the river boating industry in *Life on the Mississippi*, which was read in union halls decades later. He supported the labor movement, especially one of the most important unions, the Knights of Labor. In a speech to them, he said:

Who are the oppressors? The few: the King, the capitalist, and a handful of other overseers and superintendents. Who are the oppressed? The many: the nations of the earth; the valuable personages; the workers; they that make the bread that the soft-handed and idle eat.

RELIGION

Twain was a Presbyterian. He was critical of organized religion and certain elements of Christianity through his later life. He wrote, for example, "Faith is believing what you know ain't so", and "If Christ were here now there is one thing he would not be – a Christian".With anti-Catholic sentiment rampant in 19th century America, Twain noted he was "educated to enmity toward everything that is Catholic".As an adult, he engaged in religious discussions and attended services, his theology developing as he wrestled with the deaths of loved ones and with his own mortality.

Twain generally avoided publishing his most controversial opinions on religion in his lifetime, and they are known from essays and stories that were published later. In the essay *Three Statements of the Eighties* in the 1880s, Twain stated that he believed in an almighty God, but not in any messages, revelations, holy scriptures such as the Bible, Providence, or retribution in the afterlife.

He did state that "the goodness, the justice, and the mercy of God are manifested in His works", but also that "the universe is governed by strict and immutable laws", which determine "small matters", such as who dies in a pestilence. At other times, he wrote or spoke in ways that contradicted a strict deist view, for example, plainly professing a belief in Providence. In some later writings in the 1890s, he was less optimistic about the goodness of God, observing that "if our Maker *is* all-powerful for good or evil, He is not in His right mind". At other times, he conjectured sardonically that perhaps God had created the world with all its tortures for some purpose of His own, but was otherwise indifferent to humanity, which was too petty and insignificant to deserve His attention anyway.

In 1901, Twain criticized the actions of the missionary Dr. William Scott Ament (1851–1909) because Ament and other missionaries had collected indemnities from Chinese subjects in the aftermath of the Boxer Uprising of 1900. Twain's response to hearing of Ament's methods was published in the *North American Review* in February 1901: *To the Person Sitting in Darkness*, and deals with examples of imperialism in China, South Africa, and with the U.S. occupation of the Philippines. A subsequent article, "To My Missionary Critics" published in *The North American Review* in April 1901, unapologetically continues his attack, but with the focus shifted from Ament to his missionary superiors, the American Board of Commissioners for Foreign Missions.

After his death, Twain's family suppressed some of his work that was especially irreverent toward conventional religion, notably *Letters from the Earth*, which was not published until his daughter Clara reversed her position in 1962 in response to Soviet propaganda about the withholding.

The anti-religious *The Mysterious Stranger* was published in 1916. *Little Bessie*, a story ridiculing Christianity, was first published in the 1972 collection *Mark Twain's Fables of Man*.

He raised money to build a Presbyterian Church in Nevada in 1864.

Twain created a reverent portrayal of Joan of Arc, a subject over which he had obsessed for forty years, studied for a dozen years and spent two years writing about. In 1900 and again in 1908 he stated, "I like *Joan of Arc* best of all my books, it is the best".

Those who knew Twain well late in life recount that he dwelt on the subject of the afterlife, his daughter Clara saying: "Sometimes he believed death ended everything, but most of the time he felt sure of a life beyond."

Twain's frankest views on religion appeared in his final work *Autobiography of Mark Twain*, the publication of which started in November 2010, 100 years after his death. In it, he said:

> There is one notable thing about our Christianity: bad, bloody, merciless, money-grabbing, and predatory as it is – in our country particularly and in all other Christian countries in a somewhat modified degree – it is still a hundred times better than the Christianity of the Bible, with its prodigious crime – the invention of Hell. Measured by our Christianity of to-day, bad as it is, hypocritical as it is, empty and hollow as it is, neither the Deity nor his Son is a Christian, nor qualified for that moderately high place. Ours is a terrible religion. The fleets of the world could swim in spacious comfort in the innocent blood it has spilled.

Twain was a Freemason. He belonged to Polar Star Lodge No. 79 A.F.&A.M., based in St. Louis. He was initiated an Entered Apprentice on May 22, 1861, passed to the degree of Fellow Craft on June 12, and raised to the degree of Master Mason on July 10.

Twain visited Salt Lake City for two days and met there members of The Church of Jesus Christ of Latter-day Saints. They also gave him a Book of Mormon. He later wrote in *Roughing It* about that book:

> The book seems to be merely a prosy detail of imaginary history, with the Old Testament for a model; followed by a tedious plagiarism of the New Testament.

MARK TWAIN BIBLIOGRAPHY

Samuel Langhorne Clemens (November 30, 1835 – April 21, 1910), well known by his pen name Mark Twain, was an American author and humorist. Twain is noted for his novels *Adventures of Huckleberry Finn* (1884), which has been called "the Great American Novel," and *The Adventures of Tom Sawyer* (1876). He also wrote poetry, short stories, essays, and non-fiction.

NOVELS

- *The Gilded Age: A Tale of Today* (1873)
- *The Prince and the Pauper* (1881)
- *A Connecticut Yankee in King Arthur's Court* (1889)
- *The American Claimant* (1892)
- *Pudd'nhead Wilson* (1894)
- *Personal Recollections of Joan of Arc* (1896)
- *The Mysterious Stranger* (1916, posthumous)

Tom Sawyer and Huckleberry Finn

1. *The Adventures of Tom Sawyer* 1876
2. *Adventures of Huckleberry Finn* (1884)
3. *Tom Sawyer Abroad* (1894)
4. *Tom Sawyer, Detective* (1896)
5. "Schoolhouse Hill" (6 chapters) in The Mysterious Stranger (c.1898, unfinished)
6. "Huck Finn and Tom Sawyer among the Indians" (c. 1884, 9 chapters, unfinished)
7. "Huck Finn" (1903, unfinished)
8. "Tom Sawyer's Conspiracy" (10 chapters, unfinished)
9. "Tom Sawyer's Gang Plans a Naval Battle" (unfinished)

Adam and Eve

- "Extracts from Adam's Diary", illustrated by Frederick Strothmann (1904)
- "Eve's Diary", illus. Lester Ralph (1906)
- *The Private Life of Adam and Eve: Being Extracts from Their Diaries, Translated from the Original Mss.* (Harper, 1931), LCCN 31-27192 – posthumous issue of the 1904 and 1906 works bound as one, as Twain had requested in a recently discovered letter

SHORT STORIES

- "The Celebrated Jumping Frog of Calaveras County" (1865)
- "Advice to Little Girls" (1865)
- "General Washington's Negro Body-Servant" (1868)
- "My Late Senatorial Secretaryship" (1868)
- "A Ghost Story" (1870)
- "A True Story, Repeated Word for Word As I Heard It" (1874) [70-73]
- "Some Learned Fables for Good Old Boys and Girls" (1875) [77-83]

- "A Literary Nightmare" (1876)
- "A Murder, a Mystery, and a Marriage" (1876)
- "The Invalid's Story" (1877)
- "The Great Revolution in Pitcairn" (1879)
- "1601: Conversation, as it was by the Social Fireside, in the Time of the Tudors" (1880)
- "The Stolen White Elephant" (1882)
- "Luck" (1891)
- "Those Extraordinary Twins" (1892)
- "The £1,000,000 Note" (1893)
- "The Man That Corrupted Hadleyburg" (1900)
- "A Double Barrelled Detective Story" (1902)
- "A Dog's Tale" (1904)
- "The War Prayer" (1905)
- "A Horse's Tale" (1907)
- "Captain Stormfield's Visit to Heaven" (1909)
- "My Platonic Sweetheart" (1912, posthumous)
- "The Purloining of Prince Oleomargarine" (2017, posthumous)

COLLECTIONS

Short story collections

- *The Celebrated Jumping Frog of Calaveras County and Other Sketches* (1867), short story collection
- *Mark Twain's (Burlesque) Autobiography and First Romance* (1871), short story collection
- *Sketches New and Old* (1875), short story collection
- *A True Story and the Recent Carnival of Crime* (1877), short story collection
- *Punch, Brothers, Punch! and Other Sketches* (1878), short story collection
- *Mark Twain's Library of Humor* (1888), short story collection
- *Merry Tales* (1892), short story collection
- *The £1,000,000 Bank Note and Other New Stories* (1893), short story collection
- *The $30,000 Bequest and Other Stories* (1906), short story collection
- *The Curious Republic of Gondour and Other Whimsical Sketches* (1919, posthumous), short story collection
- *The Washoe Giant in San Francisco* (1938, posthumous), short story collection

Essay collections

- *Memoranda* (1870-1871), essay collection from *Galaxy*
- *How to Tell a Story and other Essays* (1897)
- *Europe and Elsewhere* (1923, posthumous), edited by Albert Bigelow Paine
- *Letters from the Earth* (1962, posthumous)
- *A Pen Warmed Up In Hell* (1972, posthumous)
- *The Bible According to Mark Twain* (1996, posthumous)

ESSAYS

- "On the Decay of the Art of Lying" (1880)
- "The Awful German Language" (1880)

- "Advice to Youth" (1882)
- "Fenimore Cooper's Literary Offenses" (1895)
- "English As She Is Taught" (1887)
- "Concerning the Jews" (1898)
- "A Salutation Speech From the Nineteenth Century to the Twentieth" (1900)
- "To the Person Sitting in Darkness" (1901)
- "To My Missionary Critics" (1901)
- "Edmund Burke on Croker and Tammany" (1901)
- "What Is Man?" (1906)
- "Christian Science" (1907)
- "Queen Victoria's Jubilee" (1910)
- "The United States of Lyncherdom" (1923, posthumous)

NON-FICTION

- *The Innocents Abroad* (1869), travel
- *Roughing It* (1872), travel
- *Old Times on the Mississippi* (1876), travel
- *A Tramp Abroad* (1880), travel
- *Life on the Mississippi* (1883), travel
- *Following the Equator* (sometimes titled "More Tramps Abroad") (1897), travel
- *Is Shakespeare Dead?* (1909)
- *Moments with Mark Twain* (1920, posthumous)
- *Mark Twain's Notebook* (1935, posthumous)
- *Letters from Hawaii* (letters written in 1866, published as a book in 1947)

OTHER WRITINGS

- *Is He Dead?* (1898), play
- "The Battle Hymn of the Republic, Updated" (1901), satirical lyric
- *King Leopold's Soliloquy* (1905), satire
- "Little Bessie Would Assist Providence" (1908), poem
- *Slovenly Peter* (1935, posthumous), children's book
- "Some Thoughts on the Science of Onanism" (1879), a speech given to The Stomach Club

A DOG'S TALE
by Mark Twain

A DOG'S TALE

(1904)

CHAPTER I.

My father was a St. Bernard, my mother was a collie, but I am a Presbyterian. This is what my mother told me, I do not know these nice distinctions myself. To me they are only fine large words meaning nothing. My mother had a fondness for such; she liked to say them, and see other dogs look surprised and envious, as wondering how she got so much education. But, indeed, it was not real education; it was only show: she got the words by listening in the dining-room and drawing-room when there was company, and by going with the children to Sunday-school and listening there; and whenever she heard a large word she said it over to herself many times, and so was able to keep it until there was a dogmatic gathering in the neighborhood, then she would get it off, and surprise and distress them all, from pocket-pup to mastiff, which rewarded her for all her trouble. If there was a stranger he was nearly sure to be suspicious, and when he got his breath again he would ask her what it meant. And she always told him. He was never expecting this but thought he would catch her; so when she told him, he was the one that looked ashamed, whereas he had thought it was going to be she. The others were always waiting for this, and glad of it and proud of her, for they knew what was going to happen, because they had had experience. When she told the meaning of a big word they were all so taken up with admiration that it never occurred to any dog to doubt if it was the right one; and that was natural, because, for one thing, she answered up so promptly that it seemed like a dictionary speaking, and for another thing, where could they find out whether it was right or not? for she was the only cultivated dog there was. By and by, when I was older, she brought home the word Unintellectual, one time, and worked it pretty hard all the week at different gatherings, making much unhappiness and despondency; and it was at this time that I noticed that during that week she was asked for the meaning at eight different assemblages, and flashed out a fresh definition every time, which showed me that she had more presence of mind than culture, though I said nothing, of course. She had one word which she always kept on hand, and ready, like a life-preserver, a kind of emergency word to strap on when she was likely to get washed overboard in a sudden way—that was the word Synonymous. When she happened to fetch out a long word which had had its day weeks before and its prepared meanings gone to her dump-pile, if there was a stranger there of course it knocked him groggy for a couple of minutes, then he would come to, and by that time she would be away down wind on another tack, and not expecting anything; so when he'd hail and ask her to cash in, I (the only dog on the inside of her game) could see her canvas flicker a moment— but only just a moment—then it would belly out taut and full, and she would say, as calm as a summer's day, "It's synonymous with supererogation," or some godless long reptile of a word like that, and go placidly about and skim away on the next tack, perfectly comfortable, you know, and leave that stranger looking profane and embarrassed, and the initiated slatting the floor with their tails in unison and their faces transfigured with a holy joy.

And it was the same with phrases. She would drag home a whole phrase, if it had a grand sound, and play it six nights and two matinees, and explain it a new way every time—which she had to, for all she cared for was the phrase; she wasn't interested in what it meant, and knew those dogs hadn't wit enough to catch her, anyway. Yes, she was a daisy! She got so she wasn't afraid of anything, she had such confidence in the ignorance of those creatures. She even brought anecdotes that she had heard the family and the dinner-guests laugh and shout over; and as a rule she got the nub of one chestnut hitched onto another chestnut, where, of course, it didn't fit and hadn't any point; and when she delivered the nub she fell over and rolled on the floor and laughed and barked in the most insane way, while I could see that she was wondering to herself why it didn't seem as funny as it did when she first heard it. But no harm was done; the others rolled and barked too, privately ashamed of themselves for not seeing the point, and never suspecting that the fault was not with them and there wasn't any to see.

You can see by these things that she was of a rather vain and frivolous character; still, she had virtues, and enough to make up, I think. She had a kind heart and gentle ways, and never harbored resentments for injuries done her, but put them easily out of her mind and forgot them; and she taught her children her kindly way, and from her we learned also to be brave and prompt in time of danger, and not to run away, but face the peril that threatened friend or stranger, and help him the best we could without stopping to think what the cost might be to us. And she taught us not by words only, but by example, and that is the best way and the surest and the most lasting. Why, the brave things she did, the splendid things! she was just a soldier; and so modest about it—well, you couldn't help admiring her, and you couldn't help imitating her; not even a King Charles spaniel could remain entirely despicable in her society. So, as you see, there was more to her than her education.

CHAPTER II.

When I was well grown, at last, I was sold and taken away, and I never saw her again. She was broken-hearted, and so was I, and we cried; but she comforted me as well as she could, and said we were sent into this world for a wise and good purpose, and must do our duties without repining, take our life as we might find it, live it for the best good of others, and never mind about the results; they were not our affair. She said men who did like this would have a noble and beautiful reward by and by in another world, and although we animals would not go there, to do well and right without reward would give to our brief lives a worthiness and dignity which in itself would be a reward. She had gathered these things from time to time when she had gone to the Sunday-school with the children, and had laid them up in her memory more carefully than she had done with those other words and phrases; and she had studied them deeply, for her good and ours. One may see by this that she had a wise and thoughtful head, for all there was so much lightness and vanity in it.

So we said our farewells, and looked our last upon each other through our tears; and the last thing she said—keeping it for the last to make me remember it the better, I think—was, "In memory of me, when there is a time of danger to another do not think of yourself, think of your mother, and do as she would do."

Do you think I could forget that? No.

CHAPTER III.

It was such a charming home!—my new one; a fine great house, with pictures, and delicate decorations, and rich furniture, and no gloom anywhere, but all the wilderness of dainty colors lit up with flooding sunshine; and the spacious grounds around it, and the great garden—oh, greensward, and noble trees, and flowers, no end! And I was the same as a member of the family; and they loved me, and petted me, and did not give me a new name, but called me by my old one that was dear to me because my mother had given it me—Aileen Mavourneen. She got it out of a song; and the Grays knew that song, and said it was a beautiful name.

Mrs. Gray was thirty, and so sweet and so lovely, you cannot imagine it; and Sadie was ten, and just like her mother, just a darling slender little copy of her, with auburn tails down her back, and short frocks; and the baby was a year old, and plump and dimpled, and fond of me, and never could get enough of hauling on my tail, and hugging me, and laughing out its innocent happiness; and Mr. Gray was thirty-eight, and tall and slender and handsome, a little bald in front, alert, quick in his movements, business-like, prompt, decided, unsentimental, and with that kind of trim-chiseled face that just seems to glint and sparkle with frosty intellectuality! He was a renowned scientist. I do not know what the word means, but my mother would know how to use it and get effects. She would know how to depress a rat-terrier with it and make a lap-dog look sorry he came. But that is not the best one; the best one was Laboratory. My mother could organize a Trust on that one that would skin the tax-collars off the whole herd. The laboratory was not a book, or a picture, or a place to wash your hands in, as the college president's dog said—no, that is the lavatory; the laboratory is quite different, and is filled with jars, and bottles, and electrics, and wires, and strange machines; and every week other scientists came there and sat in the place, and used the machines, and discussed, and made what they called experiments and discoveries; and often I came, too, and stood around and listened, and tried to learn, for the sake of my mother, and in loving memory of her, although it was a pain to me, as realizing what she was losing out of her life and I gaining nothing at all; for try as I might, I was never able to make anything out of it at all. Other times I lay on the floor in the mistress's work-room and slept, she gently using me for a foot-stool, knowing it pleased me, for it was a caress; other times I spent an hour in the nursery, and got well tousled and made happy; other times I watched by the crib there, when the baby was asleep and the nurse out for a few minutes on the baby's affairs; other times I romped and raced through the grounds and the garden with Sadie till we were tired out, then slumbered on the grass in the shade of a tree while she read her book; other times I went visiting among the neighbor dogs—for there were some most pleasant ones not far away, and one very handsome and courteous and graceful one, a curly-haired Irish setter by the name of Robin Adair, who was a Presbyterian like me, and belonged to the Scotch minister.

The servants in our house were all kind to me and were fond of me, and so, as you see, mine was a pleasant life. There could not be a happier dog that I was, nor a gratefuller one. I will say this for myself, for it is only the truth: I tried in all ways to do well and right, and honor my mother's memory and her teachings, and earn the happiness that had come to me, as best I could.

By and by came my little puppy, and then my cup was full, my happiness was perfect. It was the dearest little waddling thing, and so smooth and soft and velvety, and had such cunning little awkward paws, and such affectionate eyes, and such a sweet and innocent face; and it made me so proud to see how the children and their mother adored it, and fondled it, and exclaimed over every little wonderful thing it did. It did seem to me that life was just too lovely to—

Then came the winter. One day I was standing a watch in the nursery. That is to say, I was asleep on the bed. The baby was asleep in the crib, which was alongside the bed, on the side next the fireplace. It was the kind of crib that has a lofty tent over it made of gauzy stuff that you can see through. The nurse was out, and we two sleepers were alone. A spark from the wood-fire was shot out, and it lit on the slope of the tent. I suppose a quiet interval followed, then a scream from the baby awoke me, and there was that tent flaming up toward the ceiling! Before I could think, I sprang to the floor in my fright, and in a second was half-way to the door; but in the next half-second my mother's farewell was sounding in my ears, and I was back on the bed again. I reached my head through the flames and dragged the baby out by the waist-band, and tugged it along, and we fell to the floor together in a cloud of smoke; I snatched a new hold, and dragged the screaming little creature along and out at the door and around the bend of the hall, and was still tugging away, all excited and happy and proud, when the master's voice shouted:

"Begone you cursed beast!" and I jumped to save myself; but he was furiously quick, and chased me up, striking furiously at me with his cane, I dodging this way and that, in terror, and at last a strong blow fell upon my left foreleg, which made me shriek and fall, for the moment, helpless; the cane went up for another blow, but never descended, for the nurse's voice rang wildly out, "The nursery's on fire!" and the master rushed away in that direction, and my other bones were saved.

The pain was cruel, but, no matter, I must not lose any time; he might come back at any moment; so I limped on three legs to the other end of the hall, where there was a dark little stairway leading up into a garret where old boxes and such things were kept, as I had heard say, and where people seldom went. I managed to climb up there, then I searched my way through the dark among the piles of things, and hid in the secretest place I could find. It was foolish to be afraid there, yet still I was; so afraid that I held in and hardly even whimpered, though it would have been such a comfort to whimper, because that eases the pain, you know. But I could lick my leg, and that did some good. For half an hour there was a commotion downstairs, and shoutings, and rushing footsteps, and then there was quiet again. Quiet for some minutes, and that was grateful to my spirit, for then my fears began to go down; and fears are worse than pains—oh, much worse. Then came a sound that froze me. They were calling me—calling me by name—hunting for me!

It was muffled by distance, but that could not take the terror out of it, and it was the most dreadful sound to me that I had ever heard. It went all about, everywhere, down there: along the halls, through all the rooms, in both stories, and in the basement and the cellar; then outside, and farther and farther away—then back, and all about the house again, and I thought it would never, never stop. But at last it did, hours and hours after the vague twilight of the garret had long ago been blotted out by black darkness.

Then in that blessed stillness my terrors fell little by little away, and I was at peace and slept. It was a good rest I had, but I woke before the twilight had come again. I was feeling fairly comfortable, and I could think out a plan now. I made a very good one; which was, to creep down, all the way down the back stairs, and hide behind the cellar door, and slip out and escape when the iceman came at dawn, while he was inside filling the refrigerator; then I would hide all day, and start on my journey when night came; my journey to—well, anywhere where they would not know me and betray me to the master. I was feeling almost cheerful now; then suddenly I thought: Why, what would life be without my puppy!

That was despair. There was no plan for me; I saw that; I must stay where I was; stay, and wait, and take what might come—it was not my affair; that was what life is—my mother had said it. Then—well, then the calling began again! All my sorrows came back. I said to myself, the master will never forgive. I did not know what I had done to make him so bitter and so unforgiving, yet I judged it was something a dog could not understand, but which was clear to a man and dreadful.

They called and called—days and nights, it seemed to me. So long that the hunger and thirst near drove me mad, and I recognized that I was getting very weak. When you are this way you sleep a great deal, and I did. Once I woke in an awful fright—it seemed to me that the calling was right there in the garret! And so it was: it was Sadie's voice, and she was crying; my name was falling from her lips all broken, poor thing, and I could not believe my ears for the joy of it when I heard her say:

"Come back to us—oh, come back to us, and forgive—it is all so sad without our—"

I broke in with SUCH a grateful little yelp, and the next moment Sadie was plunging and stumbling through the darkness and the lumber and shouting for the family to hear, "She's found, she's found!"

The days that followed—well, they were wonderful. The mother and Sadie and the servants—why, they just seemed to worship me. They couldn't seem to make me a bed that was fine enough; and as for food, they couldn't be satisfied with anything but game and delicacies that were out of season; and every day the friends and neighbors flocked in to hear about my heroism—that was the name they called it by, and it means agriculture. I remember my mother pulling it on a kennel once, and explaining it in that way, but didn't say what agriculture was, except that it was synonymous with intramural incandescence; and a dozen times a day Mrs. Gray and Sadie would tell the tale to new-comers, and say I risked my life to save the baby's, and both of us had burns to prove it, and then the company would pass me around and pet me and exclaim about me, and you could see the pride in the eyes of Sadie and her mother; and when the people wanted to know what made me limp, they looked ashamed and changed the subject, and sometimes when people hunted them this way and that way with questions about it, it looked to me as if they were going to cry.

And this was not all the glory; no, the master's friends came, a whole twenty of the most distinguished people, and had me in the laboratory, and discussed me as if I was a kind of discovery; and some of them said it was wonderful in a dumb beast, the finest exhibition of instinct they could call to mind; but the master said, with vehemence, "It's far above instinct; it's REASON, and many a man, privileged to be saved and go with you and me to a better world by right of its possession, has less of it that this poor silly quadruped that's foreordained to perish;" and then he laughed, and said: "Why, look at me—I'm a sarcasm! bless you, with all my grand intelligence, the only thing I inferred was that the dog had gone mad and was destroying the child, whereas but for the beast's intelligence—it's REASON, I tell you!—the child would have perished!"

They disputed and disputed, and I was the very center of subject of it all, and I wished my mother could know that this grand honor had come to me; it would have made her proud.

Then they discussed optics, as they called it, and whether a certain injury to the brain would produce blindness or not, but they could not agree about it, and said they must test it by experiment by and by; and next they discussed plants, and that interested me, because in the summer Sadie and I had planted seeds—I helped her dig the holes, you know—and after days and days a little shrub or a flower came up there, and it was a wonder how that could happen; but it did, and I wished I could talk—I would have told those people about it and shown then how much I knew, and been all alive with the subject; but I didn't care for the optics; it was dull, and when they came back to it again it bored me, and I went to sleep.

Pretty soon it was spring, and sunny and pleasant and lovely, and the sweet mother and the children patted me and the puppy good-by, and went away on a journey and a visit to their kin, and the master wasn't any company for us, but we played together and had good times, and the servants were kind and friendly, so we got along quite happily and counted the days and waited for the family.

And one day those men came again, and said, now for the test, and they took the puppy to the laboratory, and I limped three-leggedly along, too, feeling proud, for any attention shown to the puppy was a pleasure to me, of course. They discussed and experimented, and then suddenly the puppy shrieked, and they set him on the floor, and he went staggering around, with his head all bloody, and the master clapped his hands and shouted:

"There, I've won—confess it! He's as blind as a bat!"

And they all said:

"It's so—you've proved your theory, and suffering humanity owes you a great debt from henceforth," and they crowded around him, and wrung his hand cordially and thankfully, and praised him.

But I hardly saw or heard these things, for I ran at once to my little darling, and snuggled close to it where it lay, and licked the blood, and it put its head against mine, whimpering softly, and I knew in my heart it was a comfort to it in its pain and trouble to feel its mother's touch, though it could not see me. Then it dropped down, presently, and its little velvet nose rested upon the floor, and it was still, and did not move any more.

Soon the master stopped discussing a moment, and rang in the footman, and said, "Bury it in the far corner of the garden," and then went on with the discussion, and I trotted after the footman, very happy and grateful, for I knew the puppy was out of its pain now, because it was asleep. We went far down the garden to the farthest end, where the children and the nurse and the puppy and I used to play in the summer in the shade of a great elm, and there the footman dug a hole, and I saw he was going to plant the puppy, and I was glad, because it would grow and come up a fine handsome dog, like Robin Adair, and be a beautiful surprise for the family when they came home; so I tried to help him dig, but my lame leg was no good, being stiff, you know, and you have to have two, or it is no use. When the footman had finished and covered little Robin up, he patted my head, and there were tears in his eyes, and he said: "Poor little doggie, you saved HIS child!"

I have watched two whole weeks, and he doesn't come up! This last week a fright has been stealing upon me. I think there is something terrible about this. I do not know what it is, but the fear makes me sick, and I cannot eat, though the servants bring me the best of food; and they pet me so, and even come in the night, and cry, and say, "Poor doggie—do give it up and come home; don't break our hearts!" and all this terrifies me the more, and makes me sure something has happened. And I am so weak; since yesterday I cannot stand on my feet anymore. And within this hour the servants, looking toward the sun where it was sinking out of sight and the night chill coming on, said things I could not understand, but they carried something cold to my heart.

"Those poor creatures! They do not suspect. They will come home in the morning, and eagerly ask for the little doggie that did the brave deed, and who of us will be strong enough to say the truth to them: 'The humble little friend is gone where go the beasts that perish.'"

SELECTED SHORT STORIES

THE CELEBRATED JUMPING FROG OF CALAVERAS COUNTY

In compliance with the request of a friend of mine, who wrote me from the East, I called on good-natured, garrulous old Simon Wheeler, and inquired after my friend's friend, Leonidas W. Smiley, as requested to do, and I hereunto append the result. I have a lurking suspicion that Leonidas W. Smiley is a myth; that my friend never knew such a personage; and that he only conjectured that, if I asked old Wheeler about him, it would remind him of his infamous Jim Smiley, and he would go to work and bore me nearly to death with some infernal reminiscence of him as long and tedious as it should be useless to me. If that was the design, it certainly succeeded.

I found Simon Wheeler dozing comfortably by the bar-room stove of the old, dilapidated tavern in the ancient mining camp of Angel's, and I noticed that he was fat and bald-headed, and had an expression of winning gentleness and simplicity upon his tranquil countenance. He roused up and gave me good-day. I told him a friend of mine had commissioned me to make some inquiries about a cherished companion of his boyhood named Leonidas W. Smiley Rev. Leonidas W. Smiley a young minister of the Gospel, who he had heard was at one time a resident of Angel's Camp. I added that, if Mr. Wheeler could tell me any thing about this Rev. Leonidas W. Smiley, I would feel under many obligations to him.

Simon Wheeler backed me into a corner and blockaded me there with his chair, and then sat me down and reeled off the monotonous narrative which follows this paragraph. He never smiled, he never frowned, he never changed his voice from the gentle-flowing key to which he tuned the initial sentence, he never betrayed the slightest suspicion of enthusiasm; but all through the interminable narrative there ran a vein of impressive earnestness and sincerity, which showed me plainly that, so far from his imagining that there was any thing ridiculous or funny about his story, he regarded it as a really important matter, and admired its two heroes as men of transcendent genius in finesse. To me, the spectacle of a man drifting serenely along through such a queer yarn without ever smiling, was exquisitely absurd. As I said before, I asked him to tell me what he knew of Rev. Leonidas W. Smiley, and he replied as follows. I let him go on in his own way, and never interrupted him once:

There was a feller here once by the name of Jim Smiley, in the winter of '49 or may be it was the spring of '50 I don't recollect exactly, somehow, though what makes me think it was one or the other is because I remember the big flume wasn't finished when he first came to the camp; but any way, he was the curiosest man about always betting on any thing that turned up you ever see, if he could get any body to bet on the other side; and if he couldn't, he'd change sides. Any way that suited the other man would suit him any way just so's he got a bet, he was satisfied. But still he was lucky, uncommon lucky; he most always come out winner. He was always ready and laying for a chance; there couldn't be no solittry thing mentioned but that feller'd offer to bet on it, and -take any side you please, as I was just telling you. If there was a horse-race, you'd find him flush, or you'd find him busted at the end of it; if there was a dog-fight, he'd bet on it; if there was a cat-fight, he'd bet on it; if there was a chicken-fight, he'd bet on it; why, if there was two birds setting on a fence, he would bet you which one would fly first; or if there was a camp-meeting, he would be there reg'lar, to bet on Parson Walker, which he judged to be the best exhorter about here, and so he was, too, and a good man. If he even seen a straddle-bug start to go anywheres, he would bet you how long it would take him to get wherever he was going to, and if you took him up, he would foller that straddle-bug to Mexico but what he would find out where he was bound for and how long he was on the road. Lots of the boys here has seen that Smiley, and can tell you about him. Why, it never made no difference to him he would bet on any thing the dangdest feller. Parson Walker's wife laid very sick once, for a good while, and it seemed as if they warn's going to save her; but one morning he come in, and Smiley asked how she was, and he said she was considerable better thank the Lord for his inftnit mercy and coming on so smart that, with the blessing of Providence, she'd get well yet; and Smiley, before he thought, says, "Well, I'll risk two- and-a-half that she don't, any way."

Thish-yer Smiley had a mare the boys called her the fifteen- minute nag, but that was only in fun, you know, because, of course, she was faster than that and he used to win money on that horse, for all she was so slow and always had the asthma, or the distemper, or the consumption, or something of that kind. They used to give her two or three hundred yards start, and then pass her under way; but always at the fag-end of the race she'd get excited and desperate- like, and come cavorting and straddling up, and scattering her legs around limber, sometimes in the air, and sometimes out to one side amongst the fences, and kicking up m-o-r-e dust, and raising m-o-r-e racket with her coughing and sneezing and blowing her nose and always fetch up at the stand just about a neck ahead, as near as you could cipher it down.

And he had a little small bull pup, that to look at him you'd think he wan's worth a cent, but to set around and look ornery, and lay for a chance to steal something. But as soon as money was up on him, he was a different dog; his underjaw'd begin to stick out like the fo'castle of a steamboat, and his teeth would uncover, and shine savage like the furnaces. And a dog might tackle him, and bully- rag him, and bite him, and throw him over his shoulder two or three times, and Andrew Jackson which was the name of the pup Andrew Jackson would never let on but what he was satisfied, and hadn't expected nothing else and the bets being doubled and doubled on the other side all the time, till the money was all up; and then all of a sudden he would grab that other dog jest by the j'int of his hind leg and freeze on it not chew, you understand, but only jest grip and hang on till they thronged up the sponge, if it was a year. Smiley always come out winner on that pup, till he harnessed a dog once that didn't have no hind legs, because they'd been sawed off by a circular saw, and when the thing had gone along far enough, and the money was all up, and he come to make a snatch for his pet bolt, he saw in a minute how he'd been imposed on, and how the other dog had him in the door, so to speak, and he 'peered sur- prised, and then he looked sorter discouraged-like, and didn't try no more to win the fight, and so he got shucked out bad. He give Smiley a look, as much as to say his heart was broke, and it was his fault, for putting up a dog that hadn't no hind legs for him to take bolt of, which was his main dependence in a fight, and then he limped off a piece and laid down and died. It was a good pup, was that Andrew Jackson, and would have made a name for hisself if he'd lived, for the stuff was in him, and he had genius I know it, because he hadn't had no opportunities to speak of, and it don't stand to reason that a dog could make such a fight as he could under them circumstances, if he hadn't no talent. It always makes me feel sorry when I think of that last fight of his'n, and the way it turned out.

Well, thish-yer Smiley had rat-tarriers, and chicken cocks, and tom- cats, and all of them kind of things, till you couldn't rest, and you couldn't fetch nothing for him to bet on but he'd match you. He ketched a frog one day, and took him home, and said he cal'klated to edercate him; and so he never done nothing for three months but set in his back yard and learn that frog to jump. And you bet you he did learn him, too. He'd give him a little punch behind, and the next minute you'd see that frog whirling in the air like a doughnut see him turn one summerset, or may be a couple, if he got a good start, and come down flat-footed and all right, like a cat. He got him up so in the matter of catching flies, and kept him in practice so constant, that he'd nail a fly every time as far as he could see him. Smiley said all a frog wanted was education, and he could do most any thing and I believe him. Why, I've seen him set Dan'l Webster down here on this floor Dan'l Webster was the name of the frog and sing out, "Flies, Dan'l, flies!" and quicker'n you could wink, he'd spring straight up, and snake a fly off'n the counter there, and flop down on the floor again as solid as a gob of mud, and fall to scratching the side of his head with his hind foot as indifferent as if he hadn't no idea he'd been doin' any more'n any frog might do. You never see a frog so modest and straightforward as he was, for all he was so gifted. And when it come to fair and square jumping on a dead level, he could get over more ground at one straddle than any animal of his breed you ever see. Jumping on a dead level was his strong suit, you understand; and when it come to that, Smiley would ante up money on him as long as he had a red. Smiley was monstrous proud of his frog, and well he might be, for fellers that had traveled and been everywheres, all said he laid over any frog that ever they see.

Well, Smiley kept the beast in a little lattice box, and he used to fetch him down town sometimes and lay for a bet. One day a feller a stranger in the camp, he was come across him with his box, and says:

"What might it be that you've got in the box?"

And Smiley says, sorter indifferent like, "It might be a parrot, or it might be a canary, may be, but it an't it's only just a frog."

And the feller took it, and looked at it careful, and turned it round this way and that, and says, "H'm so 'tis. Well, what's he good for?"

"Well," Smiley says, easy and careless, "He's good enough for one thing, I should judge he can outjump any frog in Calaveras county."

The feller took the box again, and took another long, particular look, and give it back to Smiley, and says, very deliberate, "Well, I don't see no p'ints about that frog that's any better'n any other frog."

"May be you don't," Smiley says. "May be you understand frogs, and may be you don't understand 'em; may be you've had experience, and may be you an't only a amature, as it were. Anyways, I've got my opinion, and I'll risk forty dollars that he can outjump any frog in Calaveras county."

And the feller studied a minute, and then says, kinder sad like, "Well, I'm only a stranger here, and I an't got no frog; but if I had a frog, I'd bet you."

And then Smiley says, "That's all right that's all right if you'll hold my box a minute, I'll go and get you a frog." And so the feller took the box, and put up his forty dollars along with Smiley's, and set down to wait.

So he set there a good while thinking and thinking to hisself, and then he got the frog out and prized his mouth open and took a tea- spoon and filled him full of quail shot filled him pretty near up to his chin and set him on the floor. Smiley he went to the swamp and slopped around in the mud for a long time, and finally he ketched a frog, and fetched him in, and give him to this feller, and says:

"Now, if you're ready, set him alongside of Dan'l, with his fore- paws just even with Dan'l, and I'll give the word." Then he says, "One two three jump!" and him and the feller touched up the frogs from behind, and the new frog hopped off, but Dan'l give a heave, and hysted up his shoulders so like a Frenchman, but it wan's no use he couldn't budge; he was planted as solid as an anvil, and he couldn't no more stir than if he was anchored out. Smiley was a good deal surprised, and he was disgusted too, but he didn't have no idea what the matter was, of course.

The feller took the money and started away; and when he was going out at the door, he sorter jerked his thumb over his shoulders this way at Dan'l, and says again, very deliberate, "Well, I don't see no p'ints about that frog that's any better'n any other frog."

Smiley he stood scratching his head and looking down at Dan'l a long time, and at last he says, "I do wonder what in the nation that frog throw'd off for I wonder if there an't something the matter with him he 'pears to look mighty baggy, somehow." And he ketched Dan'l by the nap of the neck, and lifted him up and says, "Why, blame my cats, if he don't weigh five pound!" and turned him upside down, and he belched out a double handful of shot. And then he see how it was, and he was the maddest man he set the frog down and took out after that feller, but he never ketchd him. And-

[Here Simon Wheeler heard his name called from the front yard, and got up to see what was wanted.] And turning to me as he moved away, he said: "Just set where you are, stranger, and rest easy I an't going to be gone a second."

But, by your leave, I did not think that a continuation of the history of the enterprising vagabond Jim Smiley would be likely to afford me much information concerning the Rev. Leonidas W. Smiley, and so I started away.

At the door I met the sociable Wheeler returning, and he button- holed me and recommenced:

"Well, thish-yer Smiley had a yeller one-eyed cow that didn't have no tail, only jest a short stump like a bannanner, and "

"Oh! hang Smiley and his afflicted cow!" I muttered, good-naturedly, and bidding the old gentleman good-day, I departed.

MARK TWAIN'S (BURLESQUE) AUTOBIOGRAPHY AND FIRST ROMANCE

BURLESQUE AUTOBIOGRAPHY.

Two or three persons having at different times intimated that if I would write an autobiography they would read it, when they got leisure, I yield at last to this frenzied public demand, and herewith tender my history:

Ours is a noble old house, and stretches a long way back into antiquity. The earliest ancestor the Twains have any record of was a friend of the family by the name of Higgins. This was in the eleventh century, when our people were living in Aberdeen, county of Cork, England. Why it is that our long line has ever since borne the maternal name (except when one of them now and then took a playful refuge in an alias to avert foolishness), instead of Higgins, is a mystery which none of us has ever felt much desire to stir. It is a kind of vague, pretty romance, and we leave it alone. All the old families do that way.

Arthour Twain was a man of considerable note—a solicitor on the highway in William Rufus' time. At about the age of thirty he went to one of those fine old English places of resort called Newgate, to see about something, and never returned again. While there he died suddenly.

Augustus Twain, seems to have made something of a stir about the year 1160. He was as full of fun as he could be, and used to take his old sabre and sharpen it up, and get in a convenient place on a dark night, and stick it through people as they went by, to see them jump. He was a born humorist. But he got to going too far with it; and the first time he was found stripping one of these parties, the authorities removed one end of him, and put it up on a nice high place on Temple Bar, where it could contemplate the people and have a good time. He never liked any situation so much or stuck to it so long.

Then for the next two hundred years the family tree shows a succession of soldiers— noble, high-spirited fellows, who always went into battle singing; right behind the army, and always went out a-whooping, right ahead of it.

This is a scathing rebuke to old dead Froissart's poor witticism that our family tree never had but one limb to it, and that that one stuck out at right angles, and bore fruit winter, and summer.

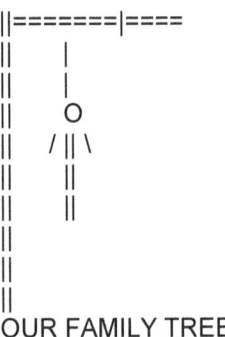

OUR FAMILY TREE

Early in the fifteenth century we have Beau Twain, called "the Scholar." He wrote a beautiful, beautiful hand. And he could imitate anybody's hand so closely that it was enough to make a person laugh his head off to see it. He had infinite sport with his talent. But by and by he took a contract to break stone for a road, and the roughness of the work spoiled his hand. Still, he enjoyed life all the time he was in the stone business, which, with inconsiderable intervals, was some forty-two years. In fact, he died in harness. During all those long years he gave such satisfaction that he never was through with one contract a week till government gave him another. He was a perfect pet. And he was always a favorite with his fellow-artists, and was a conspicuous member of their benevolent secret society, called the Chain Gang. He always wore his hair short, had a preference for striped clothes, and died lamented by the government. He was a sore loss to his country. For he was so regular.

Some years later we have the illustrious John Morgan Twain. He came over to this country with Columbus in 1492, as a passenger. He appears to have been of a crusty, uncomfortable disposition. He complained of the food all the way over, and was always threatening to go ashore unless there was a change. He wanted fresh shad. Hardly a day passed over his head that he did not go idling about the ship with his nose in the air, sneering about the commander, and saying he did not believe Columbus knew where he was going to or had ever been there before. The memorable cry of "Land ho!" thrilled every heart in the ship but his. He gazed a while through a piece of smoked glass at the penciled line lying on the distant water, and then said: "Land be hanged,—it's a raft!"

When this questionable passenger came on board the ship, he brought nothing with him but an old newspaper containing a handkerchief marked "B. G.," one cotton sock marked "L. W. C." one woollen one marked "D. F." and a night-shirt marked "O. M. R." And yet during the voyage he worried more about his "trunk," and gave himself more airs about it, than all the rest of the passengers put together.

If the ship was "down by the head," and would not steer, he would go and move his "trunk" farther aft, and then watch the effect. If the ship was "by the stern," he would suggest to Columbus to detail some men to "shift that baggage." In storms he had to be gagged, because his wailings about his "trunk" made it impossible for the men to hear the orders. The man does not appear to have been openly charged with any gravely unbecoming thing, but it is noted in the ship's log as a "curious circumstance" that albeit he brought his baggage on board the ship in a newspaper, he took it ashore in four trunks, a queensware crate, and a couple of champagne baskets. But when he came back insinuating in an insolent, swaggering way, that some of his things were missing, and was going to search the other passengers' baggage, it was too much, and they threw him overboard. They watched long and wonderingly for him to come up, but not even a bubble rose on the quietly ebbing tide. But while every one was most absorbed in gazing over the side, and the interest was momentarily increasing, it was observed with consternation that the vessel was adrift and the anchor cable hanging limp from the bow. Then in the ship's dimmed and ancient log we find this quaint note:

> "In time it was discouvered yt ye troblesome passenger hadde
> gonne downe and got ye anchor, and toke ye same and solde it to
> ye dam sauvages from ye interior, saying yt he hadde founde it,
> ye sonne of a ghun!"

Yet this ancestor had good and noble instincts, and it is with pride that we call to mind the fact that he was the first white person who ever interested himself in the work of elevating and civilizing our Indians. He built a commodious jail and put up a gallows, and to his dying day he claimed with satisfaction that he had had a more restraining and elevating influence on the Indians than any other reformer that ever labored among them. At this point the chronicle becomes less frank and chatty, and closes abruptly by saying that the old voyager went to see his gallows perform on the first white man ever hanged in America, and while there received injuries which terminated in his death.

The great grandson of the "Reformer" flourished in sixteen hundred and something, and was known in our annals as, "the old Admiral," though in history he had other titles. He was long in command of fleets of swift vessels, well armed and manned, and did great service in hurrying up merchantmen. Vessels which he followed and kept his eagle eye on, always made good fair time across the ocean. But if a ship still loitered in spite of all he could do, his indignation would grow till he could contain himself no longer—and then he would take that ship home where he lived and, keep it there carefully, expecting the owners to come for it, but they never did. And he would try to get the idleness and sloth out of the sailors of that ship by compelling them to take invigorating exercise and a bath. He called it "walking a plank." All the pupils liked it. At any rate, they never found any fault with it after trying it. When the owners were late coming for their ships, the Admiral always burned them, so that the insurance money should not be lost. At last this fine old tar was cut down in the fulness of his years and honors. And to her dying day, his poor heart-broken widow believed that if he had been cut down fifteen minutes sooner he might have been resuscitated.

Charles Henry Twain lived during the latter part of the seventeenth century, and was a zealous and distinguished missionary. He converted sixteen thousand South Sea islanders, and taught them that a dog-tooth necklace and a pair of spectacles was not enough clothing to come to divine service in. His poor flock loved him very, very dearly; and when his funeral was over, they got up in a body (and came out of the restaurant) with tears in their eyes, and saying, one to another, that he was a good tender missionary, and they wished they had some more of him.

PAH-GO-TO-WAH-WAH-PUKKETEKEEWIS (Mighty-Hunter-with-a-Hog-Eye) TWAIN adorned the middle of the eighteenth century, and aided Gen. Braddock with all his heart to resist the oppressor Washington. It was this ancestor who fired seventeen times at our Washington from behind a tree. So far the beautiful romantic narrative in the moral story-books is correct; but when that narrative goes on to say that at the seventeenth round the awe-stricken savage said solemnly that that man was being reserved by the Great Spirit for some mighty mission, and he dared not lift his sacrilegious rifle against him again, the narrative seriously impairs the integrity of history. What he did say was: "It ain't no (hic!) no use. 'At man's so drunk he can't stan' still long enough for a man to hit him. I (hic!) I can't 'ford to fool away any more am'nition on him!"

That was why he stopped at the seventeenth round, and it was, a good plain matter-of-fact reason, too, and one that easily commends itself to us by the eloquent, persuasive flavor of probability there is about it.

I always enjoyed the story-book narrative, but I felt a marring misgiving that every Indian at Braddock's Defeat who fired at a soldier a couple of times (two easily grows to seventeen in a century), and missed him, jumped to the conclusion that the Great Spirit was reserving that soldier for some grand mission; and so I somehow feared that the only reason why Washington's case is remembered and the others forgotten is, that in his the prophecy came true, and in that of the others it didn't. There are not books enough on earth to contain the record of the prophecies Indians and other unauthorized parties have made; but one may carry in his overcoat pockets the record of all the prophecies that have been fulfilled.

I will remark here, in passing, that certain ancestors of mine are so thoroughly well known in history by their aliases, that I have not felt it to be worth while to dwell upon them, or even mention them in the order of their birth. Among these may be mentioned RICHARD BRINSLEY TWAIN, alias Guy Fawkes; JOHN WENTWORTH TWAIN, alias Sixteen-String Jack; WILLIAM HOGARTH TWAIN, alias Jack Sheppard; ANANIAS TWAIN, alias Baron Munchausen; JOHN GEORGE TWAIN, alias Capt. Kydd; and then there are George Francis Train, Tom Pepper, Nebuchadnezzar and Baalam's Ass—they all belong to our family, but to a branch of it somewhat distantly removed from the honorable direct line—in fact, a collateral branch, whose members chiefly differ from the ancient stock in that, in order to acquire the notoriety we have always yearned and hungered for, they have got into a low way of going to jail instead of getting hanged.

It is not well, when writing an autobiography, to follow your ancestry down too close to your own time—it is safest to speak only vaguely of your great-grandfather, and then skip from there to yourself, which I now do.

I was born without teeth—and there Richard III had the advantage of me; but I was born without a humpback, likewise, and there I had the advantage of him. My parents were neither very poor nor conspicuously honest.

But now a thought occurs to me. My own history would really seem so tame contrasted with that of my ancestors, that it is simply wisdom to leave it unwritten until I am hanged. If some other biographies I have read had stopped with the ancestry until a like event occurred, it would have been a felicitous thing, for the reading public. How does it strike you?

AWFUL, TERRIBLE MEDIEVAL ROMANCE

CHAPTER I. THE SECRET REVEALED.

It was night. Stillness reigned in the grand old feudal castle of Klugenstein. The year 1222 was drawing to a close. Far away up in the tallest of the castle's towers a single light glimmered. A secret council was being held there. The stern old lord of Klugenstein sat in a chair of state meditating. Presently he said, with a tender accent:

"My daughter!"

A young man of noble presence, clad from head to heel in knightly mail, answered:

"Speak, father!"

"My daughter, the time is come for the revealing of the mystery that hath puzzled all your young life. Know, then, that it had its birth in the matters which I shall now unfold. My brother Ulrich is the great Duke of Brandenburgh. Our father, on his deathbed, decreed that if no son were born to Ulrich, the succession should pass to my house, provided a son were born to me. And further, in case no son were born to either, but only daughters, then the succession should pass to Ulrich's daughter, if she proved stainless; if she did not, my daughter should succeed, if she retained a blameless name. And so I, and my old wife here, prayed fervently for the good boon of a son, but the prayer was vain. You were born to us. I was in despair. I saw the mighty prize slipping from my grasp, the splendid dream vanishing away. And I had been so hopeful! Five years had Ulrich lived in wedlock, and yet his wife had borne no heir of either sex.

"'But hold,' I said, 'all is not lost.' A saving scheme had shot athwart my brain. You were born at midnight. Only the leech, the nurse, and six waiting-women knew your sex. I hanged them every one before an hour had sped. Next morning all the barony went mad with rejoicing over the proclamation that a son was born to Klugenstein, an heir to mighty Brandenburgh! And well the secret has been kept. Your mother's own sister nursed your infancy, and from that time forward we feared nothing.

"When you were ten years old, a daughter was born to Ulrich. We grieved, but hoped for good results from measles, or physicians, or other natural enemies of infancy, but were always disappointed. She lived, she throve—Heaven's malison upon her! But it is nothing. We are safe. For, Ha-ha! have we not a son? And is not our son the future Duke? Our well-beloved Conrad, is it not so?—for, woman of eight-and-twenty years— as you are, my child, none other name than that hath ever fallen to you!

"Now it hath come to pass that age hath laid its hand upon my brother, and he waxes feeble. The cares of state do tax him sore. Therefore he wills that you shall come to him and be already Duke—in act, though not yet in name. Your servitors are ready—you journey forth to-night.

"Now listen well. Remember every word I say. There is a law as old as Germany that if any woman sit for a single instant in the great ducal chair before she hath been absolutely crowned in presence of the people, SHE SHALL DIE! So heed my words. Pretend humility. Pronounce your judgments from the Premier's chair, which stands at the foot of the throne. Do this until you are crowned and safe. It is not likely that your sex will ever be discovered; but still it is the part of wisdom to make all things as safe as may be in this treacherous earthly life."

"Oh; my father, is it for this my life hath been a lie! Was it that I might cheat my unoffending cousin of her rights? Spare me, father, spare your child!"

"What, huzzy! Is this my reward for the august fortune my brain has wrought for thee? By the bones of my father, this puling sentiment of thine but ill accords with my humor.

"Betake thee to the Duke, instantly! And beware how thou meddlest with my purpose!"

Let this suffice, of the conversation. It is enough for us to know that the prayers, the entreaties and the tears of the gentle-natured girl availed nothing. They nor anything could move the stout old lord of Klugenstein. And so, at last, with a heavy heart, the daughter saw the castle gates close behind her, and found herself riding away in the darkness surrounded by a knightly array of armed vassals and a brave following of servants.

The old baron sat silent for many minutes after his daughter's departure, and then he turned to his sad wife and said:

"Dame, our matters seem speeding fairly. It is full three months since I sent the shrewd and handsome Count Detzin on his devilish mission to my brother's daughter Constance. If he fail, we are not wholly safe; but if he do succeed, no power can bar our girl from being Duchess e'en though ill-fortune should decree she never should be Duke!"

"My heart is full of bodings, yet all may still be well."

"Tush, woman! Leave the owls to croak. To bed with ye, and dream of Brandenburgh and grandeur!"

CHAPTER II. FESTIVITY AND TEARS

Six days after the occurrences related in the above chapter, the brilliant capital of the Duchy of Brandenburgh was resplendent with military pageantry, and noisy with the rejoicings of loyal multitudes; for Conrad, the young heir to the crown, was come. The old Duke's heart was full of happiness, for Conrad's handsome person and graceful bearing had won his love at once. The great halls of the palace were thronged with nobles, who welcomed Conrad bravely; and so bright and happy did all things seem, that he felt his fears and sorrows passing away and giving place to a comforting contentment.

But in a remote apartment of the palace a scene of a different nature was transpiring. By a window stood the Duke's only child, the Lady Constance. Her eyes were red and swollen, and full of tears. She was alone. Presently she fell to weeping anew, and said aloud:

"The villain Detzin is gone—has fled the dukedom! I could not believe it at first, but alas! it is too true. And I loved him so. I dared to love him though I knew the Duke my father would never let me wed him. I loved him—but now I hate him! With all my soul I hate him! Oh, what is to become of me! I am lost, lost, lost! I shall go mad!"

CHAPTER III. THE PLOT THICKENS.

A few months drifted by. All men published the praises of the young Conrad's government and extolled the wisdom of his judgments, the mercifulness of his sentences, and the modesty with which he bore himself in his great office. The old Duke soon gave everything into his hands, and sat apart and listened with proud satisfaction while his heir delivered the decrees of the crown from the seat of the premier. It seemed plain that one so loved and praised and honored of all men as Conrad was, could not be otherwise than happy. But strange enough, he was not. For he saw with dismay that the Princess Constance had begun to love him! The love of the rest of the world was happy fortune for him, but this was freighted with danger! And he saw, moreover, that the delighted Duke had discovered his daughter's passion likewise, and was already dreaming of a marriage. Every day somewhat of the deep sadness that had been in the princess' face faded away; every day hope and animation beamed brighter from her eye; and by and by even vagrant smiles visited the face that had been so troubled.

Conrad was appalled. He bitterly cursed himself for having yielded to the instinct that had made him seek the companionship of one of his own sex when he was new and a stranger in the palace—when he was sorrowful and yearned for a sympathy such as only women can give or feel. He now began to avoid, his cousin. But this only made matters worse, for, naturally enough, the more he avoided her, the more she cast herself in his way. He marvelled at this at first; and next it startled him. The girl haunted him; she hunted him; she happened upon him at all times and in all places, in the night as well as in the day. She seemed singularly anxious. There was surely a mystery somewhere.

This could not go on forever. All the world was talking about it. The Duke was beginning to look perplexed. Poor Conrad was becoming a very ghost through dread and dire distress. One day as he was emerging from a private ante-room attached to the picture gallery, Constance confronted him, and seizing both his hands, in hers, exclaimed:

"Oh, why, do you avoid me? What have I done—what have I said, to lose your kind opinion of me—for, surely I had it once? Conrad, do not despise me, but pity a tortured heart? I cannot—cannot hold the words unspoken longer, lest they kill me—I LOVE you, CONRAD! There, despise me if you must, but they would be uttered!"

Conrad was speechless. Constance hesitated a moment, and then, misinterpreting his silence, a wild gladness flamed in her eyes, and she flung her arms about his neck and said:

"You relent! you relent! You can love me—you will love me! Oh, say you will, my own, my worshipped Conrad!"

Conrad groaned aloud. A sickly pallor overspread his countenance, and he trembled like an aspen. Presently, in desperation, he thrust the poor girl from him, and cried:

"You know not what you ask! It is forever and ever impossible!" And then he fled like a criminal and left the princess stupefied with amazement. A minute afterward she was crying and sobbing there, and Conrad was crying and sobbing in his chamber. Both were in despair. Both saw ruin staring them in the face.

By and by Constance rose slowly to her feet and moved away, saying:

"To think that he was despising my love at the very moment that I thought it was melting his cruel heart! I hate him! He spurned me—did this man—he spurned me from him like a dog!"

CHAPTER IV. THE AWFUL REVELATION.

Time passed on. A settled sadness rested once more upon the countenance of the good Duke's daughter. She and Conrad were seen together no more now. The Duke grieved at this. But as the weeks wore away, Conrad's color came back to his cheeks and his old-time vivacity to his eye, and he administered the government with a clear and steadily ripening wisdom.

Presently a strange whisper began to be heard about the palace. It grew louder; it spread farther. The gossips of the city got hold of it. It swept the dukedom. And this is what the whisper said:

"The Lady Constance hath given birth to a child!"

When the lord of Klugenstein heard it, he swung his plumed helmet thrice around his head and shouted:

"Long live Duke Conrad!—for lo, his crown is sure, from this day forward! Detzin has done his errand well, and the good scoundrel shall be rewarded!"

And he spread the tidings far and wide, and for eight-and-forty hours no soul in all the barony but did dance and sing, carouse and illuminate, to celebrate the great event, and all at proud and happy old Klugenstein's expense.

CHAPTER V. THE FRIGHTFUL CATASTROPHE.

The trial was at hand. All the great lords and barons of Brandenburgh were assembled in the Hall of Justice in the ducal palace. No space was left unoccupied where there was room for a spectator to stand or sit. Conrad, clad in purple and ermine, sat in the premier's chair, and on either side sat the great judges of the realm. The old Duke had sternly commanded that the trial of his daughter should proceed, without favor, and then had taken to his bed broken-hearted. His days were numbered. Poor Conrad had begged, as for his very life, that he might be spared the misery of sitting in judgment upon his cousin's crime, but it did not avail.

The saddest heart in all that great assemblage was in Conrad's breast.

The gladdest was in his father's. For, unknown to his daughter "Conrad," the old Baron Klugenstein was come, and was among the crowd of nobles, triumphant in the swelling fortunes of his house.

After the heralds had made due proclamation and the other preliminaries had followed, the venerable Lord Chief justice said:

"Prisoner, stand forth!"

The unhappy princess rose and stood unveiled before the vast multitude. The Lord Chief Justice continued:

"Most noble lady, before the great judges of this realm it hath been charged and proven that out of holy wedlock your Grace hath given birth unto a child; and by our ancient law the penalty is death, excepting in one sole contingency, whereof his Grace the acting Duke, our good Lord Conrad, will advertise you in his solemn sentence now; wherefore, give heed."

Conrad stretched forth the reluctant sceptre, and in the self-same moment the womanly heart beneath his robe yearned pityingly toward the doomed prisoner, and the tears came into his eyes. He opened his lips to speak, but the Lord Chief Justice said quickly:

"Not there, your Grace, not there! It is not lawful to pronounce judgment upon any of the ducal line SAVE FROM THE DUCAL THRONE!"

A shudder went to the heart of poor Conrad, and a tremor shook the iron frame of his old father likewise. CONRAD HAD NOT BEEN CROWNED—dared he profane the throne? He hesitated and turned pale with fear. But it must be done. Wondering eyes were already upon him. They would be suspicious eyes if he hesitated longer. He ascended the throne. Presently he stretched forth the sceptre again, and said:

"Prisoner, in the name of our sovereign lord, Ulrich, Duke of Brandenburgh, I proceed to the solemn duty that hath devolved upon me. Give heed to my words. By the ancient law of the land, except you produce the partner of your guilt and deliver him up to the executioner, you must surely die. Embrace this opportunity—save yourself while yet you may. Name the father of your child!"

A solemn hush fell upon the great court—a silence so profound that men could hear their own hearts beat. Then the princess slowly turned, with eyes gleaming with hate, and pointing her finger straight at Conrad, said:

"Thou art the man!"

An appalling conviction of his helpless, hopeless peril struck a chill to Conrad's heart like the chill of death itself. What power on earth could save him! To disprove the charge, he must reveal that he was a woman; and for an uncrowned woman to sit in the ducal chair was death! At one and the same moment, he and his grim old father swooned and fell to, the ground.

[The remainder of this thrilling and eventful story will NOT be found in this or any other publication, either now or at any future time.]

The truth is, I have got my hero (or heroine) into such a particularly close place, that I do not see how I am ever going to get him (or her) out of it again—and therefore I will wash my hands of the whole business, and leave that person to get out the best way that offers—or else stay there. I thought it was going to be easy enough to straighten out that little difficulty, but it looks different now.

SKETCHES NEW AND OLD

MY WATCH

AN INSTRUCTIVE LITTLE TALE—

[Written about 1870.]

My beautiful new watch had run eighteen months without losing or gaining, and without breaking any part of its machinery or stopping. I had come to believe it infallible in its judgments about the time of day, and to consider its constitution and its anatomy imperishable. But at last, one night, I let it run down. I grieved about it as if it were a recognized messenger and forerunner of calamity. But by and by I cheered up, set the watch by guess, and commanded my bodings and superstitions to depart. Next day I stepped into the chief jeweler's to set it by the exact time, and the head of the establishment took it out of my hand and proceeded to set it for me. Then he said, "She is four minutes slow-regulator wants pushing up." I tried to stop him—tried to make him understand that the watch kept perfect time. But no; all this human cabbage could see was that the watch was four minutes slow, and the regulator must be pushed up a little; and so, while I danced around him in anguish, and implored him to let the watch alone, he calmly and cruelly did the shameful deed. My watch began to gain. It gained faster and faster day by day. Within the week it sickened to a raging fever, and its pulse went up to a hundred and fifty in the shade. At the end of two months it had left all the timepieces of the town far in the rear, and was a fraction over thirteen days ahead of the almanac. It was away into November enjoying the snow, while the October leaves were still turning. It hurried up house rent, bills payable, and such things, in such a ruinous way that I could not abide it. I took it to the watchmaker to be regulated. He asked me if I had ever had it repaired. I said no, it had never needed any repairing. He looked a look of vicious happiness and eagerly pried the watch open, and then put a small dice-box into his eye and peered into its machinery. He said it wanted cleaning and oiling, besides regulating—come in a week. After being cleaned and oiled, and regulated, my watch slowed down to that degree that it ticked like a tolling bell. I began to be left by trains,

I failed all appointments, I got to missing my dinner; my watch strung out three days' grace to four and let me go to protest; I gradually drifted back into yesterday, then day before, then into last week, and by and by the comprehension came upon me that all solitary and alone I was lingering along in week before last, and the world was out of sight. I seemed to detect in myself a sort of sneaking fellow-feeling for the mummy in the museum, and a desire to swap news with him. I went to a watchmaker again. He took the watch all to pieces while I waited, and then said the barrel was "swelled." He said he could reduce it in three days. After this the watch averaged well, but nothing more. For half a day it would go like the very mischief, and keep up such a barking and wheezing and whooping and sneezing and snorting, that I could not hear myself think for the disturbance; and as long as it held out there was not a watch in the land that stood any chance against it. But the rest of the day it would keep on slowing down and fooling along until all the clocks it had left behind caught up again. So at last, at the end of twenty-four hours, it would trot up to the judges' stand all right and just in time. It would show a fair and square average, and no man could say it had done more or less than its duty. But a correct average is only a mild virtue in a watch, and I took this instrument to another watchmaker. He said the king-bolt was broken. I said I was glad it was nothing more serious. To tell the plain truth, I had no idea what the king-bolt was, but I did not choose to appear ignorant to a stranger.

He repaired the king-bolt, but what the watch gained in one way it lost in another. It would run awhile and then stop awhile, and then run awhile again, and so on, using its own discretion about the intervals. And every time it went off it kicked back like a musket. I padded my breast for a few days, but finally took the watch to another watchmaker. He picked it all to pieces, and turned the ruin over and over under his glass; and then he said there appeared to be something the matter with the hair-trigger. He fixed it, and gave it a fresh start. It did well now, except that always at ten minutes to ten the hands would shut together like a pair of scissors, and from that time forth they would travel together. The oldest man in the world could not make head or tail of the time of day by such a watch, and so I went again to have the thing repaired. This person said that the crystal had got bent, and that the mainspring was not straight. He also remarked that part of the works needed half-soling. He made these things all right, and then my timepiece performed unexceptionably, save that now and then, after working along quietly for nearly eight hours, everything inside would let go all of a sudden and begin to buzz like a bee, and the hands would straightway begin to spin round and round so fast that their individuality was lost completely, and they simply seemed a delicate spider's web over the face of the watch. She would reel off the next twenty-four hours in six or seven minutes, and then stop with a bang. I went with a heavy heart to one more watchmaker, and looked on while he took her to pieces. Then I prepared to cross-question him rigidly, for this thing was getting serious. The watch had cost two hundred dollars originally, and I seemed to have paid out two or three thousand for repairs. While I waited and looked on I presently recognized in this watchmaker an old acquaintance— a steamboat engineer of other days, and not a good engineer, either. He examined all the parts carefully, just as the other watchmakers had done, and then delivered his verdict with the same confidence of manner.

He said:

"She makes too much steam—you want to hang the monkey-wrench on the safety-valve!"

I brained him on the spot, and had him buried at my own expense.

My uncle William (now deceased, alas!) used to say that a good horse was, a good horse until it had run away once, and that a good watch was a good watch until the repairers got a chance at it. And he used to wonder what became of all the unsuccessful tinkers, and gunsmiths, and shoemakers, and engineers, and blacksmiths; but nobody could ever tell him.

POLITICAL ECONOMY

Political Economy is the basis of all good government. The wisest men of all ages have brought to bear upon this subject the—

[Here I was interrupted and informed that a stranger wished to see me down at the door. I went and confronted him, and asked to know his business, struggling all the time to keep a tight rein on my seething political-economy ideas, and not let them break away from me or get tangled in their harness. And privately I wished the stranger was in the bottom of the canal with a cargo of wheat on top of him. I was all in a fever, but he was cool. He said he was sorry to disturb me, but as he was passing he noticed that I needed some lightning-rods. I said, "Yes, yes—go on—what about it?" He said there was nothing about it, in particular—nothing except that he would like to put them up for me. I am new to housekeeping; have been used to hotels and boarding-houses all my life. Like anybody else of similar experience, I try to appear (to strangers) to be an old housekeeper; consequently I said in an offhand way that I had been intending for some time to have six or eight lightning-rods put up, but—The stranger started, and looked inquiringly at me, but I was serene. I thought that if I chanced to make any mistakes, he would not catch me by my countenance. He said he would rather have my custom than any man's in town. I said, "All right," and started off to wrestle with my great subject again, when he called me back and said it would be necessary to know exactly how many "points" I wanted put up, what parts of the house I wanted them on, and what quality of rod I preferred. It was close quarters for a man not used to the exigencies of housekeeping; but I went through creditably, and he probably never suspected that I was a novice. I told him to put up eight "points," and put them all on the roof, and use the best quality of rod. He said he could furnish the "plain" article at 20 cents a foot; "coppered," 25 cents; "zinc-plated spiral-twist," at 30 cents, that would stop a streak of lightning any time, no matter where it was bound, and "render its errand harmless and its further progress apocryphal." I said apocryphal was no slouch of a word, emanating from the source it did, but, philology aside, I liked the spiral-twist and would take that brand. Then he said he could make two hundred and fifty feet answer; but to do it right, and make the best job in town of it, and attract the admiration of the just and the unjust alike, and compel all parties to say they never saw a more symmetrical and hypothetical display of lightning-rods since they were born, he supposed he really couldn't get along without four hundred, though he was not vindictive, and trusted he was willing to try. I said, go ahead and use four hundred, and make any kind of a job he pleased out of it, but let me get back to my work. So I got rid of him at last; and now, after half an hour spent in getting my train of political-economy thoughts coupled together again, I am ready to go on once more.]

richest treasures of their genius, their experience of life, and their learning. The great lights of commercial jurisprudence, international confraternity, and biological deviation, of all ages, all civilizations, and all nationalities, from Zoroaster down to Horace Greeley, have—

[Here I was interrupted again, and required to go down and confer further with that lightning-rod man. I hurried off, boiling and surging with prodigious thoughts wombed in words of such majesty that each one of them was in itself a straggling procession of syllables that might be fifteen minutes passing a given point, and once more I confronted him—he so calm and sweet, I so hot and frenzied. He was standing in the contemplative attitude of the Colossus of Rhodes, with one foot on my infant tuberose, and the other among my pansies, his hands on his hips, his hat-brim tilted forward, one eye shut and the other gazing critically and admiringly in the direction of my principal chimney. He said now there was a state of things to make a man glad to be alive; and added, "I leave it to you if you ever saw anything more deliriously picturesque than eight lightning-rods on one chimney?" I said I had no present recollection of anything that transcended it. He said that in his opinion nothing on earth but Niagara Falls was superior to it in the way of natural scenery. All that was needed now, he verily believed, to make my house a perfect balm to the eye, was to kind of touch up the other chimneys a little, and thus "add to the generous 'coup d'oeil' a soothing uniformity of achievement which would allay the excitement naturally consequent upon the 'coup d'etat.'" I asked him if he learned to talk out of a book, and if I could borrow it anywhere? He smiled pleasantly, and said that his manner of speaking was not taught in books, and that nothing but familiarity with lightning could enable a man to handle his conversational style with impunity. He then figured up an estimate, and said that about eight more rods scattered about my roof would about fix me right, and he guessed five hundred feet of stuff would do it; and added that the first eight had got a little the start of him, so to speak, and used up a mere trifle of material more than he had calculated on—a hundred feet or along there. I said I was in a dreadful hurry, and I wished we could get this business permanently mapped out, so that I could go on with my work. He said, "I could have put up those eight rods, and marched off about my business—some men would have done it. But no; I said to myself, this man is a stranger to me, and I will die before I'll wrong him; there ain't lightning-rods enough on that house, and for one I'll never stir out of my tracks till I've done as I would be done by, and told him so. Stranger, my duty is accomplished; if the recalcitrant and dephlogistic messenger of heaven strikes your—" "There, now, there," I said, "put on the other eight—add five hundred feet of spiral-twist—do anything and everything you want to do; but calm your sufferings, and try to keep your feelings where you can reach them with the dictionary. Meanwhile, if we understand each other now, I will go to work again."

I think I have been sitting here a full hour this time, trying to get back to where I was when my train of thought was broken up by the last interruption; but I believe I have accomplished it at last, and may venture to proceed again.]

      wrestled with this great subject, and the greatest among them have found it a worthy adversary, and one that always comes up fresh and smiling after every throw. The great Confucius said that he would rather be a profound political economist than chief of police. Cicero frequently said that political economy was the grandest consummation that the human mind was capable of consuming; and even our own Greeley had said vaguely but forcibly that "Political—

[Here the lightning-rod man sent up another call for me. I went down in a state of mind bordering on impatience. He said he would rather have died than interrupt me, but when he was employed to do a job, and that job was expected to be done in a clean, workmanlike manner, and when it was finished and fatigue urged him to seek the rest and recreation he stood so much in need of, and he was about to do it, but looked up and saw at a glance that all the calculations had been a little out, and if a thunder-storm were to come up, and that house, which he felt a personal interest in, stood there with nothing on earth to protect it but sixteen lightning-rods—"Let us have peace!" I shrieked. "Put up a hundred and fifty! Put some on the kitchen! Put a dozen on the barn! Put a couple on the cow! Put one on the cook!—scatter them all over the persecuted place till it looks like a zinc-plated, spiral-twisted, silver-mounted cane-brake! Move! Use up all the material you can get your hands on, and when you run out of lightning-rods put up ramrods, cam-rods, stair-rods, piston-rods—anything that will pander to your dismal appetite for artificial scenery, and bring respite to my raging brain and healing to my lacerated soul!" Wholly unmoved—further than to smile sweetly—this iron being simply turned back his wrist-bands daintily, and said he would now proceed to hump himself. Well, all that was nearly three hours ago. It is questionable whether I am calm enough yet to write on the noble theme of political economy, but I cannot resist the desire to try, for it is the one subject that is nearest to my heart and dearest to my brain of all this world's philosophy.]

economy is heaven's best boon to man." When the loose but gifted Byron lay in his Venetian exile he observed that, if it could be granted him to go back and live his misspent life over again, he would give his lucid and unintoxicated intervals to the composition, not of frivolous rhymes, but of essays upon political economy. Washington loved this exquisite science; such names as Baker, Beckwith, Judson, Smith, are imperishably linked with it; and even imperial Homer, in the ninth book of the Iliad, has said:

Fiat justitia, ruat coelum,
Post mortem unum, ante bellum,
Hic jacet hoc, ex-parte res,
Politicum e-conomico est.

The grandeur of these conceptions of the old poet, together with the felicity of the wording which clothes them, and the sublimity of the imagery whereby they are illustrated, have singled out that stanza, and made it more celebrated than any that ever—

["Now, not a word out of you—not a single word. Just state your bill and relapse into impenetrable silence for ever and ever on these premises. Nine hundred, dollars? Is that all? This check for the amount will be honored at any respectable bank in America. What is that multitude of people gathered in the street for? How?—'looking at the lightning-rods!' Bless my life, did they never see any lightning-rods before? Never saw 'such a stack of them on one establishment,' did I understand you to say? I will step down and critically observe this popular ebullition of ignorance."]

THREE DAYS LATER.—We are all about worn out. For four-and-twenty hours our bristling premises were the talk and wonder of the town. The theaters languished, for their happiest scenic inventions were tame and commonplace compared with my lightning-rods. Our street was blocked night and day with spectators, and among them were many who came from the country to see. It was a blessed relief on the second day when a thunderstorm came up and the lightning began to "go for" my house, as the historian Josephus quaintly phrases it. It cleared the galleries, so to speak. In five minutes there was not a spectator within half a mile of my place; but all the high houses about that distance away were full, windows, roof, and all. And well they might be, for all the falling stars and Fourth-of-July fireworks of a generation, put together and rained down simultaneously out of heaven in one brilliant shower upon one helpless roof, would not have any advantage of the pyrotechnic display that was making my house so magnificently conspicuous in the general gloom of the storm.

By actual count, the lightning struck at my establishment seven hundred and sixty-four times in forty minutes, but tripped on one of those faithful rods every time, and slid down the spiral-twist and shot into the earth before it probably had time to be surprised at the way the thing was done. And through all that bombardment only one patch of slates was ripped up, and that was because, for a single instant, the rods in the vicinity were transporting all the lightning they could possibly accommodate. Well, nothing was ever seen like it since the world began. For one whole day and night not a member of my family stuck his head out of the window but he got the hair snatched off it as smooth as a billiard-ball; and; if the reader will believe me, not one of us ever dreamt of stirring abroad. But at last the awful siege came to an end-because there was absolutely no more electricity left in the clouds above us within grappling distance of my insatiable rods. Then I sallied forth, and gathered daring workmen together, and not a bite or a nap did we take till the premises were utterly stripped of all their terrific armament except just three rods on the house, one on the kitchen, and one on the barn—and, behold, these remain there even unto this day. And then, and not till then, the people ventured to use our street again. I will remark here, in passing, that during that fearful time I did not continue my essay upon political economy. I am not even yet settled enough in nerve and brain to resume it.

TO WHOM IT MAY CONCERN.—Parties having need of three thousand two hundred and eleven feet of best quality zinc-plated spiral-twist lightning-rod stuff, and sixteen hundred and thirty-one silver-tipped points, all in tolerable repair (and, although much worn by use, still equal to any ordinary emergency), can hear of a bargain by addressing the publisher.

THE JUMPING FROG

[written about 1865]

IN ENGLISH. THEN IN FRENCH. THEN CLAWED BACK INTO A CIVILIZED LANGUAGE ONCE MORE BY PATIENT, UNREMUNERATED TOIL.

Even a criminal is entitled to fair play; and certainly when a man who has done no harm has been unjustly treated, he is privileged to do his best to right himself. My attention has just been called to an article some three years old in a French Magazine entitled, 'Revue des Deux Mondes' (Review of Some Two Worlds), wherein the writer treats of "Les Humoristes Americaines" (These Humorist Americans). I am one of these humorist American dissected by him, and hence the complaint I am making.

This gentleman's article is an able one (as articles go, in the French, where they always tangle up everything to that degree that when you start into a sentence you never know whether you are going to come out alive or not). It is a very good article and the writer says all manner of kind and complimentary things about me—for which I am sure I thank him with all my heart; but then why should he go and spoil all his praise by one unlucky experiment? What I refer to is this: he says my Jumping Frog is a funny story, but still he can't see why it should ever really convulse any one with laughter—and straightway proceeds to translate it into French in order to prove to his nation that there is nothing so very extravagantly funny about it. Just there is where my complaint originates. He has not translated it at all; he has simply mixed it all up; it is no more like the Jumping Frog when he gets through with it than I am like a meridian of longitude. But my mere assertion is not proof; wherefore I print the French version, that all may see that I do not speak falsely; furthermore, in order that even the unlettered may know my injury and give me their compassion, I have been at infinite pains and trouble to retranslate this French version back into English; and to tell the truth I have well-nigh worn myself out at it, having scarcely rested from my work during five days and nights. I cannot speak the French language, but I can translate very well, though not fast, I being self-educated. I ask the reader to run his eye over the original English version of the jumping Frog, and then read the French or my retranslation, and kindly take notice how the Frenchman has riddled the grammar. I think it is the worst I ever saw; and yet the French are called a polished nation. If I had a boy that put sentences together as they do, I would polish him to some purpose. Without further introduction, the Jumping Frog, as I originally wrote it, was as follows [after it will be found the French version—, and after the latter my retranslation from the French]

THE NOTORIOUS JUMPING FROG OF CALAVERAS COUNTY
[PRONOUNCED CAL-E-VA-RAS]

In compliance with the request of a friend of mine, who wrote me from the East, I called on good-natured, garrulous old Simon Wheeler, and inquired after my friend's friend, Leonidas W. Smiley, as requested to do, and I hereunto append the result. I have a lurking suspicion that Leonidas W. Smiley is a myth that my friend never knew such a personage; and that he only conjectured that if I asked old Wheeler about him, it would remind him of his infamous Jim Smiley, and he would go to work and bore me to death with some exasperating reminiscence of him as long and as tedious as it should be useless to me. If that was the design, it succeeded.

I found Simon Wheeler dozing comfortably by the bar-room stove of the dilapidated tavern in the decayed mining camp of Angel's, and I noticed that he was fat and bald-headed, and had an expression of winning gentleness and simplicity upon his tranquil countenance. He roused up, and gave me good day. I told him that a friend of mine had commissioned me to make some inquiries about a cherished companion of his boyhood named Leonidas W. Smiley—Rev. Leonidas W. Smiley, a young minister of the Gospel, who he had heard was at one time resident of Angel's Camp. I added that if Mr. Wheeler could tell me anything about this Rev. Leonidas W. Smiley, I would feel under many obligations to him.

Simon Wheeler backed me into a corner and blockaded me there with his chair, and then sat down and reeled off the monotonous narrative which follows this paragraph. He never smiled, he never frowned, he never changed his voice from the gentle flowing key to which he tuned his initial sentence, he never betrayed the slightest suspicion of enthusiasm; but all through the interminable narrative there ran a vein of impressive earnestness and sincerity, which showed me plainly that, so far from his imagining that there was anything ridiculous or funny about his story, he regarded it as a really important matter, and admired its two heroes as men of transcendent genius in 'finesse.' I let him go on in his own way, and never interrupted him once.

"Rev. Leonidas W. H'm, Reverend Le—well, there was a feller here, once by the name of Jim Smiley, in the winter of '49—or maybe it was the spring of '50—I don't recollect exactly, somehow, though what makes me think it was one or the other is because I remember the big flume warn't finished when he first come to the camp; but anyway, he was the curiousest man about always betting on anything that turned up you ever see, if he could get anybody to bet on the other side; and if he couldn't he'd change sides. Any way that suited the other man would suit him any way just so's he got a bet, he was satisfied. But still he was lucky, uncommon lucky; he most always come out winner. He was always ready and laying for a chance; there couldn't be no solit'ry thing mentioned but that feller'd offer to bet on it, and take any side you please, as I was just telling you.

If there was a horse-race, you'd find him flush or you'd find him busted at the end of it; if there was a dog-fight, he'd bet on it; if there was a cat-fight, he'd bet on it; if there was a chicken-fight, he'd bet on it; why, if there was two birds setting on a fence, he would bet you which one would fly first; or if there was a camp-meeting, he would be there reg'lar to bet on Parson Walker, which he judged to be the best exhorter about here, and so he was too, and a good man. If he even see a straddle-bug start to go anywheres, he would bet you how long it would take him to get to—to wherever he was going to, and if you took him up, he would foller that straddle-bug to Mexico but what he would find out where he was bound for and how long he was on the road. Lots of the boys here has seen that Smiley, and can tell you about him. Why, it never made no difference to him—he'd bet on any thing—the dangdest feller. Parson Walker's wife laid very sick once, for a good while, and it seemed as if they warn't going to save her; but one morning he come in, and Smiley up and asked him how she was, and he said she was considerable better—thank the Lord for his inf'nite mercy—and coming on so smart that with the blessing of Prov'dence she'd get well yet; and Smiley, before he thought, says, 'Well, I'll resk two-and-a-half she don't anyway.'

"Thish-yer Smiley had a mare—the boys called her the fifteen-minute nag, but that was only in fun, you know, because of course she was faster than that—and he used to win money on that horse, for all she was so slow and always had the asthma, or the distemper, or the consumption, or something of that kind. They used to give her two or three hundred yards' start, and then pass her under way; but always at the fag end of the race she get excited and desperate like, and come cavorting and straddling up, and scattering her legs around limber, sometimes in the air, and sometimes out to one side among the fences, and kicking up m-o-r-e dust and raising m-o-r-e racket with her coughing and sneezing and blowing her nose—and always fetch up at the stand just about a neck ahead, as near as you could cipher it down.

"And he had a little small bull-pup, that to look at him you'd think he warn't worth a cent but to set around and look ornery and lay for a chance to steal something. But as soon as money was up on him he was a different dog; his under-jaw'd begin to stick out like the fo'castle of a steamboat, and his teeth would uncover and shine like the furnaces.

And a dog might tackle him and bully-rag him, and bite him, and throw him over his shoulder two or three times, and Andrew Jackson—which was the name of the pup—Andrew Jackson would never let on but what he was satisfied, and hadn't expected nothing else—and the bets being doubled and doubled on the other side all the time, till the money was all up; and then all of a sudden he would grab that other dog jest by the j'int of his hind leg and freeze to it—not chaw, you understand, but only just grip and hang on till they threw up the sponge, if it was a year. Smiley always come out winner on that pup, till he harnessed a dog once that didn't have no hind legs, because they'd been sawed off in a circular saw, and when the thing had gone along far enough, and the money was all up, and he come to make a snatch for his pet holt, he see in a minute how he'd been imposed on, and how the other dog had him in the door, so to speak, and he 'peared surprised, and then he looked sorter discouraged-like and didn't try no more to win the fight, and so he got shucked out bad. He give Smiley a look, as much as to say his heart was broke, and it was his fault, for putting up a dog that hadn't no hind legs for him to take holt of, which was his main dependence in a fight, and then he limped off a piece and laid down and died. It was a good pup, was that Andrew Jackson, and would have made a name for hisself if he'd lived, for the stuff was in him and he had genius—I know it, because he hadn't no opportunities to speak of, and it don't stand to reason that a dog could make such a fight as he could under them circumstances if he hadn't no talent. It always makes me feel sorry when I think of that last fight of his'n, and the way it turned out.

"Well, thish-yer Smiley had rat-tarriers, and chicken cocks, and tomcats and all them kind of things, till you couldn't rest, and you couldn't fetch nothing for him to bet on but he'd match you. He ketched a frog one day, and took him home, and said he cal'lated to educate him; and so he never done nothing for three months but set in his back yard and learn that frog to jump. And you bet you he did learn him, too. He'd give him a little punch behind, and the next minute you'd see that frog whirling in the air like a doughnut—see him turn one summerset, or maybe a couple, if he got a good start, and come down flat-footed and all right, like a cat. He got him up so in the matter of ketching flies, and kep' him in practice so constant, that he'd nail a fly every time as fur as he could see him. Smiley said all a frog wanted was education, and he could do 'most anything—and I believe him. Why, I've seen him set Dan'l Webster down here on this floor—Dan'l Webster was the name of the frog—and sing out, 'Flies, Dan'l, flies!' and quicker'n you could wink he'd spring straight up and snake a fly off'n the counter there, and flop down on the floor ag'in as solid as a gob of mud, and fall to scratching the side of his head with his hind foot as indifferent as if he hadn't no idea he'd been doin' any more'n any frog might do. You never see a frog so modest and straightfor'ard as he was, for all he was so gifted. And when it come to fair and square jumping on a dead level, he could get over more ground at one straddle than any animal of his breed you ever see. Jumping on a dead level was his strong suit, you understand; and when it come to that, Smiley would ante up money on him as long as he had a red. Smiley was monstrous proud of his frog, and well he might be, for fellers that had traveled and been everywheres all said he laid over any frog that ever they see.

"Well, Smiley kep' the beast in a little lattice box, and he used to fetch him down-town sometimes and lay for a bet. One day a feller—a stranger in the camp, he was—come acrost him with his box, and says:

"'What might it be that you've got in the box?'

"And Smiley says, sorter indifferent-like, 'It might be a parrot, or it might be a canary, maybe, but it ain't—it's only just a frog.'

"And the feller took it, and looked at it careful, and turned it round this way and that, and says, 'H'm—so 'tis. Well, what's HE good for.

"'Well,' Smiley says, easy and careless, 'he's good enough for one thing, I should judge—he can outjump any frog in Calaveras County.

"The feller took the box again, and took another long, particular look, and give it back to Smiley, and says, very deliberate, 'Well,' he says, 'I don't see no p'ints about that frog that's any better'n any other frog.'

"'Maybe you don't,' Smiley says. 'Maybe you understand frogs and maybe you don't understand 'em; maybe you've had experience, and maybe you ain't only a amature, as it were. Anyways, I've got my opinion, and I'll resk forty dollars thet he can outjump any frog in Calaveras County.'

"And the feller studied a minute, and then says, kinder sad-like, 'Well, I'm only a stranger here, and I ain't got no frog; but if I had a frog, I'd bet you.

"And then Smiley says, 'That's all right—that's all right if you'll hold my box a minute, I'll go and get you a frog.' And so the feller took the box, and put up his forty dollars along with Smiley's, and set down to wait.

"So he set there a good while thinking and thinking to himself and then he got the frog out and prized his mouth open and took a teaspoon and filled him full of quail-shot— filled him pretty near up to his chin—and set him on the floor. Smiley he went to the swamp and slopped around in the mud for a long time, and finally he ketched a frog, and fetched him in, and give him to this feller and says:

"'Now, if you're ready, set him alongside of Dan'l, with his fore paws just even with Dan'l's, and I'll give the word.' Then he says, One-two-three—git' and him and the feller touches up the frogs from behind, and the new frog hopped off lively but Dan'l give a heave, and hysted up his shoulders—so—like a Frenchman, but it warn't no use—he couldn't budge; he was planted as solid as a church, and he couldn't no more stir than if he was anchored out. Smiley was a good deal surprised, and he was disgusted too, but he didn't have no idea what the matter was of course.

"The feller took the money and started away; and when he was going out at the door, he sorter jerked his thumb over his shoulder—so—at Dan'l, and says again, very deliberate, 'Well,' he says, 'I don't see no p'ints about that frog that's any better'n any other frog.'

"Smiley he stood scratching his head and looking down at Dan'l a long time, and at last he says, 'I do wonder what in the nation that frog throw'd off for—I wonder if there ain't something the matter with him—he 'pears to look mighty baggy, somehow.' And he ketched Dan'l by the nap of the neck, and hefted him, and says, 'Why blame my cats if he don't weigh five pound!' and turned him upside down and he belched out a double handful of shot. And then he see how it was, and he was the maddest man—he set the frog down and took out after that feller, but he never ketched him. And—"

[Here Simon Wheeler heard his name called from the front yard, and got up to see what was wanted.] And turning to me as he moved away, he said: "Just set where you are, stranger, and rest easy—I ain't going to be gone a second."

But, by your leave, I did not think that a continuation of the history of the enterprising vagabond Jim Smiley would be likely to afford me much information concerning the Rev. Leonidas W. Smiley, and so I started away.

At the door I met the sociable Wheeler returning, and he buttonholed me and recommenced:

"Well, thish-yer Smiley had a yaller one-eyed cow that didn't have no tail, only just a short stump like a bannanner, and—"

However, lacking both time and inclination, I did not wait to hear about the afflicted cow, but took my leave.

Now let the learned look upon this picture and say if iconoclasm can further go:

[From the Revue des Deux Mondes, of July 15th, 1872.]

THE JUMPING FROG

[From the Revue des Deux Mondes, of July 15th, 1872.]

....

LA GRENOUILLE SAUTEUSE DU COMTE DE CALAVERAS

"—Il y avait, une fois ici un individu connu sous le nom de Jim Smiley: c'était dans l'hiver de 49, peut-être bien au printemps de 50, je ne me reappelle pas exactement. Ce qui me fait croire que c'était l'un ou l'autre, c'est que je me souviens que le grand bief n'était pas achevé lorsqu'il arriva au camp pour la premiére fois, mais de toutes facons il était l'homme le plus friand de paris qui se pût voir, pariant sur tout ce qui se présentait, quand il pouvait trouver un adversaire, et, quand n'en trouvait pas il passait du côté opposé. Tout ce qui convenait à l'autre lui convenait; pourvu qu'il eût un pari, Smiley était satisfait. Et il avait une chance! une chance inouie: presque toujours il gagnait. It faut dire qu'il était toujours prêt à s'exposer, qu'on ne pouvait mentionner la moindre chose sans que ce gaillard offrît de parier là-dessus n'importe quoi et de prendre le côte que l'on voudrait, comme je vous le disais tout à l'heure. S'il y avait des courses, vous le trouviez riche ou ruiné à la fin; s'il y avait un combat de chiens, il apportait son enjeu; il l'apportait pour un combat de chats, pour un combat de coqs;—parbleu! si vous aviez vu deux oiseaux sur une haie il vous aurait offert de parier lequel s'envolerait le premier, et s'il y aviat 'meeting' au camp, il venait parier régulièrement pour le curé Walker, qu'il jugeait être le meilleur prédicateur des environs, et qui l'était en effet, et un brave homme. Il aurait rencontré une punaise de bois en chemin, qu'il aurait parié sur le temps qu'il lui faudrait pour aller où elle voudrait aller, et si vous l'aviez pris au mot, it aurait suivi la punaise jusqu'au Mexique, sans se soucier d'aller si loin, ni du temps qu'il y perdrait. Une fois la femme du curé Walker fut très malade pendant longtemps, il semblait qu'on ne la sauverait pas; mais un matin le curé arrive, et Smiley lui demande comment ella va et il dit qu'elle est bien mieux, grâce a l'infinie miséricorde tellement mieux qu'avec la bénédiction de la Providence elle s'en tirerait, et voilà que, sans y penser, Smiley répond:—Eh bien! je gage deux et demi qu'elle mourra tout de même.

"Ce Smiley avait une jument que les gars appelaient le bidet du quart d'heure, mais seulement pour plaisanter, vous comprenez, parce que, bien entendu, elle était plus vite que ca! Et il avait coutume de gagner de l'argent avec cette bête, quoi-qu'elle fût poussive, cornarde, toujours prise d'asthme, de coliques ou de consomption, ou de quelque chose d'approchant. On lui donnait 2 ou 300 'yards' au départ, puis on la dépassait sans peine; mais jamais à la fin elle ne manquait de s'échauffer, de s'exaspérer et elle arrivait, s'écartant, se défendant, ses jambes grêles en l'air devant les obstacles, quelquefois les évitant et faisant avec cela plus de poussière qu'aucun cheval, plus de bruit surtout avec ses éternumens et reniflemens.——crac! elle arrivait donc toujours première d'une tête, aussi juste qu'on peut le mesurer. Et il avait un petit bouledogue qui, à le voir, ne valait pas un sou; on aurait cru que parier contre lui c'était voler, tant il était ordinaire; mais aussitôt les enjeux faits, il devenait un autre chien. Sa mâchoire inférieure commencait à ressortir comme un gaillard d'avant, ses dents se découvcraient brillantes commes des fournaises, et un chien pouvait le taquiner, l'exciter, le mordre, le jeter deux ou trois fois par-dessus son épaule, André Jackson, c'était le nom du chien, André Jackson prenait cela tranquillement, comme s'il ne se fût jamais attendu à autre chose, et quand les paris étaient doublés et redoublés contre lui, il vous saisissait l'autre chien juste à l'articulation de la jambe de derrière, et il ne la lâchait plus, non pas qu'il la mâchât, vous concevez, mais il s'y serait tenu pendu jusqu'à ce qu'on jetât l'éponge en l'air, fallût-il attendre un an. Smiley gagnait toujours avec cette bête-là; malheureusement ils ont fini par dresser un chien qui n'avait pas de pattes de derrière, parce qu'on les avait sciées, et quand les choses furent au point qu'il voulait, et qu'il en vint à se jeter sur son morceau favori, le pauvre chien comprit en un instant qu'on s'était moqué de lui, et que l'autre le tenait. Vous n'avez jamais vu personne avoir l'air plus penaud et plus découragé; il ne fit aucun effort pour gagner le combat et fut rudement secoué, de sorte que, regardant Smiley comme pour lui dire:— Mon coeur est brisé, c'est ta faute; pourquoi m'avoir livré à un chien qui n'a pas de pattes de derrière, puisque c'est par là que je les bats?—il s'en alla en clopinant, et se coucha pour mourir. Ah! c'était un bon chien, cet André Jackson, et il se serait fait un nom, s'il avait vécu, car il y avait de l'etoffe en lui, il avait du génie, je la sais, bien que de grandes occasions lui aient manqué; mais il est impossible de supposer qu'un chien capable de se battre comme lui, certaines circonstances étant données, ait manqué de talent. Je me sens triste toutes les fois que je pense à son dernier combat et au dénoûment qu'il a eu. Eh bien! ce Smiley nourrissait des terriers à rats, et des coqs combat, et des chats, et toute sorte de choses, au point qu'il était toujours en mesure de vous tenir tête, et qu'avec sa rage de paris on n'avait plus de repos. Il attrapa un jour une grenouille et l'emporta chez lui, disant qu'il prétendait faire son éducation; vous me croirez si vous voulez, mais pendant trois mois il n'a rien fait que lui apprendre à sauter dans une cour retirée de sa maison. Et je vous réponds qu'il avait réussi. Il lui donnait un petit coup par derrière, et l'instant d'après vous voyiez la grenouille tourner en l'air comme un beignet au-dessus de la poêle, faire une culbute, quelquefois deux, lorsqu'elle était bien partie, et retomber sur ses pattes comme un chat. Il l'avait dressée dans l'art de gober des mouches, er l'y exercait continuellement, si bien qu'une mouche, du plus loin qu'elle apparaissait, était une mouche perdue. Smiley avait coutume de dire que tout ce qui manquait à une grenouille, c'était l'éducation, qu'avec l'éducation elle pouvait faire presque tout, et je le crois. Tenez, je l'ai vu poser Daniel Webster là sur se plancher,—Daniel Webster était le nom de la grenouille,—et lui chanter: Des mouches! Daniel, des mouches!—En un clin d'oeil, Daniel avait bondi et saisi une mouche ici sur le comptoir, puis sauté de nouveau par terre, où il restait vraiment à se gratter la tête avec sa patte de derrière, comme s'il n'avait pas eu la moindre idée de sa superiorité. Jamais vous n'avez grenouille vu de aussi modeste, aussi naturelle, douee comme elle l'était! Et quand il s'agissait de sauter purement et simplement sur terrain plat, elle faisait plus de chemin en un saut qu'aucune bete de son espèce que vous puissiez connaître. Sauter à plat, c'était son fort! Quand il s'agissait de cela, Smiley entassait les enjeux sur elle tant qu'il lui, restait un rouge liard. Il faut le reconnaitre, Smiley était monstrueusement fier de sa grenouille, et il en avait le droit, car des gens qui avaient voyagé, qui avaient tout vu, disaient qu'on lui ferait injure de la comparer à une autre; de facon que Smiley gardait Daniel dans une petite boîte a claire-voie qu'il emportait parfois à la Ville pour quelque pari.

"Un jour, un individu étranger au camp l'arrête aver sa boîte et lui dit:—Qu'est-ce que vous avez donc serré là dedans?

"Smiley dit d'un air indifférent:—Cela pourrait être un perroquet ou un serin, mais ce n'est rien de pareil, ce n'est qu'une grenouille.

"L'individu la prend, la regarde avec soin, la tourne d'un côté et de l'autre puis il dit.—Tiens! en effet! A quoi estelle bonne?

"—Mon Dieu! répond Smiley, toujours d'un air dégagé, elle est bonne pour une chose à mon avis, elle peut battre en sautant toute grenouille du comté de Calaveras.

"L'individu reprend la boîte, l'examine de nouveau longuement, et la rend à Smiley en disant d'un air délibéré:—Eh bien! je ne vois pas que cette grenouille ait rien de mieux qu'aucune grenouille.

"—Possible que vous ne le voyiez pas, dit Smiley, possible que vous vous entendiez en grenouilles, possible que vous ne vous y entendez point, possible que vous avez de l'expérience, et possible que vous ne soyez qu'un amateur. De toute manière, je parie quarante dollars qu'elle battra en sautant n'importe quelle grenouille du comté de Calaveras.

"L'individu réfléchit une seconde et dit comme attristé:—Je ne suis qu'un étranger ici, je n'ai pas de grenouille; mais, si j'en avais une, je tiendrais le pari.

"—Fort bien! répond Smiley. Rien de plus facile. Si vous voulez tenir ma boîte une minute, j'irai vous chercher une grenouille.—Voilà donc l'individu qui garde la boîte, qui met ses quarante dollars sur ceux de Smiley et qui attend. Il attend assez longtemps, réflechissant tout seul, et figurez-vous qu'il prend Daniel, lui ouvre la bouche de force at avec une cuiller à thé l'emplit de menu plomb de chasse, mais l'emplit jusqu'au menton, puis il le pose par terre. Smiley pendant ce temps était à barboter dans une mare. Finalement il attrape une grenouille, l'apporte à cet individu et dit:—Maintenant, si vous êtes prêt, mettez-la tout contra Daniel, avec leurs pattes de devant sur la même ligne, et je donnerai le signal; puis il ajoute:—Un, deux, trois, sautez!

"Lui et l'individu touchent leurs grenouilles par derrière, et la grenouille neuve se met à sautiller, mais Daniel se soulève lourdement, hausse les épaules ainsi, comme un Francais; à quoi bon? il ne pouvait bouger, il était planté solide comma une enclume, il n'avancait pas plus que si on l'eût mis à l'ancre. Smiley fut surpris et dégoûté, mais il ne se doutait pas du tour, bien entendu. L'individu empoche l'argent, s'en va, et en s'en allant est-ce qu'il ne donna pas un coup de pouce par-dessus l'épaule, comma ca, au pauvre Daniel, en disant de son air délibéré:—Eh bien! je ne vois pas qua cette grenouille ait rien de muiex qu'une autre.

"Smiley se gratta longtemps la tête, les yeux fixés sur Daniel; jusqu'à ce qu'enfin il dit:— Je me demande comment diable il se fait que cette bête ait refusé . . . Est-ce qu'elle aurait quelque chose? . . . On croirait qu'elle est enfleé.

"Il empoigne Daniel par la peau du cou, le souléve et dit:—Le loup me croque, s'il ne pèse pas cinq livres.

"Il le retourne, et le malheureux crache deux poignées de plomb. Quand Smiley reconnut ce qui en était, il fut comme fou. Vous le voyez d'ici poser sa grenouille par terra et courir aprés cet individu, mais il ne le rattrapa jamais, et ...."

[Translation of the above back from the French:]

THE FROG JUMPING OF THE COUNTY OF CALAVERAS

It there was one time here an individual known under the name of Jim Smiley; it was in the winter of '89, possibly well at the spring of '50, I no me recollect not exactly. This which me makes to believe that it was the one or the other, it is that I shall remember that the grand flume is not achieved when he arrives at the camp for the first time, but of all sides he was the man the most fond of to bet which one have seen, betting upon all that which is presented, when he could find an adversary; and when he not of it could not, he passed to the side opposed. All that which convenienced to the other to him convenienced also; seeing that he had a bet Smiley was satisfied. And he had a chance! a chance even worthless; nearly always he gained. It must to say that he was always near to himself expose, but one no could mention the least thing without that this gaillard offered to bet the bottom, no matter what, and to take the side that one him would, as I you it said all at the hour (tout à l'heure). If it there was of races, you him find rich or ruined at the end; if it, there is a combat of dogs, he bring his bet; he himself laid always for a combat of cats, for a combat of cocks —by-blue! If you have see two birds upon a fence, he you should have offered of to bet which of those birds shall fly the first; and if there is meeting at the camp (meeting au camp) he comes to bet regularly for the curé Walker, which he judged to be the best predicator of the neighborhood (prédicateur des environs) and which he was in effect, and a brave man. He would encounter a bug of wood in the road, whom he will bet upon the time which he shall take to go where she would go—and if you him have take at the word, he will follow the bug as far as Mexique, without himself caring to go so far; neither of the time which he there lost. One time the woman of the cure Walker is very sick during long time, it seemed that one not her saved not; but one morning the cure arrives, and Smiley him demanded how she goes, and he said that she is well better, grace to the Infinite misery (lui demande comment elle va, et il dit qu'elle est bien mieux, grâce a l'infinie miséricorde) so much better that with the benediction of the Providence she herself of it would pull out (elle s'en tirerait); and behold that without there thinking Smiley responds: "Well, I gage two-and-half that she will die all of same."

This Smiley had an animal which the boys called the nag of the quarter of hour, but solely for pleasantry, you comprehend, because, well understand, she was more fast as that! [Now why that exclamation?—M. T.] And it was custom of to gain of the silver with this beast, notwithstanding she was poussive, cornarde, always taken of asthma, of colics or of consumption, or something of approaching. One him would give two or three hundred yards at the departure, then one him passed without pain; but never at the last she not fail of herself échauffer, of herself exasperate, and she arrives herself écartant, se defendant, her legs greles in the air before the obstacles, sometimes them elevating and making with this more of dust than any horse, more of noise above with his eternumens and reniflemens—crac! she arrives then always first by one head, as just as one can it measure. And he had a small bulldog (bouledogue!) who, to him see, no value, not a cent; one would believe that to bet against him it was to steal, so much he was ordinary; but as soon as the game made, she becomes another dog. Her jaw inferior commence to project like a deck of before, his teeth themselves discover brilliant like some furnaces, and a dog could him tackle (le taquiner), him excite, him murder (le mordre), him throw two or three times over his shoulder, André Jackson—this was the name of the dog—André Jackson takes that tranquilly, as if he not himself was never expecting other thing, and when the bets were doubled and redoubled against him, he you seize the other dog just at the articulation of the leg of behind, and he not it leave more, not that he it masticate, you conceive, but he himself there shall be holding during until that one throws the sponge in the air, must he wait a year. Smiley gained always with this beast-là; unhappily they have finished by elevating a dog who no had not of feet of behind, because one them had sawed; and when things were at the point that he would, and that he came to himself throw upon his morsel favorite, the poor dog comprehended in an instant that he himself was deceived in him, and that the other dog him had. You no have never seen person having the air more penaud and more discouraged; he not made no effort to gain the combat, and was rudely shucked.

Eh bien! this Smiley nourished some terriers à rats, and some cocks of combat, and some cats, and all sorts of things; and with his rage of betting one no had more of repose. He trapped one day a frog and him imported with him (et l'emporta chez lui) saying that he pretended to make his education. You me believe if you will, but during three months he not has nothing done but to him apprehend to jump (apprendre à sauter) in a court retired of her mansion (de sa maison). And I you respond that he have succeeded. He him gives a small blow by behind, and the instant after you shall see the frog turn in the air like a grease-biscuit, make one summersault, sometimes two, when she was well started, and refall upon his feet like a cat. He him had accomplished in the art of to gobble the flies (gober des mouches), and him there exercised continually —so well that a fly at the most far that she appeared was a fly lost. Smiley had custom to say that all which lacked to a frog it was the education, but with the education she could do nearly all—and I him believe. Tenez, I him have seen pose Daniel Webster there upon this plank—Daniel Webster was the name of the frog—and to him sing, "Some flies, Daniel, some flies!"—in a flash of the eye Daniel had bounded and seized a fly here upon the counter, then jumped anew at the earth, where he rested truly to himself scratch the head with his behind foot, as if he no had not the least idea of his superiority. Never you not have seen frog as modest, as natural, sweet as she was. And when he himself agitated to jump purely and simply upon plain earth, she does more ground in one jump than any beast of his species than you can know. To jump plain-this was his strong. When he himself agitated for that, Smiley multiplied the bets upon her as long as there to him remained a red. It must to know, Smiley was monstrously proud of his frog, and he of it was right, for some men who were traveled, who had all seen, said that they to him would be injurious to him compare, to another frog. Smiley guarded Daniel in a little box latticed which he carried bytimes to the village for some bet.

One day an individual stranger at the camp him arrested with his box and him said:

"What is this that you have them shut up there within?"

Smiley said, with an air indifferent:

"That could be a paroquet, or a syringe (ou un serin), but this no is nothing of such, it not is but a frog."

The individual it took, it regarded with care, it turned from one side and from the other, then he said:

"Tiens! in effect!—At what is she good?"

"My God!" respond Smiley, always with an air disengaged, "she is good for one thing, to my notice (à mon avis), she can batter in jumping (elle peut battre en sautant) all frogs of the county of Calaveras."

The individual retook the box, it examined of new longly, and it rendered to Smiley in saying with an air deliberate:

"Eh bien! I no saw not that that frog had nothing of better than each frog." (Je ne vois pas que cette grenouille ait rien de mieux qu'aucune grenouille.) [If that isn't grammar gone to seed, then I count myself no judge.—M. T.]

"Possible that you not it saw not," said Smiley, "possible that you—you comprehend frogs; possible that you not you there comprehend nothing; possible that you had of the experience, and possible that you not be but an amateur. Of all manner (De toute manière) I bet forty dollars that she batter in jumping no matter which frog of the county of Calaveras."

The individual reflected a second, and said like sad:

"I not am but a stranger here, I no have not a frog; but if I of it had one, I would embrace the bet."

"Strong well!" respond Smiley; "nothing of more facility. If you will hold my box a minute, I go you to search a frog (j'irai vous chercher)."

Behold, then, the individual, who guards the box, who puts his forty dollars upon those of Smiley, and who attends (et qui attend). He attended enough long times, reflecting all solely. And figure you that he takes Daniel, him opens the mouth by force and with a teaspoon him fills with shot of the hunt, even him fills just to the chin, then he him puts by the earth. Smiley during these times was at slopping in a swamp. Finally he trapped (attrape) a frog, him carried to that individual, and said:

"Now if you be ready, put him all against Daniel with their before feet upon the same line, and I give the signal"—then he added: "One, two, three—advance!"

Him and the individual touched their frogs by behind, and the frog new put to jump smartly, but Daniel himself lifted ponderously, exalted the shoulders thus, like a Frenchman—to what good? he not could budge, he is planted solid like a church, he not advance no more than if one him had put at the anchor.

Smiley was surprised and disgusted, but he no himself doubted not of the turn being intended (mais il ne se doutait pas du tour, bien entendu). The individual empocketed the silver, himself with it went, and of it himself in going is it that he no gives not a jerk of thumb over the shoulder—like that—at the poor Daniel, in saying with his air deliberate—(L'individu empoche l'argent, s'en va et en s'en allant est-ce qu'il ne donne pas un coup de pouce par-dessus l'épaule, comme ça, au pauvre Daniel, en disant de son air délibéré):

"Eh bien! I no see not that that frog has nothing of better than another."

Smiley himself scratched longtimes the head, the eyes fixed upon Daniel, until that which at last he said:

"I me demand how the devil it makes itself that this beast has refused. Is it that she had something? One would believe that she is stuffed."

He grasped Daniel by the skin of the neck, him lifted and said:

"The wolf me bite if he no weigh not five pounds:"

He him reversed and the unhappy belched two handfuls of shot (et le malheureux, etc.). When Smiley recognized how it was, he was like mad. He deposited his frog by the earth and ran after that individual, but he not him caught never.

Such is the Jumping Frog, to the distorted French eye. I claim that I never put together such an odious mixture of bad grammar and delirium tremens in my life. And what has a poor foreigner like me done, to be abused and misrepresented like this? When I say, "Well, I don't see no p'ints about that frog that's any better'n any other frog," is it kind, is it just, for this Frenchman to try to make it appear that I said, "Eh bien! I no saw not that that frog had nothing of better than each frog"? I have no heart to write more. I never felt so about anything before.

HARTFORD, March, 1875.

JOURNALISM IN TENNESSEE

[written about 1871]

The editor of the Memphis Avalanche swoops thus mildly down upon a correspondent who posted him as a Radical:—"While he was writing the first word, the middle, dotting his i's, crossing his t's, and punching his period, he knew he was concocting a sentence that was saturated with infamy and reeking with falsehood."—Exchange.

I was told by the physician that a Southern climate would improve my health, and so I went down to Tennessee, and got a berth on the Morning Glory and Johnson County War-Whoop as associate editor. When I went on duty I found the chief editor sitting tilted back in a three-legged chair with his feet on a pine table. There was another pine table in the room and another afflicted chair, and both were half buried under newspapers and scraps and sheets of manuscript. There was a wooden box of sand, sprinkled with cigar stubs and "old soldiers," and a stove with a door hanging by its upper hinge. The chief editor had a long-tailed black cloth frock-coat on, and white linen pants. His boots were small and neatly blacked. He wore a ruffled shirt, a large seal-ring, a standing collar of obsolete pattern, and a checkered neckerchief with the ends hanging down. Date of costume about 1848. He was smoking a cigar, and trying to think of a word, and in pawing his hair he had rumpled his locks a good deal. He was scowling fearfully, and I judged that he was concocting a particularly knotty editorial. He told me to take the exchanges and skim through them and write up the "Spirit of the Tennessee Press," condensing into the article all of their contents that seemed of interest.

I wrote as follows:

SPIRIT OF THE TENNESSEE PRESS

The editors of the Semi-Weekly Earthquake evidently labor under a misapprehension with regard to the Ballyhack railroad. It is not the object of the company to leave Buzzardville off to one side. On the contrary, they consider it one of the most important points along the line, and consequently can have no desire to slight it. The gentlemen of the Earthquake will, of course, take pleasure in making the correction.

John W. Blossom, Esq., the able editor of the Higginsville Thunderbolt and Battle Cry of Freedom, arrived in the city yesterday. He is stopping at the Van Buren House.

We observe that our contemporary of the Mud Springs Morning Howl has fallen into the error of supposing that the election of Van Werter is not an established fact, but he will have discovered his mistake before this reminder reaches him, no doubt. He was doubtless misled by incomplete election returns.

It is pleasant to note that the city of Blathersville is endeavoring to contract with some New York gentlemen to pave its well-nigh impassable streets with the Nicholson pavement. The Daily Hurrah urges the measure with ability, and seems confident of ultimate success.

I passed my manuscript over to the chief editor for acceptance, alteration, or destruction. He glanced at it and his face clouded. He ran his eye down the pages, and his countenance grew portentous. It was easy to see that something was wrong. Presently he sprang up and said:

"Thunder and lightning! Do you suppose I am going to speak of those cattle that way? Do you suppose my subscribers are going to stand such gruel as that? Give me the pen!"

I never saw a pen scrape and scratch its way so viciously, or plow through another man's verbs and adjectives so relentlessly. While he was in the midst of his work, somebody shot at him through the open window, and marred the symmetry of my ear.

"Ah," said he, "that is that scoundrel Smith, of the Moral Volcano—he was due yesterday." And he snatched a navy revolver from his belt and fired—Smith dropped, shot in the thigh. The shot spoiled Smith's aim, who was just taking a second chance and he crippled a stranger. It was me. Merely a finger shot off.

Then the chief editor went on with his erasure; and interlineations. Just as he finished them a hand grenade came down the stove-pipe, and the explosion shivered the stove into a thousand fragments. However, it did no further damage, except that a vagrant piece knocked a couple of my teeth out.

"That stove is utterly ruined," said the chief editor.

I said I believed it was.

"Well, no matter—don't want it this kind of weather. I know the man that did it. I'll get him. Now, here is the way this stuff ought to be written."

I took the manuscript. It was scarred with erasures and interlineations till its mother wouldn't have known it if it had had one. It now read as follows:

SPIRIT OF THE TENNESSEE PRESS

The inveterate liars of the Semi-Weekly Earthquake are evidently endeavoring to palm off upon a noble and chivalrous people another of their vile and brutal falsehoods with regard to that most glorious conception of the nineteenth century, the Ballyhack railroad. The idea that Buzzardville was to be left off at one side originated in their own fulsome brains—or rather in the settlings which they regard as brains. They had better swallow this lie if they want to save their abandoned reptile carcasses the cowhiding they so richly deserve.

That ass, Blossom, of the Higginsville Thunderbolt and Battle Cry of Freedom, is down here again sponging at the Van Buren.

We observe that the besotted blackguard of the Mud Springs Morning Howl is giving out, with his usual propensity for lying, that Van Werter is not elected. The heaven-born mission of journalism is to disseminate truth; to eradicate error; to educate, refine, and elevate the tone of public morals and manners, and make all men more gentle, more virtuous, more charitable, and in all ways better, and holier, and happier; and yet this blackhearted scoundrel degrades his great office persistently to the dissemination of falsehood, calumny, vituperation, and vulgarity.

Blathersville wants a Nicholson pavement—it wants a jail and a poorhouse more. The idea of a pavement in a one-horse town composed of two gin-mills, a blacksmith shop, and that mustard-plaster of a newspaper, the Daily Hurrah! The crawling insect, Buckner, who edits the Hurrah, is braying about his business with his customary imbecility, and imagining that he is talking sense.

"Now that is the way to write—peppery and to the point. Mush-and-milk journalism gives me the fan-tods."

About this time a brick came through the window with a splintering crash, and gave me a considerable of a jolt in the back. I moved out of range—I began to feel in the way.

The chief said, "That was the Colonel, likely. I've been expecting him for two days. He will be up now right away."

He was correct. The Colonel appeared in the door a moment afterward with a dragoon revolver in his hand.

He said, "Sir, have I the honor of addressing the poltroon who edits this mangy sheet?"

"You have. Be seated, sir. Be careful of the chair, one of its legs is gone. I believe I have the honor of addressing the putrid liar, Colonel Blatherskite Tecumseh?"

"Right, Sir. I have a little account to settle with you. If you are at leisure we will begin."

"I have an article on the 'Encouraging Progress of Moral and Intellectual Development in America' to finish, but there is no hurry. Begin."

Both pistols rang out their fierce clamor at the same instant. The chief lost a lock of his hair, and the Colonel's bullet ended its career in the fleshy part of my thigh. The Colonel's left shoulder was clipped a little. They fired again. Both missed their men this time, but I got my share, a shot in the arm. At the third fire both gentlemen were wounded slightly, and I had a knuckle chipped. I then said, I believed I would go out and take a walk, as this was a private matter, and I had a delicacy about participating in it further. But both gentlemen begged me to keep my seat, and assured me that I was not in the way.

They then talked about the elections and the crops while they reloaded, and I fell to tying up my wounds. But presently they opened fire again with animation, and every shot took effect—but it is proper to remark that five out of the six fell to my share. The sixth one mortally wounded the Colonel, who remarked, with fine humor, that he would have to say good morning now, as he had business uptown. He then inquired the way to the undertaker's and left.

The chief turned to me and said, "I am expecting company to dinner, and shall have to get ready. It will be a favor to me if you will read proof and attend to the customers."

I winced a little at the idea of attending to the customers, but I was too bewildered by the fusillade that was still ringing in my ears to think of anything to say.

He continued, "Jones will be here at three—cowhide him. Gillespie will call earlier, perhaps—throw him out of the window. Ferguson will be along about four—kill him. That is all for today, I believe. If you have any odd time, you may write a blistering article on the police—give the chief inspector rats. The cowhides are under the table; weapons in the drawer—ammunition there in the corner—lint and bandages up there in the pigeonholes. In case of accident, go to Lancet, the surgeon, downstairs. He advertises—we take it out in trade."

He was gone. I shuddered. At the end of the next three hours I had been through perils so awful that all peace of mind and all cheerfulness were gone from me. Gillespie had called and thrown me out of the window. Jones arrived promptly, and when I got ready to do the cowhiding he took the job off my hands. In an encounter with a stranger, not in the bill of fare, I had lost my scalp. Another stranger, by the name of Thompson, left me a mere wreck and ruin of chaotic rags. And at last, at bay in the corner, and beset by an infuriated mob of editors, blacklegs, politicians, and desperadoes, who raved and swore and flourished their weapons about my head till the air shimmered with glancing flashes of steel, I was in the act of resigning my berth on the paper when the chief arrived, and with him a rabble of charmed and enthusiastic friends. Then ensued a scene of riot and carnage such as no human pen, or steel one either, could describe. People were shot, probed, dismembered, blown up, thrown out of the window. There was a brief tornado of murky blasphemy, with a confused and frantic war-dance glimmering through it, and then all was over. In five minutes there was silence, and the gory chief and I sat alone and surveyed the sanguinary ruin that strewed the floor around us.

He said, "You'll like this place when you get used to it."

I said, "I'll have to get you to excuse me; I think maybe I might write to suit you after a while; as soon as I had had some practice and learned the language I am confident I could. But, to speak the plain truth, that sort of energy of expression has its inconveniences, and a man is liable to interruption.

"You see that yourself. Vigorous writing is calculated to elevate the public, no doubt, but then I do not like to attract so much attention as it calls forth. I can't write with comfort when I am interrupted so much as I have been to-day. I like this berth well enough, but I don't like to be left here to wait on the customers. The experiences are novel, I grant you, and entertaining, too, after a fashion, but they are not judiciously distributed. A gentleman shoots at you through the window and cripples me; a bombshell comes down the stove-pipe for your gratification and sends the stove door down my throat; a friend drops in to swap compliments with you, and freckles me with bullet-holes till my skin won't hold my principles; you go to dinner, and Jones comes with his cowhide, Gillespie throws me out of the window, Thompson tears all my clothes off, and an entire stranger takes my scalp with the easy freedom of an old acquaintance; and in less than five minutes all the blackguards in the country arrive in their war-paint, and proceed to scare the rest of me to death with their tomahawks. Take it altogether, I never had such a spirited time in all my life as I have had to-day. No; I like you, and I like your calm unruffled way of explaining things to the customers, but you see I am not used to it. The Southern heart is too impulsive; Southern hospitality is too lavish with the stranger. The paragraphs which I have written to-day, and into whose cold sentences your masterly hand has infused the fervent spirit of Tennesseean journalism, will wake up another nest of hornets. All that mob of editors will come—and they will come hungry, too, and want somebody for breakfast. I shall have to bid you adieu. I decline to be present at these festivities. I came South for my health, I will go back on the same errand, and suddenly. Tennesseean journalism is too stirring for me."

After which we parted with mutual regret, and I took apartments at the hospital.

THE STORY OF THE BAD LITTLE BOY

[written about 1865]

Once there was a bad little boy whose name was Jim—though, if you will notice, you will find that bad little boys are nearly always called James in your Sunday-school books. It was strange, but still it was true, that this one was called Jim.

He didn't have any sick mother, either—a sick mother who was pious and had the consumption, and would be glad to lie down in the grave and be at rest but for the strong love she bore her boy, and the anxiety she felt that the world might be harsh and cold toward him when she was gone. Most bad boys in the Sunday books are named James, and have sick mothers, who teach them to say, "Now, I lay me down," etc., and sing them to sleep with sweet, plaintive voices, and then kiss them good night, and kneel down by the bedside and weep. But it was different with this fellow. He was named Jim, and there wasn't anything the matter with his mother—no consumption, nor anything of that kind. She was rather stout than otherwise, and she was not pious; moreover, she was not anxious on Jim's account. She said if he were to break his neck it wouldn't be much loss. She always spanked Jim to sleep, and she never kissed him good night; on the contrary, she boxed his ears when she was ready to leave him.

Once this little bad boy stole the key of the pantry, and slipped in there and helped himself to some jam, and filled up the vessel with tar, so that his mother would never know the difference; but all at once a terrible feeling didn't come over him, and something didn't seem to whisper to him, "Is it right to disobey my mother? Isn't it sinful to do this? Where do bad little boys go who gobble up their good kind mother's jam?" and then he didn't kneel down all alone and promise never to be wicked any more, and rise up with a light, happy heart, and go and tell his mother all about it, and beg her forgiveness, and be blessed by her with tears of pride and thankfulness in her eyes. No; that is the way with all other bad boys in the books; but it happened otherwise with this Jim, strangely enough. He ate that jam, and said it was bully, in his sinful, vulgar way; and he put in the tar, and said that was bully also, and laughed, and observed "that the old woman would get up and snort" when she found it out; and when she did find it out, he denied knowing anything about it, and she whipped him severely, and he did the crying himself. Everything about this boy was curious—everything turned out differently with him from the way it does to the bad Jameses in the books.

Once he climbed up in Farmer Acorn's apple tree to steal apples, and the limb didn't break, and he didn't fall and break his arm, and get torn by the farmer's great dog, and then languish on a sickbed for weeks, and repent and become good. Oh, no; he stole as many apples as he wanted and came down all right; and he was all ready for the dog, too, and knocked him endways with a brick when he came to tear him. It was very strange—nothing like it ever happened in those mild little books with marbled backs, and with pictures in them of men with swallow-tailed coats and bell-crowned hats, and pantaloons that are short in the legs, and women with the waists of their dresses under their arms, and no hoops on. Nothing like it in any of the Sunday-school books.

Once he stole the teacher's penknife, and, when he was afraid it would be found out and he would get whipped, he slipped it into George Wilson's cap—poor Widow Wilson's son, the moral boy, the good little boy of the village, who always obeyed his mother, and never told an untruth, and was fond of his lessons, and infatuated with Sunday-school. And when the knife dropped from the cap, and poor George hung his head and blushed, as if in conscious guilt, and the grieved teacher charged the theft upon him, and was just in the very act of bringing the switch down upon his trembling shoulders, a white-haired, improbable justice of the peace did not suddenly appear in their midst, and strike an attitude and say, "Spare this noble boy—there stands the cowering culprit! I was passing the school door at recess, and, unseen myself, I saw the theft committed!" And then Jim didn't get whaled, and the venerable justice didn't read the tearful school a homily, and take George by the hand and say such a boy deserved to be exalted, and then tell him to come and make his home with him, and sweep out the office, and make fires, and run errands, and chop wood, and study law, and help his wife do household labors, and have all the balance of the time to play, and get forty cents a month, and be happy. No; it would have happened that way in the books, but didn't happen that way to Jim. No meddling old clam of a justice dropped in to make trouble, and so the model boy George got thrashed, and Jim was glad of it because, you know, Jim hated moral boys. Jim said he was "down on them milksops." Such was the coarse language of this bad, neglected boy.

But the strangest thing that ever happened to Jim was the time he went boating on Sunday, and didn't get drowned, and that other time that he got caught out in the storm when he was fishing on Sunday, and didn't get struck by lightning. Why, you might look, and look, all through the Sunday-school books from now till next Christmas, and you would never come across anything like this. Oh, no; you would find that all the bad boys who go boating on Sunday invariably get drowned; and all the bad boys who get caught out in storms when they are fishing on Sunday infallibly get struck by lightning. Boats with bad boys in them always upset on Sunday, and it always storms when bad boys go fishing on the Sabbath. How this Jim ever escaped is a mystery to me.

This Jim bore a charmed life—that must have been the way of it. Nothing could hurt him. He even gave the elephant in the menagerie a plug of tobacco, and the elephant didn't knock the top of his head off with his trunk. He browsed around the cupboard after essence-of peppermint, and didn't make a mistake and drink aqua fortis. He stole his father's gun and went hunting on the Sabbath, and didn't shoot three or four of his fingers off. He struck his little sister on the temple with his fist when he was angry, and she didn't linger in pain through long summer days, and die with sweet words of forgiveness upon her lips that redoubled the anguish of his breaking heart. No; she got over it. He ran off and went to sea at last, and didn't come back and find himself sad and alone in the world, his loved ones sleeping in the quiet churchyard, and the vine-embowered home of his boyhood tumbled down and gone to decay. Ah, no; he came home as drunk as a piper, and got into the station-house the first thing.

And he grew up and married, and raised a large family, and brained them all with an ax one night, and got wealthy by all manner of cheating and rascality; and now he is the infernalest wickedest scoundrel in his native village, and is universally respected, and belongs to the legislature.

So you see there never was a bad James in the Sunday-school books that had such a streak of luck as this sinful Jim with the charmed life.

THE STORY OF THE GOOD LITTLE BOY

[Written about 1865]

Once there was a good little boy by the name of Jacob Blivens. He always obeyed his parents, no matter how absurd and unreasonable their demands were; and he always learned his book, and never was late at Sabbath-school. He would not play hookey, even when his sober judgment told him it was the most profitable thing he could do. None of the other boys could ever make that boy out, he acted so strangely. He wouldn't lie, no matter how convenient it was. He just said it was wrong to lie, and that was sufficient for him. And he was so honest that he was simply ridiculous. The curious ways that that Jacob had, surpassed everything. He wouldn't play marbles on Sunday, he wouldn't rob birds' nests, he wouldn't give hot pennies to organ-grinders' monkeys; he didn't seem to take any interest in any kind of rational amusement. So the other boys used to try to reason it out and come to an understanding of him, but they couldn't arrive at any satisfactory conclusion. As I said before, they could only figure out a sort of vague idea that he was "afflicted," and so they took him under their protection, and never allowed any harm to come to him.

This good little boy read all the Sunday-school books; they were his greatest delight. This was the whole secret of it. He believed in the good little boys they put in the Sunday-school books; he had every confidence in them. He longed to come across one of them alive once; but he never did. They all died before his time, maybe. Whenever he read about a particularly good one he turned over quickly to the end to see what became of him, because he wanted to travel thousands of miles and gaze on him; but it wasn't any use; that good little boy always died in the last chapter, and there was a picture of the funeral, with all his relations and the Sunday-school children standing around the grave in pantaloons that were too short, and bonnets that were too large, and everybody crying into handkerchiefs that had as much as a yard and a half of stuff in them. He was always headed off in this way. He never could see one of those good little boys on account of his always dying in the last chapter.

Jacob had a noble ambition to be put in a Sunday school book. He wanted to be put in, with pictures representing him gloriously declining to lie to his mother, and her weeping for joy about it; and pictures representing him standing on the doorstep giving a penny to a poor beggar-woman with six children, and telling her to spend it freely, but not to be extravagant, because extravagance is a sin; and pictures of him magnanimously refusing to tell on the bad boy who always lay in wait for him around the corner as he came from school, and welted him over the head with a lath, and then chased him home, saying, "Hi! hi!" as he proceeded. That was the ambition of young Jacob Blivens. He wished to be put in a Sunday-school book. It made him feel a little uncomfortable sometimes when he reflected that the good little boys always died. He loved to live, you know, and this was the most unpleasant feature about being a Sunday-school-book boy. He knew it was not healthy to be good. He knew it was more fatal than consumption to be so supernaturally good as the boys in the books were he knew that none of them had ever been able to stand it long, and it pained him to think that if they put him in a book he wouldn't ever see it, or even if they did get the book out before he died it wouldn't be popular without any picture of his funeral in the back part of it. It couldn't be much of a Sunday-school book that couldn't tell about the advice he gave to the community when he was dying. So at last, of course, he had to make up his mind to do the best he could under the circumstances—to live right, and hang on as long as he could, and have his dying speech all ready when his time came.

But somehow nothing ever went right with the good little boy; nothing ever turned out with him the way it turned out with the good little boys in the books. They always had a good time, and the bad boys had the broken legs; but in his case there was a screw loose somewhere, and it all happened just the other way. When he found Jim Blake stealing apples, and went under the tree to read to him about the bad little boy who fell out of a neighbor's apple tree and broke his arm, Jim fell out of the tree, too, but he fell on him and broke his arm, and Jim wasn't hurt at all. Jacob couldn't understand that. There wasn't anything in the books like it.

And once, when some bad boys pushed a blind man over in the mud, and Jacob ran to help him up and receive his blessing, the blind man did not give him any blessing at all, but whacked him over the head with his stick and said he would like to catch him shoving him again, and then pretending to help him up. This was not in accordance with any of the books. Jacob looked them all over to see.

One thing that Jacob wanted to do was to find a lame dog that hadn't any place to stay, and was hungry and persecuted, and bring him home and pet him and have that dog's imperishable gratitude. And at last he found one and was happy; and he brought him home and fed him, but when he was going to pet him the dog flew at him and tore all the clothes off him except those that were in front, and made a spectacle of him that was astonishing. He examined authorities, but he could not understand the matter. It was of the same breed of dogs that was in the books, but it acted very differently. Whatever this boy did he got into trouble. The very things the boys in the books got rewarded for turned out to be about the most unprofitable things he could invest in.

Once, when he was on his way to Sunday-school, he saw some bad boys starting off pleasuring in a sailboat. He was filled with consternation, because he knew from his reading that boys who went sailing on Sunday invariably got drowned. So he ran out on a raft to warn them, but a log turned with him and slid him into the river. A man got him out pretty soon, and the doctor pumped the water out of him, and gave him a fresh start with his bellows, but he caught cold and lay sick abed nine weeks. But the most unaccountable thing about it was that the bad boys in the boat had a good time all day, and then reached home alive and well in the most surprising manner. Jacob Blivens said there was nothing like these things in the books. He was perfectly dumfounded.

When he got well he was a little discouraged, but he resolved to keep on trying anyhow. He knew that so far his experiences wouldn't do to go in a book, but he hadn't yet reached the allotted term of life for good little boys, and he hoped to be able to make a record yet if he could hold on till his time was fully up. If everything else failed he had his dying speech to fall back on.

He examined his authorities, and found that it was now time for him to go to sea as a cabin-boy. He called on a ship-captain and made his application, and when the captain asked for his recommendations he proudly drew out a tract and pointed to the word, "To Jacob Blivens, from his affectionate teacher." But the captain was a coarse, vulgar man, and he said, "Oh, that be blowed! that wasn't any proof that he knew how to wash dishes or handle a slush-bucket, and he guessed he didn't want him." This was altogether the most extraordinary thing that ever happened to Jacob in all his life. A compliment from a teacher, on a tract, had never failed to move the tenderest emotions of ship-captains, and open the way to all offices of honor and profit in their gift—it never had in any book that ever he had read. He could hardly believe his senses.

This boy always had a hard time of it. Nothing ever came out according to the authorities with him. At last, one day, when he was around hunting up bad little boys to admonish, he found a lot of them in the old iron-foundry fixing up a little joke on fourteen or fifteen dogs, which they had tied together in long procession, and were going to ornament with empty nitroglycerin cans made fast to their tails. Jacob's heart was touched. He sat down on one of those cans (for he never minded grease when duty was before him), and he took hold of the foremost dog by the collar, and turned his reproving eye upon wicked Tom Jones. But just at that moment Alderman McWelter, full of wrath, stepped in. All the bad boys ran away, but Jacob Blivens rose in conscious innocence and began one of those stately little Sunday-school-book speeches which always commence with "Oh, sir!" in dead opposition to the fact that no boy, good or bad, ever starts a remark with "Oh, sir." But the alderman never waited to hear the rest. He took Jacob Blivens by the ear and turned him around, and hit him a whack in the rear with the flat of his hand; and in an instant that good little boy shot out through the roof and soared away toward the sun, with the fragments of those fifteen dogs stringing after him like the tail of a kite. And there wasn't a sign of that alderman or that old iron-foundry left on the face of the earth; and, as for young Jacob Blivens, he never got a chance to make his last dying speech after all his trouble fixing it up, unless he made it to the birds; because, although the bulk of him came down all right in a tree-top in an adjoining county, the rest of him was apportioned around among four townships, and so they had to hold five inquests on him to find out whether he was dead or not, and how it occurred. You never saw a boy scattered so.—[This glycerin catastrophe is borrowed from a floating newspaper item, whose author's name I would give if I knew it.—M. T.]

Thus perished the good little boy who did the best he could, but didn't come out according to the books. Every boy who ever did as he did prospered except him. His case is truly remarkable. It will probably never be accounted for.

A COUPLE OF POEMS BY TWAIN AND MOORE

[written about 1865]

THOSE EVENING BELLS

BY THOMAS MOORE

>Those evening bells! those evening bells!
>How many a tale their music tells
>Of youth, and home, and that sweet time
>When last I heard their soothing chime.
>
>Those joyous hours are passed away;
>And many a heart that then was gay,
>Within the tomb now darkly dwells,
>And hears no more those evening bells.
>
>And so 'twill be when I am gone
>That tuneful peal will still ring on;
>While other bards shall walk these dells,
>And sing your praise, sweet evening bells.

THOSE ANNUAL BILLS

BY MARK TWAIN

>These annual bills! these annual bills!
>How many a song their discord trills
>Of "truck" consumed, enjoyed, forgot,
>Since I was skinned by last year's lot!
>
>Those joyous beans are passed away;
>Those onions blithe, O where are they?
>Once loved, lost, mourned—now vexing ILLS
>Your shades troop back in annual bills!
>
>And so 'twill be when I'm aground
>These yearly duns will still go round,
>While other bards, with frantic quills,
>Shall damn and damn these annual bills!

NIAGARA

[written about 1871]

Niagara Falls is a most enjoyable place of resort. The hotels are excellent, and the prices not at all exorbitant. The opportunities for fishing are not surpassed in the country; in fact, they are not even equaled elsewhere. Because, in other localities, certain places in the streams are much better than others; but at Niagara one place is just as good as another, for the reason that the fish do not bite anywhere, and so there is no use in your walking five miles to fish, when you can depend on being just as unsuccessful nearer home. The advantages of this state of things have never heretofore been properly placed before the public.

The weather is cool in summer, and the walks and drives are all pleasant and none of them fatiguing. When you start out to "do" the Falls you first drive down about a mile, and pay a small sum for the privilege of looking down from a precipice into the narrowest part of the Niagara River. A railway "cut" through a hill would be as comely if it had the angry river tumbling and foaming through its bottom. You can descend a staircase here a hundred and fifty feet down, and stand at the edge of the water. After you have done it, you will wonder why you did it; but you will then be too late.

The guide will explain to you, in his blood-curdling way, how he saw the little steamer, Maid of the Mist, descend the fearful rapids—how first one paddle-box was out of sight behind the raging billows and then the other, and at what point it was that her smokestack toppled overboard, and where her planking began to break and part asunder—and how she did finally live through the trip, after accomplishing the incredible feat of traveling seventeen miles in six minutes, or six miles in seventeen minutes, I have really forgotten which. But it was very extraordinary, anyhow. It is worth the price of admission to hear the guide tell the story nine times in succession to different parties, and never miss a word or alter a sentence or a gesture.

Then you drive over to Suspension Bridge, and divide your misery between the chances of smashing down two hundred feet into the river below, and the chances of having the railway-train overhead smashing down onto you. Either possibility is discomforting taken by itself, but, mixed together, they amount in the aggregate to positive unhappiness.

On the Canada side you drive along the chasm between long ranks of photographers standing guard behind their cameras, ready to make an ostentatious frontispiece of you and your decaying ambulance, and your solemn crate with a hide on it, which you are expected to regard in the light of a horse, and a diminished and unimportant background of sublime Niagara; and a great many people have the incredible effrontery or the native depravity to aid and abet this sort of crime.

Any day, in the hands of these photographers, you may see stately pictures of papa and mamma, Johnny and Bub and Sis, or a couple of country cousins, all smiling vacantly, and all disposed in studied and uncomfortable attitudes in their carriage, and all looming up in their awe-inspiring imbecility before the snubbed and diminished presentment of that majestic presence whose ministering spirits are the rainbows, whose voice is the thunder, whose awful front is veiled in clouds, who was monarch here dead and forgotten ages before this sackful of small reptiles was deemed temporarily necessary to fill a crack in the world's unnoted myriads, and will still be monarch here ages and decades of ages after they shall have gathered themselves to their blood-relations, the other worms, and been mingled with the unremembering dust.

There is no actual harm in making Niagara a background whereon to display one's marvelous insignificance in a good strong light, but it requires a sort of superhuman self-complacency to enable one to do it.

When you have examined the stupendous Horseshoe Fall till you are satisfied you cannot improve on it, you return to America by the new Suspension Bridge, and follow up the bank to where they exhibit the Cave of the Winds.

Here I followed instructions, and divested myself of all my clothing, and put on a waterproof jacket and overalls. This costume is picturesque, but not beautiful. A guide, similarly dressed, led the way down a flight of winding stairs, which wound and wound, and still kept on winding long after the thing ceased to be a novelty, and then terminated long before it had begun to be a pleasure. We were then well down under the precipice, but still considerably above the level of the river.

We now began to creep along flimsy bridges of a single plank, our persons shielded from destruction by a crazy wooden railing, to which I clung with both hands—not because I was afraid, but because I wanted to. Presently the descent became steeper and the bridge flimsier, and sprays from the American Fall began to rain down on us in fast increasing sheets that soon became blinding, and after that our progress was mostly in the nature of groping. Now a a furious wind began to rush out from behind the waterfall, which seemed determined to sweep us from the bridge, and scatter us on the rocks and among the torrents below. I remarked that I wanted to go home; but it was too late. We were almost under the monstrous wall of water thundering down from above, and speech was in vain in the midst of such a pitiless crash of sound.

In another moment the guide disappeared behind the deluge, and, bewildered by the thunder, driven helplessly by the wind, and smitten by the arrowy tempest of rain, I followed. All was darkness. Such a mad storming, roaring, and bellowing of warring wind and water never crazed my ears before. I bent my head, and seemed to receive the Atlantic on my back. The world seemed going to destruction. I could not see anything, the flood poured down savagely. I raised my head, with open mouth, and the most of the American cataract went down my throat. If I had sprung a leak now I had been lost. And at this moment I discovered that the bridge had ceased, and we must trust for a foothold to the slippery and precipitous rocks. I never was so scared before and survived it. But we got through at last, and emerged into the open day, where we could stand in front of the laced and frothy and seething world of descending water, and look at it. When I saw how much of it there was, and how fearfully in earnest it was, I was sorry I had gone behind it.

The noble Red Man has always been a friend and darling of mine. I love to read about him in tales and legends and romances. I love to read of his inspired sagacity, and his love of the wild free life of mountain and forest, and his general nobility of character, and his stately metaphorical manner of speech, and his chivalrous love for the dusky maiden, and the picturesque pomp of his dress and accoutrements. Especially the picturesque pomp of his dress and accoutrements. When I found the shops at Niagara Falls full of dainty Indian beadwork, and stunning moccasins, and equally stunning toy figures representing human beings who carried their weapons in holes bored through their arms and bodies, and had feet shaped like a pie, I was filled with emotion. I knew that now, at last, I was going to come face to face with the noble Red Man.

A lady clerk in a shop told me, indeed, that all her grand array of curiosities were made by the Indians, and that they were plenty about the Falls, and that they were friendly, and it would not be dangerous to speak to them. And sure enough, as I approached the bridge leading over to Luna Island, I came upon a noble Son of the Forest sitting under a tree, diligently at work on a bead reticule. He wore a slouch hat and brogans, and had a short black pipe in his mouth. Thus does the baneful contact with our effeminate civilization dilute the picturesque pomp which is so natural to the Indian when far removed from us in his native haunts. I addressed the relic as follows:

"Is the Wawhoo-Wang-Wang of the Whack-a-Whack happy? Does the great Speckled Thunder sigh for the war-path, or is his heart contented with dreaming of the dusky maiden, the Pride of the Forest? Does the mighty Sachem yearn to drink the blood of his enemies, or is he satisfied to make bead reticules for the pappooses of the paleface? Speak, sublime relic of bygone grandeur—venerable ruin, speak!"

The relic said:

"An' is it mesilf, Dennis Hooligan, that ye'd be takin' for a dirty Injin, ye drawlin', lantern-jawed, spider-legged divil! By the piper that played before Moses, I'll ate ye!"

I went away from there.

By and by, in the neighborhood of the Terrapin Tower, I came upon a gentle daughter of the aborigines in fringed and beaded buckskin moccasins and leggins, seated on a bench with her pretty wares about her. She had just carved out a wooden chief that had a strong family resemblance to a clothes-pin, and was now boring a hole through his abdomen to put his bow through. I hesitated a moment, and then addressed her:

"Is the heart of the forest maiden heavy? Is the Laughing Tadpole lonely? Does she mourn over the extinguished council-fires of her race, and the vanished glory of her ancestors? Or does her sad spirit wander afar toward the hunting-grounds whither her brave Gobbler-of-the-Lightnings is gone? Why is my daughter silent? Has she ought against the paleface stranger?"

The maiden said:

"Faix, an' is it Biddy Malone ye dare to be callin' names? Lave this, or I'll shy your lean carcass over the cataract, ye sniveling blaggard!"

I adjourned from there also.

"Confound these Indians!" I said. "They told me they were tame, but, if appearances go for anything, I should say they were all on the warpath."

I made one more attempt to fraternize with them, and only one. I came upon a camp of them gathered in the shade of a great tree, making wampum and moccasins, and addressed them in the language of friendship:

"Noble Red Men, Braves, Grand Sachems, War Chiefs, Squaws, and High Muck-a-Mucks, the paleface from the land of the setting sun greets you! You, Beneficent Polecat—you, Devourer of Mountains—you, Roaring Thundergust—you, Bully Boy with a Glass eye—the paleface from beyond the great waters greets you all! War and pestilence have thinned your ranks and destroyed your once proud nation. Poker and seven-up, and a vain modern expense for soap, unknown to your glorious ancestors, have depleted your purses. Appropriating, in your simplicity, the property of others has gotten you into trouble. Misrepresenting facts, in your simple innocence, has damaged your reputation with the soulless usurper. Trading for forty-rod whisky, to enable you to get drunk and happy and tomahawk your families, has played the everlasting mischief with the picturesque pomp of your dress, and here you are, in the broad light of the nineteenth century, gotten up like the ragtag and bobtail of the purlieus of New York. For shame! Remember your ancestors! Recall their mighty deeds! Remember Uncas!—and Red jacket! and Hole in the Day!—and Whoopdedoodledo! Emulate their achievements! Unfurl yourselves under my banner, noble savages, illustrious guttersnipes—"

"Down wid him!" "Scoop the blaggard!" "Burn him!" "Hang him!" "Dhround him!"

It was the quickest operation that ever was. I simply saw a sudden flash in the air of clubs, brickbats, fists, bead-baskets, and moccasins—a single flash, and they all appeared to hit me at once, and no two of them in the same place. In the next instant the entire tribe was upon me. They tore half the clothes off me; they broke my arms and legs; they gave me a thump that dented the top of my head till it would hold coffee like a saucer; and, to crown their disgraceful proceedings and add insult to injury, they threw me over the Niagara Falls, and I got wet.

About ninety or a hundred feet from the top, the remains of my vest caught on a projecting rock, and I was almost drowned before I could get loose. I finally fell, and brought up in a world of white foam at the foot of the Fall, whose celled and bubbly masses towered-up several inches above my head. Of course I got into the eddy. I sailed round and round in it forty-four times—chasing a chip and gaining on it—each round trip a half-mile—reaching for the same bush on the bank forty-four times, and just exactly missing it by a hair's-breadth every time.

At last a man walked down and sat down close to that bush, and put a pipe in his mouth, and lit a match, and followed me with one eye and kept the other on the match, while he sheltered it in his hands from the wind. Presently a puff of wind blew it out. The next time I swept around he said:

"Got a match?"

"Yes; in my other vest. Help me out, please."

"Not for Joe."

When I came round again, I said:

"Excuse the seemingly impertinent curiosity of a drowning man, but will you explain this singular conduct of yours?"

"With pleasure. I am the coroner. Don't hurry on my account. I can wait for you. But I wish I had a match."

I said: "Take my place, and I'll go and get you one."

He declined. This lack of confidence on his part created a coldness between us, and from that time forward I avoided him. It was my idea, in case anything happened to me, to so time the occurrence as to throw my custom into the hands of the opposition coroner on the American side.

At last a policeman came along, and arrested me for disturbing the peace by yelling at people on shore for help. The judge fined me, but I had the advantage of him. My money was with my pantaloons, and my pantaloons were with the Indians.

Thus I escaped. I am now lying in a very critical condition. At least I am lying anyway—critical or not critical. I am hurt all over, but I cannot tell the full extent yet, because the doctor is not done taking inventory. He will make out my manifest this evening. However, thus far he thinks only sixteen of my wounds are fatal. I don't mind the others.

Upon regaining my right mind, I said:

"It is an awful savage tribe of Indians that do the beadwork and moccasins for Niagara Falls, doctor. Where are they from?"

"Limerick, my son."

ANSWERS TO CORRESPONDENTS

[written about 1865]

"MORAL STATISTICIAN."—I don't want any of your statistics; I took your whole batch and lit my pipe with it. I hate your kind of people. You are always ciphering out how much a man's health is injured, and how much his intellect is impaired, and how many pitiful dollars and cents he wastes in the course of ninety-two years' indulgence in the fatal practice of smoking; and in the equally fatal practice of drinking coffee; and in playing billiards occasionally; and in taking a glass of wine at dinner, etc., etc., etc. And you are always figuring out how many women have been burned to death because of the dangerous fashion of wearing expansive hoops, etc., etc., etc. You never see more than one side of the question. You are blind to the fact that most old men in America smoke and drink coffee, although, according to your theory, they ought to have died young; and that hearty old Englishmen drink wine and survive it, and portly old Dutchmen both drink and smoke freely, and yet grow older and fatter all the time. And you never try to find out how much solid comfort, relaxation, and enjoyment a man derives from smoking in the course of a lifetime (which is worth ten times the money he would save by letting it alone), nor the appalling aggregate of happiness lost in a lifetime by your kind of people from not smoking. Of course you can save money by denying yourself all the little vicious enjoyments for fifty years; but then what can you do with it? What use can you put it to? Money can't save your infinitesimal soul. All the use that money can be put to is to purchase comfort and enjoyment in this life; therefore, as you are an enemy to comfort and enjoyment, where is the use of accumulating cash? It won't do for you to say that you can use it to better purpose in furnishing a good table, and in charities, and in supporting tract societies, because you know yourself that you people who have no petty vices are never known to give away a cent, and that you stint yourselves so in the matter of food that you are always feeble and hungry. And you never dare to laugh in the daytime for fear some poor wretch, seeing you in a good humor, will try to borrow a dollar of you; and in church you are always down on your knees, with your eyes buried in the cushion, when the contribution-box comes around; and you never give the revenue officer full statement of your income. Now you know these things yourself, don't you? Very well, then what is the use of your stringing out your miserable lives to a lean and withered old age? What is the use of your saving money that is so utterly worthless to you? In a word, why don't you go off somewhere and die, and not be always trying to seduce people into becoming as "ornery" and unlovable as you are yourselves, by your villainous "moral statistics"? Now I don't approve of dissipation, and I don't indulge in it, either; but I haven't a particle of confidence in a man who has no redeeming petty vices, and so I don't want to hear from you any more. I think you are the very same man who read me a long lecture last week about the degrading vice of smoking cigars, and then came back, in my absence, with your reprehensible fireproof gloves on, and carried off my beautiful parlor stove.

"YOUNG AUTHOR."—Yes, Agassiz does recommend authors to eat fish, because the phosphorus in it makes brain. So far you are correct. But I cannot help you to a decision about the amount you need to eat—at least, not with certainty. If the specimen composition you send is about your fair usual average, I should judge that perhaps a couple of whales would be all you would want for the present. Not the largest kind, but simply good, middling-sized whales.

"SIMON WHEELER," Sonora.—The following simple and touching remarks and accompanying poem have just come to hand from the rich gold-mining region of Sonora:

> To Mr. Mark Twain: The within parson, which I have set to poetry under the name and style of "He Done His Level Best," was one among the whitest men I ever see, and it ain't every man that knowed him that can find it in his heart to say he's glad the poor cuss is busted and gone home to the States. He was here in an early day, and he was the handyest man about takin' holt of anything that come along you most ever see, I judge. He was a cheerful, stirin' cretur, always doin' somethin', and no man can say he ever see him do anything by halvers. Preachin was his nateral gait, but he warn't a man to lay back and twidle his thumbs because there didn't happen to be nothin' doin' in his own especial line—no, sir, he was a man who would meander forth and stir up something for hisself. His last acts was to go his pile on "Kings-and" (calklatin' to fill, but which he didn't fill), when there was a "flush" out agin him, and naterally, you see, he went under. And so he was cleaned out as you may say, and he struck the home-trail, cheerful but flat broke. I knowed this talonted man in

Arkansaw, and if you would print this humbly tribute to his gorgis abilities, you would greatly obleege his onhappy friend.

HE DONE HIS LEVEL BEST

Was he a mining on the flat—
He done it with a zest;
Was he a leading of the choir—
He done his level best.

If he'd a reg'lar task to do,
He never took no rest;
Or if 'twas off-and-on—the same—
He done his level best.

If he was preachin' on his beat,
He'd tramp from east to west,
And north to south-in cold and heat
He done his level best.

He'd yank a sinner outen (Hades),**
And land him with the blest;
Then snatch a prayer'n waltz in again,
And do his level best.

**Here I have taken a slight liberty with the original MS. "Hades" does not make such good meter as the other word of one syllable, but it sounds better.

He'd cuss and sing and howl and pray,
And dance and drink and jest,
And lie and steal—all one to him—
He done his level best.

Whate'er this man was sot to do,
He done it with a zest;
No matter what his contract was,
HE'D DO HIS LEVEL BEST.

Verily, this man was gifted with "gorgis abilities," and it is a happiness to me to embalm the memory of their luster in these columns. If it were not that the poet crop is unusually large and rank in California this year, I would encourage you to continue writing, Simon Wheeler; but, as it is, perhaps it might be too risky in you to enter against so much opposition.

"PROFESSIONAL BEGGAR."—NO; you are not obliged to take greenbacks at par.

"MELTON MOWBRAY," Dutch Flat.—This correspondent sends a lot of doggerel, and says it has been regarded as very good in Dutch Flat. I give a specimen verse:

The Assyrian came down like a wolf on the fold,
And his cohorts were gleaming with purple and gold;
And the sheen of his spears was like stars on the sea,
When the blue wave rolls nightly on deep Galilee.**

**This piece of pleasantry, published in a San Francisco paper, was mistaken by the country journals for seriousness, and many and loud were the denunciations of the ignorance of author and editor, in not knowing that the lines in question were "written by Byron."

There, that will do. That may be very good Dutch Flat poetry, but it won't do in the metropolis. It is too smooth and blubbery; it reads like buttermilk gurgling from a jug. What the people ought to have is something spirited—something like "Johnny Comes Marching Home." However, keep on practising, and you may succeed yet. There is genius in you, but too much blubber.

"ST. CLAIR HIGGINS." Los Angeles.—"My life is a failure; I have adored, wildly, madly, and she whom I love has turned coldly from me and shed her affections upon another. What would you advise me to do?"

You should set your affections on another also—or on several, if there are enough to go round. Also, do everything you can to make your former flame unhappy. There is an absurd idea disseminated in novels, that the happier a girl is with another man, the happier it makes the old lover she has blighted. Don't allow yourself to believe any such nonsense as that. The more cause that girl finds to regret that she did not marry you, the more comfortable you will feel over it. It isn't poetical, but it is mighty sound doctrine.

"ARITHMETICUS." Virginia, Nevada.—"If it would take a cannon-ball 3 and 1/3 seconds to travel four miles, and 3 and 3/8 seconds to travel the next four, and 3 and 5/8 to travel the next four, and if its rate of progress continued to diminish in the same ratio, how long would it take it to go fifteen hundred million miles?"

I don't know.

"AMBITIOUS LEARNER," Oakland.—Yes; you are right America was not discovered by Alexander Selkirk.

"DISCARDED LOVER."—"I loved, and still love, the beautiful Edwitha Howard, and intended to marry her. Yet, during my temporary absence at Benicia, last week, alas! she married Jones. Is my happiness to be thus blasted for life? Have I no redress?"

Of course you have. All the law, written and unwritten, is on your side. The intention and not the act constitutes crime—in other words, constitutes the deed. If you call your bosom friend a fool, and intend it for an insult, it is an insult; but if you do it playfully, and meaning no insult, it is not an insult. If you discharge a pistol accidentally, and kill a man, you can go free, for you have done no murder; but if you try to kill a man, and manifestly intend to kill him, but fail utterly to do it, the law still holds that the intention constituted the crime, and you are guilty of murder. Ergo, if you had married Edwitha accidentally, and without really intending to do it, you would not actually be married to her at all, because the act of marriage could not be complete without the intention. And ergo, in the strict spirit of the law, since you deliberately intended to marry Edwitha, and didn't do it, you are married to her all the same—because, as I said before, the intention constitutes the crime. It is as clear as day that Edwitha is your wife, and your redress lies in taking a club and mutilating Jones with it as much as you can. Any man has a right to protect his own wife from the advances of other men. But you have another alternative—you were married to Edwitha first, because of your deliberate intention, and now you can prosecute her for bigamy, in subsequently marrying Jones. But there is another phase in this complicated case: You intended to marry Edwitha, and consequently, according to law, she is your wife—there is no getting around that; but she didn't marry you, and if she never intended to marry you, you are not her husband, of course. Ergo, in marrying Jones, she was guilty of bigamy, because she was the wife of another man at the time; which is all very well as far as it goes—but then, don't you see, she had no other husband when she married Jones, and consequently she was not guilty of bigamy. Now, according to this view of the case, Jones married a spinster, who was a widow at the same time and another man's wife at the same time, and yet who had no husband and never had one, and never had any intention of getting married, and therefore, of course, never had been married; and by the same reasoning you are a bachelor, because you have never been any one's husband; and a married man, because you have a wife living; and to all intents and purposes a widower, because you have been deprived of that wife; and a consummate ass for going off to Benicia in the first place, while things were so mixed. And by this time I have got myself so tangled up in the intricacies of this extraordinary case that I shall have to give up any further attempt to advise you—I might get confused and fail to make myself understood. I think I could take up the argument where I left off, and by following it closely awhile, perhaps I could prove to your satisfaction, either that you never existed at all, or that you are dead now, and consequently don't need the faithless Edwitha—I think I could do that, if it would afford you any comfort.

"ARTHUR AUGUSTUS."—No; you are wrong; that is the proper way to throw a brickbat or a tomahawk; but it doesn't answer so well for a bouquet; you will hurt somebody if you keep it up. Turn your nosegay upside down, take it by the stems, and toss it with an upward sweep. Did you ever pitch quoits? that is the idea. The practice of recklessly heaving immense solid bouquets, of the general size and weight of prize cabbages, from the dizzy altitude of the galleries, is dangerous and very reprehensible. Now, night before last, at the Academy of Music, just after Signorina _____ had finished that exquisite melody, "The Last Rose of Summer," one of these floral pile-drivers came cleaving down through the atmosphere of applause, and if she hadn't deployed suddenly to the right, it would have driven her into the floor like a shinglenail. Of course that bouquet was well meant; but how would you like to have been the target? A sincere compliment is always grateful to a lady, so long as you don't try to knock her down with it.

"YOUNG MOTHER."—And so you think a baby is a thing of beauty and a joy forever? Well, the idea is pleasing, but not original; every cow thinks the same of its own calf. Perhaps the cow may not think it so elegantly, but still she thinks it nevertheless. I honor the cow for it. We all honor this touching maternal instinct wherever we find it, be it in the home of luxury or in the humble coW-shed. But really, madam, when I come to examine the matter in all its bearings, I find that the correctness of your assertion does not assert itself in all cases. A soiled baby, with a neglected nose, cannot be conscientiously regarded as a thing of beauty; and inasmuch as babyhood spans but three short years, no baby is competent to be a joy "forever." It pains me thus to demolish two-thirds of your pretty sentiment in a single sentence; but the position I hold in this chair requires that I shall not permit you to deceive and mislead the public with your plausible figures of speech. I know a female baby, aged eighteen months, in this city, which cannot hold out as a "joy" twenty-four hours on a stretch, let alone "forever." And it possesses some of the most remarkable eccentricities of character and appetite that have ever fallen under my notice. I will set down here a statement of this infant's operations (conceived, planned, and carried out by itself, and without suggestion or assistance from its mother or any one else), during a single day; and what I shall say can be substantiated by the sworn testimony of witnesses.

It commenced by eating one dozen large blue-mass pills, box and all; then it fell down a flight of stairs, and arose with a blue and purple knot on its forehead, after which it proceeded in quest of further refreshment and amusement. It found a glass trinket ornamented with brass-work—smashed up and ate the glass, and then swallowed the brass. Then it drank about twenty drops of laudanum, and more than a dozen tablespoonfuls of strong spirits of camphor. The reason why it took no more laudanum was because there was no more to take. After this it lay down on its back, and shoved five or six inches of a silver-headed whalebone cane down its throat; got it fast there, and it was all its mother could do to pull the cane out again, without pulling out some of the child with it. Then, being hungry for glass again, it broke up several wine glasses, and fell to eating and swallowing the fragments, not minding a cut or two. Then it ate a quantity of butter, pepper, salt, and California matches, actually taking a spoonful of butter, a spoonful of salt, a spoonful of pepper, and three or four lucifer matches at each mouthful. (I will remark here that this thing of beauty likes painted German lucifers, and eats all she can get of them; but she prefers California matches, which I regard as a compliment to our home manufactures of more than ordinary value, coming, as it does, from one who is too young to flatter.) Then she washed her head with soap and water, and afterward ate what soap was left, and drank as much of the suds as she had room for; after which she sallied forth and took the cow familiarly by the tail, and got kicked heels over head. At odd times during the day, when this joy forever happened to have nothing particular on hand, she put in the time by climbing up on places, and falling down off them, uniformly damaging her self in the operation. As young as she is, she speaks many words tolerably distinctly; and being plain-spoken in other respects, blunt and to the point, she opens conversation with all strangers, male or female, with the same formula, "How do, Jim?"

Not being familiar with the ways of children, it is possible that I have been magnifying into matter of surprise things which may not strike any one who is familiar with infancy as being at all astonishing. However, I cannot believe that such is the case, and so I repeat that my report of this baby's performances is strictly true; and if any one doubts it, I can produce the child. I will further engage that she will devour anything that is given her (reserving to myself only the right to exclude anvils), and fall down from any place to which she may be elevated (merely stipulating that her preference for alighting on her head shall be respected, and, therefore, that the elevation chosen shall be high enough to enable her to accomplish this to her satisfaction). But I find I have wandered from my subject; so, without further argument, I will reiterate my conviction that not all babies are things of beauty and joys forever.

"ARITHMETICUS." Virginia, Nevada.—"I am an enthusiastic student of mathematics, and it is so vexatious to me to find my progress constantly impeded by these mysterious arithmetical technicalities. Now do tell me what the difference is between geometry and conchology?"

Here you come again with your arithmetical conundrums, when I am suffering death with a cold in the head. If you could have seen the expression of scorn that darkened my countenance a moment ago, and was instantly split from the center in every direction like a fractured looking-glass by my last sneeze, you never would have written that disgraceful question. Conchology is a science which has nothing to do with mathematics; it relates only to shells. At the same time, however, a man who opens oysters for a hotel, or shells a fortified town, or sucks eggs, is not, strictly speaking, a conchologist-a fine stroke of sarcasm that, but it will be lost on such an unintellectual clam as you. Now compare conchology and geometry together, and you will see what the difference is, and your question will be answered. But don't torture me with any more arithmetical horrors until you know I am rid of my cold. I feel the bitterest animosity toward you at this moment—bothering me in this way, when I can do nothing but sneeze and rage and snort pocket-handkerchiefs to atoms. If I had you in range of my nose now I would blow your brains out.

TO RAISE POULTRY

[Being a letter written to a Poultry Society that had conferred a complimentary membership upon the author. Written about 1870.]

Seriously, from early youth I have taken an especial interest in the subject of poultry-raising, and so this membership touches a ready sympathy in my breast. Even as a schoolboy, poultry-raising was a study with me, and I may say without egotism that as early as the age of seventeen I was acquainted with all the best and speediest methods of raising chickens, from raising them off a roost by burning lucifer matches under their noses, down to lifting them off a fence on a frosty night by insinuating the end of a warm board under their heels. By the time I was twenty years old, I really suppose I had raised more poultry than any one individual in all the section round about there. The very chickens came to know my talent by and by. The youth of both sexes ceased to paw the earth for worms, and old roosters that came to crow, "remained to pray," when I passed by.

I have had so much experience in the raising of fowls that I cannot but think that a few hints from me might be useful to the society. The two methods I have already touched upon are very simple, and are only used in the raising of the commonest class of fowls; one is for summer, the other for winter. In the one case you start out with a friend along about eleven o'clock on a summer's night (not later, because in some states—especially in California and Oregon—chickens always rouse up just at midnight and crow from ten to thirty minutes, according to the ease or difficulty they experience in getting the public waked up), and your friend carries with him a sack. Arrived at the henroost (your neighbor's, not your own), you light a match and hold it under first one and then another pullet's nose until they are willing to go into that bag without making any trouble about it. You then return home, either taking the bag with you or leaving it behind, according as circumstances shall dictate. N. B.—I have seen the time when it was eligible and appropriate to leave the sack behind and walk off with considerable velocity, without ever leaving any word where to send it.

In the case of the other method mentioned for raising poultry, your friend takes along a covered vessel with a charcoal fire in it, and you carry a long slender plank. This is a frosty night, understand. Arrived at the tree, or fence, or other henroost (your own if you are an idiot), you warm the end of your plank in your friend's fire vessel, and then raise it aloft and ease it up gently against a slumbering chicken's foot. If the subject of your attentions is a true bird, he will infallibly return thanks with a sleepy cluck or two, and step out and take up quarters on the plank, thus becoming so conspicuously accessory before the fact to his own murder as to make it a grave question in our minds as it once was in the mind of Blackstone, whether he is not really and deliberately committing suicide in the second degree. [But you enter into a contemplation of these legal refinements subsequently not then.]

When you wish to raise a fine, large, donkey-voiced Shanghai rooster, you do it with a lasso, just as you would a bull. It is because he must be choked, and choked effectually, too. It is the only good, certain way, for whenever he mentions a matter which he is cordially interested in, the chances are ninety-nine in a hundred that he secures somebody else's immediate attention to it too, whether it be day or night.

The Black Spanish is an exceedingly fine bird and a costly one. Thirty-five dollars is the usual figure, and fifty a not uncommon price for a specimen. Even its eggs are worth from a dollar to a dollar and a half apiece, and yet are so unwholesome that the city physician seldom or never orders them for the workhouse. Still I have once or twice procured as high as a dozen at a time for nothing, in the dark of the moon. The best way to raise the Black Spanish fowl is to go late in the evening and raise coop and all. The reason I recommend this method is that, the birds being so valuable, the owners do not permit them to roost around promiscuously, but put them in a coop as strong as a fireproof safe and keep it in the kitchen at night. The method I speak of is not always a bright and satisfying success, and yet there are so many little articles of *vertu* about a kitchen, that if you fail on the coop you can generally bring away something else. I brought away a nice steel trap one night, worth ninety cents.

But what is the use in my pouring out my whole intellect on this subject? I have shown the Western New York Poultry Society that they have taken to their bosom a party who is not a spring chicken by any means, but a man who knows all about poultry, and is just as high up in the most efficient methods of raising it as the president of the institution himself. I thank these gentlemen for the honorary membership they have conferred upon me, and shall stand at all times ready and willing to testify my good feeling and my official zeal by deeds as well as by this hastily penned advice and information. Whenever they are ready to go to raising poultry, let them call for me any evening after eleven o'clock, and I shall be on hand promptly.

EXPERIENCE OF THE MCWILLIAMSES WITH MEMBRANOUS CROUP

[As related to the author of this book by Mr. McWilliams, a pleasant New York gentleman whom the said author met by chance on a journey.]

Well, to go back to where I was before I digressed to explain to you how that frightful and incurable disease, membranous croup,[Diphtheria D.W.] was ravaging the town and driving all mothers mad with terror, I called Mrs. McWilliams's attention to little Penelope, and said:

"Darling, I wouldn't let that child be chewing that pine stick if I were you."

"Precious, where is the harm in it?" said she, but at the same time preparing to take away the stick for women cannot receive even the most palpably judicious suggestion without arguing it; that is married women.

I replied:

"Love, it is notorious that pine is the least nutritious wood that a child can eat."

My wife's hand paused, in the act of taking the stick, and returned itself to her lap. She bridled perceptibly, and said:

"Hubby, you know better than that. You know you do. Doctors all say that the turpentine in pine wood is good for weak back and the kidneys."

"Ah—I was under a misapprehension. I did not know that the child's kidneys and spine were affected, and that the family physician had recommended—"

"Who said the child's spine and kidneys were affected?"

"My love, you intimated it."

"The idea! I never intimated anything of the kind."

"Why, my dear, it hasn't been two minutes since you said—"

"Bother what I said! I don't care what I did say. There isn't any harm in the child's chewing a bit of pine stick if she wants to, and you know it perfectly well. And she shall chew it, too. So there, now!"

"Say no more, my dear. I now see the force of your reasoning, and I will go and order two or three cords of the best pine wood to-day. No child of mine shall want while I—"

"Oh, please go along to your office and let me have some peace. A body can never make the simplest remark but you must take it up and go to arguing and arguing and arguing till you don't know what you are talking about, and you never do."

"Very well, it shall be as you say. But there is a want of logic in your last remark which—"

However, she was gone with a flourish before I could finish, and had taken the child with her. That night at dinner she confronted me with a face as white as a sheet:

"Oh, Mortimer, there's another! Little Georgi Gordon is taken."

"Membranous croup?"

"Membranous croup."

"Is there any hope for him?"

"None in the wide world. Oh, what is to become of us!"

By and by a nurse brought in our Penelope to say good night and offer the customary prayer at the mother's knee. In the midst of "Now I lay me down to sleep," she gave a slight cough! My wife fell back like one stricken with death. But the next moment she was up and brimming with the activities which terror inspires.

She commanded that the child's crib be removed from the nursery to our bedroom; and she went along to see the order executed. She took me with her, of course. We got matters arranged with speed. A cot-bed was put up in my wife's dressing room for the nurse. But now Mrs. McWilliams said we were too far away from the other baby, and what if he were to have the symptoms in the night—and she blanched again, poor thing.

We then restored the crib and the nurse to the nursery and put up a bed for ourselves in a room adjoining.

Presently, however, Mrs. McWilliams said suppose the baby should catch it from Penelope? This thought struck a new panic to her heart, and the tribe of us could not get the crib out of the nursery again fast enough to satisfy my wife, though she assisted in her own person and well-nigh pulled the crib to pieces in her frantic hurry.

We moved down-stairs; but there was no place there to stow the nurse, and Mrs. McWilliams said the nurse's experience would be an inestimable help. So we returned, bag and baggage, to our own bedroom once more, and felt a great gladness, like storm-buffeted birds that have found their nest again.

Mrs. McWilliams sped to the nursery to see how things were going on there. She was back in a moment with a new dread. She said:

"What can make Baby sleep so?"

I said:

"Why, my darling, Baby always sleeps like a graven image."

"I know. I know; but there's something peculiar about his sleep now. He seems to—to— he seems to breathe so regularly. Oh, this is dreadful."

"But, my dear, he always breathes regularly."

"Oh, I know it, but there's something frightful about it now. His nurse is too young and inexperienced. Maria shall stay there with her, and be on hand if anything happens."

"That is a good idea, but who will help you?"

"You can help me all I want. I wouldn't allow anybody to do anything but myself, anyhow, at such a time as this."

I said I would feel mean to lie abed and sleep, and leave her to watch and toil over our little patient all the weary night. But she reconciled me to it. So old Maria departed and took up her ancient quarters in the nursery.

Penelope coughed twice in her sleep.

"Oh, why don't that doctor come! Mortimer, this room is too warm. This room is certainly too warm. Turn off the register-quick!"

I shut it off, glancing at the thermometer at the same time, and wondering to myself if 70 was too warm for a sick child.

The coachman arrived from down-town now with the news that our physician was ill and confined to his bed. Mrs. McWilliams turned a dead eye upon me, and said in a dead voice:

"There is a Providence in it. It is foreordained. He never was sick before. Never. We have not been living as we ought to live, Mortimer. Time and time again I have told you so. Now you see the result. Our child will never get well. Be thankful if you can forgive yourself; I never can forgive myself."

I said, without intent to hurt, but with heedless choice of words, that I could not see that we had been living such an abandoned life.

"Mortimer! Do you want to bring the judgment upon Baby, too!"

Then she began to cry, but suddenly exclaimed:

"The doctor must have sent medicines!"

I said:

"Certainly. They are here. I was only waiting for you to give me a chance."

"Well do give them to me! Don't you know that every moment is precious now? But what was the use in sending medicines, when he knows that the disease is incurable?"

I said that while there was life there was hope.

"Hope! Mortimer, you know no more what you are talking about than the child unborn. If you would—As I live, the directions say give one teaspoonful once an hour! Once an hour!—as if we had a whole year before us to save the child in! Mortimer, please hurry. Give the poor perishing thing a tablespoonful, and try to be quick!"

"Why, my dear, a tablespoonful might—"

"Don't drive me frantic! . . . There, there, there, my precious, my own; it's nasty bitter stuff, but it's good for Nelly—good for mother's precious darling; and it will make her well. There, there, there, put the little head on mamma's breast and go to sleep, and pretty soon—oh, I know she can't live till morning! Mortimer, a tablespoonful every half-hour will—Oh, the child needs belladonna, too; I know she does—and aconite. Get them, Mortimer. Now do let me have my way. You know nothing about these things."

We now went to bed, placing the crib close to my wife's pillow. All this turmoil had worn upon me, and within two minutes I was something more than half asleep. Mrs. McWilliams roused me:

"Darling, is that register turned on?"

"No."

"I thought as much. Please turn it on at once. This room is cold."

I turned it on, and presently fell asleep again. I was aroused once more:

"Dearie, would you mind moving the crib to your side of the bed? It is nearer the register."

I moved it, but had a collision with the rug and woke up the child. I dozed off once more, while my wife quieted the sufferer. But in a little while these words came murmuring remotely through the fog of my drowsiness:

"Mortimer, if we only had some goose grease—will you ring?"

I climbed dreamily out, and stepped on a cat, which responded with a protest and would have got a convincing kick for it if a chair had not got it instead.

"Now, Mortimer, why do you want to turn up the gas and wake up the child again?"

"Because I want to see how much I am hurt, Caroline."

"Well, look at the chair, too—I have no doubt it is ruined. Poor cat, suppose you had—"

"Now I am not going to suppose anything about the cat. It never would have occurred if Maria had been allowed to remain here and attend to these duties, which are in her line and are not in mine."

"Now, Mortimer, I should think you would be ashamed to make a remark like that. It is a pity if you cannot do the few little things I ask of you at such an awful time as this when our child—"

"There, there, I will do anything you want. But I can't raise anybody with this bell. They're all gone to bed. Where is the goose grease?"

"On the mantelpiece in the nursery. If you'll step there and speak to Maria—"

I fetched the goose grease and went to sleep again. Once more I was called:

"Mortimer, I so hate to disturb you, but the room is still too cold for me to try to apply this stuff. Would you mind lighting the fire? It is all ready to touch a match to."

I dragged myself out and lit the fire, and then sat down disconsolate.

"Mortimer, don't sit there and catch your death of cold. Come to bed."

As I was stepping in she said:

"But wait a moment. Please give the child some more of the medicine."

Which I did. It was a medicine which made a child more or less lively; so my wife made use of its waking interval to strip it and grease it all over with the goose oil. I was soon asleep once more, but once more I had to get up.

"Mortimer, I feel a draft. I feel it distinctly. There is nothing so bad for this disease as a draft. Please move the crib in front of the fire."

I did it; and collided with the rug again, which I threw in the fire. Mrs. McWilliams sprang out of bed and rescued it and we had some words. I had another trifling interval of sleep, and then got up, by request, and constructed a flax-seed poultice. This was placed upon the child's breast and left there to do its healing work.

A wood-fire is not a permanent thing. I got up every twenty minutes and renewed ours, and this gave Mrs. McWilliams the opportunity to shorten the times of giving the medicines by ten minutes, which was a great satisfaction to her. Now and then, between times, I reorganized the flax-seed poultices, and applied sinapisms and other sorts of blisters where unoccupied places could be found upon the child. Well, toward morning the wood gave out and my wife wanted me to go down cellar and get some more. I said:

"My dear, it is a laborious job, and the child must be nearly warm enough, with her extra clothing. Now mightn't we put on another layer of poultices and—"

I did not finish, because I was interrupted. I lugged wood up from below for some little time, and then turned in and fell to snoring as only a man can whose strength is all gone and whose soul is worn out. Just at broad daylight I felt a grip on my shoulder that brought me to my senses suddenly. My wife was glaring down upon me and gasping. As soon as she could command her tongue she said:

"It is all over! All over! The child's perspiring! What shall we do?"

"Mercy, how you terrify me! I don't know what we ought to do. Maybe if we scraped her and put her in the draft again—"

"Oh, idiot! There is not a moment to lose! Go for the doctor. Go yourself. Tell him he must come, dead or alive."

I dragged that poor sick man from his bed and brought him. He looked at the child and said she was not dying. This was joy unspeakable to me, but it made my wife as mad as if he had offered her a personal affront. Then he said the child's cough was only caused by some trifling irritation or other in the throat. At this I thought my wife had a mind to show him the door. Now the doctor said he would make the child cough harder and dislodge the trouble. So he gave her something that sent her into a spasm of coughing, and presently up came a little wood splinter or so.

"This child has no membranous croup," said he. "She has been chewing a bit of pine shingle or something of the kind, and got some little slivers in her throat. They won't do her any hurt."

"No," said I, "I can well believe that. Indeed, the turpentine that is in them is very good for certain sorts of diseases that are peculiar to children. My wife will tell you so."

But she did not. She turned away in disdain and left the room; and since that time there is one episode in our life which we never refer to. Hence the tide of our days flows by in deep and untroubled serenity.

> [Very few married men have such an experience as McWilliams's, and so the author of this book thought that maybe the novelty of it would give it a passing interest to the reader.]

MY FIRST LITERARY VENTURE

[written about 1865]

I was a very smart child at the age of thirteen—an unusually smart child, I thought at the time. It was then that I did my first newspaper scribbling, and most unexpectedly to me it stirred up a fine sensation in the community. It did, indeed, and I was very proud of it, too. I was a printer's "devil," and a progressive and aspiring one. My uncle had me on his paper (the Weekly Hannibal Journal, two dollars a year in advance—five hundred subscribers, and they paid in cordwood, cabbages, and unmarketable turnips), and on a lucky summer's day he left town to be gone a week, and asked me if I thought I could edit one issue of the paper judiciously. Ah! didn't I want to try! Higgins was the editor on the rival paper. He had lately been jilted, and one night a friend found an open note on the poor fellow's bed, in which he stated that he could not longer endure life and had drowned himself in Bear Creek. The friend ran down there and discovered Higgins wading back to shore. He had concluded he wouldn't.

The village was full of it for several days, but Higgins did not suspect it. I thought this was a fine opportunity. I wrote an elaborately wretched account of the whole matter, and then illustrated it with villainous cuts engraved on the bottoms of wooden type with a jackknife—one of them a picture of Higgins wading out into the creek in his shirt, with a lantern, sounding the depth of the water with a walking-stick. I thought it was desperately funny, and was densely unconscious that there was any moral obliquity about such a publication. Being satisfied with this effort I looked around for other worlds to conquer, and it struck me that it would make good, interesting matter to charge the editor of a neighboring country paper with a piece of gratuitous rascality and "see him squirm."

I did it, putting the article into the form of a parody on the "Burial of Sir John Moore"— and a pretty crude parody it was, too.

Then I lampooned two prominent citizens outrageously—not because they had done anything to deserve, but merely because I thought it was my duty to make the paper lively.

Next I gently touched up the newest stranger—the lion of the day, the gorgeous journeyman tailor from Quincy. He was a simpering coxcomb of the first water, and the "loudest" dressed man in the state. He was an inveterate woman-killer. Every week he wrote lushy "poetry" for the journal, about his newest conquest. His rhymes for my week were headed, "To MARY IN H—l," meaning to Mary in Hannibal, of course. But while setting up the piece I was suddenly riven from head to heel by what I regarded as a perfect thunderbolt of humor, and I compressed it into a snappy footnote at the bottom— thus: "We will let this thing pass, just this once; but we wish Mr. J. Gordon Runnels to understand distinctly that we have a character to sustain, and from this time forth when he wants to commune with his friends in h—l, he must select some other medium than the columns of this journal!"

The paper came out, and I never knew any little thing attract so much attention as those playful trifles of mine.

For once the Hannibal Journal was in demand—a novelty it had not experienced before. The whole town was stirred. Higgins dropped in with a double-barreled shotgun early in the forenoon. When he found that it was an infant (as he called me) that had done him the damage, he simply pulled my ears and went away; but he threw up his situation that night and left town for good. The tailor came with his goose and a pair of shears; but he despised me, too, and departed for the South that night. The two lampooned citizens came with threats of libel, and went away incensed at my insignificance. The country editor pranced in with a war-whoop next day, suffering for blood to drink; but he ended by forgiving me cordially and inviting me down to the drug store to wash away all animosity in a friendly bumper of "Fahnestock's Vermifuge." It was his little joke. My uncle was very angry when he got back—unreasonably so, I thought, considering what an impetus I had given the paper, and considering also that gratitude for his preservation ought to have been uppermost in his mind, inasmuch as by his delay he had so wonderfully escaped dissection, tomahawking, libel, and getting his head shot off.

But he softened when he looked at the accounts and saw that I had actually booked the unparalleled number of thirty-three new subscribers, and had the vegetables to show for it, cordwood, cabbage, beans, and unsalable turnips enough to run the family for two years!

HOW THE AUTHOR WAS SOLD IN NEWARK

[written about 1869]

It is seldom pleasant to tell on oneself, but some times it is a sort of relief to a man to make a confession. I wish to unburden my mind now, and yet I almost believe that I am moved to do it more because I long to bring censure upon another man than because I desire to pour balm upon my wounded heart. (I don't know what balm is, but I believe it is the correct expression to use in this connection—never having seen any balm.) You may remember that I lectured in Newark lately for the young gentlemen of the————- Society? I did at any rate. During the afternoon of that day I was talking with one of the young gentlemen just referred to, and he said he had an uncle who, from some cause or other, seemed to have grown permanently bereft of all emotion. And with tears in his eyes, this young man said, "Oh, if I could only see him laugh once more! Oh, if I could only see him weep!" I was touched. I could never withstand distress.

I said: "Bring him to my lecture. I'll start him for you."

"Oh, if you could but do it! If you could but do it, all our family would bless you for evermore—for he is so very dear to us. Oh, my benefactor, can you make him laugh? can you bring soothing tears to those parched orbs?"

I was profoundly moved. I said: "My son, bring the old party round. I have got some jokes in that lecture that will make him laugh if there is any laugh in him; and if they miss fire, I have got some others that will make him cry or kill him, one or the other." Then the young man blessed me, and wept on my neck, and went after his uncle. He placed him in full view, in the second row of benches, that night, and I began on him. I tried him with mild jokes, then with severe ones; I dosed him with bad jokes and riddled him with good ones; I fired old stale jokes into him, and peppered him fore and aft with red-hot new ones; I warmed up to my work, and assaulted him on the right and left, in front and behind; I fumed and sweated and charged and ranted till I was hoarse and sick and frantic and furious; but I never moved him once—I never started a smile or a tear! Never a ghost of a smile, and never a suspicion of moisture! I was astounded. I closed the lecture at last with one despairing shriek—with one wild burst of humor, and hurled a joke of supernatural atrocity full at him!

Then I sat down bewildered and exhausted.

The president of the society came up and bathed my head with cold water, and said: "What made you carry on so toward the last?"

I said: "I was trying to make that confounded old fool laugh, in the second row."

And he said: "Well, you were wasting your time, because he is deaf and dumb, and as blind as a badger!"

Now, was that any way for that old man's nephew to impose on a stranger and orphan like me? I ask you as a man and brother, if that was any way for him to do?

THE OFFICE BORE

[written about 1869]

He arrives just as regularly as the clock strikes nine in the morning. And so he even beats the editor sometimes, and the porter must leave his work and climb two or three pairs of stairs to unlock the "Sanctum" door and let him in. He lights one of the office pipes—not reflecting, perhaps, that the editor may be one of those "stuck-up" people who would as soon have a stranger defile his tooth-brush as his pipe-stem. Then he begins to loll—for a person who can consent to loaf his useless life away in ignominious indolence has not the energy to sit up straight. He stretches full length on the sofa awhile; then draws up to half length; then gets into a chair, hangs his head back and his arms abroad, and stretches his legs till the rims of his boot-heels rest upon the floor; by and by sits up and leans forward, with one leg or both over the arm of the chair. But it is still observable that with all his changes of position, he never assumes the upright or a fraudful affectation of dignity. From time to time he yawns, and stretches, and scratches himself with a tranquil, mangy enjoyment, and now and then he grunts a kind of stuffy, overfed grunt, which is full of animal contentment. At rare and long intervals, however, he sighs a sigh that is the eloquent expression of a secret confession, to wit "I am useless and a nuisance, a cumberer of the earth." The bore and his comrades—for there are usually from two to four on hand, day and night—mix into the conversation when men come in to see the editors for a moment on business; they hold noisy talks among themselves about politics in particular, and all other subjects in general—even warming up, after a fashion, sometimes, and seeming to take almost a real interest in what they are discussing. They ruthlessly call an editor from his work with such a remark as: "Did you see this, Smith, in the Gazette?" and proceed to read the paragraph while the sufferer reins in his impatient pen and listens; they often loll and sprawl round the office hour after hour, swapping anecdotes and relating personal experiences to each other— hairbreadth escapes, social encounters with distinguished men, election reminiscences, sketches of odd characters, etc. And through all those hours they never seem to comprehend that they are robbing the editors of their time, and the public of journalistic excellence in next day's paper. At other times they drowse, or dreamily pore over exchanges, or droop limp and pensive over the chair-arms for an hour. Even this solemn silence is small respite to the editor, for the next uncomfortable thing to having people look over his shoulders, perhaps, is to have them sit by in silence and listen to the scratching of his pen. If a body desires to talk private business with one of the editors, he must call him outside, for no hint milder than blasting-powder or nitroglycerin would be likely to move the bores out of listening-distance. To have to sit and endure the presence of a bore day after day; to feel your cheerful spirits begin to sink as his footstep sounds on the stair, and utterly vanish away as his tiresome form enters the door; to suffer through his anecdotes and die slowly to his reminiscences; to feel always the fetters of his clogging presence; to long hopelessly for one single day's privacy; to note with a shudder, by and by, that to contemplate his funeral in fancy has ceased to soothe, to imagine him undergoing in strict and fearful detail the tortures of the ancient Inquisition has lost its power to satisfy the heart, and that even to wish him millions and millions and millions of miles in Tophet is able to bring only a fitful gleam of joy; to have to endure all this, day after day, and week after week, and month after month, is an affliction that transcends any other that men suffer. Physical pain is pastime to it, and hanging a pleasure excursion.

JOHNNY GREER

"The church was densely crowded that lovely summer Sabbath," said the Sunday-school superintendent, "and all, as their eyes rested upon the small coffin, seemed impressed by the poor black boy's fate. Above the stillness the pastor's voice rose, and chained the interest of every ear as he told, with many an envied compliment, how that the brave, noble, daring little Johnny Greer, when he saw the drowned body sweeping down toward the deep part of the river whence the agonized parents never could have recovered it in this world, gallantly sprang into the stream, and, at the risk of his life, towed the corpse to shore, and held it fast till help came and secured it. Johnny Greer was sitting just in front of me. A ragged street-boy, with eager eye, turned upon him instantly, and said in a hoarse whisper

"'No; but did you, though?'

"'Yes.'

"'Towed the carkiss ashore and saved it yo'self?'

"'Yes.'

"'Cracky! What did they give you?'

"'Nothing.'

"'W-h-a-t [with intense disgust]! D'you know what I'd 'a' done? I'd 'a' anchored him out in the stream, and said, Five dollars, gents, or you carn't have yo' nigger.'"

THE FACTS IN THE CASE OF THE GREAT BEEF CONTRACT

[written about 1867]

In as few words as possible I wish to lay before the nation what share, howsoever small, I have had in this matter—this matter which has so exercised the public mind, engendered so much ill-feeling, and so filled the newspapers of both continents with distorted statements and extravagant comments.

The origin of this distressful thing was this—and I assert here that every fact in the following *résumé* can be amply proved by the official records of the General Government.

John Wilson Mackenzie, of Rotterdam, Chemung County, New Jersey, deceased, contracted with the General Government, on or about the 10th day of October, 1861, to furnish to General Sherman the sum total of thirty barrels of beef.

Very well.

He started after Sherman with the beef, but when he got to Washington Sherman had gone to Manassas; so he took the beef and followed him there, but arrived too late; he followed him to Nashville, and from Nashville to Chattanooga, and from Chattanooga to Atlanta—but he never could overtake him. At Atlanta he took a fresh start and followed him clear through his march to the sea. He arrived too late again by a few days; but hearing that Sherman was going out in the Quaker City excursion to the Holy Land, he took shipping for Beirut, calculating to head off the other vessel. When he arrived in Jerusalem with his beef, he learned that Sherman had not sailed in the Quaker City, but had gone to the Plains to fight the Indians. He returned to America and started for the Rocky Mountains. After sixty-eight days of arduous travel on the Plains, and when he had got within four miles of Sherman's headquarters, he was tomahawked and scalped, and the Indians got the beef.

They got all of it but one barrel. Sherman's army captured that, and so, even in death, the bold navigator partly fulfilled his contract. In his will, which he had kept like a journal, he bequeathed the contract to his son Bartholomew. Bartholomew W. made out the following bill, and then died:

THE UNITED STATES

In account with JOHN WILSON MACKENZIE, of New Jersey,	
deceased,	Dr.
To thirty barrels of beef for General Sherman, at $100,	$3,000
To traveling expenses and transportation	14,000
Total	$17,000
Rec'd Pay't.	

He died then; but he left the contract to Wm. J. Martin, who tried to collect it, but died before he got through. He left it to Barker J. Allen, and he tried to collect it also. He did not survive. Barker J. Allen left it to Anson G. Rogers, who attempted to collect it, and got along as far as the Ninth Auditor's Office, when Death, the great Leveler, came all unsummoned, and foreclosed on him also. He left the bill to a relative of his in Connecticut, Vengeance Hopkins by name, who lasted four weeks and two days, and made the best time on record, coming within one of reaching the Twelfth Auditor. In his will he gave the contract bill to his uncle, by the name of O-be-joyful Johnson. It was too undermining for Joyful. His last words were: "Weep not for me—I am willing to go." And so he was, poor soul. Seven people inherited the contract after that; but they all died. So it came into my hands at last. It fell to me through a relative by the name of Hubbard—Bethlehem Hubbard, of Indiana. He had had a grudge against me for a long time; but in his last moments he sent for me, and forgave me everything, and, weeping, gave me the beef contract.

This ends the history of it up to the time that I succeeded to the property. I will now endeavor to set myself straight before the nation in everything that concerns my share in the matter. I took this beef contract, and the bill for mileage and transportation, to the President of the United States.

He said, "Well, sir, what can I do for you?"

I said, "Sire, on or about the 10th day of October, 1861, John Wilson Mackenzie, of Rotterdam, Chemung County, New Jersey, deceased, contracted with the General Government to furnish to General Sherman, the sum total of thirty barrels of beef—"

He stopped me there, and dismissed me from his presence—kindly, but firmly. The next day I called on the Secretary of State.

He said, "Well, sir?"

I said, "Your Royal Highness: on or about the 10th day of October, 1861, John Wilson Mackenzie of Rotterdam, Chemung County, New Jersey, deceased, contracted with the General Government to furnish to General Sherman the sum total of thirty barrels of beef—"

"That will do, sir—that will do; this office has nothing to do with contracts for beef."

I was bowed out. I thought the matter all over and finally, the following day, I visited the Secretary of the Navy, who said, "Speak quickly, sir; do not keep me waiting."

I said, "Your Royal Highness, on or about the 10th day of October, 1861, John Wilson Mackenzie of Rotterdam, Chemung County, New Jersey, deceased, contracted with the General Government to General Sherman the sum total of thirty barrels of beef—"

Well, it was as far as I could get. He had nothing to do with beef contracts for General Sherman either. I began to think it was a curious kind of government. It looked somewhat as if they wanted to get out of paying for that beef. The following day I went to the Secretary of the Interior.

I said, "Your Imperial Highness, on or about the 10th day of October—"

"That is sufficient, sir. I have heard of you before. Go, take your infamous beef contract out of this establishment. The Interior Department has nothing whatever to do with subsistence for the army."

I went away. But I was exasperated now. I said I would haunt them; I would infest every department of this iniquitous government till that contract business was settled. I would collect that bill, or fall, as fell my predecessors, trying. I assailed the Postmaster-General; I besieged the Agricultural Department; I waylaid the Speaker of the House of Representatives. They had nothing to do with army contracts for beef. I moved upon the Commissioner of the Patent Office.

I said, "Your August Excellency, on or about—"

"Perdition! have you got here with your incendiary beef contract, at last? We have nothing to do with beef contracts for the army, my dear sir."

"Oh, that is all very well—but somebody has got to pay for that beef. It has got to be paid now, too, or I'll confiscate this old Patent Office and everything in it."

"But, my dear sir—"

"It don't make any difference, sir. The Patent Office is liable for that beef, I reckon; and, liable or not liable, the Patent Office has got to pay for it."

Never mind the details. It ended in a fight. The Patent Office won. But I found out something to my advantage. I was told that the Treasury Department was the proper place for me to go to. I went there. I waited two hours and a half, and then I was admitted to the First Lord of the Treasury.

I said, "Most noble, grave, and reverend Signor, on or about the 10th day of October, 1861, John Wilson Macken—"

"That is sufficient, sir. I have heard of you. Go to the First Auditor of the Treasury."

I did so. He sent me to the Second Auditor. The Second Auditor sent me to the Third, and the Third sent me to the First Comptroller of the Corn-Beef Division. This began to look like business. He examined his books and all his loose papers, but found no minute of the beef contract. I went to the Second Comptroller of the Corn-Beef Division. He examined his books and his loose papers, but with no success. I was encouraged. During that week I got as far as the Sixth Comptroller in that division; the next week I got through the Claims Department; the third week I began and completed the Mislaid Contracts Department, and got a foothold in the Dead Reckoning Department. I finished that in three days. There was only one place left for it now. I laid siege to the Commissioner of Odds and Ends. To his clerk, rather—he was not there himself. There were sixteen beautiful young ladies in the room, writing in books, and there were seven well-favored young clerks showing them how. The young women smiled up over their shoulders, and the clerks smiled back at them, and all went merry as a marriage bell. Two or three clerks that were reading the newspapers looked at me rather hard, but went on reading, and nobody said anything. However, I had been used to this kind of alacrity from Fourth Assistant Junior Clerks all through my eventful career, from the very day I entered the first office of the Corn-Beef Bureau clear till I passed out of the last one in the Dead Reckoning Division. I had got so accomplished by this time that I could stand on one foot from the moment I entered an office till a clerk spoke to me, without changing more than two, or maybe three, times.

So I stood there till I had changed four different times. Then I said to one of the clerks who was reading:

"Illustrious Vagrant, where is the Grand Turk?"

"What do you mean, sir? whom do you mean? If you mean the Chief of the Bureau, he is out."

"Will he visit the harem to-day?"

The young man glared upon me awhile, and then went on reading his paper. But I knew the ways of those clerks. I knew I was safe if he got through before another New York mail arrived. He only had two more papers left. After a while he finished them, and then he yawned and asked me what I wanted.

"Renowned and honored Imbecile: on or about—"

"You are the beef-contract man. Give me your papers."

He took them, and for a long time he ransacked his odds and ends. Finally he found the Northwest Passage, as I regarded it—he found the long lost record of that beef contract—he found the rock upon which so many of my ancestors had split before they ever got to it. I was deeply moved. And yet I rejoiced—for I had survived. I said with emotion, "Give it me. The government will settle now." He waved me back, and said there was something yet to be done first.

"Where is this John Wilson Mackenzie?" said he.

"Dead."

"When did he die?"

"He didn't die at all—he was killed."

"How?"

"Tomahawked."

"Who tomahawked him?"

"Why, an Indian, of course. You didn't suppose it was the superintendent of a Sunday-school, did you?"

"No. An Indian, was it?"

"The same."

"Name of the Indian?"

"His name? I don't know his name."

"Must have his name. Who saw the tomahawking done?"

"I don't know."

"You were not present yourself, then?"

"Which you can see by my hair. I was absent.

"Then how do you know that Mackenzie is dead?"

"Because he certainly died at that time, and I have every reason to believe that he has been dead ever since. I know he has, in fact."

"We must have proofs. Have you got the Indian?"

"Of course not."

"Well, you must get him. Have you got the tomahawk?"

"I never thought of such a thing."

"You must get the tomahawk. You must produce the Indian and the tomahawk. If Mackenzie's death can be proven by these, you can then go before the commission appointed to audit claims with some show of getting your bill under such headway that your children may possibly live to receive the money and enjoy it. But that man's death must be proven. However, I may as well tell you that the government will never pay that transportation and those traveling expenses of the lamented Mackenzie. It may possibly pay for the barrel of beef that Sherman's soldiers captured, if you can get a relief bill through Congress making an appropriation for that purpose; but it will not pay for the twenty-nine barrels the Indians ate."

"Then there is only a hundred dollars due me, and that isn't certain! After all Mackenzie's travels in Europe, Asia, and America with that beef; after all his trials and tribulations and transportation; after the slaughter of all those innocents that tried to collect that bill! Young man, why didn't the First Comptroller of the Corn-Beef Division tell me this?"

"He didn't know anything about the genuineness of your claim."

"Why didn't the Second tell me? why didn't the Third? why didn't all those divisions and departments tell me?"

"None of them knew. We do things by routine here. You have followed the routine and found out what you wanted to know. It is the best way. It is the only way. It is very regular, and very slow, but it is very certain."

"Yes, certain death." It has been, to the most of our tribe. I begin to feel that I, too, am called.

"Young man, you love the bright creature yonder with the gentle blue eyes and the steel pens behind her ears—I see it in your soft glances; you wish to marry her—but you are poor. Here, hold out your hand—here is the beef contract; go, take her and be happy! Heaven bless you, my children!"

This is all I know about the great beef contract that has created so much talk in the community. The clerk to whom I bequeathed it died. I know nothing further about the contract, or any one connected with it. I only know that if a man lives long enough he can trace a thing through the Circumlocution Office of Washington and find out, after much labor and trouble and delay, that which he could have found out on the first day if the business of the Circumlocution Office were as ingeniously systematized as it would be if it were a great private mercantile institution.

THE CASE OF GEORGE FISHER

—[Some years ago, about 1867, when this was first published, few people believed it, but considered it a mere extravaganza. In these latter days it seems hard to realize that there was ever a time when the robbing of our government was a novelty. The very man who showed me where to find the documents for this case was at that very time spending hundreds of thousands of dollars in Washington for a mail steamship concern, in the effort to procure a subsidy for the company—a fact which was a long time in coming to the surface, but leaked out at last and underwent Congressional investigation.]

This is history. It is not a wild extravaganza, like "John Wilson Mackenzie's Great Beef Contract," but is a plain statement of facts and circumstances with which the Congress of the United States has interested itself from time to time during the long period of half a century.

I will not call this matter of George Fisher's a great deathless and unrelenting swindle upon the government and people of the United States—for it has never been so decided, and I hold that it is a grave and solemn wrong for a writer to cast slurs or call names when such is the case—but will simply present the evidence and let the reader deduce his own verdict. Then we shall do nobody injustice, and our consciences shall be clear.

On or about the 1st day of September, 1813, the Creek war being then in progress in Florida, the crops, herds, and houses of Mr. George Fisher, a citizen, were destroyed, either by the Indians or by the United States troops in pursuit of them. By the terms of the law, if the Indians destroyed the property, there was no relief for Fisher; but if the troops destroyed it, the Government of the United States was debtor to Fisher for the amount involved.

George Fisher must have considered that the Indians destroyed the property, because, although he lived several years afterward, he does not appear to have ever made any claim upon the government.

In the course of time Fisher died, and his widow married again. And by and by, nearly twenty years after that dimly remembered raid upon Fisher's corn-fields, the widow Fisher's new husband petitioned Congress for pay for the property, and backed up the petition with many depositions and affidavits which purported to prove that the troops, and not the Indians, destroyed the property; that the troops, for some inscrutable reason, deliberately burned down "houses" (or cabins) valued at $600, the same belonging to a peaceable private citizen, and also destroyed various other property belonging to the same citizen. But Congress declined to believe that the troops were such idiots (after overtaking and scattering a band of Indians proved to have been found destroying

Fisher's property) as to calmly continue the work of destruction themselves; and make a complete job of what the Indians had only commenced. So Congress denied the petition of the heirs of George Fisher in 1832, and did not pay them a cent.

We hear no more from them officially until 1848, sixteen years after their first attempt on the Treasury, and a full generation after the death of the man whose fields were destroyed. The new generation of Fisher heirs then came forward and put in a bill for damages. The Second Auditor awarded them $8,873, being half the damage sustained by Fisher. The Auditor said the testimony showed that at least half the destruction was done by the Indians "before the troops started in pursuit," and of course the government was not responsible for that half.

2. That was in April, 1848. In December, 1848, the heirs of George Fisher, deceased, came forward and pleaded for a "revision" of their bill of damages. The revision was made, but nothing new could be found in their favor except an error of $100 in the former calculation. However, in order to keep up the spirits of the Fisher family, the Auditor concluded to go back and allow interest from the date of the first petition (1832) to the date when the bill of damages was awarded. This sent the Fishers home happy with sixteen years' interest on $8,873—the same amounting to $8,997.94. Total, $17,870.94.

3. For an entire year the suffering Fisher family remained quiet—even satisfied, after a fashion. Then they swooped down upon the government with their wrongs once more. That old patriot, Attorney-General Toucey, burrowed through the musty papers of the Fishers and discovered one more chance for the desolate orphans—interest on that original award of $8,873 from date of destruction of the property (1813) up to 1832! Result, $10,004.89 for the indigent Fishers. So now we have: First, $8,873 damages; second, interest on it from 1832 to 1848, $8,997.94; third, interest on it dated back to 1813, $10,004.89. Total, $27,875.83! What better investment for a great-grandchild than to get the Indians to burn a corn-field for him sixty or seventy years before his birth, and plausibly lay it on lunatic United States troops?

4. Strange as it may seem, the Fishers let Congress alone for five years—or, what is perhaps more likely, failed to make themselves heard by Congress for that length of time. But at last, in 1854, they got a hearing. They persuaded Congress to pass an act requiring the Auditor to re-examine their case. But this time they stumbled upon the misfortune of an honest Secretary of the Treasury (Mr. James Guthrie), and he spoiled everything. He said in very plain language that the Fishers were not only not entitled to another cent, but that those children of many sorrows and acquainted with grief had been paid too much already.

5. Therefore another interval of rest and silence ensued—an interval which lasted four years—viz till 1858. The "right man in the right place" was then Secretary of War—John B. Floyd, of peculiar renown! Here was a master intellect; here was the very man to succor the suffering heirs of dead and forgotten Fisher. They came up from Florida with a rush—a great tidal wave of Fishers freighted with the same old musty documents about the same immortal corn-fields of their ancestor. They straight-way got an act passed transferring the Fisher matter from the dull Auditor to the ingenious Floyd. What did Floyd do? He said, "IT WAS PROVED that the Indians destroyed everything they could before the troops entered in pursuit." He considered, therefore, that what they destroyed must have consisted of "the houses with all their contents, and the liquor" (the

most trifling part of the destruction, and set down at only $3,200 all told), and that the government troops then drove them off and calmly proceeded to destroy:—

Two hundred and twenty acres of corn in the field, thirty-five acres of wheat, and nine hundred and eighty-six head of live stock! [What a singularly intelligent army we had in those days, according to Mr. Floyd—though not according to the Congress of 1832.]

So Mr. Floyd decided that the Government was not responsible for that $3,200 worth of rubbish which the Indians destroyed, but was responsible for the property destroyed by the troops—which property consisted of (I quote from the printed United States Senate document):

	Dollars
Corn at Bassett's Creek,	3,000
Cattle,	5,000
Stock hogs,	1,050
Drove hogs,	1,204
Wheat,	350
Hides,	4,000
Corn on the Alabama River,	3,500
Total,	18,104

That sum, in his report, Mr. Floyd calls the "full value of the property destroyed by the troops."

He allows that sum to the starving Fishers, TOGETHER WITH INTEREST FROM 1813. From this new sum total the amounts already paid to the Fishers were deducted, and then the cheerful remainder (a fraction under forty thousand dollars) was handed to them and again they retired to Florida in a condition of temporary tranquillity. Their ancestor's farm had now yielded them altogether nearly sixty-seven thousand dollars in cash.

6. Does the reader suppose that that was the end of it? Does he suppose those diffident Fishers were satisfied? Let the evidence show. The Fishers were quiet just two years. Then they came swarming up out of the fertile swamps of Florida with their same old documents, and besieged Congress once more. Congress capitulated on the 1st of June, 1860, and instructed Mr. Floyd to overhaul those papers again, and pay that bill. A Treasury clerk was ordered to go through those papers and report to Mr. Floyd what amount was still due the emaciated Fishers.

This clerk (I can produce him whenever he is wanted) discovered what was apparently a glaring and recent forgery in the papers; whereby a witness's testimony as to the price of corn in Florida in 1813 was made to name double the amount which that witness had originally specified as the price! The clerk not only called his superior's attention to this thing, but in making up his brief of the case called particular attention to it in writing. That part of the brief never got before Congress, nor has Congress ever yet had a hint of forgery existing among the Fisher papers. Nevertheless, on the basis of the double prices (and totally ignoring the clerk's assertion that the figures were manifestly and unquestionably a recent forgery), Mr. Floyd remarks in his new report that "the testimony, particularly in regard to the corn crops, DEMANDS A MUCH HIGHER ALLOWANCE than any heretofore made by the Auditor or myself." So he estimates the crop at sixty bushels to the acre (double what Florida acres produce), and then virtuously allows pay for only half the crop, but allows two dollars and a half a bushel for that half, when there are rusty old books and documents in the Congressional library to show just what the Fisher testimony showed before the forgery—viz., that in the fall of 1813 corn was only worth from $1.25 to $1.50 a bushel. Having accomplished this, what does Mr. Floyd do next? Mr. Floyd ("with an earnest desire to execute truly the legislative will," as he piously remarks) goes to work and makes out an entirely new bill of Fisher damages, and in this new bill he placidly ignores the Indians altogether—puts no particle of the destruction of the Fisher property upon them, but, even repenting him of charging them with burning the cabins and drinking the whisky and breaking the crockery, lays the entire damage at the door of the imbecile United States troops down to the very last item! And not only that, but uses the forgery to double the loss of corn at "Bassett's Creek," and uses it again to absolutely treble the loss of corn on the "Alabama River." This new and ably conceived and executed bill of Mr. Floyd's figures up as follows (I copy again from the printed United States Senate document):

**THE UNITED STATES IN ACCOUNT WITH THE
LEGAL REPRESENTATIVES OF GEORGE FISHER, DECEASED.**

1813—	DOL
To 550 head of cattle, at 10 dollars,	5,500
To 86 head of drove hogs,	1,204
To 350 head of stock hogs,	1,750
To 100 ACRES OF CORN ON BASSETT'S CREEK,	6,000
To 8 barrels of whisky,	350
To 2 barrels of brandy,	280
To 1 barrel of rum,	70
To dry-goods and merchandise in store,	1,100
To 35 acres of wheat,	350
To 2,000 hides,	4,000
To furs and hats in store,	600
To crockery ware in store,	100
To smith's and carpenter's tools,	250
To houses burned and destroyed,	600
To 4 dozen bottles of wine,	48
1814—	
To 120 acres of corn on Alabama River,	9,500
To crops of peas, fodder, etc	3,250
Total,	34,952

To interest on $22,202, from July 1813

to November 1860, 47 years and 4 months,	63,053.68
To interest on $12,750, from September 1814 to November 1860, 46 years and 2 months,	35,317.50
Total,	133,323.18

He puts everything in this time. He does not even allow that the Indians destroyed the crockery or drank the four dozen bottles of (currant) wine. When it came to supernatural comprehensiveness in "gobbling," John B. Floyd was without his equal, in his own or any other generation. Subtracting from the above total the $67,000 already paid to George Fisher's implacable heirs, Mr. Floyd announced that the government was still indebted to them in the sum of sixty-six thousand five hundred and nineteen dollars and eighty-five cents, "which," Mr. Floyd complacently remarks, "will be paid, accordingly, to the administrator of the estate of George Fisher, deceased, or to his attorney in fact."

But, sadly enough for the destitute orphans, a new President came in just at this time, Buchanan and Floyd went out, and they never got their money. The first thing Congress did in 1861 was to rescind the resolution of June 1, 1860, under which Mr. Floyd had been ciphering. Then Floyd (and doubtless the heirs of George Fisher likewise) had to give up financial business for a while, and go into the Confederate army and serve their country.

Were the heirs of George Fisher killed? No. They are back now at this very time (July, 1870), beseeching Congress through that blushing and diffident creature, Garrett Davis, to commence making payments again on their interminable and insatiable bill of damages for corn and whisky destroyed by a gang of irresponsible Indians, so long ago that even government red-tape has failed to keep consistent and intelligent track of it.

Now the above are facts. They are history. Any one who doubts it can send to the Senate Document Department of the Capitol for H. R. Ex. Doc. No. 21, 36th Congress, 2d Session; and for S. Ex. Doc. No. 106, 41st Congress, 2d Session, and satisfy himself. The whole case is set forth in the first volume of the Court of Claims Reports.

It is my belief that as long as the continent of America holds together, the heirs of George Fisher, deceased, will still make pilgrimages to Washington from the swamps of Florida, to plead for just a little more cash on their bill of damages (even when they received the last of that sixty-seven thousand dollars, they said it was only one fourth what the government owed them on that fruitful corn-field), and as long as they choose to come they will find Garrett Davises to drag their vampire schemes before Congress. This is not the only hereditary fraud (if fraud it is—which I have before repeatedly remarked is not proven) that is being quietly handed down from generation to generation of fathers and sons, through the persecuted Treasury of the United States.

DISGRACEFUL PERSECUTION OF A BOY

In San Francisco, the other day, "A well-dressed boy, on his way to Sunday-school, was arrested and thrown into the city prison for stoning Chinamen."

What a commentary is this upon human justice! What sad prominence it gives to our human disposition to tyrannize over the weak! San Francisco has little right to take credit to herself for her treatment of this poor boy. What had the child's education been? How should he suppose it was wrong to stone a Chinaman? Before we side against him, along with outraged San Francisco, let us give him a chance—let us hear the testimony for the defense.

He was a "well-dressed" boy, and a Sunday-school scholar, and therefore the chances are that his parents were intelligent, well-to-do people, with just enough natural villainy in their composition to make them yearn after the daily papers, and enjoy them; and so this boy had opportunities to learn all through the week how to do right, as well as on Sunday.

It was in this way that he found out that the great commonwealth of California imposes an unlawful mining-tax upon John the foreigner, and allows Patrick the foreigner to dig gold for nothing—probably because the degraded Mongol is at no expense for whisky, and the refined Celt cannot exist without it.

It was in this way that he found out that a respectable number of the tax-gatherers—it would be unkind to say all of them—collect the tax twice, instead of once; and that, inasmuch as they do it solely to discourage Chinese immigration into the mines, it is a thing that is much applauded, and likewise regarded as being singularly facetious.

It was in this way that he found out that when a white man robs a sluice-box (by the term white man is meant Spaniards, Mexicans, Portuguese, Irish, Hondurans, Peruvians, Chileans, etc., etc.), they make him leave the camp; and when a Chinaman does that thing, they hang him.

It was in this way that he found out that in many districts of the vast Pacific coast, so strong is the wild, free love of justice in the hearts of the people, that whenever any secret and mysterious crime is committed, they say, "Let justice be done, though the heavens fall," and go straightway and swing a Chinaman.

It was in this way that he found out that by studying one half of each day's "local items," it would appear that the police of San Francisco were either asleep or dead, and by studying the other half it would seem that the reporters were gone mad with admiration of the energy, the virtue, the high effectiveness, and the dare-devil intrepidity of that very police-making exultant mention of how "the Argus-eyed officer So-and-so" captured a wretched knave of a Chinaman who was stealing chickens, and brought him gloriously to the city prison; and how "the gallant officer Such-and-such-a-one" quietly kept an eye on the movements of an "unsuspecting, almond-eyed son of Confucius" (your reporter is nothing if not facetious), following him around with that far-off look of vacancy and unconsciousness always so finely affected by that inscrutable being, the forty-dollar policeman, during a waking interval, and captured him at last in the very act of placing his hands in a suspicious manner upon a paper of tacks, left by the owner in an exposed situation; and how one officer performed this prodigious thing, and another officer that, and another the other—and pretty much every one of these performances having for a dazzling central incident a Chinaman guilty of a shilling's worth of crime, an unfortunate, whose misdemeanor must be hurrahed into something enormous in order to keep the public from noticing how many really important rascals went uncaptured in the mean time, and how overrated those glorified policemen actually are.

It was in this way that the boy found out that the legislature, being aware that the Constitution has made America an asylum for the poor and the oppressed of all nations, and that, therefore, the poor and oppressed who fly to our shelter must not be charged a disabling admission fee, made a law that every Chinaman, upon landing, must be vaccinated upon the wharf, and pay to the state's appointed officer ten dollars for the service, when there are plenty of doctors in San Francisco who would be glad enough to do it for him for fifty cents.

It was in this way that the boy found out that a Chinaman had no rights that any man was bound to respect; that he had no sorrows that any man was bound to pity; that neither his life nor his liberty was worth the purchase of a penny when a white man needed a scapegoat; that nobody loved Chinamen, nobody befriended them, nobody spared them suffering when it was convenient to inflict it; everybody, individuals, communities, the majesty of the state itself, joined in hating, abusing, and persecuting these humble strangers.

And, therefore, what could have been more natural than for this sunny-hearted-boy, tripping along to Sunday-school, with his mind teeming with freshly learned incentives to high and virtuous action, to say to himself:

"Ah, there goes a Chinaman! God will not love me if I do not stone him."

And for this he was arrested and put in the city jail.

Everything conspired to teach him that it was a high and holy thing to stone a Chinaman, and yet he no sooner attempts to do his duty than he is punished for it—he, poor chap, who has been aware all his life that one of the principal recreations of the police, out toward the Gold Refinery, is to look on with tranquil enjoyment while the butchers of Brannan Street set their dogs on unoffending Chinamen, and make them flee for their lives.

—[I have many such memories in my mind, but am thinking just at present of one particular one, where the Brannan Street butchers set their dogs on a Chinaman who was quietly passing with a basket of clothes on his head; and while the dogs mutilated his flesh, a butcher increased the hilarity of the occasion by knocking some of the Chinaman's teeth down his throat with half a brick. This incident sticks in my memory with a more malevolent tenacity, perhaps, on account of the fact that I was in the employ of a San Francisco journal at the time, and was not allowed to publish it because it might offend some of the peculiar element that subscribed for the paper.]

Keeping in mind the tuition in the humanities which the entire "Pacific coast" gives its youth, there is a very sublimity of incongruity in the virtuous flourish with which the good city fathers of San Francisco proclaim (as they have lately done) that "The police are positively ordered to arrest all boys, of every description and wherever found, who engage in assaulting Chinamen."

Still, let us be truly glad they have made the order, notwithstanding its inconsistency; and let us rest perfectly confident the police are glad, too. Because there is no personal peril in arresting boys, provided they be of the small kind, and the reporters will have to laud their performances just as loyally as ever, or go without items.

The new form for local items in San Francisco will now be: "The ever-vigilant and efficient officer So-and-so succeeded, yesterday afternoon, in arresting Master Tommy Jones, after a determined resistance," etc., etc., followed by the customary statistics and final hurrah, with its unconscious sarcasm: "We are happy in being able to state that this is the forty-seventh boy arrested by this gallant officer since the new ordinance went into effect. The most extraordinary activity prevails in the police department. Nothing like it has been seen since we can remember."

THE JUDGE'S "SPIRITED WOMAN"

"I was sitting here," said the judge, "in this old pulpit, holding court, and we were trying a big, wicked-looking Spanish desperado for killing the husband of a bright, pretty Mexican woman. It was a lazy summer day, and an awfully long one, and the witnesses were tedious. None of us took any interest in the trial except that nervous, uneasy devil of a Mexican woman—because you know how they love and how they hate, and this one had loved her husband with all her might, and now she had boiled it all down into hate, and stood here spitting it at that Spaniard with her eyes; and I tell you she would stir me up, too, with a little of her summer lightning, occasionally. Well, I had my coat off and my heels up, lolling and sweating, and smoking one of those cabbage cigars the San Francisco people used to think were good enough for us in those times; and the lawyers they all had their coats off, and were smoking and whittling, and the witnesses the same, and so was the prisoner. Well, the fact is, there warn't any interest in a murder trial then, because the fellow was always brought in not guilty,' the jury expecting him to do as much for them some time; and, although the evidence was straight and square against this Spaniard, we knew we could not convict him without seeming to be rather high-handed and sort of reflecting on every gentleman in the community; for there warn't any carriages and liveries then, and so the only 'style' there was, was to keep your private graveyard. But that woman seemed to have her heart set on hanging that Spaniard; and you'd ought to have seen how she would glare on him a minute, and then look up at me in her pleading way, and then turn and for the next five minutes search the jury's faces, and by and by drop her face in her hands for just a little while as if she was most ready to give up; but out she'd come again directly, and be as live and anxious as ever. But when the jury announced the verdict—Not Guilty—and I told the prisoner he was acquitted and free to go, that woman rose up till she appeared to be as tall and grand as a seventy-four-gun ship, and says she:

"'Judge, do I understand you to say that this man is not guilty that murdered my husband without any cause before my own eyes and my little children's, and that all has been done to him that ever justice and the law can do?'

"'The same,' says I.

"And then what do you reckon she did? Why, she turned on that smirking Spanish fool like a wildcat, and out with a 'navy' and shot him dead in open court!"

"That was spirited, I am willing to admit."

"Wasn't it, though?" said the judge admiringly.

"I wouldn't have missed it for anything. I adjourned court right on the spot, and we put on our coats and went out and took up a collection for her and her cubs, and sent them over the mountains to their friends. Ah, she was a spirited wench!"

INFORMATION WANTED

"WASHINGTON, December 10, 1867.

"Could you give me any information respecting such islands, if any, as the government is going to purchase?"

It is an uncle of mine that wants to know. He is an industrious man and well disposed, and wants to make a living in an honest, humble way, but more especially he wants to be quiet. He wishes to settle down, and be quiet and unostentatious. He has been to the new island St. Thomas, but he says he thinks things are unsettled there. He went there early with an attache of the State Department, who was sent down with money to pay for the island. My uncle had his money in the same box, and so when they went ashore, getting a receipt, the sailors broke open the box and took all the money, not making any distinction between government money, which was legitimate money to be stolen, and my uncle's, which was his own private property, and should have been respected. But he came home and got some more and went back. And then he took the fever. There are seven kinds of fever down there, you know; and, as his blood was out of order by reason of loss of sleep and general wear and tear of mind, he failed to cure the first fever, and then somehow he got the other six. He is not a kind of man that enjoys fevers, though he is well meaning and always does what he thinks is right, and so he was a good deal annoyed when it appeared he was going to die.

But he worried through, and got well and started a farm. He fenced it in, and the next day that great storm came on and washed the most of it over to Gibraltar, or around there somewhere. He only said, in his patient way, that it was gone, and he wouldn't bother about trying to find out where it went to, though it was his opinion it went to Gibraltar.

Then he invested in a mountain, and started a farm up there, so as to be out of the way when the sea came ashore again. It was a good mountain, and a good farm, but it wasn't any use; an earthquake came the next night and shook it all down. It was all fragments, you know, and so mixed up with another man's property that he could not tell which were his fragments without going to law; and he would not do that, because his main object in going to St. Thomas was to be quiet. All that he wanted was to settle down and be quiet.

He thought it all over, and finally he concluded to try the low ground again, especially as he wanted to start a brickyard this time. He bought a flat, and put out a hundred thousand bricks to dry preparatory to baking them. But luck appeared to be against him. A volcano shoved itself through there that night, and elevated his brickyard about two thousand feet in the air. It irritated him a good deal. He has been up there, and he says the bricks are all baked right enough, but he can't get them down. At first, he thought maybe the government would get the bricks down for him, because since government bought the island, it ought to protect the property where a man has invested in good faith; but all he wants is quiet, and so he is not going to apply for the subsidy he was thinking about.

He went back there last week in a couple of ships of war, to prospect around the coast for a safe place for a farm where he could be quiet; but a great "tidal wave" came, and hoisted both of the ships out into one of the interior counties, and he came near losing his life. So he has given up prospecting in a ship, and is discouraged.

Well, now he don't know what to do. He has tried Alaska; but the bears kept after him so much, and kept him so much on the jump, as it were, that he had to leave the country. He could not be quiet there with those bears prancing after him all the time. That is how he came to go to the new island we have bought—St. Thomas. But he is getting to think St. Thomas is not quiet enough for a man of his turn of mind, and that is why he wishes me to find out if government is likely to buy some more islands shortly. He has heard that government is thinking about buying Porto Rico. If that is true, he wishes to try Porto Rico, if it is a quiet place. How is Porto Rico for his style of man? Do you think the government will buy it?

SOME LEARNED FABLES, FOR GOOD OLD BOYS AND GIRLS IN THREE PARTS

PART FIRST
HOW THE ANIMALS OF THE WOOD SENT OUT A SCIENTIFIC EXPEDITION

Once the creatures of the forest held a great convention and appointed a commission consisting of the most illustrious scientists among them to go forth, clear beyond the forest and out into the unknown and unexplored world, to verify the truth of the matters already taught in their schools and colleges and also to make discoveries. It was the most imposing enterprise of the kind the nation had ever embarked in. True, the government had once sent Dr. Bull Frog, with a picked crew, to hunt for a northwesterly passage through the swamp to the right-hand corner of the wood, and had since sent out many expeditions to hunt for Dr. Bull Frog; but they never could find him, and so government finally gave him up and ennobled his mother to show its gratitude for the services her son had rendered to science. And once government sent Sir Grass Hopper to hunt for the sources of the rill that emptied into the swamp; and afterward sent out many expeditions to hunt for Sir Grass, and at last they were successful—they found his body, but if he had discovered the sources meantime, he did not let on. So government acted handsomely by deceased, and many envied his funeral.

But these expeditions were trifles compared with the present one; for this one comprised among its servants the very greatest among the learned; and besides it was to go to the utterly unvisited regions believed to lie beyond the mighty forest—as we have remarked before. How the members were banqueted, and glorified, and talked about! Everywhere that one of them showed himself, straightway there was a crowd to gape and stare at him.

Finally they set off, and it was a sight to see the long procession of dry-land Tortoises heavily laden with savants, scientific instruments, Glow-Worms and Fire-Flies for signal service, provisions, Ants and Tumble-Bugs to fetch and carry and delve, Spiders to carry the surveying chain and do other engineering duty, and so forth and so on; and after the Tortoises came another long train of ironclads—stately and spacious Mud Turtles for marine transportation service; and from every Tortoise and every Turtle flaunted a flaming gladiolus or other splendid banner; at the head of the column a great band of Bumble-Bees, Mosquitoes, Katy-Dids, and Crickets discoursed martial music; and the entire train was under the escort and protection of twelve picked regiments of the Army Worm.

At the end of three weeks the expedition emerged from the forest and looked upon the great Unknown World. Their eyes were greeted with an impressive spectacle. A vast level plain stretched before them, watered by a sinuous stream; and beyond there towered up against the sky a long and lofty barrier of some kind, they did not know what. The Tumble-Bug said he believed it was simply land tilted up on its edge, because he knew he could see trees on it. But Professor Snail and the others said:

"You are hired to dig, sir—that is all. We need your muscle, not your brains. When we want your opinion on scientific matters, we will hasten to let you know. Your coolness is intolerable, too—loafing about here meddling with august matters of learning, when the other laborers are pitching camp. Go along and help handle the baggage."

The Tumble-Bug turned on his heel uncrushed, unabashed, observing to himself, "If it isn't land tilted up, let me die the death of the unrighteous."

Professor Bull Frog (nephew of the late explorer) said he believed the ridge was the wall that inclosed the earth. He continued:

"Our fathers have left us much learning, but they had not traveled far, and so we may count this a noble new discovery. We are safe for renown now, even though our labors began and ended with this single achievement. I wonder what this wall is built of? Can it be fungus? Fungus is an honorable good thing to build a wall of."

Professor Snail adjusted his field-glass and examined the rampart critically. Finally he said:

"'The fact that it is not diaphanous convinces me that it is a dense vapor formed by the calorification of ascending moisture dephlogisticated by refraction. A few endiometrical experiments would confirm this, but it is not necessary. The thing is obvious."

So he shut up his glass and went into his shell to make a note of the discovery of the world's end, and the nature of it.

"Profound mind!" said Professor Angle-Worm to Professor Field-Mouse; "profound mind! nothing can long remain a mystery to that august brain."

Night drew on apace, the sentinel crickets were posted, the Glow-Worm and Fire-Fly lamps were lighted, and the camp sank to silence and sleep. After breakfast in the morning, the expedition moved on. About noon a great avenue was reached, which had in it two endless parallel bars of some kind of hard black substance, raised the height of the tallest Bull Frog above the general level. The scientists climbed up on these and examined and tested them in various ways. They walked along them for a great distance, but found no end and no break in them. They could arrive at no decision. There was nothing in the records of science that mentioned anything of this kind. But at last the bald and venerable geographer, Professor Mud Turtle, a person who, born poor, and of a drudging low family, had, by his own native force raised himself to the headship of the geographers of his generation, said:

"'My friends, we have indeed made a discovery here. We have found in a palpable, compact, and imperishable state what the wisest of our fathers always regarded as a mere thing of the imagination. Humble yourselves, my friends, for we stand in a majestic presence. These are parallels of latitude!"

Every heart and every head was bowed, so awful, so sublime was the magnitude of the discovery. Many shed tears.

The camp was pitched and the rest of the day given up to writing voluminous accounts of the marvel, and correcting astronomical tables to fit it. Toward midnight a demoniacal shriek was heard, then a clattering and rumbling noise, and the next instant a vast terrific eye shot by, with a long tail attached, and disappeared in the gloom, still uttering triumphant shrieks.

The poor camp laborers were stricken to the heart with fright, and stampeded for the high grass in a body. But not the scientists. They had no superstitions. They calmly proceeded to exchange theories. The ancient geographer's opinion was asked. He went into his shell and deliberated long and profoundly. When he came out at last, they all knew by his worshiping countenance that he brought light. Said he:

"Give thanks for this stupendous thing which we have been permitted to witness. It is the Vernal Equinox!"

There were shoutings and great rejoicings.

"But," said the Angle-Worm, uncoiling after reflection, "this is dead summer-time."

"Very well," said the Turtle, "we are far from our region; the season differs with the difference of time between the two points."

"Ah, true. True enough. But it is night. How should the sun pass in the night?"

"In these distant regions he doubtless passes always in the night at this hour."

"Yes, doubtless that is true. But it being night, how is it that we could see him?"

"It is a great mystery. I grant that. But I am persuaded that the humidity of the atmosphere in these remote regions is such that particles of daylight adhere to the disk and it was by aid of these that we were enabled to see the sun in the dark."

This was deemed satisfactory, and due entry was made of the decision.

But about this moment those dreadful shriekings were heard again; again the rumbling and thundering came speeding up out of the night; and once more a flaming great eye flashed by and lost itself in gloom and distance.

The camp laborers gave themselves up for lost. The savants were sorely perplexed. Here was a marvel hard to account for. They thought and they talked, they talked and they thought. Finally the learned and aged Lord Grand-Daddy-Longlegs, who had been sitting in deep study, with his slender limbs crossed and his stemmy arms folded, said:

"Deliver your opinions, brethren, and then I will tell my thought—for I think I have solved this problem."

"So be it, good your lordship," piped the weak treble of the wrinkled and withered Professor Woodlouse, "for we shall hear from your lordship's lips naught but wisdom." [Here the speaker threw in a mess of trite, threadbare, exasperating quotations from the ancient poets and philosophers, delivering them with unction in the sounding grandeurs of the original tongues, they being from the Mastodon, the Dodo, and other dead languages.] "Perhaps I ought not to presume to meddle with matters pertaining to astronomy at all, in such a presence as this, I who have made it the business of my life to delve only among the riches of the extinct languages and unearth the opulence of their ancient lore; but still, as unacquainted as I am with the noble science of astronomy, I beg with deference and humility to suggest that inasmuch as the last of these wonderful apparitions proceeded in exactly the opposite direction from that pursued by the first, which you decide to be the Vernal Equinox, and greatly resembled it in all particulars, is it not possible, nay certain, that this last is the Autumnal Equi—"

"O-o-o!" "O-o-o! go to bed! go to bed!" with annoyed derision from everybody. So the poor old Woodlouse retreated out of sight, consumed with shame.

Further discussion followed, and then the united voice of the commission begged Lord Longlegs to speak. He said:

"Fellow-scientists, it is my belief that we have witnessed a thing which has occurred in perfection but once before in the knowledge of created beings. It is a phenomenon of inconceivable importance and interest, view it as one may, but its interest to us is vastly heightened by an added knowledge of its nature which no scholar has heretofore possessed or even suspected. This great marvel which we have just witnessed, fellow-savants (it almost takes my breath away), is nothing less than the transit of Venus!"

Every scholar sprang to his feet pale with astonishment. Then ensued tears, handshakings, frenzied embraces, and the most extravagant jubilations of every sort.

But by and by, as emotion began to retire within bounds, and reflection to return to the front, the accomplished Chief Inspector Lizard observed:

"But how is this? Venus should traverse the sun's surface, not the earth's."

The arrow went home. It carried sorrow to the breast of every apostle of learning there, for none could deny that this was a formidable criticism. But tranquilly the venerable Duke crossed his limbs behind his ears and said:

"My friend has touched the marrow of our mighty discovery. Yes—all that have lived before us thought a transit of Venus consisted of a flight across the sun's face; they thought it, they maintained it, they honestly believed it, simple hearts, and were justified in it by the limitations of their knowledge; but to us has been granted the inestimable boon of proving that the transit occurs across the earth's face, for we have SEEN it!"

The assembled wisdom sat in speechless adoration of this imperial intellect. All doubts had instantly departed, like night before the lightning.

The Tumble-Bug had just intruded, unnoticed. He now came reeling forward among the scholars, familiarly slapping first one and then another on the shoulder, saying "Nice ('ic) nice old boy!" and smiling a smile of elaborate content. Arrived at a good position for speaking, he put his left arm akimbo with his knuckles planted in his hip just under the edge of his cut-away coat, bent his right leg, placing his toe on the ground and resting his heel with easy grace against his left shin, puffed out his aldermanic stomach, opened his lips, leaned his right elbow on Inspector Lizard's shoulder, and—

But the shoulder was indignantly withdrawn and the hard-handed son of toil went to earth. He floundered a bit, but came up smiling, arranged his attitude with the same careful detail as before, only choosing Professor Dogtick's shoulder for a support, opened his lips and—

Went to earth again. He presently scrambled up once more, still smiling, made a loose effort to brush the dust off his coat and legs, but a smart pass of his hand missed entirely, and the force of the unchecked impulse slewed him suddenly around, twisted his legs together, and projected him, limber and sprawling, into the lap of the Lord Longlegs. Two or three scholars sprang forward, flung the low creature head over heels into a corner, and reinstated the patrician, smoothing his ruffled dignity with many soothing and regretful speeches. Professor Bull Frog roared out:

"No more of this, sirrah Tumble-Bug! Say your say and then get you about your business with speed! Quick—what is your errand? Come move off a trifle; you smell like a stable; what have you been at?"

"Please ('ic!) please your worship I chanced to light upon a find. But no m(e-uck!) matter 'bout that. There's b('ic !) been another find which—beg pardon, your honors, what was that th('ic!) thing that ripped by here first?"

"It was the Vernal Equinox."

"Inf('ic !)fernal equinox. 'At's all right. D('ic !) Dunno him. What's other one?"

"The transit of Venus.

"G('ic !) Got me again. No matter. Las' one dropped something."

"Ah, indeed! Good luck! Good news! Quick what is it?"

"M('ic!) Mosey out 'n' see. It'll pay."

No more votes were taken for four-and-twenty hours. Then the following entry was made:

"The commission went in a body to view the find. It was found to consist of a hard, smooth, huge object with a rounded summit surmounted by a short upright projection resembling a section of a cabbage stalk divided transversely. This projection was not solid, but was a hollow cylinder plugged with a soft woody substance unknown to our region—that is, it had been so plugged, but unfortunately this obstruction had been heedlessly removed by Norway Rat, Chief of the Sappers and Miners, before our arrival. The vast object before us, so mysteriously conveyed from the glittering domains of space, was found to be hollow and nearly filled with a pungent liquid of a brownish hue, like rainwater that has stood for some time. And such a spectacle as met our view!

Norway Rat was perched upon the summit engaged in thrusting his tail into the cylindrical projection, drawing it out dripping, permitting the struggling multitude of laborers to suck the end of it, then straightway reinserting it and delivering the fluid to the mob as before. Evidently this liquor had strangely potent qualities; for all that partook of it were immediately exalted with great and pleasurable emotions, and went staggering about singing ribald songs, embracing, fighting, dancing, discharging irruptions of profanity, and defying all authority. Around us struggled a massed and uncontrolled mob—uncontrolled and likewise uncontrollable, for the whole army, down to the very sentinels, were mad like the rest, by reason of the drink. We were seized upon by these reckless creatures, and within the hour we, even we, were undistinguishable from the rest—the demoralization was complete and universal. In time the camp wore itself out with its orgies and sank into a stolid and pitiable stupor, in whose mysterious bonds rank was forgotten and strange bedfellows made, our eyes, at the resurrection, being blasted and our souls petrified with the incredible spectacle of that intolerable stinking scavenger, the Tumble-Bug, and the illustrious patrician my Lord Grand Daddy, Duke of Longlegs, lying soundly steeped in sleep, and clasped lovingly in each other's arms, the like whereof hath not been seen in all the ages that tradition compasseth, and doubtless none shall ever in this world find faith to master the belief of it save only we that have beheld the damnable and unholy vision. Thus inscrutable be the ways of God, whose will be done!

"This day, by order, did the engineer-in-chief, Herr Spider, rig the necessary tackle for the overturning of the vast reservoir, and so its calamitous contents were discharged in a torrent upon the thirsty earth, which drank it up, and now there is no more danger, we reserving but a few drops for experiment and scrutiny, and to exhibit to the king and subsequently preserve among the wonders of the museum. What this liquid is has been determined. It is without question that fierce and most destructive fluid called lightning. It was wrested, in its container, from its storehouse in the clouds, by the resistless might of the flying planet, and hurled at our feet as she sped by. An interesting discovery here results. Which is, that lightning, kept to itself, is quiescent; it is the assaulting contact of the thunderbolt that releases it from captivity, ignites its awful fires, and so produces an instantaneous combustion and explosion which spread disaster and desolation far and wide in the earth."

After another day devoted to rest and recovery, the expedition proceeded upon its way. Some days later it went into camp in a pleasant part of the plain, and the savants sallied forth to see what they might find. Their reward was at hand. Professor Bull Frog discovered a strange tree, and called his comrades. They inspected it with profound interest. It was very tall and straight, and wholly devoid of bark, limbs, or foliage. By triangulation Lord Longlegs determined its altitude; Herr Spider measured its circumference at the base and computed the circumference at its top by a mathematical demonstration based upon the warrant furnished by the uniform degree of its taper upward. It was considered a very extraordinary find; and since it was a tree of a hitherto unknown species, Professor Woodlouse gave it a name of a learned sound, being none other than that of Professor Bull Frog translated into the ancient Mastodon language, for it had always been the custom with discoverers to perpetuate their names and honor themselves by this sort of connection with their discoveries.

Now Professor Field-Mouse having placed his sensitive ear to the tree, detected a rich, harmonious sound issuing from it. This surprising thing was tested and enjoyed by each scholar in turn, and great was the gladness and astonishment of all. Professor Woodlouse was requested to add to and extend the tree's name so as to make it suggest the musical quality it possessed—which he did, furnishing the addition Anthem Singer, done into the Mastodon tongue.

By this time Professor Snail was making some telescopic inspections. He discovered a great number of these trees, extending in a single rank, with wide intervals between, as far as his instrument would carry, both southward and northward. He also presently discovered that all these trees were bound together, near their tops, by fourteen great ropes, one above another, which ropes were continuous, from tree to tree, as far as his vision could reach. This was surprising. Chief Engineer Spider ran aloft and soon reported that these ropes were simply a web hung there by some colossal member of his own species, for he could see its prey dangling here and there from the strands, in the shape of mighty shreds and rags that had a woven look about their texture and were no doubt the discarded skins of prodigious insects which had been caught and eaten. And then he ran along one of the ropes to make a closer inspection, but felt a smart sudden burn on the soles of his feet, accompanied by a paralyzing shock, wherefore he let go and swung himself to the earth by a thread of his own spinning, and advised all to hurry at once to camp, lest the monster should appear and get as much interested in the savants as they were in him and his works. So they departed with speed, making notes about the gigantic web as they went. And that evening the naturalist of the expedition built a beautiful model of the colossal spider, having no need to see it in order to do this, because he had picked up a fragment of its vertebra by the tree, and so knew exactly what the creature looked like and what its habits and its preferences were by this simple evidence alone. He built it with a tail, teeth, fourteen legs, and a snout, and said it ate grass, cattle, pebbles, and dirt with equal enthusiasm. This animal was regarded as a very precious addition to science. It was hoped a dead one might be found to stuff. Professor Woodlouse thought that he and his brother scholars, by lying hid and being quiet, might maybe catch a live one. He was advised to try it. Which was all the attention that was paid to his suggestion. The conference ended with the naming the monster after the naturalist, since he, after God, had created it.

"And improved it, mayhap," muttered the Tumble-Bug, who was intruding again, according to his idle custom and his unappeasable curiosity.

END OF PART FIRST

SOME LEARNED FABLES FOR GOOD OLD BOYS AND GIRLS
PART SECOND
HOW THE ANIMALS OF THE WOOD COMPLETED THEIR SCIENTIFIC LABORS

A week later the expedition camped in the midst of a collection of wonderful curiosities. These were a sort of vast caverns of stone that rose singly and in bunches out of the plain by the side of the river which they had first seen when they emerged from the forest. These caverns stood in long, straight rows on opposite sides of broad aisles that were bordered with single ranks of trees. The summit of each cavern sloped sharply both ways. Several horizontal rows of great square holes, obstructed by a thin, shiny, transparent substance, pierced the frontage of each cavern. Inside were caverns within caverns; and one might ascend and visit these minor compartments by means of curious winding ways consisting of continuous regular terraces raised one above another. There were many huge, shapeless objects in each compartment which were considered to have been living creatures at one time, though now the thin brown skin was shrunken and loose, and rattled when disturbed. Spiders were here in great number, and their cobwebs, stretched in all directions and wreathing the great skinny dead together, were a pleasant spectacle, since they inspired with life and wholesome cheer a scene which would otherwise have brought to the mind only a sense of forsakenness and desolation. Information was sought of these spiders, but in vain. They were of a different nationality from those with the expedition, and their language seemed but a musical, meaningless jargon. They were a timid, gentle race, but ignorant, and heathenish worshipers of unknown gods. The expedition detailed a great detachment of missionaries to teach them the true religion, and in a week's time a precious work had been wrought among those darkened creatures, not three families being by that time at peace with each other or having a settled belief in any system of religion whatever. This encouraged the expedition to establish a colony of missionaries there permanently, that the work of grace might go on.

But let us not outrun our narrative. After close examination of the fronts of the caverns, and much thinking and exchanging of theories, the scientists determined the nature of these singular formations. They said that each belonged mainly to the Old Red Sandstone period; that the cavern fronts rose in innumerable and wonderfully regular strata high in the air, each stratum about five frog-spans thick, and that in the present discovery lay an overpowering refutation of all received geology; for between every two layers of Old Red Sandstone reposed a thin layer of decomposed limestone; so instead of there having been but one Old Red Sandstone period there had certainly been not less than a hundred and seventy-five! And by the same token it was plain that there had also been a hundred and seventy-five floodings of the earth and depositings of limestone strata! The unavoidable deduction from which pair of facts was the overwhelming truth that the world, instead of being only two hundred thousand years old, was older by millions upon millions of years! And there was another curious thing: every stratum of Old Red Sandstone was pierced and divided at mathematically regular intervals by vertical strata of limestone. Up-shootings of igneous rock through fractures in water formations were common; but here was the first instance where water-formed rock had been so projected. It was a great and noble discovery, and its value to science was considered to be inestimable.

A critical examination of some of the lower strata demonstrated the presence of fossil ants and tumble-bugs (the latter accompanied by their peculiar goods), and with high gratification the fact was enrolled upon the scientific record; for this was proof that these vulgar laborers belonged to the first and lowest orders of created beings, though at the same time there was something repulsive in the reflection that the perfect and exquisite creature of the modern uppermost order owed its origin to such ignominious beings through the mysterious law of Development of Species.

The Tumble-Bug, overhearing this discussion, said he was willing that the parvenus of these new times should find what comfort they might in their wise-drawn theories, since as far as he was concerned he was content to be of the old first families and proud to point back to his place among the old original aristocracy of the land.

"Enjoy your mushroom dignity, stinking of the varnish of yesterday's veneering, since you like it," said he; "suffice it for the Tumble-Bugs that they come of a race that rolled their fragrant spheres down the solemn aisles of antiquity, and left their imperishable works embalmed in the Old Red Sandstone to proclaim it to the wasting centuries as they file along the highway of Time!"

"Oh, take a walk!" said the chief of the expedition, with derision.

The summer passed, and winter approached. In and about many of the caverns were what seemed to be inscriptions. Most of the scientists said they were inscriptions, a few said they were not. The chief philologist, Professor Woodlouse, maintained that they were writings, done in a character utterly unknown to scholars, and in a language equally unknown. He had early ordered his artists and draftsmen to make facsimiles of all that were discovered; and had set himself about finding the key to the hidden tongue. In this work he had followed the method which had always been used by decipherers previously. That is to say, he placed a number of copies of inscriptions before him and studied them both collectively and in detail. To begin with, he placed the following copies together:

THE AMERICAN HOTEL.	MEALS AT ALL HOURS.
THE SHADES.	NO SMOKING.
BOATS FOR HIRE CHEAP	UNION PRAYER MEETING, 4 P.M.
BILLIARDS.	THE WATERSIDE JOURNAL.

THE A1 BARBER SHOP.	TELEGRAPH OFFICE.
KEEP OFF THE GRASS.	TRY BRANDRETH'S PILLS.
COTTAGES FOR RENT DURING	THE WATERING SEASON.
FOR SALE CHEAP.	FOR SALE CHEAP.
FOR SALE CHEAP.	FOR SALE CHEAP.

At first it seemed to the professor that this was a sign-language, and that each word was represented by a distinct sign; further examination convinced him that it was a written language, and that every letter of its alphabet was represented by a character of its own; and finally he decided that it was a language which conveyed itself partly by letters, and partly by signs or hieroglyphics. This conclusion was forced upon him by the discovery of several specimens of the following nature:

He observed that certain inscriptions were met with in greater frequency than others. Such as "FOR SALE CHEAP"; "BILLIARDS"; "S. T.—1860—X"; "KENO"; "ALE ON DRAUGHT." Naturally, then, these must be religious maxims. But this idea was cast aside by and by, as the mystery of the strange alphabet began to clear itself. In time, the professor was enabled to translate several of the inscriptions with considerable plausibility, though not to the perfect satisfaction of all the scholars. Still, he made constant and encouraging progress.

Finally a cavern was discovered with these inscriptions upon it:

WATERSIDE MUSEUM.
Open at All Hours.
Admission 50 cents.
WONDERFUL COLLECTION OF
WAX-WORKS, ANCIENT FOSSILS,
ETC.

Professor Woodlouse affirmed that the word "Museum" was equivalent to the phrase "lumgath molo," or "Burial Place." Upon entering, the scientists were well astonished. But what they saw may be best conveyed in the language of their own official report:

"Erect, in a row, were a sort of rigid great figures which struck us instantly as belonging to the long extinct species of reptile called MAN, described in our ancient records. This was a peculiarly gratifying discovery, because of late times it has become fashionable to regard this creature as a myth and a superstition, a work of the inventive imaginations of our remote ancestors. But here, indeed, was Man perfectly preserved, in a fossil state. And this was his burial place, as already ascertained by the inscription. And now it began to be suspected that the caverns we had been inspecting had been his ancient haunts in that old time that he roamed the earth—for upon the breast of each of these tall fossils was an inscription in the character heretofore noticed. One read, 'CAPTAIN KIDD THE PIRATE'; another, 'QUEEN VICTORIA'; another, 'ABE LINCOLN'; another, 'GEORGE WASHINGTON,' etc.

"With feverish interest we called for our ancient scientific records to discover if perchance the description of Man there set down would tally with the fossils before us. Professor Woodlouse read it aloud in its quaint and musty phraseology, to wit:

"'In ye time of our fathers Man still walked ye earth, as by tradition we know. It was a creature of exceeding great size, being compassed about with a loose skin, sometimes of one color, sometimes of many, the which it was able to cast at will; which being done, the hind legs were discovered to be armed with short claws like to a mole's but broader, and ye forelegs with fingers of a curious slimness and a length much more prodigious than a frog's, armed also with broad talons for scratching in ye earth for its food. It had a sort of feathers upon its head such as hath a rat, but longer, and a beak suitable for seeking its food by ye smell thereof. When it was stirred with happiness, it leaked water from its eyes; and when it suffered or was sad, it manifested it with a horrible hellish cackling clamor that was exceeding dreadful to hear and made one long that it might rend itself and perish, and so end its troubles. Two Mans being together, they uttered noises at each other like this: "Haw-haw-haw—dam good, dam good," together with other sounds of more or less likeness to these, wherefore ye poets conceived that they talked, but poets be always ready to catch at any frantic folly, God he knows. Sometimes this creature goeth about with a long stick ye which it putteth to its face and bloweth fire and smoke through ye same with a sudden and most damnable bruit and noise that doth fright its prey to death, and so seizeth it in its talons and walketh away to its habitat, consumed with a most fierce and devilish joy.'

"Now was the description set forth by our ancestors wonderfully indorsed and confirmed by the fossils before us, as shall be seen. The specimen marked 'Captain Kidd' was examined in detail. Upon its head and part of its face was a sort of fur like that upon the tail of a horse. With great labor its loose skin was removed, whereupon its body was discovered to be of a polished white texture, thoroughly petrified. The straw it had eaten, so many ages gone by, was still in its body, undigested—and even in its legs.

"Surrounding these fossils were objects that would mean nothing to the ignorant, but to the eye of science they were a revelation. They laid bare the secrets of dead ages. These musty Memorials told us when Man lived, and what were his habits. For here, side by side with Man, were the evidences that he had lived in the earliest ages of creation, the companion of the other low orders of life that belonged to that forgotten time. Here was the fossil nautilus that sailed the primeval seas; here was the skeleton of the mastodon, the ichthyosaurus, the cave-bear, the prodigious elk. Here, also, were the charred bones of some of these extinct animals and of the young of Man's own species, split lengthwise, showing that to his taste the marrow was a toothsome luxury. It was plain that Man had robbed those bones of their contents, since no toothmark of any beast was upon them albeit the Tumble-Bug intruded the remark that 'no beast could mark a bone with its teeth, anyway.' Here were proofs that Man had vague, groveling notions of art; for this fact was conveyed by certain things marked with the untranslatable words, 'FLINT HATCHETS, KNIVES, ARROW-HEADS, AND BONE ORNAMENTS OF PRIMEVAL MAN.' Some of these seemed to be rude weapons chipped out of flint, and in a secret place was found some more in process of construction, with this untranslatable legend, on a thin, flimsy material, lying by:

"'Jones, if you don't want to be discharged from the Musseum, make the next primeaveal weppons more careful—you couldn't even fool one of these sleepy old syentific grannys from the Coledge with the last ones. And mind you the animles you carved on some of the Bone Ornaments is a blame sight too good for any primeaveal man that was ever fooled.— Varnum, Manager.'

"Back of the burial place was a mass of ashes, showing that Man always had a feast at a funeral—else why the ashes in such a place; and showing, also, that he believed in God and the immortality of the soul —else why these solemn ceremonies?

"To, sum up. We believe that Man had a written language. We know that he indeed existed at one time, and is not a myth; also, that he was the companion of the cave-bear, the mastodon, and other extinct species; that he cooked and ate them and likewise the young of his own kind; also, that he bore rude weapons, and knew something of art; that he imagined he had a soul, and pleased himself with the fancy that it was immortal. But let us not laugh; there may be creatures in existence to whom we and our vanities and profundities may seem as ludicrous."

END OF PART SECOND

SOME LEARNED FABLES FOR GOOD OLD BOYS AND GIRLS

PART THIRD

Near the margin of the great river the scientists presently found a huge, shapely stone, with this inscription:

"In 1847, in the spring, the river overflowed its banks and covered the whole township. The depth was from two to six feet. More than 900 head of cattle were lost, and many homes destroyed. The Mayor ordered this memorial to be erected to perpetuate the event. God spare us the repetition of it!"

With infinite trouble, Professor Woodlouse succeeded in making a translation of this inscription, which was sent home, and straightway an enormous excitement was created about it. It confirmed, in a remarkable way, certain treasured traditions of the ancients. The translation was slightly marred by one or two untranslatable words, but these did not impair the general clearness of the meaning. It is here presented:

"One thousand eight hundred and forty-seven years ago, the (fires?) descended and consumed the whole city. Only some nine hundred souls were saved, all others destroyed. The (king?) commanded this stone to be set up to . . . (untranslatable) . . . prevent the repetition of it."

This was the first successful and satisfactory translation that had been made of the mysterious character left behind him by extinct man, and it gave Professor Woodlouse such reputation that at once every seat of learning in his native land conferred a degree of the most illustrious grade upon him, and it was believed that if he had been a soldier and had turned his splendid talents to the extermination of a remote tribe of reptiles, the king would have ennobled him and made him rich. And this, too, was the origin of that school of scientists called Manologists, whose specialty is the deciphering of the ancient records of the extinct bird termed Man. [For it is now decided that Man was a bird and not a reptile.] But Professor Woodlouse began and remained chief of these, for it was granted that no translations were ever so free from error as his. Others made mistakes—he seemed incapable of it. Many a memorial of the lost race was afterward found, but none ever attained to the renown and veneration achieved by the "Mayoritish Stone" it being so called from the word "Mayor" in it, which, being translated "King," "Mayoritish Stone" was but another way of saying "King Stone."

Another time the expedition made a great "find." It was a vast round flattish mass, ten frog-spans in diameter and five or six high. Professor Snail put on his spectacles and examined it all around, and then climbed up and inspected the top. He said:

"The result of my perlustration and perscontation of this isoperimetrical protuberance is a belief at it is one of those rare and wonderful creations left by the Mound Builders. The fact that this one is lamellibranchiate in its formation, simply adds to its interest as being possibly of a different kind from any we read of in the records of science, but yet in no manner marring its authenticity. Let the megalophonous grasshopper sound a blast and summon hither the perfunctory and circumforaneous Tumble-Bug, to the end that excavations may be made and learning gather new treasures."

Not a Tumble-Bug could be found on duty, so the Mound was excavated by a working party of Ants. Nothing was discovered. This would have been a great disappointment, had not the venerable Longlegs explained the matter. He said:

"It is now plain to me that the mysterious and forgotten race of Mound Builders did not always erect these edifices as mausoleums, else in this case, as in all previous cases, their skeletons would be found here, along with the rude implements which the creatures used in life. Is not this manifest?"

"True! true!" from everybody.

"Then we have made a discovery of peculiar value here; a discovery which greatly extends our knowledge of this creature in place of diminishing it; a discovery which will add luster to the achievements of this expedition and win for us the commendations of scholars everywhere. For the absence of the customary relics here means nothing less than this: The Mound Builder, instead of being the ignorant, savage reptile we have been taught to consider him, was a creature of cultivation and high intelligence, capable of not only appreciating worthy achievements of the great and noble of his species, but of commemorating them! Fellow-scholars, this stately Mound is not a sepulcher, it is a monument!"

A profound impression was produced by this.

But it was interrupted by rude and derisive laughter—and the Tumble-Bug appeared.

"A monument!" quoth he. "A monument setup by a Mound Builder! Aye, so it is! So it is, indeed, to the shrewd keen eye of science; but to an ignorant poor devil who has never seen a college, it is not a Monument, strictly speaking, but is yet a most rich and noble property; and with your worship's good permission I will proceed to manufacture it into spheres of exceeding grace and—"

The Tumble-Bug was driven away with stripes, and the draftsmen of the expedition were set to making views of the Monument from different standpoints, while Professor Woodlouse, in a frenzy of scientific zeal, traveled all over it and all around it hoping to find an inscription. But if there had ever been one, it had decayed or been removed by some vandal as a relic.

The views having been completed, it was now considered safe to load the precious Monument itself upon the backs of four of the largest Tortoises and send it home to the king's museum, which was done; and when it arrived it was received with enormous éclat and escorted to its future abiding-place by thousands of enthusiastic citizens, King Bullfrog XVI. himself attending and condescending to sit enthroned upon it throughout the progress.

The growing rigor of the weather was now admonishing the scientists to close their labors for the present, so they made preparations to journey homeward. But even their last day among the Caverns bore fruit; for one of the scholars found in an out-of-the-way corner of the Museum or "Burial Place" a most strange and extraordinary thing. It was nothing less than a double Man-Bird lashed together breast to breast by a natural ligament, and labeled with the untranslatable words, "Siamese Twins." The official report concerning this thing closed thus:

"Wherefore it appears that there were in old times two distinct species of this majestic fowl, the one being single and the other double. Nature has a reason for all things. It is plain to the eye of science that the Double-Man originally inhabited a region where dangers abounded; hence he was paired together to the end that while one part slept the other might watch; and likewise that, danger being discovered, there might always be a double instead of a single power to oppose it. All honor to the mystery-dispelling eye of godlike Science!"

And near the Double Man-Bird was found what was plainly an ancient record of his, marked upon numberless sheets of a thin white substance and bound together. Almost the first glance that Professor Woodlouse threw into it revealed this following sentence, which he instantly translated and laid before the scientists, in a tremble, and it uplifted every soul there with exultation and astonishment:

"In truth it is believed by many that the lower animals reason and talk together."

When the great official report of the expedition appeared, the above sentence bore this comment:

"Then there are lower animals than Man! This remarkable passage can mean nothing else. Man himself is extinct, but they may still exist. What can they be? Where do they inhabit? One's enthusiasm bursts all bounds in the contemplation of the brilliant field of discovery and investigation here thrown open to science. We close our labors with the humble prayer that your Majesty will immediately appoint a commission and command it to rest not nor spare expense until the search for this hitherto unsuspected race of the creatures of God shall be crowned with success."

The expedition then journeyed homeward after its long absence and its faithful endeavors, and was received with a mighty ovation by the whole grateful country. There were vulgar, ignorant carpers, of course, as there always are and always will be; and naturally one of these was the obscene Tumble-Bug. He said that all he had learned by his travels was that science only needed a spoonful of supposition to build a mountain of demonstrated fact out of; and that for the future he meant to be content with the knowledge that nature had made free to all creatures and not go prying into the august secrets of the Deity.

MY LATE SENATORIAL SECRETARYSHIP

[written about 1867]

I am not a private secretary to a senator any more now. I held the berth two months in security and in great cheerfulness of spirit, but my bread began to return from over the waters then—that is to say, my works came back and revealed themselves. I judged it best to resign. The way of it was this. My employer sent for me one morning tolerably early, and, as soon as I had finished inserting some conundrums clandestinely into his last great speech upon finance, I entered the presence. There was something portentous in his appearance. His cravat was untied, his hair was in a state of disorder, and his countenance bore about it the signs of a suppressed storm. He held a package of letters in his tense grasp, and I knew that the dreaded Pacific mail was in. He said:

"I thought you were worthy of confidence."

I said, "Yes, sir."

He said, "I gave you a letter from certain of my constituents in the State of Nevada, asking the establishment of a post-office at Baldwin's Ranch, and told you to answer it, as ingeniously as you could, with arguments which should persuade them that there was no real necessity for an office at that place."

I felt easier. "Oh, if that is all, sir, I did do that."

"Yes, you did. I will read your answer for your own humiliation:

'WASHINGTON, Nov. 24

'Messrs. Smith, Jones, and others.

'GENTLEMEN: What the mischief do you suppose you want with a post-office at Baldwin's Ranch? It would not do you any good. If any letters came there, you couldn't read them, you know; and, besides, such letters as ought to pass through, with money in them, for other localities, would not be likely to get through, you must perceive at once; and that would make trouble for us all. No, don't bother about a post-office in your camp. I have your best interests at heart, and feel that it would only be an ornamental folly. What you want is a nice jail, you know—a nice, substantial jail and a free school. These will be a lasting benefit to you. These will make you really contented and happy. I will move in the matter at once.

'Very truly, etc.,
Mark Twain,

'For James W. N———, U. S. Senator.'

"That is the way you answered that letter. Those people say they will hang me, if I ever enter that district again; and I am perfectly satisfied they will, too."

"Well, sir, I did not know I was doing any harm. I only wanted to convince them."

"Ah. Well, you did convince them, I make no manner of doubt. Now, here is another specimen. I gave you a petition from certain gentlemen of Nevada, praying that I would get a bill through Congress incorporating the Methodist Episcopal Church of the State of Nevada. I told you to say, in reply, that the creation of such a law came more properly within the province of the state legislature; and to endeavor to show them that, in the present feebleness of the religious element in that new commonwealth, the expediency of incorporating the church was questionable. What did you write?

"'WASHINGTON, Nov. 24.

"'Rev. John Halifax and others.

"'GENTLEMEN: You will have to go to the state legislature about that speculation of yours—Congress don't know anything about religion. But don't you hurry to go there, either; because this thing you propose to do out in that new country isn't expedient—in fact, it is ridiculous. Your religious people there are too feeble, in intellect, in morality, in piety in everything, pretty much. You had better drop this—you can't make it work. You can't issue stock on an incorporation like that—or if you could, it would only keep you in trouble all the time. The other denominations would abuse it, and "bear" it, and "sell it short," and break it down. They would do with it just as they would with one of your silver-mines out there—they would try to make all the world believe it was "wildcat." You ought not to do anything that is calculated to bring a sacred thing into disrepute. You ought to be ashamed of yourselves—that is what I think about it. You close your petition with the words: "And we will ever pray." I think you had better—you need to do it.

"'Very truly, etc.,
"'MARK TWAIN,

"'For James W. N———, U. S. Senator.'

"That luminous epistle finishes me with the religious element among my constituents. But that my political murder might be made sure, some evil instinct prompted me to hand you this memorial from the grave company of elders composing the board of aldermen of the city of San Francisco, to try your hand upon—a memorial praying that the city's right to the water-lots upon the city front might be established by law of Congress. I told you this was a dangerous matter to move in. I told you to write a non-committal letter to the aldermen—an ambiguous letter—a letter that should avoid, as far as possible, all real consideration and discussion of the water-lot question. If there is any feeling left in you—any shame—surely this letter you wrote, in obedience to that order, ought to evoke it, when its words fall upon your ears:

'WASHINGTON, Nov. 27

'The Honorable Board of Aldermen, etc.

'GENTLEMEN: George Washington, the revered Father of his Country, is dead. His long and brilliant career is closed, alas! forever. He was greatly respected in this section of the country, and his untimely decease cast a gloom over the whole community. He died on the 14th day of December, 1799. He passed peacefully away from the scene of his honors and his great achievements, the most lamented hero and the best beloved that ever earth hath yielded unto Death. At such a time as this, you speak of water-lots! what a lot was his!

'What is fame! Fame is an accident. Sir Isaac Newton discovered an apple falling to the ground—a trivial discovery, truly, and one which a million men had made before him—but his parents were influential, and so they tortured that small circumstance into something wonderful, and, lo! the simple world took up the shout and, in almost the twinkling of an eye, that man was famous. Treasure these thoughts.

'Poesy, sweet poesy, who shall estimate what the world owes to thee!

"Mary had a little lamb, its fleece was white as
snow—And everywhere that Mary went, the lamb was sure to go."

"Jack and Gill went up the hill
To draw a pail of water;
Jack fell down and broke his crown,
And Gill came tumbling after."

'For simplicity, elegance of diction, and freedom from immoral tendencies, I regard those two poems in the light of gems. They are suited to all grades of intelligence, to every sphere of life —to the field, to the nursery, to the guild. Especially should no Board of Aldermen be without them.

'Venerable fossils! write again. Nothing improves one so much as friendly correspondence. Write again—and if there is anything in this memorial of yours that refers to anything in particular, do not be backward about explaining it. We shall always be happy to hear you chirp.

'Very truly, etc.,
'"MARK TWAIN,

'For James W. N——-, U. S. Senator.'

"That is an atrocious, a ruinous epistle! Distraction!"

"Well, sir, I am really sorry if there is anything wrong about it—but—but it appears to me to dodge the water-lot question."

"Dodge the mischief! Oh!—but never mind. As long as destruction must come now, let it be complete. Let it be complete—let this last of your performances, which I am about to read, make a finality of it. I am a ruined man. I had my misgivings when I gave you the letter from Humboldt, asking that the post route from Indian Gulch to Shakespeare Gap and intermediate points be changed partly to the old Mormon trail. But I told you it was a delicate question, and warned you to deal with it deftly—to answer it dubiously, and leave them a little in the dark. And your fatal imbecility impelled you to make this disastrous reply. I should think you would stop your ears, if you are not dead to all shame:

'"WASHINGTON, Nov. 30.

'"Messers. Perkins, Wagner, et at.

'"GENTLEMEN: It is a delicate question about this Indian trail, but, handled with proper deftness and dubiousness, I doubt not we shall succeed in some measure or otherwise, because the place where the route leaves the Lassen Meadows, over beyond where those two Shawnee chiefs, Dilapidated Vengeance and Biter-of-the-Clouds, were scalped last winter, this being the favorite direction to some, but others preferring something else in consequence of things, the Mormon trail leaving Mosby's at three in the morning, and passing through Jawbone Flat to Blucher, and then down by Jug-Handle, the road passing to the right of it, and naturally leaving it on the right, too, and Dawson's on the left of the trail where it passes to the left of said Dawson's and onward thence to Tomahawk, thus making the route cheaper, easier of access to all who can get at it, and compassing all the desirable objects so considered by others, and, therefore, conferring the most good upon the greatest number, and, consequently, I am encouraged to hope we shall. However, I shall be ready, and happy, to afford you still further information upon the subject, from time to time, as you may desire it and the Post-office Department be enabled to furnish it to me.

"'Very truly, etc.,
"'MARK TWAIN,

"'For James W. N———, U. S. Senator.'

"There—now what do you think of that?"

"Well, I don't know, sir. It—well, it appears to me—to be dubious enough."

"Du—leave the house! I am a ruined man. Those Humboldt savages never will forgive me for tangling their brains up with this inhuman letter. I have lost the respect of the Methodist Church, the board of aldermen—"

"Well, I haven't anything to say about that, because I may have missed it a little in their cases, but I was too many for the Baldwin's Ranch people, General!"

"Leave the house! Leave it forever and forever, too."

I regarded that as a sort of covert intimation that my service could be dispensed with, and so I resigned. I never will be a private secretary to a senator again. You can't please that kind of people. They don't know anything. They can't appreciate a party's efforts.

A FASHION ITEM

[written about 1867]

At General G——'s reception the other night, the most fashionably dressed lady was Mrs. G. C. She wore a pink satin dress, plain in front but with a good deal of rake to it—to the train, I mean; it was said to be two or three yards long. One could see it creeping along the floor some little time after the woman was gone. Mrs. C. wore also a white bodice, cut bias, with Pompadour sleeves, flounced with ruches; low neck, with the inside handkerchief not visible, with white kid gloves. She had on a pearl necklace, which glinted lonely, high up the midst of that barren waste of neck and shoulders. Her hair was frizzled into a tangled chaparral, forward of her ears, aft it was drawn together, and compactly bound and plaited into a stump like a pony's tail, and furthermore was canted upward at a sharp angle, and ingeniously supported by a red velvet crupper, whose forward extremity was made fast with a half-hitch around a hairpin on the top of her head. Her whole top hamper was neat and becoming. She had a beautiful complexion when she first came, but it faded out by degrees in an unaccountable way. However, it is not lost for good. I found the most of it on my shoulder afterward. (I stood near the door when she squeezed out with the throng.) There were other ladies present, but I only took notes of one as a specimen. I would gladly enlarge upon the subject were I able to do it justice.

RILEY—NEWSPAPER CORRESPONDENT

One of the best men in Washington—or elsewhere—is RILEY, correspondent of one of the great San Francisco dailies.

Riley is full of humor, and has an unfailing vein of irony, which makes his conversation to the last degree entertaining (as long as the remarks are about somebody else). But notwithstanding the possession of these qualities, which should enable a man to write a happy and an appetizing letter, Riley's newspaper letters often display a more than earthly solemnity, and likewise an unimaginative devotion to petrified facts, which surprise and distress all men who know him in his unofficial character. He explains this curious thing by saying that his employers sent him to Washington to write facts, not fancy, and that several times he has come near losing his situation by inserting humorous remarks which, not being looked for at headquarters, and consequently not understood, were thought to be dark and bloody speeches intended to convey signals and warnings to murderous secret societies, or something of that kind, and so were scratched out with a shiver and a prayer and cast into the stove. Riley says that sometimes he is so afflicted with a yearning to write a sparkling and absorbingly readable letter that he simply cannot resist it, and so he goes to his den and revels in the delight of untrammeled scribbling; and then, with suffering such as only a mother can know, he destroys the pretty children of his fancy and reduces his letter to the required dismal accuracy. Having seen Riley do this very thing more than once, I know whereof I speak. Often I have laughed with him over a happy passage, and grieved to see him plow his pen through it. He would say, "I had to write that or die; and I've got to scratch it out or starve. They wouldn't stand it, you know."

I think Riley is about the most entertaining company I ever saw. We lodged together in many places in Washington during the winter of '67-8, moving comfortably from place to place, and attracting attention by paying our board—a course which cannot fail to make a person conspicuous in Washington. Riley would tell all about his trip to California in the early days, by way of the Isthmus and the San Juan River; and about his baking bread in San Francisco to gain a living, and setting up tenpins, and practising law, and opening oysters, and delivering lectures, and teaching French, and tending bar, and reporting for the newspapers, and keeping dancing-schools, and interpreting Chinese in the courts— which latter was lucrative, and Riley was doing handsomely and laying up a little money when people began to find fault because his translations were too "free," a thing for which Riley considered he ought not to be held responsible, since he did not know a word of the Chinese tongue, and only adopted interpreting as a means of gaining an honest livelihood. Through the machinations of enemies he was removed from the position of official interpreter, and a man put in his place who was familiar with the Chinese language, but did not know any English. And Riley used to tell about publishing a newspaper up in what is Alaska now, but was only an iceberg then, with a population composed of bears, walruses, Indians, and other animals; and how the iceberg got adrift at last, and left all his paying subscribers behind, and as soon as the commonwealth floated out of the jurisdiction of Russia the people rose and threw off their allegiance and ran up the English flag, calculating to hook on and become an English colony as they drifted along down the British Possessions; but a land breeze and a crooked current carried them by, and they ran up the Stars and Stripes and steered for California, missed the connection again and swore allegiance to Mexico, but it wasn't any use; the anchors came home every time, and away they went with the northeast trades drifting off sideways toward the Sandwich Islands, whereupon they ran up the Cannibal flag and had a grand human barbecue in honor of it, in which it was noticed that the better a man liked a friend the better he enjoyed him; and as soon as they got fairly within the tropics the weather got so fearfully hot that the iceberg began to melt, and it got so sloppy under foot that it was almost impossible for ladies to get about at all; and at last, just as they came in sight of the islands, the melancholy remnant of the once majestic iceberg canted first to one side and then to the other, and then plunged under forever, carrying the national archives along with it—and not only the archives and the populace, but some eligible town lots which had increased in value as fast as they diminished in size in the tropics, and which Riley could have sold at thirty cents a pound and made himself rich if he could have kept the province afloat ten hours longer and got her into port.

Riley is very methodical, untiringly accommodating, never forgets anything that is to be attended to, is a good son, a stanch friend, and a permanent reliable enemy. He will put himself to any amount of trouble to oblige a body, and therefore always has his hands full of things to be done for the helpless and the shiftless. And he knows how to do nearly everything, too. He is a man whose native benevolence is a well-spring that never goes dry. He stands always ready to help whoever needs help, as far as he is able—and not simply with his money, for that is a cheap and common charity, but with hand and brain, and fatigue of limb and sacrifice of time. This sort of men is rare.

Riley has a ready wit, a quickness and aptness at selecting and applying quotations, and a countenance that is as solemn and as blank as the back side of a tombstone when he is delivering a particularly exasperating joke. One night a negro woman was burned to death in a house next door to us, and Riley said that our landlady would be oppressively emotional at breakfast, because she generally made use of such opportunities as offered, being of a morbidly sentimental turn, and so we should find it best to let her talk along and say nothing back—it was the only way to keep her tears out of the gravy.

Riley said there never was a funeral in the neighborhood but that the gravy was watery for a week.

And, sure enough, at breakfast the landlady was down in the very sloughs of woe—entirely brokenhearted. Everything she looked at reminded her of that poor old negro woman, and so the buckwheat cakes made her sob, the coffee forced a groan, and when the beefsteak came on she fetched a wail that made our hair rise. Then she got to talking about deceased, and kept up a steady drizzle till both of us were soaked through and through. Presently she took a fresh breath and said, with a world of sobs:

"Ah, to think of it, only to think of it!—the poor old faithful creature. For she was so faithful. Would you believe it, she had been a servant in that selfsame house and that selfsame family for twenty seven years come Christmas, and never a cross word and never a lick! And, oh, to think she should meet such a death at last!—a-sitting over the red hot stove at three o'clock in the morning and went to sleep and fell on it and was actually roasted! Not just frizzled up a bit, but literally roasted to a crisp! Poor faithful creature, how she was cooked! I am but a poor woman, but even if I have to scrimp to do it, I will put up a tombstone over that lone sufferer's grave—and Mr. Riley if you would have the goodness to think up a little epitaph to put on it which would sort of describe the awful way in which she met her—"

"Put it, 'Well done, good and faithful servant,'" said Riley, and never smiled.

A FINE OLD MAN

John Wagner, the oldest man in Buffalo—one hundred and four years old—recently walked a mile and a half in two weeks.

He is as cheerful and bright as any of these other old men that charge around so persistently and tiresomely in the newspapers, and in every way as remarkable.

Last November he walked five blocks in a rainstorm, without any shelter but an umbrella, and cast his vote for Grant, remarking that he had voted for forty-seven presidents—which was a lie.

His "second crop" of rich brown hair arrived from New York yesterday, and he has a new set of teeth coming from—Philadelphia.

He is to be married next week to a girl one hundred and two years old, who still takes in washing.

They have been engaged eighty years, but their parents persistently refused their consent until three days ago.

John Wagner is two years older than the Rhode Island veteran, and yet has never tasted a drop of liquor in his life—unless—unless you count whisky.

SCIENCE V.S. LUCK

[written about 1867]

At that time, in Kentucky (said the Hon. Mr. K——); the law was very strict against what is termed "games of chance." About a dozen of the boys were detected playing "seven up" or "old sledge" for money, and the grand jury found a true bill against them. Jim Sturgis was retained to defend them when the case came up, of course. The more he studied over the matter, and looked into the evidence, the plainer it was that he must lose a case at last—there was no getting around that painful fact. Those boys had certainly been betting money on a game of chance. Even public sympathy was roused in behalf of Sturgis. People said it was a pity to see him mar his successful career with a big prominent case like this, which must go against him.

But after several restless nights an inspired idea flashed upon Sturgis, and he sprang out of bed delighted. He thought he saw his way through. The next day he whispered around a little among his clients and a few friends, and then when the case came up in court he acknowledged the seven-up and the betting, and, as his sole defense, had the astounding effrontery to put in the plea that old sledge was not a game of chance! There was the broadest sort of a smile all over the faces of that sophisticated audience. The judge smiled with the rest. But Sturgis maintained a countenance whose earnestness was even severe. The opposite counsel tried to ridicule him out of his position, and did not succeed. The judge jested in a ponderous judicial way about the thing, but did not move him. The matter was becoming grave. The judge lost a little of his patience, and said the joke had gone far enough. Jim Sturgis said he knew of no joke in the matter— his clients could not be punished for indulging in what some people chose to consider a game of chance until it was *proven* that it was a game of chance. Judge and counsel said that would be an easy matter, and forthwith called Deacons Job, Peters, Burke, and Johnson, and Dominies Wirt and Miggles, to testify; and they unanimously and with strong feeling put down the legal quibble of Sturgis by pronouncing that old sledge was a game of chance.

"What do you call it now?" said the judge.

"I call it a game of science!" retorted Sturgis; "and I'll prove it, too!"

They saw his little game.

He brought in a cloud of witnesses, and produced an overwhelming mass of testimony, to show that old sledge was not a game of chance but a game of science.

Instead of being the simplest case in the world, it had somehow turned out to be an excessively knotty one. The judge scratched his head over it awhile, and said there was no way of coming to a determination, because just as many men could be brought into court who would testify on one side as could be found to testify on the other. But he said he was willing to do the fair thing by all parties, and would act upon any suggestion Mr. Sturgis would make for the solution of the difficulty.

Mr. Sturgis was on his feet in a second.

"Impanel a jury of six of each, Luck versus Science. Give them candles and a couple of decks of cards. Send them into the jury-room, and just abide by the result!"

There was no disputing the fairness of the proposition. The four deacons and the two dominies were sworn in as the "chance" jurymen, and six inveterate old seven-up professors were chosen to represent the "science" side of the issue. They retired to the jury-room.

In about two hours Deacon Peters sent into court to borrow three dollars from a friend. [Sensation.] In about two hours more Dominie Miggles sent into court to borrow a "stake" from a friend. [Sensation.] During the next three or four hours the other dominie and the other deacons sent into court for small loans. And still the packed audience waited, for it was a prodigious occasion in Bull's Corners, and one in which every father of a family was necessarily interested.

The rest of the story can be told briefly. About daylight the jury came in, and Deacon Job, the foreman, read the following:

VERDICT:

We, the jury in the case of the Commonwealth of Kentucky vs. John Wheeler et al., have carefully considered the points of the case, and tested the merits of the several theories advanced, and do hereby unanimously decide that the game commonly known as old sledge or seven-up is eminently a game of science and not of chance. In demonstration whereof it is hereby and herein stated, iterated, reiterated, set forth, and made manifest that, during the entire night, the "chance" men never won a game or turned a jack, although both feats were common and frequent to the opposition; and furthermore, in support of this our verdict, we call attention to the significant fact that the "chance" men are all busted, and the "science" men have got the money. It is the deliberate opinion of this jury, that the "chance" theory concerning seven-up is a pernicious doctrine, and calculated to inflict untold suffering and pecuniary loss upon any community that takes stock in it.

"That is the way that seven-up came to be set apart and particularized in the statute-books of Kentucky as being a game not of chance but of science, and therefore not punishable under the law," said Mr. K———. "That verdict is of record, and holds good to this day."

THE LATE BENJAMIN FRANKLIN

[written about 1870]

["Never put off till to-morrow what you can do day after to-morrow just as well."—B. F.]

This party was one of those persons whom they call Philosophers. He was twins, being born simultaneously in two different houses in the city of Boston. These houses remain unto this day, and have signs upon them worded in accordance with the facts. The signs are considered well enough to have, though not necessary, because the inhabitants point out the two birthplaces to the stranger anyhow, and sometimes as often as several times in the same day. The subject of this memoir was of a vicious disposition, and early prostituted his talents to the invention of maxims and aphorisms calculated to inflict suffering upon the rising generation of all subsequent ages. His simplest acts, also, were contrived with a view to their being held up for the emulation of boys forever—boys who might otherwise have been happy. It was in this spirit that he became the son of a soap-boiler, and probably for no other reason than that the efforts of all future boys who tried to be anything might be looked upon with suspicion unless they were the sons of soap-boilers. With a malevolence which is without parallel in history, he would work all day, and then sit up nights, and let on to be studying algebra by the light of a smoldering fire, so that all other boys might have to do that also, or else have Benjamin Franklin thrown up to them.

Not satisfied with these proceedings, he had a fashion of living wholly on bread and water, and studying astronomy at meal-time—a thing which has brought affliction to millions of boys since, whose fathers had read Franklin's pernicious biography.

His maxims were full of animosity toward boys. Nowadays a boy cannot follow out a single natural instinct without tumbling over some of those everlasting aphorisms and hearing from Franklin on the spot. If he buys two cents' worth of peanuts, his father says, "Remember what Franklin has said, my son—'A grout a day's a penny a year'"; and the comfort is all gone out of those peanuts. If he wants to spin his top when he has done work, his father quotes, "Procrastination is the thief of time." If he does a virtuous action, he never gets anything for it, because "Virtue is its own reward." And that boy is hounded to death and robbed of his natural rest, because Franklin, said once, in one of his inspired flights of malignity:

> Early to bed and early to rise
> Makes a man healthy and wealthy and wise.

As if it were any object to a boy to be healthy and wealthy and wise on such terms. The sorrow that that maxim has cost me, through my parents, experimenting on me with it, tongue cannot tell. The legitimate result is my present state of general debility, indigence, and mental aberration. My parents used to have me up before nine o'clock in the morning sometimes when I was a boy. If they had let me take my natural rest where would I have been now? Keeping store, no doubt, and respected by all.

And what an adroit old adventurer the subject of this memoir was! In order to get a chance to fly his kite on Sunday he used to hang a key on the string and let on to be fishing for lightning. And a guileless public would go home chirping about the "wisdom" and the "genius" of the hoary Sabbath-breaker. If anybody caught him playing "mumblepeg" by himself, after the age of sixty, he would immediately appear to be ciphering out how the grass grew—as if it was any of his business. My grandfather knew him well, and he says Franklin was always fixed—always ready. If a body, during his old age, happened on him unexpectedly when he was catching flies, or making mud-pies, or sliding on a cellar door, he would immediately look wise, and rip out a maxim, and walk off with his nose in the air and his cap turned wrong side before, trying to appear absent-minded and eccentric. He was a hard lot.

He invented a stove that would smoke your head off in four hours by the clock. One can see the almost devilish satisfaction he took in it by his giving it his name.

He was always proud of telling how he entered Philadelphia for the first time, with nothing in the world but two shillings in his pocket and four rolls of bread under his arm. But really, when you come to examine it critically, it was nothing. Anybody could have done it.

To the subject of this memoir belongs the honor of recommending the army to go back to bows and arrows in place of bayonets and muskets. He observed, with his customary force, that the bayonet was very well under some circumstances, but that he doubted whether it could be used with accuracy at a long range.

Benjamin Franklin did a great many notable things for his country, and made her young name to be honored in many lands as the mother of such a son. It is not the idea of this memoir to ignore that or cover it up. No; the simple idea of it is to snub those pretentious maxims of his, which he worked up with a great show of originality out of truisms that had become wearisome platitudes as early as the dispersion from Babel; and also to snub his stove, and his military inspirations, his unseemly endeavor to make himself conspicuous when he entered Philadelphia, and his flying his kite and fooling away his time in all sorts of such ways when he ought to have been foraging for soap-fat, or constructing candles.

I merely desired to do away with somewhat of the prevalent calamitous idea among heads of families that Franklin acquired his great genius by working for nothing, studying by moonlight, and getting up in the night instead of waiting till morning like a Christian; and that this program, rigidly inflicted, will make a Franklin of every father's fool. It is time these gentlemen were finding out that these execrable eccentricities of instinct and conduct are only the evidences of genius, not the creators of it. I wish I had been the father of my parents long enough to make them comprehend this truth, and thus prepare them to let their son have an easier time of it. When I was a child I had to boil soap, notwithstanding my father was wealthy, and I had to get up early and study geometry at breakfast, and peddle my own poetry, and do everything just as Franklin did, in the solemn hope that I would be a Franklin some day. And here I am.

MR. BLOKE'S ITEM

[written about 1865]

Our esteemed friend, Mr. John William Bloke, of Virginia City, walked into the office where we are sub-editor at a late hour last night, with an expression of profound and heartfelt suffering upon his countenance, and, sighing heavily, laid the following item reverently upon the desk, and walked slowly out again. He paused a moment at the door, and seemed struggling to command his feelings sufficiently to enable him to speak, and then, nodding his head toward his manuscript, ejaculated in a broken voice, "Friend of mine—oh! how sad!" and burst into tears. We were so moved at his distress that we did not think to call him back and endeavor to comfort him until he was gone, and it was too late. The paper had already gone to press, but knowing that our friend would consider the publication of this item important, and cherishing the hope that to print it would afford a melancholy satisfaction to his sorrowing heart, we stopped the press at once and inserted it in our columns:

> DISTRESSING ACCIDENT.—Last evening, about six o'clock, as Mr. William Schuyler, an old and respectable citizen of South Park, was leaving his residence to go down-town, as has been his usual custom for many years with the exception only of a short interval in the spring of 1850, during which he was confined to his bed by injuries received in attempting to stop a runaway horse by thoughtlessly placing himself directly in its wake and throwing up his hands and shouting, which if he had done so even a single moment sooner, must inevitably have frightened the animal still more instead of checking its speed, although disastrous enough to himself as it was, and rendered more melancholy and distressing by reason of the presence of his wife's mother, who was there and saw the sad occurrence notwithstanding it is at least likely, though not necessarily so, that she should be reconnoitering in another direction when incidents occur, not being vivacious and on the lookout, as a general thing, but even the reverse, as her own mother is said to have stated, who is no more, but died in the full hope of a glorious resurrection, upwards of three years ago; aged eighty-six, being a Christian woman and without guile, as it were, or property, in consequence of the fire of 1849, which destroyed every single thing she had in the world. But such is life. Let us all take warning by this solemn occurrence, and let us endeavor so to conduct ourselves that when we come to die we can do it. Let us place our hands upon our heart, and say with earnestness and sincerity that from this day forth we will beware of the intoxicating bowl.— 'First Edition of the Californian.'

The head editor has been in here raising the mischief, and tearing his hair and kicking the furniture about, and abusing me like a pickpocket. He says that every time he leaves me in charge of the paper for half an hour I get imposed upon by the first infant or the first idiot that comes along. And he says that that distressing item of Mr. Bloke's is nothing but a lot of distressing bosh, and has no point to it, and no sense in it, and no information in it, and that there was no sort of necessity for stopping the press to publish it.

Now all this comes of being good-hearted. If I had been as unaccommodating and unsympathetic as some people, I would have told Mr. Bloke that I wouldn't receive his communication at such a late hour; but no, his snuffling distress touched my heart, and I jumped at the chance of doing something to modify his misery. I never read his item to see whether there was anything wrong about it, but hastily wrote the few lines which preceded it, and sent it to the printers. And what has my kindness done for me? It has done nothing but bring down upon me a storm of abuse and ornamental blasphemy.

Now I will read that item myself, and see if there is any foundation for all this fuss. And if there is, the author of it shall hear from me.

I have read it, and I am bound to admit that it seems a little mixed at a first glance. However, I will peruse it once more.

I have read it again, and it does really seem a good deal more mixed than ever.

I have read it over five times, but if I can get at the meaning of it I wish I may get my just deserts. It won't bear analysis. There are things about it which I cannot understand at all. It don't say whatever became of William Schuyler. It just says enough about him to get one interested in his career, and then drops him. Who is William Schuyler, anyhow, and what part of South Park did he live in, and if he started down-town at six o'clock, did he ever get there, and if he did, did anything happen to him? Is he the individual that met with the "distressing accident"? Considering the elaborate circumstantiality of detail observable in the item, it seems to me that it ought to contain more information than it does. On the contrary, it is obscure—and not only obscure, but utterly incomprehensible. Was the breaking of Mr. Schuyler's leg, fifteen years ago, the "distressing accident" that plunged Mr. Bloke into unspeakable grief, and caused him to come up here at dead of night and stop our press to acquaint the world with the circumstance? Or did the "distressing accident" consist in the destruction of Schuyler's mother-in-law's property in early times? Or did it consist in the death of that person herself three years ago (albeit it does not appear that she died by accident)? In a word, what did that "distressing accident" consist in? What did that driveling ass of a Schuyler stand in the wake of a runaway horse for, with his shouting and gesticulating, if he wanted to stop him? And how the mischief could he get run over by a horse that had already passed beyond him? And what are we to take "warning" by? And how is this extraordinary chapter of incomprehensibilities going to be a "lesson" to us? And, above all, what has the intoxicating "bowl" got to do with it, anyhow? It is not stated that Schuyler drank, or that his wife drank, or that his mother-in-law drank, or that the horse drank—wherefore, then, the reference to the intoxicating bowl? It does seem to me that if Mr. Bloke had let the intoxicating bowl alone himself, he never would have got into so much trouble about this exasperating imaginary accident. I have read this absurd item over and over again, with all its insinuating plausibility, until my head swims; but I can make neither head nor tail of it. There certainly seems to have been an accident of some kind or other, but it is impossible to determine what the nature of it was, or who was the sufferer by it. I do not like to do it, but I feel compelled to request that the next time anything happens to one of Mr. Bloke's friends, he will append such explanatory notes to his account of it as will enable me to find out what sort of an accident it was and whom it happened to. I had rather all his friends should die than that I should be driven to the verge of lunacy again in trying to cipher out the meaning of another such production as the above.

A MEDIEVAL ROMANCE [WRITTEN ABOUT 1868]

CHAPTER I. THE SECRET REVEALED.

It was night. Stillness reigned in the grand old feudal castle of Klugenstein. The year 1222 was drawing to a close. Far away up in the tallest of the castle's towers a single light glimmered. A secret council was being held there. The stern old lord of Klugenstein sat in a chair of state meditating. Presently he said, with a tender accent:

"My daughter!"

A young man of noble presence, clad from head to heel in knightly mail, answered:

"Speak, father!"

"My daughter, the time is come for the revealing of the mystery that hath puzzled all your young life. Know, then, that it had its birth in the matters which I shall now unfold. My brother Ulrich is the great Duke of Brandenburgh. Our father, on his deathbed, decreed that if no son were born to Ulrich, the succession should pass to my house, provided a son were born to me. And further, in case no son were born to either, but only daughters, then the succession should pass to Ulrich's daughter, if she proved stainless; if she did not, my daughter should succeed, if she retained a blameless name. And so I, and my old wife here, prayed fervently for the good boon of a son, but the prayer was vain. You were born to us. I was in despair. I saw the mighty prize slipping from my grasp—the splendid dream vanishing away. And I had been so hopeful! Five years had Ulrich lived in wedlock, and yet his wife had borne no heir of either sex.

"'But hold,' I said, 'all is not lost.' A saving scheme had shot athwart my brain. You were born at midnight. Only the leech, the nurse, and six waiting-women knew your sex. I hanged them every one before an hour had sped. Next morning all the barony went mad with rejoicing over the proclamation that a son was born to Klugenstein—an heir to mighty Brandenburgh! And well the secret has been kept. Your mother's own sister nursed your infancy, and from that time forward we feared nothing.

"When you were ten years old, a daughter was born to Ulrich. We grieved, but hoped for good results from measles, or physicians, or other natural enemies of infancy, but were always disappointed. She lived, she throve—Heaven's malison upon her! But it is nothing. We are safe. For, Ha-ha! have we not a son? And is not our son the future Duke? Our well-beloved Conrad, is it not so?—for, woman of eight-and-twenty years—as you are, my child, none other name than that hath ever fallen to you!

"Now it hath come to pass that age hath laid its hand upon my brother, and he waxes feeble. The cares of state do tax him sore, therefore he wills that you shall come to him and be already—Duke in act, though not yet in name. Your servitors are ready—you journey forth to-night.

"Now listen well. Remember every word I say. There is a law as old as Germany, that if any woman sit for a single instant in the great ducal chair before she hath been absolutely crowned in presence of the people, SHE SHALL DIE! So heed my words.

Pretend humility. Pronounce your judgments from the Premier's chair, which stands at the foot of the throne. Do this until you are crowned and safe. It is not likely that your sex will ever be discovered, but still it is the part of wisdom to make all things as safe as may be in this treacherous earthly life."

"Oh, my father, is it for this my life hath been a lie! Was it that I might cheat my unoffending cousin of her rights? Spare me, father, spare your child!"

"What, hussy! Is this my reward for the august fortune my brain has wrought for thee? By the bones of my father, this puling sentiment of thine but ill accords with my humor.

"Betake thee to the Duke, instantly! And beware how thou meddlest with my purpose!"

Let this suffice, of the conversation. It is enough for us to know that the prayers, the entreaties, and the tears of the gentle-natured girl availed nothing. Neither they nor anything could move the stout old lord of Klugenstein. And so, at last, with a heavy heart, the daughter saw the castle gates close behind her, and found herself riding away in the darkness surrounded by a knightly array of armed vassals and a brave following of servants.

The old baron sat silent for many minutes after his daughter's departure, and then he turned to his sad wife and said:

"Dame, our matters seem speeding fairly. It is full three months since I sent the shrewd and handsome Count Detzin on his devilish mission to my brother's daughter Constance. If he fail, we are not wholly safe; but if he do succeed, no power can bar our girl from being Duchess e'en though ill-fortune should decree she never should be Duke!"

"My heart is full of bodings, yet all may still be well."

"Tush, woman! Leave the owls to croak. To bed with ye, and dream of Brandenburgh and grandeur!"

CHAPTER II.FESTIVITY AND TEARS

Six days after the occurrences related in the above chapter, the brilliant capital of the Duchy of Brandenburgh was resplendent with military pageantry, and noisy with the rejoicings of loyal multitudes, for Conrad, the young heir to the crown, was come. The old duke's heart was full of happiness, for Conrad's handsome person and graceful bearing had won his love at once. The great halls of the palace were thronged with nobles, who welcomed Conrad bravely; and so bright and happy did all things seem, that he felt his fears and sorrows passing away and giving place to a comforting contentment.

But in a remote apartment of the palace a scene of a different nature was transpiring. By a window stood the duke's only child, the Lady Constance. Her eyes were red and swollen, and full of tears. She was alone. Presently she fell to weeping anew, and said aloud:

"The villain Detzin is gone—has fled the dukedom! I could not believe it at first, but alas! it is too true. And I loved him so. I dared to love him though I knew the duke, my father, would never let me wed him. I loved him—but now I hate him! With all my soul I hate him! Oh, what is to become of me! I am lost, lost, lost! I shall go mad!"

CHAPTER III. THE PLOT THICKENS

Few months drifted by. All men published the praises of the young Conrad's government and extolled the wisdom of his judgments, the mercifulness of his sentences, and the modesty with which he bore himself in his great office. The old duke soon gave everything into his hands, and sat apart and listened with proud satisfaction while his heir delivered the decrees of the crown from the seat of the premier. It seemed plain that one so loved and praised and honored of all men as Conrad was, could not be otherwise than happy. But, strangely enough, he was not. For he saw with dismay that the Princess Constance had begun to love him! The love of the rest of the world was happy fortune for him, but this was freighted with danger! And he saw, moreover, that the delighted duke had discovered his daughter's passion likewise, and was already dreaming of a marriage. Every day somewhat of the deep sadness that had been in the princess's face faded away; every day hope and animation beamed brighter from her eye; and by and by even vagrant smiles visited the face that had been so troubled.

Conrad was appalled. He bitterly cursed himself for having yielded to the instinct that had made him seek the companionship of one of his own sex when he was new and a stranger in the palace—when he was sorrowful and yearned for a sympathy such as only women can give or feel. He now began to avoid his cousin. But this only made matters worse, for, naturally enough, the more he avoided her the more she cast herself in his way. He marveled at this at first, and next it startled him. The girl haunted him; she hunted him; she happened upon him at all times and in all places, in the night as well as in the day. She seemed singularly anxious. There was surely a mystery somewhere.

This could not go on forever. All the world was talking about it. The duke was beginning to look perplexed. Poor Conrad was becoming a very ghost through dread and dire distress. One day as he was emerging from a private ante-room attached to the picture-gallery, Constance confronted him, and seizing both his hands, in hers, exclaimed:

"Oh, why do you avoid me? What have I done—what have I said, to lose your kind opinion of me—for surely I had it once? Conrad, do not despise me, but pity a tortured heart? I cannot,—cannot hold the words unspoken longer, lest they kill me—I LOVE YOU, CONRAD! There, despise me if you must, but they would be uttered!"

Conrad was speechless. Constance hesitated a moment, and then, misinterpreting his silence, a wild gladness flamed in her eyes, and she flung her arms about his neck and said:

"You relent! you relent! You can love me—you will love me! Oh, say you will, my own, my worshipped Conrad!"

Conrad groaned aloud. A sickly pallor overspread his countenance, and he trembled like an aspen. Presently, in desperation, he thrust the poor girl from him, and cried:

"You know not what you ask! It is forever and ever impossible!" And then he fled like a criminal, and left the princess stupefied with amazement. A minute afterward she was crying and sobbing there, and Conrad was crying and sobbing in his chamber. Both were in despair. Both saw ruin staring them in the face.

By and by Constance rose slowly to her feet and moved away, saying:

"To think that he was despising my love at the very moment that I thought it was melting his cruel heart! I hate him! He spurned me—did this man—he spurned me from him like a dog!"

CHAPTER IV.

THE AWFUL REVELATION

Time passed on. A settled sadness rested once more upon the countenance of the good duke's daughter. She and Conrad were seen together no more now. The duke grieved at this. But as the weeks wore away, Conrad's color came back to his cheeks and his old-time vivacity to his eye, and he administered the government with a clear and steadily ripening wisdom.

Presently a strange whisper began to be heard about the palace. It grew louder; it spread farther. The gossips of the city got hold of it. It swept the dukedom. And this is what the whisper said:

"The Lady Constance hath given birth to a child!"

When the lord of Klugenstein heard it, he swung his plumed helmet thrice around his head and shouted:

"Long live Duke Conrad!—for lo, his crown is sure from this day forward! Detzin has done his errand well, and the good scoundrel shall be rewarded!"

And he spread the tidings far and wide, and for eight-and-forty hours no soul in all the barony but did dance and sing, carouse and illuminate, to celebrate the great event, and all at proud and happy old Klugenstein's expense.

CHAPTER V.THE FRIGHTFUL CATASTROPHE

The trial was at hand. All the great lords and barons of Brandenburgh were assembled in the Hall of Justice in the ducal palace. No space was left unoccupied where there was room for a spectator to stand or sit. Conrad, clad in purple and ermine, sat in the Premier's chair, and on either side sat the great judges of the realm. The old Duke had sternly commanded that the trial of his daughter should proceed without favor, and then had taken to his bed broken-hearted. His days were numbered. Poor Conrad had begged, as for his very life, that he might be spared the misery of sitting in judgment upon his cousin's crime, but it did not avail.

The saddest heart in all that great assemblage was in Conrad's breast.

The gladdest was in his father's, for unknown to his daughter "Conrad," the old Baron Klugenstein was come, and was among the crowd of nobles, triumphant in the swelling fortunes of his house.

After the heralds had made due proclamation and the other preliminaries had followed, the venerable Lord Chief justice said:

"Prisoner, stand forth!"

The unhappy princess rose, and stood unveiled before the vast multitude. The Lord Chief Justice continued:

"Most noble lady, before the great judges of this realm it hath been charged and proven that out of holy wedlock your Grace hath given birth unto a child; and by our ancient law the penalty is death, excepting in one sole contingency whereof his Grace the acting Duke, our good Lord Conrad, will advertise you in his solemn sentence now; wherefore, give heed."

Conrad stretched forth the reluctant sceptre, and in the selfsame moment the womanly heart beneath his robe yearned pityingly toward the doomed prisoner, and the tears came into his eyes. He opened his lips to speak, but the Lord Chief Justice said quickly:

"Not there, your Grace, not there! It is not lawful to pronounce judgment upon any of the ducal line SAVE FROM THE DUCAL THRONE!"

A shudder went to the heart of poor Conrad, and a tremor shook the iron frame of his old father likewise. CONRAD HAD NOT BEEN CROWNED—dared he profane the throne? He hesitated and turned pale with fear. But it must be done. Wondering eyes were already upon him. They would be suspicious eyes if he hesitated longer. He ascended the throne. Presently he stretched forth the sceptre again, and said:

"Prisoner, in the name of our sovereign lord, Ulrich, Duke of Brandenburgh, I proceed to the solemn duty that hath devolved upon me. Give heed to my words. By the ancient law of the land, except you produce the partner of your guilt and deliver him up to the executioner, you must surely die. Embrace this opportunity—save yourself while yet you may. Name the father of your child!"

A solemn hush fell upon the great court—a silence so profound that men could hear their own hearts beat. Then the princess slowly turned, with eyes gleaming with hate, and pointing her finger straight at Conrad, said:

"Thou art the man!"

An appalling conviction of his helpless, hopeless peril struck a chill to Conrad's heart like the chill of death itself. What power on earth could save him! To disprove the charge he must reveal that he was a woman; and for an uncrowned woman to sit in the ducal chair was death! At one and the same moment he and his grim old father swooned and fell to the ground.

The remainder of this thrilling and eventful story will NOT be found in this or any other publication, either now or at any future time.

The truth is, I have got my hero (or heroine) into such a particularly close place that I do not see how I am ever going to get him (or her) out of it again—and therefore I will wash my hands of the whole business, and leave that person to get out the best way that offers—or else stay there. I thought it was going to be easy enough to straighten out that little difficulty, but it looks different now.

PETITION CONCERNING COPYRIGHT

TO THE HONORABLE THE SENATE AND HOUSE OF REPRESENTATIVES IN CONGRESS ASSEMBLED

Whereas, The Constitution guarantees equal rights to all, backed by the Declaration of Independence; and

Whereas, Under our laws, the right of property in real estate is perpetual; and

Whereas, Under our laws, the right of property in the literary result of a citizen's intellectual labor is restricted to forty-two years; and

Whereas, Forty-two years seems an exceedingly just and righteous term, and a sufficiently long one for the retention of property;

Therefore, Your petitioner, having the good of his country solely at heart, humbly prays that "equal rights" and fair and equal treatment may be meted out to all citizens, by the restriction of rights in all property, real estate included, to the beneficent term of forty-two years. Then shall all men bless your honorable body and be happy. And for this will your petitioner ever pray.

MARK TWAIN.

A PARAGRAPH NOT ADDED TO THE PETITION

The charming absurdity of restricting property-rights in books to forty-two years sticks prominently out in the fact that hardly any man's books ever live forty-two years, or even the half of it; and so, for the sake of getting a shabby advantage of the heirs of about one Scott or Burns or Milton in a hundred years, the lawmakers of the "Great" Republic are content to leave that poor little pilfering edict upon the statute-books. It is like an emperor lying in wait to rob a phoenix's nest, and waiting the necessary century to get the chance.

AFTER-DINNER SPEECH

[AT A FOURTH OF JULY GATHERING, IN LONDON, OF AMERICANS]

MR. CHAIRMAN AND LADIES AND GENTLEMEN: I thank you for the compliment which has just been tendered me, and to show my appreciation of it I will not afflict you with many words. It is pleasant to celebrate in this peaceful way, upon this old mother soil, the anniversary of an experiment which was born of war with this same land so long ago, and wrought out to a successful issue by the devotion of our ancestors. It has taken nearly a hundred years to bring the English and Americans into kindly and mutually appreciative relations, but I believe it has been accomplished at last. It was a great step when the two last misunderstandings were settled by arbitration instead of cannon. It is another great step when England adopts our sewing-machines without claiming the invention—as usual. It was another when they imported one of our sleeping-cars the other day. And it warmed my heart more than I can tell, yesterday, when I witnessed the spectacle of an Englishman ordering an American sherry cobbler of his own free will and accord—and not only that but with a great brain and a level head reminding the barkeeper not to forget the strawberries. With a common origin, a common language, a common literature, a common religion and—common drinks, what is longer needful to the cementing of the two nations together in a permanent bond of brotherhood?

This is an age of progress, and ours is a progressive land. A great and glorious land, too—a land which has developed a Washington, a Franklin, a William M. Tweed, a Longfellow, a Motley, a Jay Gould, a Samuel C. Pomeroy, a recent Congress which has never had its equal (in some respects), and a United States Army which conquered sixty Indians in eight months by tiring them out—which is much better than uncivilized slaughter, God knows. We have a criminal jury system which is superior to any in the world; and its efficiency is only marred by the difficulty of finding twelve men every day who don't know anything and can't read. And I may observe that we have an insanity plea that would have saved Cain. I think I can say, and say with pride, that we have some legislatures that bring higher prices than any in the world.

I refer with effusion to our railway system, which consents to let us live, though it might do the opposite, being our owners. It only destroyed three thousand and seventy lives last year by collisions, and twenty-seven thousand two hundred and sixty by running over heedless and unnecessary people at crossings. The companies seriously regretted the killing of these thirty thousand people, and went so far as to pay for some of them—voluntarily, of course, for the meanest of us would not claim that we possess a court treacherous enough to enforce a law against a railway company. But, thank Heaven, the railway companies are generally disposed to do the right and kindly thing without compulsion. I know of an instance which greatly touched me at the time. After an accident the company sent home the remains of a dear distant old relative of mine in a basket, with the remark, "Please state what figure you hold him at—and return the basket." Now there couldn't be anything friendlier than that.

But I must not stand here and brag all night. However, you won't mind a body bragging a little about his country on the fourth of July. It is a fair and legitimate time to fly the eagle. I will say only one more word of brag—and a hopeful one. It is this. We have a form of government which gives each man a fair chance and no favor. With us no individual is born with a right to look down upon his neighbor and hold him in contempt. Let such of us as are not dukes find our consolation in that. And we may find hope for the future in the fact that as unhappy as is the condition of our political morality to-day, England has risen up out of a far fouler since the days when Charles I. ennobled courtesans and all political place was a matter of bargain and sale. There is hope for us yet.

[At least the above is the speech which I was going to make, but our minister, General Schenck, presided, and after the blessing, got up and made a great long inconceivably dull harangue, and wound up by saying that inasmuch as speech-making did not seem to exhilarate the guests much, all further oratory would be dispensed with during the evening, and we could just sit and talk privately to our elbow-neighbors and have a good sociable time. It is known that in consequence of that remark forty-four perfected speeches died in the womb. The depression, the gloom, the solemnity that reigned over the banquet from that time forth will be a lasting memory with many that were there. By that one thoughtless remark General Schenck lost forty-four of the best friends he had in England. More than one said that night, "And this is the sort of person that is sent to represent us in a great sister empire!"]

LIONIZING MURDERERS

I had heard so much about the celebrated fortune-teller Madame— —, that I went to see her yesterday. She has a dark complexion naturally, and this effect is heightened by artificial aids which cost her nothing. She wears curls—very black ones, and I had an impression that she gave their native attractiveness a lift with rancid butter. She wears a reddish check handkerchief, cast loosely around her neck, and it was plain that her other one is slow getting back from the wash. I presume she takes snuff. At any rate, something resembling it had lodged among the hairs sprouting from her upper lip. I know she likes garlic—I knew that as soon as she sighed. She looked at me searchingly for nearly a minute, with her black eyes, and then said:

"It is enough. Come!"

She started down a very dark and dismal corridor—I stepping close after her. Presently she stopped, and said that, as the way was so crooked and dark, perhaps she had better get a light. But it seemed ungallant to allow a woman to put herself to so much trouble for me, and so I said:

"It is not worth while, madam. If you will heave another sigh, I think I can follow it."

So we got along all right. Arrived at her official and mysterious den, she asked me to tell her the date of my birth, the exact hour of that occurrence, and the color of my grandmother's hair. I answered as accurately as I could. Then she said:

"Young man, summon your fortitude—do not tremble. I am about to reveal the past."

"Information concerning the future would be, in a general way, more—"

"Silence! You have had much trouble, some joy, some good fortune, some bad. Your great grandfather was hanged."

"That is a I—"

"Silence! Hanged sir. But it was not his fault. He could not help it."

"I am glad you do him justice."

"Ah—grieve, rather, that the jury did. He was hanged. His star crosses yours in the fourth division, fifth sphere. Consequently you will be hanged also."

"In view of this cheerful—"

"I must have silence. Yours was not, in the beginning, a criminal nature, but circumstances changed it. At the age of nine you stole sugar. At the age of fifteen you stole money. At twenty you stole horses. At twenty-five you committed arson. At thirty, hardened in crime, you became an editor. You are now a public lecturer. Worse things are in store for you. You will be sent to Congress. Next, to the penitentiary. Finally, happiness will come again—all will be well—you will be hanged."

I was now in tears. It seemed hard enough to go to Congress; but to be hanged—this was too sad, too dreadful. The woman seemed surprised at my grief. I told her the thoughts that were in my mind. Then she comforted me.

"Why, man," she said, "hold up your head—you have nothing to grieve about. Listen.

—[In this paragraph the fortune-teller details the exact history of the Pike-Brown assassination case in New Hampshire, from the succoring and saving of the stranger Pike by the Browns, to the subsequent hanging and coffining of that treacherous miscreant. She adds nothing, invents nothing, exaggerates nothing (see any New England paper for November, 1869). This Pike-Brown case is selected merely as a type, to illustrate a custom that prevails, not in New Hampshire alone, but in every state in the Union—I mean the sentimental custom of visiting, petting, glorifying, and snuffling over murderers like this Pike, from the day they enter the jail under sentence of death until they swing from the gallows. The following extract from the Temple Bar (1866) reveals the fact that this custom is not confined to the United States.—"on December 31, 1841, a man named John Johnes, a shoemaker, murdered his sweetheart, Mary Hallam, the daughter of a respectable laborer, at Mansfield, in the county of Nottingham. He was executed on March 23, 1842. He was a man of unsteady habits, and gave way to violent fits of passion. The girl declined his addresses, and he said if he did not have her no one else should. After he had inflicted the first wound, which was not immediately fatal, she begged for her life, but seeing him resolved, asked for time to pray. He said that he would pray for both, and completed the crime. The wounds were inflicted by a shoemaker's knife, and her throat was cut barbarously. After this he dropped on his knees some time, and prayed God to have mercy on two unfortunate lovers. He made no attempt to escape, and confessed the crime. After his imprisonment he behaved in a most decorous manner; he won upon the good opinion of the jail chaplain, and he was visited by the Bishop of Lincoln. It does not appear that he expressed any contrition for the crime, but seemed to pass away with triumphant certainty that he was going to rejoin his victim in heaven. He was visited by some pious and benevolent ladies of Nottingham, some of whom declared he was a child of God, if ever there was one. One of the ladies sent him a white camellia to wear at his execution."]

"You will live in New Hampshire. In your sharp need and distress the Brown family will succor you—such of them as Pike the assassin left alive. They will be benefactors to you. When you shall have grown fat upon their bounty, and are grateful and happy, you will desire to make some modest return for these things, and so you will go to the house some night and brain the whole family with an ax. You will rob the dead bodies of your benefactors, and disburse your gains in riotous living among the rowdies and courtesans of Boston. Then you will be arrested, tried, condemned to be hanged, thrown into prison. Now is your happy day. You will be converted—you will be converted just as soon as every effort to compass pardon, commutation, or reprieve has failed—and then!—Why, then, every morning and every afternoon, the best and purest young ladies of the village will assemble in your cell and sing hymns. This will show that assassination is respectable. Then you will write a touching letter, in which you will forgive all those recent Browns. This will excite the public admiration. No public can withstand magnanimity. Next, they will take you to the scaffold, with great éclat, at the head of an imposing procession composed of clergymen, officials, citizens generally, and young ladies walking pensively two and two, and bearing bouquets and immortelles. You will mount the scaffold, and while the great concourse stand uncovered in your presence, you will read your sappy little speech which the minister has written for you. And then, in the midst of a grand and impressive silence, they will swing you into per—Paradise, my son. There will not be a dry eye on the ground. You will be a hero! Not a rough there but will envy you. Not a rough there but will resolve to emulate you. And next, a great procession will follow you to the tomb—will weep over your remains—the young ladies will sing again the hymns made dear by sweet associations connected with the jail, and, as a last tribute of affection, respect, and appreciation of your many sterling qualities, they will walk two and two around your bier, and strew wreaths of flowers on it. And lo! you are canonized.

Think of it, son—ingrate, assassin, robber of the dead, drunken brawler among thieves and harlots in the slums of Boston one month, and the pet of the pure and innocent daughters of the land the next! A bloody and hateful devil—a bewept, bewailed, and sainted martyr—all in a month! Fool!—so noble a fortune, and yet you sit here grieving!"

"No, madam," I said, "you do me wrong, you do, indeed. I am perfectly satisfied. I did not know before that my great-grandfather was hanged, but it is of no consequence. He has probably ceased to bother about it by this time—and I have not commenced yet. I confess, madam, that I do something in the way of editing and lecturing, but the other crimes you mention have escaped my memory. Yet I must have committed them—you would not deceive a stranger. But let the past be as it was, and let the future be as it may—these are nothing. I have only cared for one thing. I have always felt that I should be hanged some day, and somehow the thought has annoyed me considerably; but if you can only assure me that I shall be hanged in New Hampshire—"

"Not a shadow of a doubt!"

"Bless you, my benefactress!—excuse this embrace—you have removed a great load from my breast. To be hanged in New Hampshire is happiness—it leaves an honored name behind a man, and introduces him at once into the best New Hampshire society in the other world."

I then took leave of the fortune-teller. But, seriously, is it well to glorify a murderous villain on the scaffold, as Pike was glorified in New Hampshire? Is it well to turn the penalty for a bloody crime into a reward? Is it just to do it? Is it safe?

A NEW CRIME

LEGISLATION NEEDED

This country, during the last thirty or forty years, has produced some of the most remarkable cases of insanity of which there is any mention in history. For instance, there was the Baldwin case, in Ohio, twenty-two years ago. Baldwin, from his boyhood up, had been of a vindictive, malignant, quarrelsome nature. He put a boy's eye out once, and never was heard upon any occasion to utter a regret for it. He did many such things. But at last he did something that was serious. He called at a house just after dark one evening, knocked, and when the occupant came to the door, shot him dead, and then tried to escape, but was captured. Two days before, he had wantonly insulted a helpless cripple, and the man he afterward took swift vengeance upon with an assassin bullet had knocked him down. Such was the Baldwin case. The trial was long and exciting; the community was fearfully wrought up. Men said this spiteful, bad-hearted villain had caused grief enough in his time, and now he should satisfy the law. But they were mistaken; Baldwin was insane when he did the deed—they had not thought of that. By the argument of counsel it was shown that at half past ten in the morning on the day of the murder, Baldwin became insane, and remained so for eleven hours and a half exactly. This just covered the case comfortably, and he was acquitted. Thus, if an unthinking and excited community had been listened to instead of the arguments of counsel, a poor crazy creature would have been held to a fearful responsibility for a mere freak of madness. Baldwin went clear, and although his relatives and friends were naturally incensed against the community for their injurious suspicions and remarks, they said let it go for this time, and did not prosecute. The Baldwins were very wealthy. This same Baldwin had momentary fits of insanity twice afterward, and on both occasions killed people he had grudges against. And on both these occasions the circumstances of the killing were so aggravated, and the murders so seemingly heartless and treacherous, that if Baldwin had not been insane he would have been hanged without the shadow of a doubt. As it was, it required all his political and family influence to get him clear in one of the cases, and cost him not less than ten thousand dollars to get clear in the other. One of these men he had notoriously been threatening to kill for twelve years. The poor creature happened, by the merest piece of ill fortune, to come along a dark alley at the very moment that Baldwin's insanity came upon him, and so he was shot in the back with a gun loaded with slugs.

Take the case of Lynch Hackett, of Pennsylvania. Twice, in public, he attacked a German butcher by the name of Bemis Feldner, with a cane, and both times Feldner whipped him with his fists. Hackett was a vain, wealthy, violent gentleman, who held his blood and family in high esteem, and believed that a reverent respect was due to his great riches. He brooded over the shame of his chastisement for two weeks, and then, in a momentary fit of insanity, armed himself to the teeth, rode into town, waited a couple of hours until he saw Feldner coming down the street with his wife on his arm, and then, as the couple passed the doorway in which he had partially concealed himself, he drove a knife into Feldner's neck, killing him instantly. The widow caught the limp form and eased it to the earth. Both were drenched with blood. Hackett jocosely remarked to her that as a professional butcher's recent wife she could appreciate the artistic neatness of the job that left her in condition to marry again, in case she wanted to. This remark, and another which he made to a friend, that his position in society made the killing of an obscure citizen simply an "eccentricity" instead of a crime, were shown to be evidences of insanity, and so Hackett escaped punishment. The jury were hardly inclined to accept these as proofs at first, inasmuch as the prisoner had never been insane before the murder, and under the tranquilizing effect of the butchering had immediately regained his right mind; but when the defense came to show that a third cousin of Hackett's wife's stepfather was insane, and not only insane, but had a nose the very counterpart of Hackett's, it was plain that insanity was hereditary in the family, and Hackett had come by it by legitimate inheritance.

Of course the jury then acquitted him. But it was a merciful providence that Mrs. H.'s people had been afflicted as shown, else Hackett would certainly have been hanged.

However, it is not possible to recount all the marvelous cases of insanity that have come under the public notice in the last thirty or forty years. There was the Durgin case in New Jersey three years ago. The servant girl, Bridget Durgin, at dead of night, invaded her mistress's bedroom and carved the lady literally to pieces with a knife. Then she dragged the body to the middle of the floor, and beat and banged it with chairs and such things. Next she opened the feather beds, and strewed the contents around, saturated everything with kerosene, and set fire to the general wreck. She now took up the young child of the murdered woman in her blood smeared hands and walked off, through the snow, with no shoes on, to a neighbor's house a quarter of a mile off, and told a string of wild, incoherent stories about some men coming and setting fire to the house; and then she cried piteously, and without seeming to think there was anything suggestive about the blood upon her hands, her clothing, and the baby, volunteered the remark that she was afraid those men had murdered her mistress! Afterward, by her own confession and other testimony, it was proved that the mistress had always been kind to the girl, consequently there was no revenge in the murder; and it was also shown that the girl took nothing away from the burning house, not even her own shoes, and consequently robbery was not the motive.

Now, the reader says, "Here comes that same old plea of insanity again." But the reader has deceived himself this time. No such plea was offered in her defense. The judge sentenced her, nobody persecuted the governor with petitions for her pardon, and she was promptly hanged.

There was that youth in Pennsylvania, whose curious confession was published some years ago. It was simply a conglomeration of incoherent drivel from beginning to end, and so was his lengthy speech on the scaffold afterward. For a whole year he was haunted with a desire to disfigure a certain young woman, so that no one would marry her. He did not love her himself, and did not want to marry her, but he did not want anybody else to do it. He would not go anywhere with her, and yet was opposed to anybody else's escorting her. Upon one occasion he declined to go to a wedding with her, and when she got other company, lay in wait for the couple by the road, intending to make them go back or kill the escort. After spending sleepless nights over his ruling desire for a full year, he at last attempted its execution—that is, attempted to disfigure the young woman. It was a success. It was permanent. In trying to shoot her cheek (as she sat at the supper-table with her parents and brothers and sisters) in such a manner as to mar its comeliness, one of his bullets wandered a little out of the course, and she dropped dead. To the very last moment of his life he bewailed the ill luck that made her move her face just at the critical moment. And so he died, apparently about half persuaded that somehow it was chiefly her own fault that she got killed. This idiot was hanged. The plea of insanity was not offered.

Insanity certainly is on the increase in the world, and crime is dying out. There are no longer any murders—none worth mentioning, at any rate. Formerly, if you killed a man, it was possible that you were insane—but now, if you, having friends and money, kill a man, it is evidence that you are a lunatic. In these days, too, if a person of good family and high social standing steals anything, they call it kleptomania, and send him to the lunatic asylum. If a person of high standing squanders his fortune in dissipation, and closes his career with strychnine or a bullet, "Temporary Aberration" is what was the trouble with him.

Is not this insanity plea becoming rather common? Is it not so common that the reader confidently expects to see it offered in every criminal case that comes before the courts? And is it not so cheap, and so common, and often so trivial, that the reader smiles in derision when the newspaper mentions it? And is it not curious to note how very often it wins acquittal for the prisoner? Of late years it does not seem possible for a man to so conduct himself, before killing another man, as not to be manifestly insane. If he talks about the stars, he is insane. If he appears nervous and uneasy an hour before the killing, he is insane. If he weeps over a great grief, his friends shake their heads, and fear that he is "not right." If, an hour after the murder, he seems ill at ease, preoccupied, and excited, he is, unquestionably insane.

Really, what we want now, is not laws against crime, but a law against insanity. There is where the true evil lies.

A CURIOUS DREAM [WRITTEN ABOUT 1870.]

CONTAINING A MORAL

Night before last I had a singular dream. I seemed to be sitting on a doorstep (in no particular city perhaps) ruminating, and the time of night appeared to be about twelve or one o'clock. The weather was balmy and delicious. There was no human sound in the air, not even a footstep. There was no sound of any kind to emphasize the dead stillness, except the occasional hollow barking of a dog in the distance and the fainter answer of a further dog. Presently up the street I heard a bony clack-clacking, and guessed it was the castanets of a serenading party. In a minute more a tall skeleton, hooded, and half clad in a tattered and moldy shroud, whose shreds were flapping about the ribby latticework of its person, swung by me with a stately stride and disappeared in the gray gloom of the starlight. It had a broken and worm-eaten coffin on its shoulder and a bundle of something in its hand. I knew what the clack-clacking was then; it was this party's joints working together, and his elbows knocking against his sides as he walked. I may say I was surprised. Before I could collect my thoughts and enter upon any speculations as to what this apparition might portend, I heard another one coming for I recognized his clack-clack. He had two-thirds of a coffin on his shoulder, and some foot and head boards under his arm. I mightily wanted to peer under his hood and speak to him, but when he turned and smiled upon me with his cavernous sockets and his projecting grin as he went by, I thought I would not detain him. He was hardly gone when I heard the clacking again, and another one issued from the shadowy half-light. This one was bending under a heavy gravestone, and dragging a shabby coffin after him by a string. When he got to me he gave me a steady look for a moment or two, and then rounded to and backed up to me, saying:

"Ease this down for a fellow, will you?"

I eased the gravestone down till it rested on the ground, and in doing so noticed that it bore the name of "John Baxter Copmanhurst," with "May, 1839," as the date of his death. Deceased sat wearily down by me, and wiped his os frontis with his major maxillary—chiefly from former habit I judged, for I could not see that he brought away any perspiration.

"It is too bad, too bad," said he, drawing the remnant of the shroud about him and leaning his jaw pensively on his hand. Then he put his left foot up on his knee and fell to scratching his anklebone absently with a rusty nail which he got out of his coffin.

"What is too bad, friend?"

"Oh, everything, everything. I almost wish I never had died."

"You surprise me. Why do you say this? Has anything gone wrong? What is the matter?"

"Matter! Look at this shroud-rags. Look at this gravestone, all battered up. Look at that disgraceful old coffin. All a man's property going to ruin and destruction before his eyes, and ask him if anything is wrong? Fire and brimstone!"

"Calm yourself, calm yourself," I said. "It is too bad—it is certainly too bad, but then I had not supposed that you would much mind such matters, situated as you are."

"Well, my dear sir, I do mind them. My pride is hurt, and my comfort is impaired—destroyed, I might say. I will state my case—I will put it to you in such a way that you can comprehend it, if you will let me," said the poor skeleton, tilting the hood of his shroud back, as if he were clearing for action, and thus unconsciously giving himself a jaunty and festive air very much at variance with the grave character of his position in life—so to speak—and in prominent contrast with his distressful mood.

"Proceed," said I.

"I reside in the shameful old graveyard a block or two above you here, in this street—there, now, I just expected that cartilage would let go!—third rib from the bottom, friend, hitch the end of it to my spine with a string, if you have got such a thing about you, though a bit of silver wire is a deal pleasanter, and more durable and becoming, if one keeps it polished—to think of shredding out and going to pieces in this way, just on account of the indifference and neglect of one's posterity!"—and the poor ghost grated his teeth in a way that gave me a wrench and a shiver—for the effect is mightily increased by the absence of muffling flesh and cuticle. "I reside in that old graveyard, and have for these thirty years; and I tell you things are changed since I first laid this old tired frame there, and turned over, and stretched out for a long sleep, with a delicious sense upon me of being done with bother, and grief, and anxiety, and doubt, and fear, forever and ever, and listening with comfortable and increasing satisfaction to the sexton's work, from the startling clatter of his first spadeful on my coffin till it dulled away to the faint patting that shaped the roof of my new home—delicious! My! I wish you could try it to-night!" and out of my reverie deceased fetched me a rattling slap with a bony hand.

"Yes, sir, thirty years ago I laid me down there, and was happy. For it was out in the country then—out in the breezy, flowery, grand old woods, and the lazy winds gossiped with the leaves, and the squirrels capered over us and around us, and the creeping things visited us, and the birds filled the tranquil solitude with music. Ah, it was worth ten years of a man's life to be dead then! Everything was pleasant. I was in a good neighborhood, for all the dead people that lived near me belonged to the best families in the city. Our posterity appeared to think the world of us. They kept our graves in the very best condition; the fences were always in faultless repair, head-boards were kept painted or whitewashed, and were replaced with new ones as soon as they began to look rusty or decayed; monuments were kept upright, railings intact and bright, the rose-bushes and shrubbery trimmed, trained, and free from blemish, the walks clean and smooth and graveled. But that day is gone by. Our descendants have forgotten us. My grandson lives in a stately house built with money made by these old hands of mine, and I sleep in a neglected grave with invading vermin that gnaw my shroud to build them nests withal! I and friends that lie with me founded and secured the prosperity of this fine city, and the stately bantling of our loves leaves us to rot in a dilapidated cemetery which neighbors curse and strangers scoff at. See the difference between the old time and this—for instance: Our graves are all caved in now; our head-boards have rotted away and tumbled down; our railings reel this way and that, with one foot in the air, after a fashion of unseemly levity; our monuments lean wearily, and our gravestones bow their heads discouraged; there be no adornments any more—no roses, nor shrubs, nor graveled walks, nor anything that is a comfort to the eye; and even the paintless old board fence that did make a show of holding us sacred from companionship with beasts and the defilement of heedless feet, has tottered till it overhangs the street, and only advertises the presence of our dismal resting-place and invites yet more derision to it. And now we cannot hide our poverty and tatters in the friendly woods, for the city has stretched its withering arms abroad and taken us in, and all that remains of the cheer of our old home is the cluster of lugubrious forest trees that stand, bored and weary of a city life, with their feet in our coffins, looking into the hazy distance and wishing they were there. I tell you it is disgraceful!

"You begin to comprehend—you begin to see how it is. While our descendants are living sumptuously on our money, right around us in the city, we have to fight hard to keep skull and bones together. Bless you, there isn't a grave in our cemetery that doesn't leak—not one. Every time it rains in the night we have to climb out and roost in the trees, and sometimes we are wakened suddenly by the chilly water trickling down the back of our necks. Then I tell you there is a general heaving up of old graves and kicking over of old monuments, and scampering of old skeletons for the trees! Bless me, if you had gone along there some such nights after twelve you might have seen as many as fifteen of us roosting on one limb, with our joints rattling drearily and the wind wheezing through our ribs! Many a time we have perched there for three or four dreary hours, and then come down, stiff and chilled through and drowsy, and borrowed each other's skulls to bail out our graves with—if you will glance up in my mouth now as I tilt my head back, you can see that my head-piece is half full of old dry sediment—how top-heavy and stupid it makes me sometimes! Yes, sir, many a time if you had happened to come along just before the dawn you'd have caught us bailing out the graves and hanging our shrouds on the fence to dry. Why, I had an elegant shroud stolen from there one morning—think a party by the name of Smith took it, that resides in a plebeian graveyard over yonder—I think so because the first time I ever saw him he hadn't anything on but a check shirt, and the last time I saw him, which was at a social gathering in the new cemetery, he was the best-dressed corpse in the company—and it is a significant fact that he left when he saw me; and presently an old woman from here missed her coffin— she generally took it with her when she went anywhere, because she was liable to take cold and bring on the spasmodic rheumatism that originally killed her if she exposed herself to the night air much. She was named Hotchkiss—Anna Matilda Hotchkiss—you might know her? She has two upper front teeth, is tall, but a good deal inclined to stoop, one rib on the left side gone, has one shred of rusty hair hanging from the left side of her head, and one little tuft just above and a little forward of her right ear, has her underjaw wired on one side where it had worked loose, small bone of left forearm gone—lost in a fight—has a kind of swagger in her gait and a 'gallus' way of going with her arms akimbo and her nostrils in the air—has been pretty free and easy, and is all damaged and battered up till she looks like a queensware crate in ruins—maybe you have met her?"

"God forbid!" I involuntarily ejaculated, for somehow I was not looking for that form of question, and it caught me a little off my guard. But I hastened to make amends for my rudeness, and say, "I simply meant I had not had the honor—for I would not deliberately speak discourteously of a friend of yours. You were saying that you were robbed—and it was a shame, too—but it appears by what is left of the shroud you have on that it was a costly one in its day. How did—"

A most ghastly expression began to develop among the decayed features and shriveled integuments of my guest's face, and I was beginning to grow uneasy and distressed, when he told me he was only working up a deep, sly smile, with a wink in it, to suggest that about the time he acquired his present garment a ghost in a neighboring cemetery missed one. This reassured me, but I begged him to confine himself to speech thenceforth, because his facial expression was uncertain. Even with the most elaborate care it was liable to miss fire. Smiling should especially be avoided. What he might honestly consider a shining success was likely to strike me in a very different light. I said I liked to see a skeleton cheerful, even decorously playful, but I did not think smiling was a skeleton's best hold.

"Yes, friend," said the poor skeleton, "the facts are just as I have given them to you. Two of these old graveyards—the one that I resided in and one further along—have been deliberately neglected by our descendants of to-day until there is no occupying them any longer. Aside from the osteological discomfort of it—and that is no light matter this rainy weather—the present state of things is ruinous to property. We have got to move or be content to see our effects wasted away and utterly destroyed.

"Now, you will hardly believe it, but it is true, nevertheless, that there isn't a single coffin in good repair among all my acquaintance—now that is an absolute fact. I do not refer to low people who come in a pine box mounted on an express-wagon, but I am talking about your high-toned, silver-mounted burial-case, your monumental sort, that travel under black plumes at the head of a procession and have choice of cemetery lots—I mean folks like the Jarvises, and the Bledsoes and Burlings, and such. They are all about ruined. The most substantial people in our set, they were. And now look at them— utterly used up and poverty-stricken. One of the Bledsoes actually traded his monument to a late barkeeper for some fresh shavings to put under his head. I tell you it speaks volumes, for there is nothing a corpse takes so much pride in as his monument. He loves to read the inscription. He comes after a while to believe what it says himself, and then you may see him sitting on the fence night after night enjoying it. Epitaphs are cheap, and they do a poor chap a world of good after he is dead, especially if he had hard luck while he was alive. I wish they were used more. Now I don't complain, but confidentially I do think it was a little shabby in my descendants to give me nothing but this old slab of a gravestone—and all the more that there isn't a compliment on it. It used to have:

GONE TO HIS JUST REWARD'

on it, and I was proud when I first saw it, but by and by I noticed that whenever an old friend of mine came along he would hook his chin on the railing and pull a long face and read along down till he came to that, and then he would chuckle to himself and walk off, looking satisfied and comfortable. So I scratched it off to get rid of those fools. But a dead man always takes a deal of pride in his monument. Yonder goes half a dozen of the Jarvises now, with the family monument along. And Smithers and some hired specters went by with his awhile ago. Hello, Higgins, good-by, old friend! That's Meredith Higgins—died in '44—belongs to our set in the cemetery—fine old family— great-grandmother was an Injun—I am on the most familiar terms with him—he didn't hear me was the reason he didn't answer me. And I am sorry, too, because I would have liked to introduce you. You would admire him. He is the most disjointed, sway-backed, and generally distorted old skeleton you ever saw, but he is full of fun. When he laughs it sounds like rasping two stones together, and he always starts it off with a cheery screech like raking a nail across a window-pane. Hey, Jones! That is old Columbus Jones—shroud cost four hundred dollars—entire trousseau, including monument, twenty-seven hundred. This was in the spring of '26. It was enormous style for those days. Dead people came all the way from the Alleghanies to see his things—the party that occupied the grave next to mine remembers it well. Now do you see that individual going along with a piece of a head-board under his arm, one leg-bone below his knee gone, and not a thing in the world on? That is Barstow Dalhousie, and next to Columbus Jones he was the most sumptuously outfitted person that ever entered our cemetery. We are all leaving. We cannot tolerate the treatment we are receiving at the hands of our descendants. They open new cemeteries, but they leave us to our ignominy. They mend the streets, but they never mend anything that is about us or belongs to us. Look at that coffin of mine—yet I tell you in its day it was a piece of furniture that would have attracted attention in any drawing-room in this city. You may have it if you want it—I can't afford to repair it. Put a new bottom in her, and part of a new top, and a bit of fresh lining along the left side, and you'll find her about as comfortable as any receptacle of her species you ever tried. No thanks—no, don't mention it— you have been civil to me, and I would give you all the property I have got before I would seem ungrateful. Now this winding-sheet is a kind of a sweet thing in its way, if you would like to—No? Well, just as you say, but I wished to be fair and liberal—there's nothing mean about me. Good-by, friend, I must be going. I may have a good way to go to-night—don't know. I only know one thing for certain, and that is that I am on the emigrant trail now, and I'll never sleep in that crazy old cemetery again. I will travel till I find respectable quarters, if I have to hoof it to New Jersey. All the boys are going. It was decided in public conclave, last night, to emigrate, and by the time the sun rises there won't be a bone left in our old habitations. Such cemeteries may suit my surviving friends, but they do not suit the remains that have the honor to make these remarks. My opinion is the general opinion. If you doubt it, go and see how the departing ghosts upset things before they started. They were almost riotous in their demonstrations of distaste. Hello, here are some of the Bledsoes, and if you will give me a lift with this tombstone I guess I will join company and jog along with them—mighty respectable old family, the Bledsoes, and used to always come out in six-horse hearses and all that sort of thing fifty years ago when I walked these streets in daylight. Good-by, friend."

And with his gravestone on his shoulder he joined the grisly procession, dragging his damaged coffin after him, for notwithstanding he pressed it upon me so earnestly, I utterly refused his hospitality. I suppose that for as much as two hours these sad outcasts went clacking by, laden with their dismal effects, and all that time I sat pitying them. One or two of the youngest and least dilapidated among them inquired about midnight trains on the railways, but the rest seemed unacquainted with that mode of travel, and merely asked about common public roads to various towns and cities, some of which are not on the map now, and vanished from it and from the earth as much as thirty years ago, and some few of them never had existed anywhere but on maps, and private ones in real-estate agencies at that. And they asked about the condition of the cemeteries in these towns and cities, and about the reputation the citizens bore as to reverence for the dead.

This whole matter interested me deeply, and likewise compelled my sympathy for these homeless ones. And it all seeming real, and I not knowing it was a dream, I mentioned to one shrouded wanderer an idea that had entered my head to publish an account of this curious and very sorrowful exodus, but said also that I could not describe it truthfully, and just as it occurred, without seeming to trifle with a grave subject and exhibit an irreverence for the dead that would shock and distress their surviving friends. But this bland and stately remnant of a former citizen leaned him far over my gate and whispered in my ear, and said:

"Do not let that disturb you. The community that can stand such graveyards as those we are emigrating from can stand anything a body can say about the neglected and forsaken dead that lie in them."

At that very moment a cock crowed, and the weird procession vanished and left not a shred or a bone behind. I awoke, and found myself lying with my head out of the bed and "sagging" downward considerably—a position favorable to dreaming dreams with morals in them, maybe, but not poetry.

NOTE.—The reader is assured that if the cemeteries in his town are kept in good order, this Dream is not leveled at his town at all, but is leveled particularly and venomously at the next town.

A TRUE STORY

REPEATED WORD FOR WORD AS I HEARD IT—[WRITTEN ABOUT 1876]

It was summer-time, and twilight. We were sitting on the porch of the farmhouse, on the summit of the hill, and "Aunt Rachel" was sitting respectfully below our level, on the steps—for she was our Servant, and colored. She was of mighty frame and stature; she was sixty years old, but her eye was undimmed and her strength unabated. She was a cheerful, hearty soul, and it was no more trouble for her to laugh than it is for a bird to sing. She was under fire now, as usual when the day was done. That is to say, she was being chaffed without mercy, and was enjoying it. She would let off peal after peal of laughter, and then sit with her face in her hands and shake with throes of enjoyment which she could no longer get breath enough to express. At such a moment as this a thought occurred to me, and I said:

"Aunt Rachel, how is it that you've lived sixty years and never had any trouble?"

She stopped quaking. She paused, and there was moment of silence. She turned her face over her shoulder toward me, and said, without even a smile her voice:

"Misto C——, is you in 'arnest?"

It surprised me a good deal; and it sobered my manner and my speech, too. I said:

"Why, I thought—that is, I meant—why, you can't have had any trouble. I've never heard you sigh, and never seen your eye when there wasn't a laugh in it."

She faced fairly around now, and was full earnestness.

"Has I had any trouble? Misto C——, I's gwyne to tell you, den I leave it to you. I was bawn down 'mongst de slaves; I knows all 'bout slavery, 'case I ben one of 'em my own se'f. Well sah, my ole man—dat's my husban'—he was lovin' an' kind to me, jist as kind as you is to yo' own wife. An' we had chil'en—seven chil'en—an' we loved dem chil'en jist de same as you loves yo' chil'en. Dey was black, but de Lord can't make chil'en so black but what dey mother loves 'em an' wouldn't give 'em up, no, not for anything dat's in dis whole world.

"Well, sah, I was raised in ole Fo'ginny, but my mother she was raised in Maryland; an' my souls she was turrible when she'd git started! My lan! but she'd make de fur fly! When she'd git into dem tantrums, she always had one word dat she said. She'd straighten herse'f up an' put her fists in her hips an' say, 'I want you to understan' dat I wa'n't bawn in the mash to be fool' by trash! I's one o' de ole Blue Hen's Chickens, I is!' Ca'se you see, dat's what folks dat's bawn in Maryland calls deyselves, an' dey's proud of it. Well, dat was her word. I don't ever forgit it, beca'se she said it so much, an' beca'se she said it one day when my little Henry tore his wris' awful, and most busted 'is head, right up at de top of his forehead, an' de niggers didn't fly aroun' fas' enough to tend to him. An' when dey talk' back at her, she up an' she says, Look-a-heah!' she says, 'I want you niggers to understan' dat I wa'n't bawn in de mash be fool' by trash! I's one o' de ole Blue Hen's chickens, I is!' an' den she clar' dat kitchen an' bandage' up de chile herse'f. So I says dat word, too, when I's riled.

"Well, bymeby my ole mistis say she's broke, an' she got to sell all de niggers on de place. An' when I heah dat dey gwyne to sell us all off at oction in Richmon', oh, de good gracious! I know what dat mean!"

Aunt Rachel had gradually risen, while she warmed to her subject, and now she towered above us, black against the stars.

"Dey put chains on us an' put us on a stan' as high as dis po'ch—twenty foot high—an' all de people stood aroun', crowds an' crowds. An' dey'd come up dah an' look at us all roun', an' squeeze our arm, an' make us git up an' walk, an' den say, Dis one too ole,' or 'Dis one lame,' or Dis one don't 'mount to much.' An' dey sole my ole man, an' took him away, an' dey begin to sell my chil'en an' take dem away, an' I begin to cry; an' de man say, 'Shet up yo' damn blubberin',' an' hit me on de mouf wid his han'. An' when de las' one was gone but my little Henry, I grab' him clost up to my breas' so, an' I ris up an' says, 'You sha'nt take him away,' I says; 'I'll kill de man dat tetches him!' I says. But my little Henry whisper an' say 'I gwyne to run away, an' den I work an' buy yo' freedom.' Oh, bless de chile, he always so good! But dey got him—dey got him, de men did; but I took and tear de clo'es mos' off of 'em an' beat 'em over de head wid my chain; an' dey give it to me too, but I didn't mine dat.

"Well, dah was my ole man gone, an' all my chil'en, all my seven chil'en—an' six of 'em I hain't set eyes on ag'in to dis day, an' dat's twenty-two year ago las' Easter. De man dat bought me b'long' in Newbern, an' he took me dah. Well, bymeby de years roll on an' de waw come. My marster he was a Confedrit colonel, an' I was his family's cook. So when de Unions took dat town, dey all run away an' lef' me all by myse'f wid de other niggers in dat mons'us big house. So de big Union officers move in dah, an' dey ask me would I cook for dem. 'Lord bless you,' says I, 'dat what I's for.'

"Dey wa'n't no small-fry officers, mine you, dey was de biggest dey is; an' de way dey made dem sojers mosey roun'! De Gen'l he tole me to boss dat kitchen; an' he say, 'If anybody come meddlin' wid you, you jist make em walk chalk; don't you be afeared,' he say; 'you's 'mong frens now.'

"Well, I thinks to myse'f, if my little Henry ever got a chance to run away, he'd make to de Norf, o' course. So one day I comes in dah whar de big officers was, in de parlor, an' I drops a kurtchy, so, an' I up an' tole 'em 'bout my Henry, dey a-listenin' to my troubles jist de same as if I was white folks; an' I says, 'What I come for is beca'se if he got away and got up Norf whar you gemmen comes from, you might 'a' seen him, maybe, an' could tell me so as I could fine him ag'in; he was very little, an' he had a sk-yar on his lef' wris' an' at de top of his forehead.' Den dey look mournful, an' de Gen'l says, 'How long sence you los' him?' an' I say, 'Thirteen year.' Den de Gen'l say, 'He wouldn't be little no mo' now—he's a man!'

"I never thought o' dat befo'! He was only dat little feller to me yit. I never thought 'bout him growin' up an' bein' big. But I see it den. None o' de gemmen had run acrost him, so dey couldn't do nothin' for me. But all dat time, do' I didn't know it, my Henry was run off to de Norf, years an' years, an' he was a barber, too, an' worked for hisse'f. An' bymeby, when de waw come he ups an' he says: 'I's done barberin',' he says, 'I's gwyne to fine my ole mammy, less'n she's dead.' So he sole out an' went to whar dey was recruitin', an' hired hisse'f out to de colonel for his servant; an' den he went all froo de battles everywhah, huntin' for his ole mammy; yes, indeedy, he'd hire to fust one officer an' den another, tell he'd ransacked de whole Souf; but you see I didn't know *nuffin* bout dis. How was *I* gwyne to know it?

"Well, one night we had a big sojer ball; de sojers dah at Newbern was always havin' balls an' carryin' on. Dey had 'em in my kitchen, heaps o' times, 'ca'se it was so big. Mine you, I was down on sich doin's; beca'se my place was wid de officers, an' it rasp me to have dem common sojers cavortin' roun' in my kitchen like dat. But I alway' stood aroun' an kep' things straight, I did; an' sometimes dey'd git my dander up, an' den I'd make 'em clar dat kitchen, mine I TELL you!

"Well, one night—it was a Friday night—dey comes a whole platoon f'm a nigger ridgment da was on guard at de house—de house was head quarters, you know-an' den I was jist a-bilin' mad? I was jist a-boomin'! I swelled aroun', an swelled aroun'; I jist was a-itchin' for em to do somefin for to start me. An' dey was a-waltzin' an a dancin'! my but dey was havin' a time! an I jist a-swellin' an' a-swellin' up! Pooty soon, 'long comes sich a spruce young nigger a-sailin' down de room wid a yaller wench roun' de wais'; an' roun' an' roun' an roun' dey went, enough to make a body drunk to look at 'em; an' when dey got abreas' o' me, dey went to kin' o' balancin' aroun' fust on one leg an' den on t'other, an' smilin' at my big red turban, an' makin' fun, an' I ups an' says 'Git along wid you!—rubbage!'

De young man's face kin' o' changed, all of a sudden, for 'bout a second, but den he went to smilin' ag'in, same as he was befo'. Well, 'bout dis time, in comes some niggers dat played music and b'long' to de ban', an' dey never could git along widout puttin' on airs. An' de very fust air dey put on dat night, I lit into em! Dey laughed, an' dat made me wuss. De res' o' de niggers got to laughin', an' den my soul alive but I was hot! My eye was jist a-blazin'! I jist straightened myself up so—jist as I is now, plum to de ceilin', mos'—an' I digs my fists into my hips, an' I says, 'Look-a-heah!' I says, 'I want you niggers to understan' dat I wa'n't bawn in de mash to be fool' by trash! I's one o' de ole Blue hen's Chickens, I is!'—an' den I see dat young man stan' a-starin' an' stiff, lookin' kin' o' up at de ceilin' like he fo'got somefin, an' couldn't 'member it no mo'. Well, I jist march' on dem niggers—so, lookin' like a gen'l—an' dey jist cave' away befo' me an' out at de do'. An' as dis young man a-goin' out, I heah him say to another nigger, Jim,' he says, 'you go 'long an' tell de cap'n I be on han' 'bout eight o'clock in de mawnin'; dey's somefin on my mine,' he says; 'I don't sleep no mo' dis night. You go 'long,' he says, 'an' leave me by my own se'f.'

"Dis was 'bout one o'clock in de mawnin'. Well, 'bout seven, I was up an' on han', gittin' de officers' breakfast. I was a-stoopin' down by de stove—jist so, same as if yo' foot was de stove—an' I'd opened de stove do' wid my right han'—so, pushin' it back, jist as I pushes yo' foot—an' I'd jist got de pan o' hot biscuits in my han' an' was 'bout to raise up, when I see a black face come aroun' under mine, an' de eyes a-lookin' up into mine, jist as I's a-lookin' up clost under yo' face now; an' I jist stopped right dah, an' never budged! jist gazed an' gazed so; an' de pan begin to tremble, an' all of a sudden I knowed! De pan drop' on de flo' an' I grab his lef' han' an' shove back his sleeve—jist so, as I's doin' to you—an' den I goes for his forehead an' push de hair back so, an' 'Boy!' I says, 'if you an't my Henry, what is you doin' wid dis welt on yo' wris' an' dat sk-yar on yo' forehead? De Lord God ob heaven be praise', I got my own ag'in!'

"Oh no' Misto C———, I hain't had no trouble. An' no joy!"

THE SIAMESE TWINS

[Written about 1868.]

I do not wish to write of the personal habits of these strange creatures solely, but also of certain curious details of various kinds concerning them, which, belonging only to their private life, have never crept into print. Knowing the Twins intimately, I feel that I am peculiarly well qualified for the task I have taken upon myself.

The Siamese Twins are naturally tender and affectionate in disposition, and have clung to each other with singular fidelity throughout a long and eventful life. Even as children they were inseparable companions; and it was noticed that they always seemed to prefer each other's society to that of any other persons. They nearly always played together; and, so accustomed was their mother to this peculiarity, that, whenever both of them chanced to be lost, she usually only hunted for one of them—satisfied that when she found that one she would find his brother somewhere in the immediate neighborhood. And yet these creatures were ignorant and unlettered—barbarians themselves and the offspring of barbarians, who knew not the light of philosophy and science. What a withering rebuke is this to our boasted civilization, with its quarrelings, its wranglings, and its separations of brothers!

As men, the Twins have not always lived in perfect accord; but still there has always been a bond between them which made them unwilling to go away from each other and dwell apart. They have even occupied the same house, as a general thing, and it is believed that they have never failed to even sleep together on any night since they were born. How surely do the habits of a lifetime become second nature to us! The Twins always go to bed at the same time; but Chang usually gets up about an hour before his brother. By an understanding between themselves, Chang does all the indoor work and Eng runs all the errands. This is because Eng likes to go out; Chang's habits are sedentary. However, Chang always goes along. Eng is a Baptist, but Chang is a Roman Catholic; still, to please his brother, Chang consented to be baptized at the same time that Eng was, on condition that it should not "count." During the war they were strong partisans, and both fought gallantly all through the great struggle—Eng on the Union side and Chang on the Confederate. They took each other prisoners at Seven Oaks, but the proofs of capture were so evenly balanced in favor of each, that a general army court had to be assembled to determine which one was properly the captor and which the captive. The jury was unable to agree for a long time; but the vexed question was finally decided by agreeing to consider them both prisoners, and then exchanging them. At one time Chang was convicted of disobedience of orders, and sentenced to ten days in the guard-house, but Eng, in spite of all arguments, felt obliged to share his imprisonment, notwithstanding he himself was entirely innocent; and so, to save the blameless brother from suffering, they had to discharge both from custody—the just reward of faithfulness.

Upon one occasion the brothers fell out about something, and Chang knocked Eng down, and then tripped and fell on him, whereupon both clinched and began to beat and gouge each other without mercy. The bystanders interfered, and tried to separate them, but they could not do it, and so allowed them to fight it out. In the end both were disabled, and were carried to the hospital on one and the same shutter.

Their ancient habit of going always together had its drawbacks when they reached man's estate, and entered upon the luxury of courting. Both fell in love with the same girl. Each tried to steal clandestine interviews with her, but at the critical moment the other would always turn up. By and by Eng saw, with distraction, that Chang had won the girl's affections; and, from that day forth, he had to bear with the agony of being a witness to all their dainty billing and cooing. But with a magnanimity that did him infinite credit, he succumbed to his fate, and gave countenance and encouragement to a state of things that bade fair to sunder his generous heart-strings. He sat from seven every evening until two in the morning, listening to the fond foolishness of the two lovers, and to the concussion of hundreds of squandered kisses—for the privilege of sharing only one of which he would have given his right hand. But he sat patiently, and waited, and gaped, and yawned, and stretched, and longed for two o'clock to come. And he took long walks with the lovers on moonlight evenings—sometimes traversing ten miles, notwithstanding he was usually suffering from rheumatism. He is an inveterate smoker; but he could not smoke on these occasions, because the young lady was painfully sensitive to the smell of tobacco. Eng cordially wanted them married, and done with it; but although Chang often asked the momentous question, the young lady could not gather sufficient courage to answer it while Eng was by. However, on one occasion, after having walked some sixteen miles, and sat up till nearly daylight, Eng dropped asleep, from sheer exhaustion, and then the question was asked and answered. The lovers were married. All acquainted with the circumstance applauded the noble brother-in-law. His unwavering faithfulness was the theme of every tongue. He had stayed by them all through their long and arduous courtship; and when at last they were married, he lifted his hands above their heads, and said with impressive unction, "Bless ye, my children, I will never desert ye!" and he kept his word. Fidelity like this is all too rare in this cold world.

By and by Eng fell in love with his sister-in-law's sister, and married her, and since that day they have all lived together, night and day, in an exceeding sociability which is touching and beautiful to behold, and is a scathing rebuke to our boasted civilization.

The sympathy existing between these two brothers is so close and so refined that the feelings, the impulses, the emotions of the one are instantly experienced by the other. When one is sick, the other is sick; when one feels pain, the other feels it; when one is angered, the other's temper takes fire. We have already seen with what happy facility they both fell in love with the same girl. Now Chang is bitterly opposed to all forms of intemperance, on principle; but Eng is the reverse—for, while these men's feelings and emotions are so closely wedded, their reasoning faculties are unfettered; their thoughts are free. Chang belongs to the Good Templars, and is a hard-working, enthusiastic supporter of all temperance reforms. But, to his bitter distress, every now and then Eng gets drunk, and, of course, that makes Chang drunk too. This unfortunate thing has been a great sorrow to Chang, for it almost destroys his usefulness in his favorite field of effort. As sure as he is to head a great temperance procession Eng ranges up alongside of him, prompt to the minute, and drunk as a lord; but yet no more dismally and hopelessly drunk than his brother, who has not tasted a drop. And so the two begin to hoot and yell, and throw mud and bricks at the Good Templars; and, of course, they break up the procession. It would be manifestly wrong to punish Chang for what Eng does, and, therefore, the Good Templars accept the untoward situation, and suffer in silence and sorrow. They have officially and deliberately examined into the matter, and find Chang blameless. They have taken the two brothers and filled Chang full of warm water and sugar and Eng full of whisky, and in twenty-five minutes it was not possible to tell which was the drunkest. Both were as drunk as loons—and on hot whisky punches, by the smell of their breath. Yet all the while Chang's moral principles were unsullied, his conscience clear; and so all just men were forced to confess that he was not morally, but only physically, drunk. By every right and by every moral evidence the man was strictly sober; and, therefore, it caused his friends all the more anguish to see him shake hands with the pump and try to wind his watch with his night-key.

There is a moral in these solemn warnings—or, at least, a warning in these solemn morals; one or the other. No matter, it is somehow. Let us heed it; let us profit by it.

I could say more of an instructive nature about these interesting beings, but let what I have written suffice.

Having forgotten to mention it sooner, I will remark in conclusion that the ages of the Siamese Twins are respectively fifty-one and fifty-three years.

SPEECH AT THE SCOTTISH BANQUET IN LONDON

[Written about 1872.]

At the anniversary festival of the Scottish Corporation of London on Monday evening, in response to the toast of "The Ladies," MARK TWAIN replied. The following is his speech as reported in the London Observer:

I am proud, indeed, of the distinction of being chosen to respond to this especial toast, to 'The Ladies,' or to women if you please, for that is the preferable term, perhaps; it is certainly the older, and therefore the more entitled to reverence [Laughter.] I have noticed that the Bible, with that plain, blunt honesty which is such a conspicuous characteristic of the Scriptures, is always particular to never refer to even the illustrious mother of all mankind herself as a 'lady,' but speaks of her as a woman. [Laughter.] It is odd, but you will find it is so. I am peculiarly proud of this honor, because I think that the toast to women is one which, by right and by every rule of gallantry, should take precedence of all others—of the army, of the navy, of even royalty itself—perhaps, though the latter is not necessary in this day and in this land, for the reason that, tacitly, you do drink a broad general health to all good women when you drink the health of the Queen of England and the Princess of Wales. [Loud cheers.] I have in mind a poem just now which is familiar to you all, familiar to everybody. And what an inspiration that was (and how instantly the present toast recalls the verses to all our minds) when the most noble, the most gracious, the purest, and sweetest of all poets says:

"Woman! O woman!—er— Wom—"

[Laughter.] However, you remember the lines; and you remember how feelingly, how daintily, how almost imperceptibly the verses raise up before you, feature by feature, the ideal of a true and perfect woman; and how, as you contemplate the finished marvel, your homage grows into worship of the intellect that could create so fair a thing out of mere breath, mere words. And you call to mind now, as I speak, how the poet, with stern fidelity to the history of all humanity, delivers this beautiful child of his heart and his brain over to the trials and sorrows that must come to all, sooner or later, that abide in the earth, and how the pathetic story culminates in that apostrophe—so wild, so regretful, so full of mournful retrospection. The lines run thus:

"Alas!—alas!—a—alas! ——Alas!————alas!"

—and so on. [Laughter.] I do not remember the rest; but, taken together, it seems to me that poem is the noblest tribute to woman that human genius has ever brought forth—[laughter]—and I feel that if I were to talk hours I could not do my great theme completer or more graceful justice than I have now done in simply quoting that poet's matchless words. [Renewed laughter.] The phases of the womanly nature are infinite in their variety. Take any type of woman, and you shall find in it something to respect, something to admire, something to love. And you shall find the whole joining you heart and hand. Who was more patriotic than Joan of Arc? Who was braver? Who has given us a grander instance of self-sacrificing devotion? Ah! you remember, you remember well, what a throb of pain, what a great tidal wave of grief swept over us all when Joan of Arc fell at Waterloo. [Much laughter.] Who does not sorrow for the loss of Sappho, the sweet singer of Israel? [Laughter.] Who among us does not miss the gentle ministrations, the softening influences, the humble piety of Lucretia Borgia? [Laughter.] Who can join in the heartless libel that says woman is extravagant in dress when he can look back and call to mind our simple and lowly mother Eve arrayed in her modification of the Highland costume. [Roars of laughter.] Sir, women have been soldiers, women have been painters, women have been poets. As long as language lives the name of Cleopatra will live.

And, not because she conquered George III.—[laughter]—but because she wrote those divine lines:

"Let dogs delight to bark and bite, For God hath made them so."

[More laughter.] The story of the world is adorned with the names of illustrious ones of our own sex—some of them sons of St. Andrew, too—Scott, Bruce, Burns, the warrior Wallace, Ben Nevis—[laughter]—the gifted Ben Lomond, and the great new Scotchman, Ben Disraeli.* [Great laughter.] Out of the great plains of history tower whole mountain ranges of sublime women—the Queen of Sheba, Josephine, Semiramis, Sairey Gamp; the list is endless—[laughter]—but I will not call the mighty roll, the names rise up in your own memories at the mere suggestion, luminous with the glory of deeds that cannot die, hallowed by the loving worship of the good and the true of all epochs and all climes. [Cheers.] Suffice it for our pride and our honor that we in our day have added to it such names as those of Grace Darling and Florence Nightingale. [Cheers.] Woman is all that she should be—gentle, patient, long suffering, trustful, unselfish, full of generous impulses. It is her blessed mission to comfort the sorrowing, plead for the erring, encourage the faint of purpose, succor the distressed, uplift the fallen, befriend the friendless—in a word, afford the healing of her sympathies and a home in her heart for all the bruised and persecuted children of misfortune that knock at its hospitable door. [Cheers.] And when I say, God bless her, there is none among us who has known the ennobling affection of a wife, or the steadfast devotion of a mother, but in his heart will say, Amen! [Loud and prolonged cheering.]

—[* Mr. Benjamin Disraeli, at that time Prime Minister of England, had just been elected Lord Rector of Glasgow University, and had made a speech which gave rise to a world of discussion.]

A GHOST STORY

I took a large room, far up Broadway, in a huge old building whose upper stories had been wholly unoccupied for years until I came. The place had long been given up to dust and cobwebs, to solitude and silence. I seemed groping among the tombs and invading the privacy of the dead, that first night I climbed up to my quarters. For the first time in my life a superstitious dread came over me; and as I turned a dark angle of the stairway and an invisible cobweb swung its slazy woof in my face and clung there, I shuddered as one who had encountered a phantom.

I was glad enough when I reached my room and locked out the mold and the darkness. A cheery fire was burning in the grate, and I sat down before it with a comforting sense of relief. For two hours I sat there, thinking of bygone times; recalling old scenes, and summoning half-forgotten faces out of the mists of the past; listening, in fancy, to voices that long ago grew silent for all time, and to once familiar songs that nobody sings now. And as my reverie softened down to a sadder and sadder pathos, the shrieking of the winds outside softened to a wail, the angry beating of the rain against the panes diminished to a tranquil patter, and one by one the noises in the street subsided, until the hurrying footsteps of the last belated straggler died away in the distance and left no sound behind.

The fire had burned low. A sense of loneliness crept over me. I arose and undressed, moving on tiptoe about the room, doing stealthily what I had to do, as if I were environed by sleeping enemies whose slumbers it would be fatal to break. I covered up in bed, and lay listening to the rain and wind and the faint creaking of distant shutters, till they lulled me to sleep.

I slept profoundly, but how long I do not know. All at once I found myself awake, and filled with a shuddering expectancy. All was still. All but my own heart—I could hear it beat. Presently the bedclothes began to slip away slowly toward the foot of the bed, as if some one were pulling them! I could not stir; I could not speak. Still the blankets slipped deliberately away, till my breast was uncovered. Then with a great effort I seized them and drew them over my head. I waited, listened, waited. Once more that steady pull began, and once more I lay torpid a century of dragging seconds till my breast was naked again. At last I roused my energies and snatched the covers back to their place and held them with a strong grip. I waited. By and by I felt a faint tug, and took a fresh grip. The tug strengthened to a steady strain—it grew stronger and stronger. My hold parted, and for the third time the blankets slid away. I groaned. An answering groan came from the foot of the bed! Beaded drops of sweat stood upon my forehead. I was more dead than alive. Presently I heard a heavy footstep in my room—the step of an elephant, it seemed to me—it was not like anything human. But it was moving from me—there was relief in that. I heard it approach the door—pass out without moving bolt or lock—and wander away among the dismal corridors, straining the floors and joists till they creaked again as it passed—and then silence reigned once more.

When my excitement had calmed, I said to myself, "This is a dream—simply a hideous dream." And so I lay thinking it over until I convinced myself that it was a dream, and then a comforting laugh relaxed my lips and I was happy again. I got up and struck a light; and when I found that the locks and bolts were just as I had left them, another soothing laugh welled in my heart and rippled from my lips. I took my pipe and lit it, and was just sitting down before the fire, when—down went the pipe out of my nerveless fingers, the blood forsook my cheeks, and my placid breathing was cut short with a gasp! In the ashes on the hearth, side by side with my own bare footprint, was another, so vast that in comparison mine was but an infant's! Then I had had a visitor, and the elephant tread was explained.

I put out the light and returned to bed, palsied with fear. I lay a long time, peering into the darkness, and listening.—Then I heard a grating noise overhead, like the dragging of a heavy body across the floor; then the throwing down of the body, and the shaking of my windows in response to the concussion. In distant parts of the building I heard the muffled slamming of doors. I heard, at intervals, stealthy footsteps creeping in and out among the corridors, and up and down the stairs. Sometimes these noises approached my door, hesitated, and went away again. I heard the clanking of chains faintly, in remote passages, and listened while the clanking grew nearer—while it wearily climbed the stairways, marking each move by the loose surplus of chain that fell with an accented rattle upon each succeeding step as the goblin that bore it advanced. I heard muttered sentences; half-uttered screams that seemed smothered violently; and the swish of invisible garments, the rush of invisible wings. Then I became conscious that my chamber was invaded—that I was not alone. I heard sighs and breathings about my bed, and mysterious whisperings. Three little spheres of soft phosphorescent light appeared on the ceiling directly over my head, clung and glowed there a moment, and then dropped—two of them upon my face and one upon the pillow. They spattered, liquidly, and felt warm. Intuition told me they had turned to gouts of blood as they fell—I needed no light to satisfy myself of that. Then I saw pallid faces, dimly luminous, and white uplifted hands, floating bodiless in the air—floating a moment and then disappearing. The whispering ceased, and the voices and the sounds, and a solemn stillness followed. I waited and listened. I felt that I must have light or die. I was weak with fear. I slowly raised myself toward a sitting posture, and my face came in contact with a clammy hand! All strength went from me apparently, and I fell back like a stricken invalid. Then I heard the rustle of a garment—it seemed to pass to the door and go out.

When everything was still once more, I crept out of bed, sick and feeble, and lit the gas with a hand that trembled as if it were aged with a hundred years. The light brought some little cheer to my spirits. I sat down and fell into a dreamy contemplation of that great footprint in the ashes. By and by its outlines began to waver and grow dim. I glanced up and the broad gas-flame was slowly wilting away. In the same moment I heard that elephantine tread again. I noted its approach, nearer and nearer, along the musty halls, and dimmer and dimmer the light waned. The tread reached my very door and paused—the light had dwindled to a sickly blue, and all things about me lay in a spectral twilight. The door did not open, and yet I felt a faint gust of air fan my cheek, and presently was conscious of a huge, cloudy presence before me. I watched it with fascinated eyes. A pale glow stole over the Thing; gradually its cloudy folds took shape—an arm appeared, then legs, then a body, and last a great sad face looked out of the vapor. Stripped of its filmy housings, naked, muscular and comely, the majestic Cardiff Giant loomed above me!

All my misery vanished—for a child might know that no harm could come with that benignant countenance. My cheerful spirits returned at once, and in sympathy with them the gas flamed up brightly again. Never a lonely outcast was so glad to welcome company as I was to greet the friendly giant. I said:

"Why, is it nobody but you? Do you know, I have been scared to death for the last two or three hours? I am most honestly glad to see you. I wish I had a chair—Here, here, don't try to sit down in that thing—"

But it was too late. He was in it before I could stop him and down he went—I never saw a chair shivered so in my life.

"Stop, stop, you'll ruin ev—"

Too late again. There was another crash, and another chair was resolved into its original elements.

"Confound it, haven't you got any judgment at all? Do you want to ruin all the furniture on the place? Here, here, you petrified fool—"

But it was no use. Before I could arrest him he had sat down on the bed, and it was a melancholy ruin.

"Now what sort of a way is that to do? First you come lumbering about the place bringing a legion of vagabond goblins along with you to worry me to death, and then when I overlook an indelicacy of costume which would not be tolerated anywhere by cultivated people except in a respectable theater, and not even there if the nudity were of your sex, you repay me by wrecking all the furniture you can find to sit down on. And why will you? You damage yourself as much as you do me. You have broken off the end of your spinal column, and littered up the floor with chips of your hams till the place looks like a marble yard. You ought to be ashamed of yourself—you are big enough to know better."

"Well, I will not break any more furniture. But what am I to do? I have not had a chance to sit down for a century." And the tears came into his eyes.

"Poor devil," I said, "I should not have been so harsh with you. And you are an orphan, too, no doubt. But sit down on the floor here—nothing else can stand your weight—and besides, we cannot be sociable with you away up there above me; I want you down where I can perch on this high counting-house stool and gossip with you face to face."

So he sat down on the floor, and lit a pipe which I gave him, threw one of my red blankets over his shoulders, inverted my sitz-bath on his head, helmet fashion, and made himself picturesque and comfortable. Then he crossed his ankles, while I renewed the fire, and exposed the flat, honeycombed bottoms of his prodigious feet to the grateful warmth.

"What is the matter with the bottom of your feet and the back of your legs, that they are gouged up so?"

"Infernal chilblains—I caught them clear up to the back of my head, roosting out there under Newell's farm. But I love the place; I love it as one loves his old home. There is no peace for me like the peace I feel when I am there."

We talked along for half an hour, and then I noticed that he looked tired, and spoke of it.

"Tired?" he said. "Well, I should think so. And now I will tell you all about it, since you have treated me so well. I am the spirit of the Petrified Man that lies across the street there in the museum. I am the ghost of the Cardiff Giant. I can have no rest, no peace, till they have given that poor body burial again. Now what was the most natural thing for me to do, to make men satisfy this wish? Terrify them into it!— haunt the place where the body lay! So I haunted the museum night after night. I even got other spirits to help me. But it did no good, for nobody ever came to the museum at midnight. Then it occurred to me to come over the way and haunt this place a little. I felt that if I ever got a hearing I must succeed, for I had the most efficient company that perdition could furnish. Night after night we have shivered around through these mildewed halls, dragging chains, groaning, whispering, tramping up and down stairs, till, to tell you the truth, I am almost worn out. But when I saw a light in your room to-night I roused my energies again and went at it with a deal of the old freshness. But I am tired out—entirely fagged out. Give me, I beseech you, give me some hope!"

I lit off my perch in a burst of excitement, and exclaimed:

"This transcends everything! everything that ever did occur! Why you poor blundering old fossil, you have had all your trouble for nothing—you have been haunting a plaster cast of yourself—the real Cardiff Giant is in Albany!—[A fact. The original fraud was ingeniously and fraudfully duplicated, and exhibited in New York as the "only genuine" Cardiff Giant (to the unspeakable disgust of the owners of the real colossus) at the very same time that the latter was drawing crowds at a museum in Albany,]—Confound it, don't you know your own remains?"

I never saw such an eloquent look of shame, of pitiable humiliation, overspread a countenance before.

The Petrified Man rose slowly to his feet, and said:

"Honestly, is that true?"

"As true as I am sitting here."

He took the pipe from his mouth and laid it on the mantel, then stood irresolute a moment (unconsciously, from old habit, thrusting his hands where his pantaloons pockets should have been, and meditatively dropping his chin on his breast) and finally said:

"Well—I never felt so absurd before. The Petrified Man has sold everybody else, and now the mean fraud has ended by selling its own ghost! My son, if there is any charity left in your heart for a poor friendless phantom like me, don't let this get out. Think how you would feel if you had made such an ass of yourself."

I heard his stately tramp die away, step by step down the stairs and out into the deserted street, and felt sorry that he was gone, poor fellow—and sorrier still that he had carried off my red blanket and my bath-tub.

THE CAPITOLINE VENUS

CHAPTER I.

[Scene-An Artist's Studio in Rome.]

"Oh, George, I do love you!"

"Bless your dear heart, Mary, I know that—why is your father so obdurate?"

"George, he means well, but art is folly to him—he only understands groceries. He thinks you would starve me."

"Confound his wisdom—it savors of inspiration. Why am I not a money-making bowelless grocer, instead of a divinely gifted sculptor with nothing to eat?"

"Do not despond, Georgy, dear—all his prejudices will fade away as soon as you shall have acquired fifty thousand dol—"

"Fifty thousand demons! Child, I am in arrears for my board!"

CHAPTER II.

 [Scene-A Dwelling in Rome.]

"My dear sir, it is useless to talk. I haven't anything against you, but I can't let my daughter marry a hash of love, art, and starvation—I believe you have nothing else to offer."

"Sir, I am poor, I grant you. But is fame nothing? The Hon. Bellamy Foodle of Arkansas says that my new statue of America is a clever piece of sculpture, and he is satisfied that my name will one day be famous."

"Bosh! What does that Arkansas ass know about it? Fame's nothing—the market price of your marble scarecrow is the thing to look at. It took you six months to chisel it, and you can't sell it for a hundred dollars. No, sir! Show me fifty thousand dollars and you can have my daughter—otherwise she marries young Simper. You have just six months to raise the money in. Good morning, sir."

"Alas! Woe is me!"

CHAPTER III.

[Scene-The Studio.]

"Oh, John, friend of my boyhood, I am the unhappiest of men."

"You're a simpleton!"

"I have nothing left to love but my poor statue of America—and see, even she has no sympathy for me in her cold marble countenance—so beautiful and so heartless!"

"You're a dummy!"

"Oh, John!"

"Oh, fudge! Didn't you say you had six months to raise the money in?"

"Don't deride my agony, John. If I had six centuries what good would it do? How could it help a poor wretch without name, capital, or friends?"

"Idiot! Coward! Baby! Six months to raise the money in—and five will do!"

"Are you insane?"

"Six months—an abundance. Leave it to me. I'll raise it."

"What do you mean, John? How on earth can you raise such a monstrous sum for me?"

"Will you let that be my business, and not meddle? Will you leave the thing in my hands? Will you swear to submit to whatever I do? Will you pledge me to find no fault with my actions?"

"I am dizzy—bewildered—but I swear."

John took up a hammer and deliberately smashed the nose of America! He made another pass and two of her fingers fell to the floor—another, and part of an ear came away—another, and a row of toes was mangled and dismembered—another, and the left leg, from the knee down, lay a fragmentary ruin!

John put on his hat and departed.

George gazed speechless upon the battered and grotesque nightmare before him for the space of thirty seconds, and then wilted to the floor and went into convulsions.

John returned presently with a carriage, got the broken-hearted artist and the broken-legged statue aboard, and drove off, whistling low and tranquilly.

He left the artist at his lodgings, and drove off and disappeared down the Via Quirinalis with the statue.

CHAPTER IV.

[Scene—The Studio.]

"The six months will be up at two o'clock to-day! Oh, agony! My life is blighted. I would that I were dead. I had no supper yesterday. I have had no breakfast to-day. I dare not enter an eating-house. And hungry? —don't mention it! My bootmaker duns me to death—my tailor duns me—my landlord haunts me. I am miserable. I haven't seen John since that awful day. She smiles on me tenderly when we meet in the great thoroughfares, but her old flint of a father makes her look in the other direction in short order. Now who is knocking at that door? Who is come to persecute me? That malignant villain the bootmaker, I'll warrant. Come in!"

"Ah, happiness attend your highness—Heaven be propitious to your grace! I have brought my lord's new boots—ah, say nothing about the pay, there is no hurry, none in the world. Shall be proud if my noble lord will continue to honor me with his custom—ah, adieu!"

"Brought the boots himself! Don't want his pay! Takes his leave with a bow and a scrape fit to honor majesty withal! Desires a continuance of my custom! Is the world coming to an end? Of all the—come in!"

"Pardon, signore, but I have brought your new suit of clothes for—"

"Come in!"

"A thousand pardons for this intrusion, your worship. But I have prepared the beautiful suite of rooms below for you—this wretched den is but ill suited to—"

"Come in!"

"I have called to say that your credit at our bank, some time since unfortunately interrupted, is entirely and most satisfactorily restored, and we shall be most happy if you will draw upon us for any—"

"COME IN!"

"My noble boy, she is yours! She'll be here in a moment! Take her—marry her—love her—be happy!—God bless you both! Hip, hip, hur—"

"COME IN!!!!!"

"Oh, George, my own darling, we are saved!"

"Oh, Mary, my own darling, we are saved—but I'll swear I don't know why nor how!"

CHAPTER V.

[Scene-A Roman Cafe.]

One of a group of American gentlemen reads and translates from the weekly edition of 'Il Slangwhanger di Roma' as follows:

WONDERFUL DISCOVERY—Some six months ago Signor John Smitthe, an American gentleman now some years a resident of Rome, purchased for a trifle a small piece of ground in the Campagna, just beyond the tomb of the Scipio family, from the owner, a bankrupt relative of the Princess Borghese. Mr. Smitthe afterward went to the Minister of the Public Records and had the piece of ground transferred to a poor American artist named George Arnold, explaining that he did it as payment and satisfaction for pecuniary damage accidentally done by him long since upon property belonging to Signor Arnold, and further observed that he would make additional satisfaction by improving the ground for Signor A., at his own charge and cost. Four weeks ago, while making some necessary excavations upon the property, Signor Smitthe unearthed the most remarkable ancient statue that has ever been added to the opulent art treasures of Rome. It was an exquisite figure of a woman, and though sadly stained by the soil and the mold of ages, no eye can look unmoved upon its ravishing beauty. The nose, the left leg from the knee down, an ear, and also the toes of the right foot and two fingers of one of the hands were gone, but otherwise the noble figure was in a remarkable state of preservation. The government at once took military possession of the statue, and appointed a commission of art-critics, antiquaries, and cardinal princes of the church to assess its value and determine the remuneration that must go to the owner of the ground in which it was found. The whole affair was kept a profound secret until last night. In the mean time the commission sat with closed doors and deliberated. Last night they decided unanimously that the statue is a Venus, and the work of some unknown but sublimely gifted artist of the third century before Christ. They consider it the most faultless work of art the world has any knowledge of.

At midnight they held a final conference and decided that the Venus was worth the enormous sum of ten million francs! In accordance with Roman law and Roman usage, the government being half-owner in all works of art found in the Campagna, the State has naught to do but pay five million francs to Mr. Arnold and take permanent possession of the beautiful statue. This morning the Venus will be removed to the Capitol, there to remain, and at noon the commission will wait upon Signor Arnold with His Holiness the Pope's order upon the Treasury for the princely sum of five million francs in gold!

Chorus of Voices.—"Luck! It's no name for it!"

Another Voice.—"Gentlemen, I propose that we immediately form an American joint-stock company for the purchase of lands and excavations of statues here, with proper connections in Wall Street to bull and bear the stock."

All.—"Agreed."

CHAPTER VI.

[Scene—The Roman Capitol Ten Years Later.]

"Dearest Mary, this is the most celebrated statue in the world. This is the renowned 'Capitoline Venus' you've heard so much about. Here she is with her little blemishes 'restored' (that is, patched) by the most noted Roman artists—and the mere fact that they did the humble patching of so noble a creation will make their names illustrious while the world stands. How strange it seems—this place! The day before I last stood here, ten happy years ago, I wasn't a rich man bless your soul, I hadn't a cent. And yet I had a good deal to do with making Rome mistress of this grandest work of ancient art the world contains."

"The worshiped, the illustrious Capitoline Venus—and what a sum she is valued at! Ten millions of francs!"

"Yes—now she is."

"And oh, Georgy, how divinely beautiful she is!"

"Ah, yes but nothing to what she was before that blessed John Smith broke her leg and battered her nose. Ingenious Smith!—gifted Smith!—noble Smith! Author of all our bliss! Hark! Do you know what that wheeze means? Mary, that cub has got the whooping-cough. Will you never learn to take care of the children!"

THE END

The Capitoline Venus is still in the Capitol at Rome, and is still the most charming and most illustrious work of ancient art the world can boast of. But if ever it shall be your fortune to stand before it and go into the customary ecstasies over it, don't permit this true and secret history of its origin to mar your bliss—and when you read about a gigantic Petrified man being dug up near Syracuse, in the State of New York, or near any other place, keep your own counsel—and if the Barnum that buried him there offers to sell to you at an enormous sum, don't you buy. Send him to the Pope!

> [NOTE.—The above sketch was written at the time the famous swindle of the "Petrified Giant" was the sensation of the day in the United States]

SPEECH ON ACCIDENT INSURANCE

DELIVERED IN HARTFORD, AT A DINNER TO CORNELIUS WALFORD, OF LONDON

GENTLEMEN: I am glad, indeed, to assist in welcoming the distinguished guest of this occasion to a city whose fame as an insurance center has extended to all lands, and given us the name of being a quadruple band of brothers working sweetly hand in hand—the Colt's Arms Company making the destruction of our race easy and convenient, our life insurance citizens paying for the victims when they pass away, Mr. Batterson perpetuating their memory with his stately monuments, and our fire-insurance comrades taking care of their hereafter. I am glad to assist in welcoming our guest—first, because he is an Englishman, and I owe a heavy debt of hospitality to certain of his fellow-countrymen; and secondly, because he is in sympathy with insurance and has been the means of making many other men cast their sympathies in the same direction.

Certainly there is no nobler field for human effort than the insurance line of business— especially accident insurance. Ever since I have been a director in an accident-insurance company I have felt that I am a better man. Life has seemed more precious. Accidents have assumed a kindlier aspect. Distressing special providences have lost half their horror. I look upon a cripple now with affectionate interest—as an advertisement. I do not seem to care for poetry any more. I do not care for politics—even agriculture does not excite me. But to me now there is a charm about a railway collision that is unspeakable.

There is nothing more beneficent than accident insurance. I have seen an entire family lifted out of poverty and into affluence by the simple boon of a broken leg. I have had people come to me on crutches, with tears in their eyes, to bless this beneficent institution. In all my experience of life, I have seen nothing so seraphic as the look that comes into a freshly mutilated man's face when he feels in his vest pocket with his remaining hand and finds his accident ticket all right. And I have seen nothing so sad as the look that came into another splintered customer's face when he found he couldn't collect on a wooden leg.

I will remark here, by way of advertisement, that that noble charity which we have named the HARTFORD ACCIDENT INSURANCE COMPANY—[The speaker is a director of the company named.]—is an institution which is peculiarly to be depended upon. A man is bound to prosper who gives it his custom.

No man can take out a policy in it and not get crippled before the year is out. Now there was one indigent man who had been disappointed so often with other companies that he had grown disheartened, his appetite left him, he ceased to smile—life was but a weariness. Three weeks ago I got him to insure with us, and now he is the brightest, happiest spirit in this land—has a good steady income and a stylish suit of new bandages every day, and travels around on a shutter.

I will say, in conclusion, that my share of the welcome to our guest is none the less hearty because I talk so much nonsense, and I know that I can say the same for the rest of the speakers.

JOHN CHINAMAN IN NEW YORK

As I passed along by one of those monster American tea stores in New York, I found a Chinaman sitting before it acting in the capacity of a sign. Everybody that passed by gave him a steady stare as long as their heads would twist over their shoulders without dislocating their necks, and a group had stopped to stare deliberately.

Is it not a shame that we, who prate so much about civilization and humanity, are content to degrade a fellow-being to such an office as this? Is it not time for reflection when we find ourselves willing to see in such a being matter for frivolous curiosity instead of regret and grave reflection? Here was a poor creature whom hard fortune had exiled from his natural home beyond the seas, and whose troubles ought to have touched these idle strangers that thronged about him; but did it? Apparently not. Men calling themselves the superior race, the race of culture and of gentle blood, scanned his quaint Chinese hat, with peaked roof and ball on top, and his long queue dangling down his back; his short silken blouse, curiously frogged and figured (and, like the rest of his raiment, rusty, dilapidated, and awkwardly put on); his blue cotton, tight-legged pants, tied close around the ankles; and his clumsy blunt-toed shoes with thick cork soles; and having so scanned him from head to foot, cracked some unseemly joke about his outlandish attire or his melancholy face, and passed on. In my heart I pitied the friendless Mongol. I wondered what was passing behind his sad face, and what distant scene his vacant eye was dreaming of. Were his thoughts with his heart, ten thousand miles away, beyond the billowy wastes of the Pacific? among the ricefields and the plumy palms of China? under the shadows of remembered mountain peaks, or in groves of bloomy shrubs and strange forest trees unknown to climes like ours? And now and then, rippling among his visions and his dreams, did he hear familiar laughter and half-forgotten voices, and did he catch fitful glimpses of the friendly faces of a bygone time? A cruel fate it is, I said, that is befallen this bronzed wanderer. In order that the group of idlers might be touched at least by the words of the poor fellow, since the appeal of his pauper dress and his dreary exile was lost upon them, I touched him on the shoulder and said:

"Cheer up—don't be downhearted. It is not America that treats you in this way, it is merely one citizen, whose greed of gain has eaten the humanity out of his heart. America has a broader hospitality for the exiled and oppressed. America and Americans are always ready to help the unfortunate. Money shall be raised—you shall go back to China—you shall see your friends again. What wages do they pay you here?"

"Divil a cint but four dollars a week and find meself; but it's aisy, barrin' the troublesome furrin clothes that's so expinsive."

The exile remains at his post. The New York tea merchants who need picturesque signs are not likely to run out of Chinamen.

HOW I EDITED AN AGRICULTURAL PAPER

[Written about 1870.]

I did not take temporary editorship of an agricultural paper without misgivings. Neither would a landsman take command of a ship without misgivings. But I was in circumstances that made the salary an object. The regular editor of the paper was going off for a holiday, and I accepted the terms he offered, and took his place.

The sensation of being at work again was luxurious, and I wrought all the week with unflagging pleasure. We went to press, and I waited a day with some solicitude to see whether my effort was going to attract any notice. As I left the office, toward sundown, a group of men and boys at the foot of the stairs dispersed with one impulse, and gave me passageway, and I heard one or two of them say: "That's him!" I was naturally pleased by this incident. The next morning I found a similar group at the foot of the stairs, and scattering couples and individuals standing here and there in the street and over the way, watching me with interest. The group separated and fell back as I approached, and I heard a man say, "Look at his eye!" I pretended not to observe the notice I was attracting, but secretly I was pleased with it, and was purposing to write an account of it to my aunt. I went up the short flight of stairs, and heard cheery voices and a ringing laugh as I drew near the door, which I opened, and caught a glimpse of two young rural-looking men, whose faces blanched and lengthened when they saw me, and then they both plunged through the window with a great crash. I was surprised.

In about half an hour an old gentleman, with a flowing beard and a fine but rather austere face, entered, and sat down at my invitation. He seemed to have something on his mind. He took off his hat and set it on the floor, and got out of it a red silk handkerchief and a copy of our paper.

He put the paper on his lap, and while he polished his spectacles with his handkerchief he said, "Are you the new editor?"

I said I was.

"Have you ever edited an agricultural paper before?"

"No," I said; "this is my first attempt."

"Very likely. Have you had any experience in agriculture practically?"

"No; I believe I have not."

"Some instinct told me so," said the old gentleman, putting on his spectacles, and looking over them at me with asperity, while he folded his paper into a convenient shape. "I wish to read you what must have made me have that instinct. It was this editorial. Listen, and see if it was you that wrote it:

"'Turnips should never be pulled, it injures them. It is much better to send a boy up and let him shake the tree.'

"Now, what do you think of that?—for I really suppose you wrote it?"

"Think of it? Why, I think it is good. I think it is sense. I have no doubt that every year millions and millions of bushels of turnips are spoiled in this township alone by being pulled in a half-ripe condition, when, if they had sent a boy up to shake the tree—"

"Shake your grandmother! Turnips don't grow on trees!"

"Oh, they don't, don't they? Well, who said they did? The language was intended to be figurative, wholly figurative. Anybody that knows anything will know that I meant that the boy should shake the vine."

Then this old person got up and tore his paper all into small shreds, and stamped on them, and broke several things with his cane, and said I did not know as much as a cow; and then went out and banged the door after him, and, in short, acted in such a way that I fancied he was displeased about something. But not knowing what the trouble was, I could not be any help to him.

Pretty soon after this a long, cadaverous creature, with lanky locks hanging down to his shoulders, and a week's stubble bristling from the hills and valleys of his face, darted within the door, and halted, motionless, with finger on lip, and head and body bent in listening attitude. No sound was heard.

Still he listened. No sound. Then he turned the key in the door, and came elaborately tiptoeing toward me till he was within long reaching distance of me, when he stopped and, after scanning my face with intense interest for a while, drew a folded copy of our paper from his bosom, and said:

"There, you wrote that. Read it to me—quick! Relieve me. I suffer."

I read as follows; and as the sentences fell from my lips I could see the relief come, I could see the drawn muscles relax, and the anxiety go out of the face, and rest and peace steal over the features like the merciful moonlight over a desolate landscape:

> The guano is a fine bird, but great care is necessary in rearing it. It should not be imported earlier than June or later than September. In the winter it should be kept in a warm place, where it can hatch out its young.

> It is evident that we are to have a backward season for grain. Therefore it will be well for the farmer to begin setting out his corn-stalks and planting his buckwheat cakes in July instead of August. Concerning the pumpkin. This berry is a favorite with the natives of the interior of New England, who prefer it to the gooseberry for the making of fruit-cake, and who likewise give it the preference over the raspberry for feeding cows, as being more filling and fully as satisfying. The pumpkin is the only esculent of the orange family that will thrive in the North, except the gourd and one or two varieties of the squash. But the custom of planting it in the front yard with the shrubbery is fast going out of vogue, for it is now generally conceded that, the pumpkin as a shade tree is a failure.

Now, as the warm weather approaches, and the ganders begin to spawn—

The excited listener sprang toward me to shake hands, and said:

"There, there—that will do. I know I am all right now, because you have read it just as I did, word, for word. But, stranger, when I first read it this morning, I said to myself, I never, never believed it before, notwithstanding my friends kept me under watch so strict, but now I believe I am crazy; and with that I fetched a howl that you might have heard two miles, and started out to kill somebody—because, you know, I knew it would come to that sooner or later, and so I might as well begin. I read one of them paragraphs over again, so as to be certain, and then I burned my house down and started. I have crippled several people, and have got one fellow up a tree, where I can get him if I want him.

But I thought I would call in here as I passed along and make the thing perfectly certain; and now it is certain, and I tell you it is lucky for the chap that is in the tree. I should have killed him sure, as I went back. Good-by, sir, good-by; you have taken a great load off my mind. My reason has stood the strain of one of your agricultural articles, and I know that nothing can ever unseat it now. Good-by, sir."

I felt a little uncomfortable about the cripplings and arsons this person had been entertaining himself with, for I could not help feeling remotely accessory to them. But these thoughts were quickly banished, for the regular editor walked in! [I thought to myself, Now if you had gone to Egypt as I recommended you to, I might have had a chance to get my hand in; but you wouldn't do it, and here you are. I sort of expected you.]

The editor was looking sad and perplexed and dejected.

He surveyed the wreck which that old rioter and those two young farmers had made, and then said "This is a sad business—a very sad business. There is the mucilage-bottle broken, and six panes of glass, and a spittoon, and two candlesticks. But that is not the worst. The reputation of the paper is injured—and permanently, I fear. True, there never was such a call for the paper before, and it never sold such a large edition or soared to such celebrity;—but does one want to be famous for lunacy, and prosper upon the infirmities of his mind? My friend, as I am an honest man, the street out here is full of people, and others are roosting on the fences, waiting to get a glimpse of you, because they think you are crazy. And well they might after reading your editorials. They are a disgrace to journalism. Why, what put it into your head that you could edit a paper of this nature? You do not seem to know the first rudiments of agriculture. You speak of a furrow and a harrow as being the same thing; you talk of the moulting season for cows; and you recommend the domestication of the pole-cat on account of its playfulness and its excellence as a ratter! Your remark that clams will lie quiet if music be played to them was superfluous—entirely superfluous. Nothing disturbs clams. Clams always lie quiet. Clams care nothing whatever about music. Ah, heavens and earth, friend! if you had made the acquiring of ignorance the study of your life, you could not have graduated with higher honor than you could to-day. I never saw anything like it. Your observation that the horse-chestnut as an article of commerce is steadily gaining in favor is simply calculated to destroy this journal. I want you to throw up your situation and go. I want no more holiday—I could not enjoy it if I had it. Certainly not with you in my chair. I would always stand in dread of what you might be going to recommend next. It makes me lose all patience every time I think of your discussing oyster-beds under the head of 'Landscape Gardening.' I want you to go. Nothing on earth could persuade me to take another holiday. Oh! why didn't you tell me you didn't know anything about agriculture?"

"Tell you, you corn-stalk, you cabbage, you son of a cauliflower? It's the first time I ever heard such an unfeeling remark. I tell you I have been in the editorial business going on fourteen years, and it is the first time I ever heard of a man's having to know anything in order to edit a newspaper. You turnip! Who write the dramatic critiques for the second-rate papers? Why, a parcel of promoted shoemakers and apprentice apothecaries, who know just as much about good acting as I do about good farming and no more. Who review the books? People who never wrote one. Who do up the heavy leaders on finance? Parties who have had the largest opportunities for knowing nothing about it. Who criticize the Indian campaigns? Gentlemen who do not know a war-whoop from a wigwam, and who never have had to run a foot-race with a tomahawk, or pluck arrows out of the several members of their families to build the evening camp-fire with. Who write the temperance appeals, and clamor about the flowing bowl? Folks who will never draw another sober breath till they do it in the grave. Who edit the agricultural papers, you—yam? Men, as a general thing, who fail in the poetry line, yellow-colored novel line, sensation, drama line, city-editor line, and finally fall back on agriculture as a temporary reprieve from the poorhouse. You try to tell me anything about the newspaper business! Sir, I have been through it from Alpha to Omaha, and I tell you that the less a man knows the bigger the noise he makes and the higher the salary he commands. Heaven knows if I had but been ignorant instead of cultivated, and impudent instead of diffident, I could have made a name for myself in this cold, selfish world. I take my leave, sir. Since I have been treated as you have treated me, I am perfectly willing to go. But I have done my duty. I have fulfilled my contract as far as I was permitted to do it. I said I could make your paper of interest to all classes—and I have. I said I could run your circulation up to twenty thousand copies, and if I had had two more weeks I'd have done it. And I'd have given you the best class of readers that ever an agricultural paper had—not a farmer in it, nor a solitary individual who could tell a watermelon-tree from a peach-vine to save his life. You are the loser by this rupture, not me, Pie-plant. Adios."

I then left.

THE PETRIFIED MAN

Now, to show how really hard it is to foist a moral or a truth upon an unsuspecting public through a burlesque without entirely and absurdly missing one's mark, I will here set down two experiences of my own in this thing. In the fall of 1862, in Nevada and California, the people got to running wild about extraordinary petrifactions and other natural marvels. One could scarcely pick up a paper without finding in it one or two glorified discoveries of this kind. The mania was becoming a little ridiculous. I was a brand-new local editor in Virginia City, and I felt called upon to destroy this growing evil; we all have our benignant, fatherly moods at one time or another, I suppose. I chose to kill the petrifaction mania with a delicate, a very delicate satire. But maybe it was altogether too delicate, for nobody ever perceived the satire part of it at all. I put my scheme in the shape of the discovery of a remarkably petrified man.

I had had a temporary falling out with Mr.——, the new coroner and justice of the peace of Humboldt, and thought I might as well touch him up a little at the same time and make him ridiculous, and thus combine pleasure with business. So I told, in patient, belief-compelling detail, all about the finding of a petrified-man at Gravelly Ford (exactly a hundred and twenty miles, over a breakneck mountain trail from where —— lived); how all the savants of the immediate neighborhood had been to examine it (it was notorious that there was not a living creature within fifty miles of there, except a few starving Indians, some crippled grasshoppers, and four or five buzzards out of meat and too feeble to get away); how those savants all pronounced the petrified man to have been in a state of complete petrifaction for over ten generations; and then, with a seriousness that I ought to have been ashamed to assume, I stated that as soon as Mr.——heard the news he summoned a jury, mounted his mule, and posted off, with noble reverence for official duty, on that awful five days' journey, through alkali, sage brush, peril of body, and imminent starvation, to hold an inquest on this man that had been dead and turned to everlasting stone for more than three hundred years!

And then, my hand being "in," so to speak, I went on, with the same unflinching gravity, to state that the jury returned a verdict that deceased came to his death from protracted exposure. This only moved me to higher flights of imagination, and I said that the jury, with that charity so characteristic of pioneers, then dug a grave, and were about to give the petrified man Christian burial, when they found that for ages a limestone sediment had been trickling down the face of the stone against which he was sitting, and this stuff had run under him and cemented him fast to the "bed-rock"; that the jury (they were all silver-miners) canvassed the difficulty a moment, and then got out their powder and fuse, and proceeded to drill a hole under him, in order to blast him from his position, when Mr.——, "with that delicacy so characteristic of him, forbade them, observing that it would be little less than sacrilege to do such a thing."

From beginning to end the "Petrified Man" squib was a string of roaring absurdities, albeit they were told with an unfair pretense of truth that even imposed upon me to some extent, and I was in some danger of believing in my own fraud. But I really had no desire to deceive anybody, and no expectation of doing it. I depended on the way the petrified man was sitting to explain to the public that he was a swindle. Yet I purposely mixed that up with other things, hoping to make it obscure—and I did. I would describe the position of one foot, and then say his right thumb was against the side of his nose; then talk about his other foot, and presently come back and say the fingers of his right hand were spread apart; then talk about the back of his head a little, and return and say the left thumb was hooked into the right little finger; then ramble off about something else, and by and by drift back again and remark that the fingers of the left hand were spread like those of the right. But I was too ingenious. I mixed it up rather too much; and so all that description of the attitude, as a key to the humbuggery of the article, was entirely lost, for nobody but me ever discovered and comprehended the peculiar and suggestive position of the petrified man's hands.

As a satire on the petrifaction mania, or anything else, my Petrified Man was a disheartening failure; for everybody received him in innocent good faith, and I was stunned to see the creature I had begotten to pull down the wonder-business with, and bring derision upon it, calmly exalted to the grand chief place in the list of the genuine marvels our Nevada had produced. I was so disappointed at the curious miscarriage of my scheme, that at first I was angry, and did not like to think about it; but by and by, when the exchanges began to come in with the Petrified Man copied and guilelessly glorified, I began to feel a soothing secret satisfaction; and as my gentleman's field of travels broadened, and by the exchanges I saw that he steadily and implacably penetrated territory after territory, state after state, and land after land, till he swept the great globe and culminated in sublime and unimpeached legitimacy in the august London Lancet, my cup was full, and I said I was glad I had done it. I think that for about eleven months, as nearly as I can remember, Mr.——'s daily mail-bag continued to be swollen by the addition of half a bushel of newspapers hailing from many climes with the Petrified Man in them, marked around with a prominent belt of ink. I sent them to him. I did it for spite, not for fun.

He used to shovel them into his back yard and curse. And every day during all those months the miners, his constituents (for miners never quit joking a person when they get started), would call on him and ask if he could tell them where they could get hold of a paper with the Petrified Man in it. He could have accommodated a continent with them. I hated——-in those days, and these things pacified me and pleased me. I could not have gotten more real comfort out of him without killing him.

MY BLOODY MASSACRE

The other burlesque I have referred to was my fine satire upon the financial expedients of "cooking dividends," a thing which became shamefully frequent on the Pacific coast for a while. Once more, in my self-complacent simplicity I felt that the time had arrived for me to rise up and be a reformer. I put this reformatory satire in the shape of a fearful "Massacre at Empire City." The San Francisco papers were making a great outcry about the iniquity of the Daney Silver-Mining Company, whose directors had declared a "cooked" or false dividend, for the purpose of increasing the value of their stock, so that they could sell out at a comfortable figure, and then scramble from under the tumbling concern. And while abusing the Daney, those papers did not forget to urge the public to get rid of all their silver stocks and invest in sound and safe San Francisco stocks, such as the Spring Valley Water Company, etc. But right at this unfortunate juncture, behold the Spring Valley cooked a dividend too! And so, under the insidious mask of an invented "bloody massacre," I stole upon the public unawares with my scathing satire upon the dividend-cooking system. In about half a column of imaginary human carnage I told how a citizen had murdered his wife and nine children, and then committed suicide. And I said slyly, at the bottom, that the sudden madness of which this melancholy massacre was the result had been brought about by his having allowed himself to be persuaded by the California papers to sell his sound and lucrative Nevada silver stocks, and buy into Spring Valley just in time to get cooked along with that company's fancy dividend, and sink every cent he had in the world.

Ah, it was a deep, deep satire, and most ingeniously contrived. But I made the horrible details so carefully and conscientiously interesting that the public devoured them greedily, and wholly overlooked the following distinctly stated facts, to wit: The murderer was perfectly well known to every creature in the land as a bachelor, and consequently he could not murder his wife and nine children; he murdered them "in his splendid dressed-stone mansion just in the edge of the great pine forest between Empire City and Dutch Nick's," when even the very pickled oysters that came on our tables knew that there was not a "dressed-stone mansion" in all Nevada Territory; also that, so far from there being a "great pine forest between Empire City and Dutch Nick's," there wasn't a solitary tree within fifteen miles of either place; and, finally, it was patent and notorious that Empire City and Dutch Nick's were one and the same place, and contained only six houses anyhow, and consequently there could be no forest between them; and on top of all these absurdities I stated that this diabolical murderer, after inflicting a wound upon himself that the reader ought to have seen would kill an elephant in the twinkling of an eye, jumped on his horse and rode four miles, waving his wife's reeking scalp in the air, and thus performing entered Carson City with tremendous éclat, and dropped dead in front of the chief saloon, the envy and admiration of all beholders.

Well, in all my life I never saw anything like the sensation that little satire created. It was the talk of the town, it was the talk of the territory. Most of the citizens dropped gently into it at breakfast, and they never finished their meal. There was something about those minutely faithful details that was a sufficing substitute for food. Few people that were able to read took food that morning. Dan and I (Dan was my reportorial associate) took our seats on either side of our customary table in the "Eagle Restaurant," and, as I unfolded the shred they used to call a napkin in that establishment, I saw at the next table two stalwart innocents with that sort of vegetable dandruff sprinkled about their clothing which was the sign and evidence that they were in from the Truckee with a load of hay. The one facing me had the morning paper folded to a long, narrow strip, and I knew, without any telling, that that strip represented the column that contained my pleasant financial satire. From the way he was excitedly mumbling, I saw that the heedless son of a hay-mow was skipping with all his might, in order to get to the bloody details as quickly as possible; and so he was missing the guide-boards I had set up to warn him that the whole thing was a fraud. Presently his eyes spread wide open, just as his jaws swung asunder to take in a potato approaching it on a fork; the potato halted, the face lit up redly, and the whole man was on fire with excitement. Then he broke into a disjointed checking off of the particulars—his potato cooling in mid-air meantime, and his mouth making a reach for it occasionally, but always bringing up suddenly against a new and still more direful performance of my hero. At last he looked his stunned and rigid comrade impressively in the face, and said, with an expression of concentrated awe:

"Jim, he b'iled his baby, and he took the old 'oman's skelp. Cuss'd if I want any breakfast!"

And he laid his lingering potato reverently down, and he and his friend departed from the restaurant empty but satisfied.

He never got down to where the satire part of it began. Nobody ever did. They found the thrilling particulars sufficient. To drop in with a poor little moral at the fag-end of such a gorgeous massacre was like following the expiring sun with a candle and hope to attract the world's attention to it.

The idea that anybody could ever take my massacre for a genuine occurrence never once suggested itself to me, hedged about as it was by all those telltale absurdities and impossibilities concerning the "great pine forest," the "dressed-stone mansion," etc. But I found out then, and never have forgotten since, that we never read the dull explanatory surroundings of marvelously exciting things when we have no occasion to suppose that some irresponsible scribbler is trying to defraud us; we skip all that, and hasten to revel in the blood-curdling particulars and be happy.

THE UNDERTAKER'S CHAT

"Now that corpse," said the undertaker, patting the folded hands of deceased approvingly, "was a brick—every way you took him he was a brick. He was so real accommodating, and so modest-like and simple in his last moments. Friends wanted metallic burial-case—nothing else would do. I couldn't get it. There warn't going to be time—anybody could see that.

"Corpse said never mind, shake him up some kind of a box he could stretch out in comfortable, he warn't particular 'bout the general style of it. Said he went more on room than style, anyway in a last final container.

"Friends wanted a silver door-plate on the coffin, signifying who he was and wher' he was from. Now you know a fellow couldn't roust out such a gaily thing as that in a little country-town like this. What did corpse say?

"Corpse said, whitewash his old canoe and dob his address and general destination onto it with a blacking-brush and a stencil-plate, 'long with a verse from some likely hymn or other, and p'int him for the tomb, and mark him C. O. D., and just let him flicker. He warn't distressed any more than you be—on the contrary, just as ca'm and collected as a hearse-horse; said he judged that wher' he was going to a body would find it considerable better to attract attention by a picturesque moral character than a natty burial-case with a swell door-plate on it.

"Splendid man, he was. I'd druther do for a corpse like that 'n any I've tackled in seven year. There's some satisfaction in buryin' a man like that. You feel that what you're doing is appreciated. Lord bless you, so's he got planted before he sp'iled, he was perfectly satisfied; said his relations meant well, perfectly well, but all them preparations was bound to delay the thing more or less, and he didn't wish to be kept layin' around. You never see such a clear head as what he had—and so ca'm and so cool. Jist a hunk of brains—that is what he was. Perfectly awful. It was a ripping distance from one end of that man's head to t'other. Often and over again he's had brain-fever a-raging in one place, and the rest of the pile didn't know anything about it—didn't affect it any more than an Injun Insurrection in Arizona affects the Atlantic States. Well, the relations they wanted a big funeral, but corpse said he was down on flummery—didn't want any procession—fill the hearse full of mourners, and get out a stern line and tow him behind. He was the most down on style of any remains I ever struck. A beautiful, simpleminded creature—it was what he was, you can depend on that. He was just set on having things the way he wanted them, and he took a solid comfort in laying his little plans. He had me measure him and take a whole raft of directions; then he had the minister stand up behind a long box with a table-cloth over it, to represent the coffin, and read his funeral sermon, saying 'Angcore, angcore!' at the good places, and making him scratch out every bit of brag about him, and all the hifalutin; and then he made them trot out the choir, so's he could help them pick out the tunes for the occasion, and he got them to sing 'Pop Goes the Weasel,' because he'd always liked that tune when he was downhearted, and solemn music made him sad; and when they sung that with tears in their eyes (because they all loved him), and his relations grieving around, he just laid there as happy as a bug, and trying to beat time and showing all over how much he enjoyed it; and presently he got worked up and excited, and tried to join in, for, mind you, he was pretty proud of his abilities in the singing line; but the first time he opened his mouth and was just going to spread himself his breath took a walk.

"I never see a man snuffed out so sudden. Ah, it was a great loss—a powerful loss to this poor little one-horse town. Well, well, well, I hain't got time to be palavering along here—got to nail on the lid and mosey along with him; and if you'll just give me a lift we'll skeet him into the hearse and meander along. Relations bound to have it so—don't pay no attention to dying injunctions, minute a corpse's gone; but, if I had my way, if I didn't respect his last wishes and tow him behind the hearse I'll be cuss'd. I consider that whatever a corpse wants done for his comfort is little enough matter, and a man hain't got no right to deceive him or take advantage of him; and whatever a corpse trusts me to do I'm a-going to do, you know, even if it's to stuff him and paint him yaller and keep him for a keepsake—you hear me!"

He cracked his whip and went lumbering away with his ancient ruin of a hearse, and I continued my walk with a valuable lesson learned—that a healthy and wholesome cheerfulness is not necessarily impossible to any occupation. The lesson is likely to be lasting, for it will take many months to obliterate the memory of the remarks and circumstances that impressed it.

CONCERNING CHAMBERMAIDS

Against all chambermaids, of whatsoever age or nationality, I launch the curse of bachelordom! Because:

They always put the pillows at the opposite end of the bed from the gas-burner, so that while you read and smoke before sleeping (as is the ancient and honored custom of bachelors), you have to hold your book aloft, in an uncomfortable position, to keep the light from dazzling your eyes.

When they find the pillows removed to the other end of the bed in the morning, they receive not the suggestion in a friendly spirit; but, glorying in their absolute sovereignty, and unpitying your helplessness, they make the bed just as it was originally, and gloat in secret over the pang their tyranny will cause you.

Always after that, when they find you have transposed the pillows, they undo your work, and thus defy and seek to embitter the life that God has given you.

If they cannot get the light in an inconvenient position any other way, they move the bed.

If you pull your trunk out six inches from the wall, so that the lid will stay up when you open it, they always shove that trunk back again. They do it on purpose.

If you want the spittoon in a certain spot, where it will be handy, they don't, and so they move it.

They always put your other boots into inaccessible places. They chiefly enjoy depositing them as far under the bed as the wall will permit. It is because this compels you to get down in an undignified attitude and make wild sweeps for them in the dark with the bootjack, and swear.

They always put the matchbox in some other place. They hunt up a new place for it every day, and put up a bottle, or other perishable glass thing, where the box stood before. This is to cause you to break that glass thing, groping in the dark, and get yourself into trouble.

They are for ever and ever moving the furniture. When you come in in the night you can calculate on finding the bureau where the wardrobe was in the morning. And when you go out in the morning, if you leave the slop-bucket by the door and rocking-chair by the window, when you come in at midnight or thereabout, you will fall over that rocking-chair, and you will proceed toward the window and sit down in that slop-tub. This will disgust you. They like that.

No matter where you put anything, they are not going to let it stay there. They will take it and move it the first chance they get. It is their nature. And, besides, it gives them pleasure to be mean and contrary this way. They would die if they couldn't be villains.

They always save up all the old scraps of printed rubbish you throw on the floor, and stack them up carefully on the table, and start the fire with your valuable manuscripts. If there is any one particular old scrap that you are more down on than any other, and which you are gradually wearing your life out trying to get rid of, you may take all the pains you possibly can in that direction, but it won't be of any use, because they will always fetch that old scrap back and put it in the same old place again every time. It does them good.

And they use up more hair-oil than any six men. If charged with purloining the same, they lie about it. What do they care about a hereafter? Absolutely nothing.

If you leave the key in the door for convenience' sake, they will carry it down to the office and give it to the clerk. They do this under the vile pretense of trying to protect your property from thieves; but actually they do it because they want to make you tramp back down-stairs after it when you come home tired, or put you to the trouble of sending a waiter for it, which waiter will expect you to pay him something. In which case I suppose the degraded creatures divide.

They keep always trying to make your bed before you get up, thus destroying your rest and inflicting agony upon you; but after you get up, they don't come any more till next day.

They do all the mean things they can think of, and they do them just out of pure cussedness, and nothing else.

Chambermaids are dead to every human instinct.

If I can get a bill through the legislature abolishing chambermaids, I mean to do it.

AURELIA'S UNFORTUNATE YOUNG MAN

[Written about 1865.]

The facts in the following case came to me by letter from a young lady who lives in the beautiful city of San José; she is perfectly unknown to me, and simply signs herself "Aurelia Maria," which may possibly be a fictitious name. But no matter, the poor girl is almost heartbroken by the misfortunes she has undergone, and so confused by the conflicting counsels of misguided friends and insidious enemies that she does not know what course to pursue in order to extricate herself from the web of difficulties in which she seems almost hopelessly involved. In this dilemma she turns to me for help, and supplicates for my guidance and instruction with a moving eloquence that would touch the heart of a statue. Hear her sad story:

She says that when she was sixteen years old she met and loved, with all the devotion of a passionate nature, a young man from New Jersey, named Williamson Breckinridge Caruthers, who was some six years her senior. They were engaged, with the free consent of their friends and relatives, and for a time it seemed as if their career was destined to be characterized by an immunity from sorrow beyond the usual lot of humanity. But at last the tide of fortune turned; young Caruthers became infected with smallpox of the most virulent type, and when he recovered from his illness his face was pitted like a waffle-mold, and his comeliness gone forever. Aurelia thought to break off the engagement at first, but pity for her unfortunate lover caused her to postpone the marriage-day for a season, and give him another trial.

The very day before the wedding was to have taken place, Breckinridge, while absorbed in watching the flight of a balloon, walked into a well and fractured one of his legs, and it had to be taken off above the knee. Again Aurelia was moved to break the engagement, but again love triumphed, and she set the day forward and gave him another chance to reform.

And again misfortune overtook the unhappy youth. He lost one arm by the premature discharge of a Fourth of July cannon, and within three months he got the other pulled out by a carding-machine. Aurelia's heart was almost crushed by these latter calamities. She could not but be deeply grieved to see her lover passing from her by piecemeal, feeling, as she did, that he could not last forever under this disastrous process of reduction, yet knowing of no way to stop its dreadful career, and in her tearful despair she almost regretted, like brokers who hold on and lose, that she had not taken him at first, before he had suffered such an alarming depreciation. Still, her brave soul bore her up, and she resolved to bear with her friend's unnatural disposition yet a little longer.

Again the wedding-day approached, and again disappointment overshadowed it; Caruthers fell ill with the erysipelas, and lost the use of one of his eyes entirely. The friends and relatives of the bride, considering that she had already put up with more than could reasonably be expected of her, now came forward and insisted that the match should be broken off; but after wavering awhile, Aurelia, with a generous spirit which did her credit, said she had reflected calmly upon the matter, and could not discover that Breckinridge was to blame.

So she extended the time once more, and he broke his other leg.

It was a sad day for the poor girl when she saw the surgeons reverently bearing away the sack whose uses she had learned by previous experience, and her heart told her the bitter truth that some more of her lover was gone. She felt that the field of her affections was growing more and more circumscribed every day, but once more she frowned down her relatives and renewed her betrothal.

Shortly before the time set for the nuptials another disaster occurred. There was but one man scalped by the Owens River Indians last year. That man was Williamson Breckinridge Caruthers of New Jersey. He was hurrying home with happiness in his heart, when he lost his hair forever, and in that hour of bitterness he almost cursed the mistaken mercy that had spared his head.

At last Aurelia is in serious perplexity as to what she ought to do. She still loves her Breckinridge, she writes, with truly womanly feeling—she still loves what is left of him—but her parents are bitterly opposed to the match, because he has no property and is disabled from working, and she has not sufficient means to support both comfortably. "Now, what should she do?" she asked with painful and anxious solicitude.

It is a delicate question; it is one which involves the lifelong happiness of a woman, and that of nearly two-thirds of a man, and I feel that it would be assuming too great a responsibility to do more than make a mere suggestion in the case. How would it do to build to him? If Aurelia can afford the expense, let her furnish her mutilated lover with wooden arms and wooden legs, and a glass eye and a wig, and give him another show; give him ninety days, without grace, and if he does not break his neck in the mean time, marry him and take the chances. It does not seem to me that there is much risk, anyway, Aurelia, because if he sticks to his singular propensity for damaging himself every time he sees a good opportunity, his next experiment is bound to finish him, and then you are safe, married or single. If married, the wooden legs and such other valuables as he may possess revert to the widow, and you see you sustain no actual loss save the cherished fragment of a noble but most unfortunate husband, who honestly strove to do right, but whose extraordinary instincts were against him. Try it, Maria. I have thought the matter over carefully and well, and it is the only chance I see for you. It would have been a happy conceit on the part of Caruthers if he had started with his neck and broken that first; but since he has seen fit to choose a different policy and string himself out as long as possible, I do not think we ought to upbraid him for it if he has enjoyed it. We must do the best we can under the circumstances, and try not to feel exasperated at him.

"AFTER" JENKINS

A grand affair of a ball—the Pioneers'—came off at the Occidental some time ago. The following notes of the costumes worn by the belles of the occasion may not be uninteresting to the general reader, and Jenkins may get an idea therefrom:

Mrs. W. M. was attired in an elegant 'pâté de foie gras,' made expressly for her, and was greatly admired. Miss S. had her hair done up. She was the center of attraction for the gentlemen and the envy of all the ladies. Mrs. G. W. was tastefully dressed in a 'tout ensemble,' and was greeted with deafening applause wherever she went. Mrs. C. N. was superbly arrayed in white kid gloves. Her modest and engaging manner accorded well with the unpretending simplicity of her costume and caused her to be regarded with absorbing interest by every one.

The charming Miss M. M. B. appeared in a thrilling waterfall, whose exceeding grace and volume compelled the homage of pioneers and emigrants alike. How beautiful she was!

The queenly Mrs. L. R. was attractively attired in her new and beautiful false teeth, and the 'bon jour' effect they naturally produced was heightened by her enchanting and well-sustained smile.

Miss R. P., with that repugnance to ostentation in dress which is so peculiar to her, was attired in a simple white lace collar, fastened with a neat pearl-button solitaire. The fine contrast between the sparkling vivacity of her natural optic, and the steadfast attentiveness of her placid glass eye, was the subject of general and enthusiastic remark.

Miss C. L. B. had her fine nose elegantly enameled, and the easy grace with which she blew it from time to time marked her as a cultivated and accomplished woman of the world; its exquisitely modulated tone excited the admiration of all who had the happiness to hear it.

ABOUT BARBERS

All things change except barbers, the ways of barbers, and the surroundings of barbers. These never change. What one experiences in a barber's shop the first time he enters one is what he always experiences in barbers' shops afterward till the end of his days. I got shaved this morning as usual. A man approached the door from Jones Street as I approached it from Main—a thing that always happens. I hurried up, but it was of no use; he entered the door one little step ahead of me, and I followed in on his heels and saw him take the only vacant chair, the one presided over by the best barber. It always happens so. I sat down, hoping that I might fall heir to the chair belonging to the better of the remaining two barbers, for he had already begun combing his man's hair, while his comrade was not yet quite done rubbing up and oiling his customer's locks. I watched the probabilities with strong interest. When I saw that No. 2 was gaining on No. 1 my interest grew to solicitude. When No. 1 stopped a moment to make change on a bath ticket for a new-comer, and lost ground in the race, my solicitude rose to anxiety. When No. 1 caught up again, and both he and his comrade were pulling the towels away and brushing the powder from their customers' cheeks, and it was about an even thing which one would say "Next!" first, my very breath stood still with the suspense. But when at the culminating moment No. 1 stopped to pass a comb a couple of times through his customer's eyebrows, I saw that he had lost the race by a single instant, and I rose indignant and quitted the shop, to keep from falling into the hands of No. 2; for I have none of that enviable firmness that enables a man to look calmly into the eyes of a waiting barber and tell him he will wait for his fellow-barber's chair.

I stayed out fifteen minutes, and then went back, hoping for better luck. Of course all the chairs were occupied now, and four men sat waiting, silent, unsociable, distraught, and looking bored, as men always do who are waiting their turn in a barber's shop. I sat down in one of the iron-armed compartments of an old sofa, and put in the time for a while reading the framed advertisements of all sorts of quack nostrums for dyeing and coloring the hair. Then I read the greasy names on the private bayrum bottles; read the names and noted the numbers on the private shaving-cups in the pigeonholes; studied the stained and damaged cheap prints on the walls, of battles, early Presidents, and voluptuous recumbent sultanas, and the tiresome and everlasting young girl putting her grandfather's spectacles on; execrated in my heart the cheerful canary and the distracting parrot that few barbers' shops are without. Finally, I searched out the least dilapidated of last year's illustrated papers that littered the foul center-table, and conned their unjustifiable misrepresentations of old forgotten events.

At last my turn came. A voice said "Next!" and I surrendered to—No. 2, of course. It always happens so. I said meekly that I was in a hurry, and it affected him as strongly as if he had never heard it. He shoved up my head, and put a napkin under it. He plowed his fingers into my collar and fixed a towel there. He explored my hair with his claws and suggested that it needed trimming. I said I did not want it trimmed. He explored again and said it was pretty long for the present style—better have a little taken off; it needed it behind especially. I said I had had it cut only a week before. He yearned over it reflectively a moment, and then asked with a disparaging manner, who cut it? I came back at him promptly with a "You did!" I had him there. Then he fell to stirring up his lather and regarding himself in the glass, stopping now and then to get close and examine his chin critically or inspect a pimple. Then he lathered one side of my face thoroughly, and was about to lather the other, when a dog-fight attracted his attention, and he ran to the window and stayed and saw it out, losing two shillings on the result in bets with the other barbers, a thing which gave me great satisfaction. He finished lathering, and then began to rub in the suds with his hand.

He now began to sharpen his razor on an old suspender, and was delayed a good deal on account of a controversy about a cheap masquerade ball he had figured at the night before, in red cambric and bogus ermine, as some kind of a king. He was so gratified with being chaffed about some damsel whom he had smitten with his charms that he used every means to continue the controversy by pretending to be annoyed at the chaffings of his fellows. This matter begot more surveyings of himself in the glass, and he put down his razor and brushed his hair with elaborate care, plastering an inverted arch of it down on his forehead, accomplishing an accurate "part" behind, and brushing the two wings forward over his ears with nice exactness. In the mean time the lather was drying on my face, and apparently eating into my vitals.

Now he began to shave, digging his fingers into my countenance to stretch the skin and bundling and tumbling my head this way and that as convenience in shaving demanded. As long as he was on the tough sides of my face I did not suffer; but when he began to rake, and rip, and tug at my chin, the tears came. He now made a handle of my nose, to assist him shaving the corners of my upper lip, and it was by this bit of circumstantial evidence that I discovered that a part of his duties in the shop was to clean the kerosene-lamps. I had often wondered in an indolent way whether the barbers did that, or whether it was the boss.

About this time I was amusing myself trying to guess where he would be most likely to cut me this time, but he got ahead of me, and sliced me on the end of the chin before I had got my mind made up. He immediately sharpened his razor—he might have done it before. I do not like a close shave, and would not let him go over me a second time. I tried to get him to put up his razor, dreading that he would make for the side of my chin, my pet tender spot, a place which a razor cannot touch twice without making trouble; but he said he only wanted to just smooth off one little roughness, and in the same moment he slipped his razor along the forbidden ground, and the dreaded pimple-signs of a close shave rose up smarting and answered to the call. Now he soaked his towel in bay rum, and slapped it all over my face nastily; slapped it over as if a human being ever yet washed his face in that way. Then he dried it by slapping with the dry part of the towel, as if a human being ever dried his face in such a fashion; but a barber seldom rubs you like a Christian. Next he poked bay rum into the cut place with his towel, then choked the wound with powdered starch, then soaked it with bay rum again, and would have gone on soaking and powdering it forevermore, no doubt, if I had not rebelled and begged off. He powdered my whole face now, straightened me up, and began to plow my hair thoughtfully with his hands. Then he suggested a shampoo, and said my hair needed it badly, very badly. I observed that I shampooed it myself very thoroughly in the bath yesterday. I "had him" again. He next recommended some of "Smith's Hair Glorifier," and offered to sell me a bottle. I declined. He praised the new perfume, "Jones's Delight of the Toilet," and proposed to sell me some of that. I declined again. He tendered me a tooth-wash atrocity of his own invention, and when I declined offered to trade knives with me.

He returned to business after the miscarriage of this last enterprise, sprinkled me all over, legs and all, greased my hair in defiance of my protest against it, rubbed and scrubbed a good deal of it out by the roots, and combed and brushed the rest, parting it behind, and plastering the eternal inverted arch of hair down on my forehead, and then, while combing my scant eyebrows and defiling them with pomade, strung out an account of the achievements of a six-ounce black-and-tan terrier of his till I heard the whistles blow for noon, and knew I was five minutes too late for the train. Then he snatched away the towel, brushed it lightly about my face, passed his comb through my eyebrows once more, and gaily sang out "Next!"

This barber fell down and died of apoplexy two hours later. I am waiting over a day for my revenge—I am going to attend his funeral.

"PARTY CRIES" IN IRELAND

Belfast is a peculiarly religious community. This may be said of the whole of the North of Ireland. About one-half of the people are Protestants and the other half Catholics. Each party does all it can to make its own doctrines popular and draw the affections of the irreligious toward them. One hears constantly of the most touching instances of this zeal. A week ago a vast concourse of Catholics assembled at Armagh to dedicate a new Cathedral; and when they started home again the roadways were lined with groups of meek and lowly Protestants who stoned them till all the region round about was marked with blood. I thought that only Catholics argued in that way, but it seems to be a mistake.

Every man in the community is a missionary and carries a brick to admonish the erring with. The law has tried to break this up, but not with perfect success. It has decreed that irritating "party cries" shall not be indulged in, and that persons uttering them shall be fined forty shillings and costs. And so, in the police court reports every day, one sees these fines recorded. Last week a girl of twelve years old was fined the usual forty shillings and costs for proclaiming in the public streets that she was "a Protestant." The usual cry is, "To hell with the Pope!" or "To hell with the Protestants!" according to the utterer's system of salvation.

One of Belfast's local jokes was very good. It referred to the uniform and inevitable fine of forty shillings and costs for uttering a party cry—and it is no economical fine for a poor man, either, by the way. They say that a policeman found a drunken man lying on the ground, up a dark alley, entertaining himself with shouting, "To hell with!" "To hell with!" The officer smelt a fine—informers get half.

"What's that you say?"

"To hell with!"

"To hell with who? To hell with what?"

"Ah, bedad, ye can finish it yourself—it's too expinsive for me!"

I think the seditious disposition, restrained by the economical instinct, is finely put in that.

THE FACTS CONCERNING THE RECENT RESIGNATION [WRITTEN ABOUT 1867]

WASHINGTON, December, 1867.

I have resigned. The government appears to go on much the same, but there is a spoke out of its wheel, nevertheless. I was clerk of the Senate Committee on Conchology and I have thrown up the position. I could see the plainest disposition on the part of the other members of the government to debar me from having any voice in the counsels of the nation, and so I could no longer hold office and retain my self-respect. If I were to detail all the outrages that were heaped upon me during the six days that I was connected with the government in an official capacity, the narrative would fill a volume. They appointed me clerk of that Committee on Conchology and then allowed me no amanuensis to play billiards with. I would have borne that, lonesome as it was, if I had met with that courtesy from the other members of the Cabinet which was my due. But I did not. Whenever I observed that the head of a department was pursuing a wrong course, I laid down everything and went and tried to set him right, as it was my duty to do; and I never was thanked for it in a single instance. I went, with the best intentions in the world, to the Secretary of the Navy, and said:

"Sir, I cannot see that Admiral Farragut is doing anything but skirmishing around there in Europe, having a sort of picnic. Now, that may be all very well, but it does not exhibit itself to me in that light. If there is no fighting for him to do, let him come home. There is no use in a man having a whole fleet for a pleasure excursion. It is too expensive. Mind, I do not object to pleasure excursions for the naval officers—pleasure excursions that are in reason—pleasure excursions that are economical. Now, they might go down the Mississippi on a raft—"

You ought to have heard him storm! One would have supposed I had committed a crime of some kind. But I didn't mind. I said it was cheap, and full of republican simplicity, and perfectly safe. I said that, for a tranquil pleasure excursion, there was nothing equal to a raft.

Then the Secretary of the Navy asked me who I was; and when I told him I was connected with the government, he wanted to know in what capacity. I said that, without remarking upon the singularity of such a question, coming, as it did, from a member of that same government, I would inform him that I was clerk of the Senate Committee on Conchology. Then there was a fine storm! He finished by ordering me to leave the premises, and give my attention strictly to my own business in future. My first impulse was to get him removed. However, that would harm others besides himself, and do me no real good, and so I let him stay.

I went next to the Secretary of War, who was not inclined to see me at all until he learned that I was connected with the government. If I had not been on important business, I suppose I could not have got in. I asked him for a light (he was smoking at the time), and then I told him I had no fault to find with his defending the parole stipulations of General Lee and his comrades in arms, but that I could not approve of his method of fighting the Indians on the Plains. I said he fought too scattering. He ought to get the Indians more together—get them together in some convenient place, where he could have provisions enough for both parties, and then have a general massacre. I said there was nothing so convincing to an Indian as a general massacre. If he could not approve of the massacre, I said the next surest thing for an Indian was soap and education. Soap and education are not as sudden as a massacre, but they are more deadly in the long run; because a half-massacred Indian may recover, but if you educate him and wash him, it is bound to finish him some time or other. It undermines his constitution; it strikes at the foundation of his being. "Sir," I said, "the time has come when blood-curdling cruelty has become necessary. Inflict soap and a spelling-book on every Indian that ravages the Plains, and let them die!"

The Secretary of War asked me if I was a member of the Cabinet, and I said I was. He inquired what position I held, and I said I was clerk of the Senate Committee on Conchology. I was then ordered under arrest for contempt of court, and restrained of my liberty for the best part of the day.

I almost resolved to be silent thenceforward, and let the Government get along the best way it could. But duty called, and I obeyed. I called on the Secretary of the Treasury. He said:

"What will you have?"

The question threw me off my guard. I said, "Rum punch."

He said: "If you have got any business here, sir, state it—and in as few words as possible."

I then said that I was sorry he had seen fit to change the subject so abruptly, because such conduct was very offensive to me; but under the circumstances I would overlook the matter and come to the point. I now went into an earnest expostulation with him upon the extravagant length of his report. I said it was expensive, unnecessary, and awkwardly constructed; there were no descriptive passages in it, no poetry, no sentiment—no heroes, no plot, no pictures—not even wood-cuts. Nobody would read it, that was a clear case. I urged him not to ruin his reputation by getting out a thing like that. If he ever hoped to succeed in literature he must throw more variety into his writings. He must beware of dry detail. I said that the main popularity of the almanac was derived from its poetry and conundrums, and that a few conundrums distributed around through his Treasury report would help the sale of it more than all the internal revenue he could put into it. I said these things in the kindest spirit, and yet the Secretary of the Treasury fell into a violent passion. He even said I was an ass. He abused me in the most vindictive manner, and said that if I came there again meddling with his business he would throw me out of the window. I said I would take my hat and go, if I could not be treated with the respect due to my office, and I did go. It was just like a new author. They always think they know more than anybody else when they are getting out their first book. Nobody can tell them anything.

During the whole time that I was connected with the government it seemed as if I could not do anything in an official capacity without getting myself into trouble. And yet I did nothing, attempted nothing, but what I conceived to be for the good of my country. The sting of my wrongs may have driven me to unjust and harmful conclusions, but it surely seemed to me that the Secretary of State, the Secretary of War, the Secretary of the Treasury, and others of my confrères had conspired from the very beginning to drive me from the Administration. I never attended but one Cabinet meeting while I was connected with the government. That was sufficient for me. The servant at the White House door did not seem disposed to make way for me until I asked if the other members of the Cabinet had arrived. He said they had, and I entered. They were all there; but nobody offered me a seat. They stared at me as if I had been an intruder. The President said:

"Well, sir, who are you?"

I handed him my card, and he read: "The HON. MARK TWAIN, Clerk of the Senate Committee on Conchology." Then he looked at me from head to foot, as if he had never heard of me before. The Secretary of the Treasury said:

"This is the meddlesome ass that came to recommend me to put poetry and conundrums in my report, as if it were an almanac."

The Secretary of War said: "It is the same visionary that came to me yesterday with a scheme to educate a portion of the Indians to death, and massacre the balance."

The Secretary of the Navy said: "I recognize this youth as the person who has been interfering with my business time and again during the week. He is distressed about Admiral Farragut's using a whole fleet for a pleasure excursion, as he terms it. His proposition about some insane pleasure excursion on a raft is too absurd to repeat."

I said: "Gentlemen, I perceive here a disposition to throw discredit upon every act of my official career; I perceive, also, a disposition to debar me from all voice in the counsels of the nation. No notice whatever was sent to me to-day. It was only by the merest chance that I learned that there was going to be a Cabinet meeting. But let these things pass. All I wish to know is, is this a Cabinet meeting or is it not?"

The President said it was.

"Then," I said, "let us proceed to business at once, and not fritter away valuable time in unbecoming fault-findings with each other's official conduct."

The Secretary of State now spoke up, in his benignant way, and said, "Young man, you are laboring under a mistake. The clerks of the Congressional committees are not members of the Cabinet. Neither are the doorkeepers of the Capitol, strange as it may seem. Therefore, much as we could desire your more than human wisdom in our deliberations, we cannot lawfully avail ourselves of it. The counsels of the nation must proceed without you; if disaster follows, as follow full well it may, be it balm to your sorrowing spirit that by deed and voice you did what in you lay to avert it. You have my blessing. Farewell."

These gentle words soothed my troubled breast, and I went away. But the servants of a nation can know no peace. I had hardly reached my den in the Capitol, and disposed my feet on the table like a representative, when one of the Senators on the Conchological Committee came in in a passion and said:

"Where have you been all day?"

I observed that, if that was anybody's affair but my own, I had been to a Cabinet meeting.

"To a Cabinet meeting? I would like to know what business you had at a Cabinet meeting?"

I said I went there to consult—allowing for the sake of argument that he was in any wise concerned in the matter. He grew insolent then, and ended by saying he had wanted me for three days past to copy a report on bomb-shells, egg-shells, clamshells, and I don't know what all, connected with conchology, and nobody had been able to find me.

This was too much. This was the feather that broke the clerical camel's back. I said, "Sir, do you suppose that I am going to work for six dollars a day? If that is the idea, let me recommend the Senate Committee on Conchology to hire somebody else. I am the slave of no faction! Take back your degrading commission. Give me liberty, or give me death!"

From that hour I was no longer connected with the government. Snubbed by the department, snubbed by the Cabinet, snubbed at last by the chairman of a committee I was endeavoring to adorn, I yielded to persecution, cast far from me the perils and seductions of my great office, and forsook my bleeding country in the hour of her peril.

But I had done the state some service, and I sent in my bill:

The United States of America in account with the Hon. Clerk of the Senate Committee on Conchology,	Dr
To consultation with Secretary of War	$50
To consultation with Secretary of Navy	$50
To consultation with Secretary of the Treasury	$50
Cabinet consultation	No charge
To mileage to and from Jerusalem, via Egypt, Algiers, Gibraltar, and Cadiz, 14,000 miles, at 20c. a mile	$2,800
To salary as Clerk of Senate Committee on Conchology, six days, at $6 per day	$36
Total	$2,986

—[Territorial delegates charge mileage both ways, although they never go back when they get here once. Why my mileage is denied me is more than I can understand.]

Not an item of this bill has been paid, except that trifle of thirty-six dollars for clerkship salary. The Secretary of the Treasury, pursuing me to the last, drew his pen through all the other items, and simply marked in the margin "Not allowed." So, the dread alternative is embraced at last. Repudiation has begun! The nation is lost.

I am done with official life for the present. Let those clerks who are willing to be imposed on remain. I know numbers of them in the departments who are never informed when there is to be a Cabinet meeting, whose advice is never asked about war, or finance, or commerce, by the heads of the nation, any more than if they were not connected with the government, and who actually stay in their offices day after day and work! They know their importance to the nation, and they unconsciously show it in their bearing, and the way they order their sustenance at the restaurant—but they work. I know one who has to paste all sorts of little scraps from the newspapers into a scrapbook—sometimes as many as eight or ten scraps a day. He doesn't do it well, but he does it as well as he can. It is very fatiguing. It is exhausting to the intellect. Yet he only gets eighteen hundred dollars a year. With a brain like his, that young man could amass thousands and thousands of dollars in some other pursuit, if he chose to do it. But no—his heart is with his country, and he will serve her as long as she has got a scrapbook left. And I know clerks that don't know how to write very well, but such knowledge as they possess they nobly lay at the feet of their country, and toil on and suffer for twenty-five hundred dollars a year. What they write has to be written over again by other clerks sometimes; but when a man has done his best for his country, should his country complain? Then there are clerks that have no clerkships, and are waiting, and waiting, and waiting for a vacancy—waiting patiently for a chance to help their country out—and while they are waiting, they only get barely two thousand dollars a year for it. It is sad—it is very, very sad. When a member of Congress has a friend who is gifted, but has no employment wherein his great powers may be brought to bear, he confers him upon his country, and gives him a clerkship in a department. And there that man has to slave his life out, fighting documents for the benefit of a nation that never thinks of him, never sympathizes with him—and all for two thousand or three thousand dollars a year. When I shall have completed my list of all the clerks in the several departments, with my statement of what they have to do, and what they get for it, you will see that there are not half enough clerks, and that what there are do not get half enough pay.

HISTORY REPEATS ITSELF

The following I find in a Sandwich Island paper which some friend has sent me from that tranquil far-off retreat. The coincidence between my own experience and that here set down by the late Mr. Benton is so remarkable that I cannot forbear publishing and commenting upon the paragraph. The Sandwich Island paper says:

How touching is this tribute of the late Hon. T. H. Benton to his mother's influence:—'My mother asked me never to use tobacco; I have never touched it from that time to the present day. She asked me not to gamble, and I have never gambled. I cannot tell who is losing in games that are being played. She admonished me, too, against liquor-drinking, and whatever capacity for endurance I have at present, and whatever usefulness I may have attained through life, I attribute to having complied with her pious and correct wishes. When I was seven years of age she asked me not to drink, and then I made a resolution of total abstinence; and that I have adhered to it through all time I owe to my mother.'

I never saw anything so curious. It is almost an exact epitome of my own moral career—after simply substituting a grandmother for a mother. How well I remember my grandmother's asking me not to use tobacco, good old soul! She said, "You're at it again, are you, you whelp? Now don't ever let me catch you chewing tobacco before breakfast again, or I lay I'll blacksnake you within an inch of your life!" I have never touched it at that hour of the morning from that time to the present day.

She asked me not to gamble. She whispered and said, "Put up those wicked cards this minute!—two pair and a jack, you numskull, and the other fellow's got a flush!"

I never have gambled from that day to this—never once—without a "cold deck" in my pocket. I cannot even tell who is going to lose in games that are being played unless I deal myself.

When I was two years of age she asked me not to drink, and then I made a resolution of total abstinence. That I have adhered to it and enjoyed the beneficent effects of it through all time, I owe to my grandmother. I have never drunk a drop from that day to this of any kind of water.

HONORED AS A CURIOSITY

If you get into conversation with a stranger in Honolulu, and experience that natural desire to know what sort of ground you are treading on by finding out what manner of man your stranger is, strike out boldly and address him as "Captain." Watch him narrowly, and if you see by his countenance that you are on the wrong track, ask him where he preaches. It is a safe bet that he is either a missionary or captain of a whaler. I became personally acquainted with seventy-two captains and ninety-six missionaries. The captains and ministers form one-half of the population; the third fourth is composed of common Kanakas and mercantile foreigners and their families; and the final fourth is made up of high officers of the Hawaiian Government. And there are just about cats enough for three apiece all around.

A solemn stranger met me in the suburbs one day, and said:

"Good morning, your reverence. Preach in the stone church yonder, no doubt!"

"No, I don't. I'm not a preacher."

"Really, I beg your pardon, captain. I trust you had a good season. How much oil—"

"Oil! Why, what do you take me for? I'm not a whaler."

"Oh! I beg a thousand pardons, your Excellency. Major-General in the household troops, no doubt? Minister of the Interior, likely? Secretary of War? First Gentleman of the Bedchamber? Commissioner of the Royal—"

"Stuff, man! I'm not connected in any way with the government."

"Bless my life! Then who the mischief are you? what the mischief are you? and how the mischief did you get here? and where in thunder did you come from?"

"I'm only a private personage—an unassuming stranger—lately arrived from America."

"No! Not a missionary! not a whaler! not a member of his Majesty's government! not even a Secretary of the Navy! Ah! Heaven! it is too blissful to be true, alas! I do but dream. And yet that noble, honest countenance—those oblique, ingenuous eyes—that massive head, incapable of—of anything; your hand; give me your hand, bright waif. Excuse these tears. For sixteen weary years I have yearned for a moment like this, and—"

Here his feelings were too much for him, and he swooned away. I pitied this poor creature from the bottom of my heart. I was deeply moved. I shed a few tears on him, and kissed him for his mother. I then took what small change he had, and "shoved."

FIRST INTERVIEW WITH ARTEMUS WARD

[Written about 1870.]

I had never seen him before. He brought letters of introduction from mutual friends in San Francisco, and by invitation I breakfasted with him. It was almost religion, there in the silver-mines, to precede such a meal with whisky cocktails. Artemus, with the true cosmopolitan instinct, always deferred to the customs of the country he was in, and so he ordered three of those abominations. Hingston was present. I said I would rather not drink a whisky cocktail. I said it would go right to my head, and confuse me so that I would be in a helpless tangle in ten minutes. I did not want to act like a lunatic before strangers. But Artemus gently insisted, and I drank the treasonable mixture under protest, and felt all the time that I was doing a thing I might be sorry for. In a minute or two I began to imagine that my ideas were clouded. I waited in great anxiety for the conversation to open, with a sort of vague hope that my understanding would prove clear, after all, and my misgivings groundless.

Artemus dropped an unimportant remark or two, and then assumed a look of superhuman earnestness, and made the following astounding speech. He said:

"Now there is one thing I ought to ask you about before I forget it. You have been here in Silver land—here in Nevada—two or three years, and, of course, your position on the daily press has made it necessary for you to go down in the mines and examine them carefully in detail, and therefore you know all about the silver-mining business. Now what I want to get at is—is, well, the way the deposits of ore are made, you know. For instance. Now, as I understand it, the vein which contains the silver is sandwiched in between casings of granite, and runs along the ground, and sticks up like a curb stone. Well, take a vein forty feet thick, for example, or eighty, for that matter, or even a hundred—say you go down on it with a shaft, straight down, you know, or with what you call 'incline' maybe you go down five hundred feet, or maybe you don't go down but two hundred—anyway, you go down, and all the time this vein grows narrower, when the casings come nearer or approach each other, you may say—that is, when they do approach, which, of course, they do not always do, particularly in cases where the nature of the formation is such that they stand apart wider than they otherwise would, and which geology has failed to account for, although everything in that science goes to prove that, all things being equal, it would if it did not, or would not certainly if it did, and then, of course, they are. Do not you think it is?"

I said to myself:

"Now I just knew how it would be—that whisky cocktail has done the business for me; I don't understand any more than a clam."

And then I said aloud:

"I—I—that is—if you don't mind, would you—would you say that over again? I ought—"

"Oh, certainly, certainly! You see I am very unfamiliar with the subject, and perhaps I don't present my case clearly, but I—"

"No, no-no, no-you state it plain enough, but that cocktail has muddled me a little. But I will—no, I do understand for that matter; but I would get the hang of it all the better if you went over it again—and I'll pay better attention this time."

He said, "Why, what I was after was this."

[Here he became even more fearfully impressive than ever, and emphasized each particular point by checking it off on his finger-ends.]

"This vein, or lode, or ledge, or whatever you call it, runs along between two layers of granite, just the same as if it were a sandwich. Very well. Now suppose you go down on that, say a thousand feet, or maybe twelve hundred (it don't really matter) before you drift, and then you start your drifts, some of them across the ledge, and others along the length of it, where the sulphurets—I believe they call them sulphurets, though why they should, considering that, so far as I can see, the main dependence of a miner does not so lie, as some suppose, but in which it cannot be successfully maintained, wherein the same should not continue, while part and parcel of the same ore not committed to either in the sense referred to, whereas, under different circumstances, the most inexperienced among us could not detect it if it were, or might overlook it if it did, or scorn the very idea of such a thing, even though it were palpably demonstrated as such. Am I not right?"

I said, sorrowfully: "I feel ashamed of myself, Mr. Ward. I know I ought to understand you perfectly well, but you see that treacherous whisky cocktail has got into my head, and now I cannot understand even the simplest proposition. I told you how it would be."

"Oh, don't mind it, don't mind it; the fault was my own, no doubt—though I did think it clear enough for—"

"Don't say a word. Clear! Why, you stated it as clear as the sun to anybody but an abject idiot; but it's that confounded cocktail that has played the mischief."

"No; now don't say that. I'll begin it all over again, and—"

"Don't now—for goodness' sake, don't do anything of the kind, because I tell you my head is in such a condition that I don't believe I could understand the most trifling question a man could ask me.

"Now don't you be afraid. I'll put it so plain this time that you can't help but get the hang of it. We will begin at the very beginning." [Leaning far across the table, with determined impressiveness wrought upon his every feature, and fingers prepared to keep tally of each point enumerated; and I, leaning forward with painful interest, resolved to comprehend or perish.] "You know the vein, the ledge, the thing that contains the metal, whereby it constitutes the medium between all other forces, whether of present or remote agencies, so brought to bear in favor of the former against the latter, or the latter against the former or all, or both, or compromising the relative differences existing within the radius whence culminate the several degrees of similarity to which—"

I said: "Oh, hang my wooden head, it ain't any use!—it ain't any use to try—I can't understand anything. The plainer you get it the more I can't get the hang of it."

I heard a suspicious noise behind me, and turned in time to see Hingston dodging behind a newspaper, and quaking with a gentle ecstasy of laughter. I looked at Ward again, and he had thrown off his dread solemnity and was laughing also. Then I saw that I had been sold—that I had been made a victim of a swindle in the way of a string of plausibly worded sentences that didn't mean anything under the sun. Artemus Ward was one of the best fellows in the world, and one of the most companionable. It has been said that he was not fluent in conversation, but, with the above experience in my mind, I differ.

CANNIBALISM IN THE CARS

[Written about 1867.]

I visited St. Louis lately, and on my way West, after changing cars at Terre Haute, Indiana, a mild, benevolent-looking gentleman of about forty-five, or maybe fifty, came in at one of the way-stations and sat down beside me. We talked together pleasantly on various subjects for an hour, perhaps, and I found him exceedingly intelligent and entertaining. When he learned that I was from Washington, he immediately began to ask questions about various public men, and about Congressional affairs; and I saw very shortly that I was conversing with a man who was perfectly familiar with the ins and outs of political life at the Capital, even to the ways and manners, and customs of procedure of Senators and Representatives in the Chambers of the national Legislature. Presently two men halted near us for a single moment, and one said to the other:

"Harris, if you'll do that for me, I'll never forget you, my boy."

My new comrade's eye lighted pleasantly. The words had touched upon a happy memory, I thought. Then his face settled into thoughtfulness—almost into gloom. He turned to me and said,

"Let me tell you a story; let me give you a secret chapter of my life—a chapter that has never been referred to by me since its events transpired. Listen patiently, and promise that you will not interrupt me."

I said I would not, and he related the following strange adventure, speaking sometimes with animation, sometimes with melancholy, but always with feeling and earnestness.

THE STRANGER'S NARRATIVE

"On the 19th of December, 1853, I started from St. Louis on the evening train bound for Chicago. There were only twenty-four passengers, all told. There were no ladies and no children. We were in excellent spirits, and pleasant acquaintanceships were soon formed. The journey bade fair to be a happy one; and no individual in the party, I think, had even the vaguest presentiment of the horrors we were soon to undergo.

"At 11 P.M. it began to snow hard. Shortly after leaving the small village of Welden, we entered upon that tremendous prairie solitude that stretches its leagues on leagues of houseless dreariness far away toward the Jubilee Settlements. The winds, unobstructed by trees or hills, or even vagrant rocks, whistled fiercely across the level desert, driving the falling snow before it like spray from the crested waves of a stormy sea. The snow was deepening fast; and we knew, by the diminished speed of the train, that the engine was plowing through it with steadily increasing difficulty. Indeed, it almost came to a dead halt sometimes, in the midst of great drifts that piled themselves like colossal graves across the track. Conversation began to flag. Cheerfulness gave place to grave concern. The possibility of being imprisoned in the snow, on the bleak prairie, fifty miles from any house, presented itself to every mind, and extended its depressing influence over every spirit.

"At two o'clock in the morning I was aroused out of an uneasy slumber by the ceasing of all motion about me. The appalling truth flashed upon me instantly—we were captives in a snow-drift! 'All hands to the rescue!' Every man sprang to obey. Out into the wild night, the pitchy darkness, the billowy snow, the driving storm, every soul leaped, with the consciousness that a moment lost now might bring destruction to us all. Shovels, hands, boards—anything, everything that could displace snow, was brought into instant requisition. It was a weird picture, that small company of frantic men fighting the banking snows, half in the blackest shadow and half in the angry light of the locomotive's reflector.

"One short hour sufficed to prove the utter uselessness of our efforts. The storm barricaded the track with a dozen drifts while we dug one away. And worse than this, it was discovered that the last grand charge the engine had made upon the enemy had broken the fore-and-aft shaft of the driving-wheel! With a free track before us we should still have been helpless. We entered the car wearied with labor, and very sorrowful. We gathered about the stoves, and gravely canvassed our situation. We had no provisions whatever—in this lay our chief distress. We could not freeze, for there was a good supply of wood in the tender. This was our only comfort. The discussion ended at last in accepting the disheartening decision of the conductor, viz., that it would be death for any man to attempt to travel fifty miles on foot through snow like that. We could not send for help, and even if we could it would not come. We must submit, and await, as patiently as we might, succor or starvation! I think the stoutest heart there felt a momentary chill when those words were uttered.

"Within the hour conversation subsided to a low murmur here and there about the car, caught fitfully between the rising and falling of the blast; the lamps grew dim; and the majority of the castaways settled themselves among the flickering shadows to think—to forget the present, if they could—to sleep, if they might.

"The eternal night—it surely seemed eternal to us—wore its lagging hours away at last, and the cold gray dawn broke in the east. As the light grew stronger the passengers began to stir and give signs of life, one after another, and each in turn pushed his slouched hat up from his forehead, stretched his stiffened limbs, and glanced out of the windows upon the cheerless prospect. It was cheer less, indeed!—not a living thing visible anywhere, not a human habitation; nothing but a vast white desert; uplifted sheets of snow drifting hither and thither before the wind—a world of eddying flakes shutting out the firmament above.

"All day we moped about the cars, saying little, thinking much. Another lingering dreary night—and hunger.

"Another dawning—another day of silence, sadness, wasting hunger, hopeless watching for succor that could not come. A night of restless slumber, filled with dreams of feasting—wakings distressed with the gnawings of hunger.

"The fourth day came and went—and the fifth! Five days of dreadful imprisonment! A savage hunger looked out at every eye. There was in it a sign of awful import—the foreshadowing of a something that was vaguely shaping itself in every heart—a something which no tongue dared yet to frame into words.

"The sixth day passed—the seventh dawned upon as gaunt and haggard and hopeless a company of men as ever stood in the shadow of death. It must out now! That thing which had been growing up in every heart was ready to leap from every lip at last! Nature had been taxed to the utmost—she must yield. RICHARD H. GASTON of Minnesota, tall, cadaverous, and pale, rose up. All knew what was coming. All prepared—every emotion, every semblance of excitement—was smothered—only a calm, thoughtful seriousness appeared in the eyes that were lately so wild.

"'Gentlemen: It cannot be delayed longer! The time is at hand! We must determine which of us shall die to furnish food for the rest!'

"MR. JOHN J. WILLIAMS of Illinois rose and said: 'Gentlemen—I nominate the Rev. James Sawyer of Tennessee.'

"MR. Wm. R. ADAMS of Indiana said: 'I nominate Mr. Daniel Slote of New York.'

"MR. CHARLES J. LANGDON: 'I nominate Mr. Samuel A. Bowen of St. Louis.'

"MR. SLOTE: 'Gentlemen—I desire to decline in favor of Mr. John A. Van Nostrand, Jun., of New Jersey.'

"MR. GASTON: 'If there be no objection, the gentleman's desire will be acceded to.'

"MR. VAN NOSTRAND objecting, the resignation of Mr. Slote was rejected. The resignations of Messrs. Sawyer and Bowen were also offered, and refused upon the same grounds.

"MR. A. L. BASCOM of Ohio: 'I move that the nominations now close, and that the House proceed to an election by ballot.'

"MR. SAWYER: 'Gentlemen—I protest earnestly against these proceedings. They are, in every way, irregular and unbecoming. I must beg to move that they be dropped at once, and that we elect a chairman of the meeting and proper officers to assist him, and then we can go on with the business before us understandingly.'

"MR. BELL of Iowa: 'Gentlemen—I object. This is no time to stand upon forms and ceremonious observances. For more than seven days we have been without food. Every moment we lose in idle discussion increases our distress. I am satisfied with the nominations that have been made—every gentleman present is, I believe—and I, for one, do not see why we should not proceed at once to elect one or more of them. I wish to offer a resolution—'

"MR. GASTON: 'It would be objected to, and have to lie over one day under the rules, thus bringing about the very delay you wish to avoid. The gentleman from New Jersey—'

"MR. VAN NOSTRAND: 'Gentlemen—I am a stranger among you; I have not sought the distinction that has been conferred upon me, and I feel a delicacy—'

"MR. MORGAN Of Alabama (interrupting): 'I move the previous question.'

"The motion was carried, and further debate shut off, of course. The motion to elect officers was passed, and under it Mr. Gaston was chosen chairman, Mr. Blake, secretary, Messrs. Holcomb, Dyer, and Baldwin a committee on nominations, and Mr. R. M. Howland, purveyor, to assist the committee in making selections.

"A recess of half an hour was then taken, and some little caucusing followed. At the sound of the gavel the meeting reassembled, and the committee reported in favor of Messrs. George Ferguson of Kentucky, Lucien Herrman of Louisiana, and W. Messick of Colorado as candidates. The report was accepted.

"MR. ROGERS of Missouri: 'Mr. President—The report being properly before the House now, I move to amend it by substituting for the name of Mr. Herrman that of Mr. Lucius Harris of St. Louis, who is well and honorably known to us all. I do not wish to be understood as casting the least reflection upon the high character and standing of the gentleman from Louisiana—far from it. I respect and esteem him as much as any gentleman here present possibly can; but none of us can be blind to the fact that he has lost more flesh during the week that we have lain here than any among us—none of us can be blind to the fact that the committee has been derelict in its duty, either through negligence or a graver fault, in thus offering for our suffrages a gentleman who, however pure his own motives may be, has really less nutriment in him—'

"THE CHAIR: 'The gentleman from Missouri will take his seat. The Chair cannot allow the integrity of the committee to be questioned save by the regular course, under the rules. What action will the House take upon the gentleman's motion?'

"MR. HALLIDAY of Virginia: 'I move to further amend the report by substituting Mr. Harvey Davis of Oregon for Mr. Messick. It may be urged by gentlemen that the hardships and privations of a frontier life have rendered Mr. Davis tough; but, gentlemen, is this a time to cavil at toughness? Is this a time to be fastidious concerning trifles? Is this a time to dispute about matters of paltry significance? No, gentlemen, bulk is what we desire—substance, weight, bulk—these are the supreme requisites now—not talent, not genius, not education. I insist upon my motion.'

"MR. MORGAN (excitedly): 'Mr. Chairman—I do most strenuously object to this amendment. The gentleman from Oregon is old, and furthermore is bulky only in bone—not in flesh. I ask the gentleman from Virginia if it is soup we want instead of solid sustenance? if he would delude us with shadows? if he would mock our suffering with an Oregonian specter? I ask him if he can look upon the anxious faces around him, if he can gaze into our sad eyes, if he can listen to the beating of our expectant hearts, and still thrust this famine-stricken fraud upon us? I ask him if he can think of our desolate state, of our past sorrows, of our dark future, and still unpityingly foist upon us this wreck, this ruin, this tottering swindle, this gnarled and blighted and sapless vagabond from Oregon's inhospitable shores? Never!' [Applause.]

"The amendment was put to vote, after a fiery debate, and lost. Mr. Harris was substituted on the first amendment. The balloting then began. Five ballots were held without a choice. On the sixth, Mr. Harris was elected, all voting for him but himself. It was then moved that his election should be ratified by acclamation, which was lost, in consequence of his again voting against himself.

"MR. RADWAY moved that the House now take up the remaining candidates, and go into an election for breakfast. This was carried.

"On the first ballot there was a tie, half the members favoring one candidate on account of his youth, and half favoring the other on account of his superior size. The President gave the casting vote for the latter, Mr. Messick. This decision created considerable dissatisfaction among the friends of Mr. Ferguson, the defeated candidate, and there was some talk of demanding a new ballot; but in the midst of it a motion to adjourn was carried, and the meeting broke up at once.

"The preparations for supper diverted the attention of the Ferguson faction from the discussion of their grievance for a long time, and then, when they would have taken it up again, the happy announcement that Mr. Harris was ready drove all thought of it to the winds.

"We improvised tables by propping up the backs of car-seats, and sat down with hearts full of gratitude to the finest supper that had blessed our vision for seven torturing days. How changed we were from what we had been a few short hours before! Hopeless, sad-eyed misery, hunger, feverish anxiety, desperation, then; thankfulness, serenity, joy too deep for utterance now. That I know was the cheeriest hour of my eventful life. The winds howled, and blew the snow wildly about our prison house, but they were powerless to distress us any more. I liked Harris. He might have been better done, perhaps, but I am free to say that no man ever agreed with me better than Harris, or afforded me so large a degree of satisfaction. Messick was very well, though rather high-flavored, but for genuine nutritiousness and delicacy of fiber, give me Harris. Messick had his good points—I will not attempt to deny it, nor do I wish to do it—but he was no more fitted for breakfast than a mummy would be, sir—not a bit. Lean?—why, bless me!—and tough? Ah, he was very tough! You could not imagine it—you could never imagine anything like it."

"Do you mean to tell me that—"

"Do not interrupt me, please. After breakfast we elected a man by the name of Walker, from Detroit, for supper. He was very good. I wrote his wife so afterward. He was worthy of all praise. I shall always remember Walker. He was a little rare, but very good. And then the next morning we had Morgan of Alabama for breakfast. He was one of the finest men I ever sat down to—handsome, educated, refined, spoke several languages fluently—a perfect gentleman—he was a perfect gentleman, and singularly juicy. For supper we had that Oregon patriarch, and he was a fraud, there is no question about it— old, scraggy, tough, nobody can picture the reality. I finally said, gentlemen, you can do as you like, but I will wait for another election. And Grimes of Illinois said, 'Gentlemen, I will wait also. When you elect a man that has something to recommend him, I shall be glad to join you again.' It soon became evident that there was general dissatisfaction with Davis of Oregon, and so, to preserve the good will that had prevailed so pleasantly since we had had Harris, an election was called, and the result of it was that Baker of Georgia was chosen. He was splendid! Well, well—after that we had Doolittle, and Hawkins, and McElroy (there was some complaint about McElroy, because he was uncommonly short and thin), and Penrod, and two Smiths, and Bailey (Bailey had a wooden leg, which was clear loss, but he was otherwise good), and an Indian boy, and an organ-grinder, and a gentleman by the name of Buckminster—a poor stick of a vagabond that wasn't any good for company and no account for breakfast. We were glad we got him elected before relief came."

"And so the blessed relief did come at last?"

"Yes, it came one bright, sunny morning, just after election. John Murphy was the choice, and there never was a better, I am willing to testify; but John Murphy came home with us, in the train that came to succor us, and lived to marry the widow Harris—"

"Relict of—"

"Relict of our first choice. He married her, and is happy and respected and prosperous yet. Ah, it was like a novel, sir—it was like a romance. This is my stopping-place, sir; I must bid you goodby. Any time that you can make it convenient to tarry a day or two with me, I shall be glad to have you. I like you, sir; I have conceived an affection for you. I could like you as well as I liked Harris himself, sir. Good day, sir, and a pleasant journey."

He was gone. I never felt so stunned, so distressed, so bewildered in my life. But in my soul I was glad he was gone. With all his gentleness of manner and his soft voice, I shuddered whenever he turned his hungry eye upon me; and when I heard that I had achieved his perilous affection, and that I stood almost with the late Harris in his esteem, my heart fairly stood still!

I was bewildered beyond description. I did not doubt his word; I could not question a single item in a statement so stamped with the earnestness of truth as his; but its dreadful details overpowered me, and threw my thoughts into hopeless confusion. I saw the conductor looking at me. I said, "Who is that man?"

"He was a member of Congress once, and a good one. But he got caught in a snow-drift in the cars, and like to have been starved to death. He got so frost-bitten and frozen up generally, and used up for want of something to eat, that he was sick and out of his head two or three months afterward. He is all right now, only he is a monomaniac, and when he gets on that old subject he never stops till he has eat up that whole car-load of people he talks about. He would have finished the crowd by this time, only he had to get out here. He has got their names as pat as A B C. When he gets them all eat up but himself, he always says: 'Then the hour for the usual election for breakfast having arrived, and there being no opposition, I was duly elected, after which, there being no objections offered, I resigned. Thus I am here.'"

I felt inexpressibly relieved to know that I had only been listening to the harmless vagaries of a madman instead of the genuine experiences of a bloodthirsty cannibal.

THE KILLING OF JULIUS CAESAR "LOCALIZED"

[Written about 1865.]

Being the only true and reliable account ever published; taken from the Roman "Daily Evening Fasces," of the date of that tremendous occurrence.

Nothing in the world affords a newspaper reporter so much satisfaction as gathering up the details of a bloody and mysterious murder and writing them up with aggravating circumstantiality. He takes a living delight in this labor of love—for such it is to him, especially if he knows that all the other papers have gone to press, and his will be the only one that will contain the dreadful intelligence. A feeling of regret has often come over me that I was not reporting in Rome when Caesar was killed—reporting on an evening paper, and the only one in the city, and getting at least twelve hours ahead of the morning-paper boys with this most magnificent "item" that ever fell to the lot of the craft. Other events have happened as startling as this, but none that possessed so peculiarly all the characteristics of the favorite "item" of the present day, magnified into grandeur and sublimity by the high rank, fame, and social and political standing of the actors in it.

However, as I was not permitted to report Caesar's assassination in the regular way, it has at least afforded me rare satisfaction to translate the following able account of it from the original Latin of the Roman Daily Evening Fasces of that date—second edition:

Our usually quiet city of Rome was thrown into a state of wild excitement yesterday by the occurrence of one of those bloody affrays which sicken the heart and fill the soul with fear, while they inspire all thinking men with forebodings for the future of a city where human life is held so cheaply and the gravest laws are so openly set at defiance. As the result of that affray, it is our painful duty, as public journalists, to record the death of one of our most esteemed citizens—a man whose name is known wherever this paper circulates, and whose fame it has been our pleasure and our privilege to extend, and also to protect from the tongue of slander and falsehood, to the best of our poor ability. We refer to Mr. J. Caesar, the Emperor-elect.

The facts of the case, as nearly as our reporter could determine them from the conflicting statements of eye-witnesses, were about as follows:—The affair was an election row, of course. Nine-tenths of the ghastly butcheries that disgrace the city nowadays grow out of the bickerings and jealousies and animosities engendered by these accursed elections. Rome would be the gainer by it if her very constables were elected to serve a century; for in our experience we have never even been able to choose a dog-pelter without celebrating the event with a dozen knockdowns and a general cramming of the station-house with drunken vagabonds overnight. It is said that when the immense majority for Caesar at the polls in the market was declared the other day, and the crown was offered to that gentleman, even his amazing unselfishness in refusing it three times was not sufficient to save him from the whispered insults of such men as Casca, of the Tenth Ward, and other hirelings of the disappointed candidate, hailing mostly from the Eleventh and Thirteenth and other outside districts, who were overheard speaking ironically and contemptuously of Mr. Caesar's conduct upon that occasion.

We are further informed that there are many among us who think they are justified in believing that the assassination of Julius Caesar was a put-up thing—a cut-and-dried arrangement, hatched by Marcus Brutus and a lot of his hired roughs, and carried out only too faithfully according to the program. Whether there be good grounds for this suspicion or not, we leave to the people to judge for themselves, only asking that they will read the following account of the sad occurrence carefully and dispassionately before they render that judgment.

The Senate was already in session, and Caesar was coming down the street toward the capitol, conversing with some personal friends, and followed, as usual, by a large number of citizens. Just as he was passing in front of Demosthenes and Thucydides' drug store, he was observing casually to a gentleman, who, our informant thinks, is a fortune-teller, that the Ides of March were come. The reply was, "Yes, they are come, but not gone yet." At this moment Artexnidorus stepped up and passed the time of day, and asked Caesar to read a schedule or a tract or something of the kind, which he had brought for his perusal. Mr. Decius Brutus also said something about an "humble suit" which he wanted read. Artexnidorus begged that attention might be paid to his first, because it was of personal consequence to Caesar. The latter replied that what concerned himself should be read last, or words to that effect. Artemidorus begged and beseeched him to read the paper instantly!— [Mark that: It is hinted by William Shakespeare, who saw the beginning and the end of the unfortunate affray, that this "schedule" was simply a note discovering to Caesar that a plot was brewing to take his life.]— However, Caesar shook him off, and refused to read any petition in the street. He then entered the capitol, and the crowd followed him.

About this time the following conversation was overheard, and we consider that, taken in connection with the events which succeeded it, it bears an appalling significance: Mr. Papilius Lena remarked to George W. Cassius (commonly known as the "Nobby Boy of the Third Ward"), a bruiser in the pay of the Opposition, that he hoped his enterprise to-day might thrive; and when Cassius asked "What enterprise?" he only closed his left eye temporarily and said with simulated indifference, "Fare you well," and sauntered toward Caesar. Marcus Brutus, who is suspected of being the ringleader of the band that killed Caesar, asked what it was that Lena had said. Cassius told him, and added in a low tone, "I fear our purpose is discovered."

Brutus told his wretched accomplice to keep an eye on Lena, and a moment after Cassius urged that lean and hungry vagrant, Casca, whose reputation here is none of the best, to be sudden, for he feared prevention. He then turned to Brutus, apparently much excited, and asked what should be done, and swore that either he or Caesar would never turn back—he would kill himself first. At this time Caesar was talking to some of the back-country members about the approaching fall elections, and paying little attention to what was going on around him. Billy Trebonius got into conversation with the people's friend and Caesar's— Mark Antony—and under some pretense or other got him away, and Brutus, Decius, Casca, Cinna, Metellus Cimber, and others of the gang of infamous desperadoes that infest Rome at present, closed around the doomed Caesar. Then Metellus Cimber knelt down and begged that his brother might be recalled from banishment, but Caesar rebuked him for his fawning conduct, and refused to grant his petition. Immediately, at Cimber's request, first Brutus and then Cassias begged for the return of the banished Publius; but Caesar still refused. He said he could not be moved; that he was as fixed as the North Star, and proceeded to speak in the most complimentary terms of the firmness of that star and its steady character. Then he said he was like it, and he believed he was the only man in the country that was; therefore, since he was "constant" that Cimber should be banished, he was also "constant" that he should stay banished, and he'd be hanged if he didn't keep him so!

Instantly seizing upon this shallow pretext for a fight, Casca sprang at Caesar and struck him with a dirk, Caesar grabbing him by the arm with his right hand, and launching a blow straight from the shoulder with his left, that sent the reptile bleeding to the earth. He then backed up against Pompey's statue, and squared himself to receive his assailants. Cassias and Cimber and Cinna rushed upon him with their daggers drawn, and the former succeeded in inflicting a wound upon his body; but before he could strike again, and before either of the others could strike at all, Caesar stretched the three miscreants at his feet with as many blows of his powerful fist. By this time the Senate was in an indescribable uproar; the throng of citizens in the lobbies had blockaded the doors in their frantic efforts to escape from the building, the sergeant-at-arms and his assistants were struggling with the assassins, venerable senators had cast aside their encumbering robes, and were leaping over benches and flying down the aisles in wild confusion toward the shelter of the committee-rooms, and a thousand voices were shouting "Po-lice! Po-lice!" in discordant tones that rose above the frightful din like shrieking winds above the roaring of a tempest. And amid it all great Caesar stood with his back against the statue, like a lion at bay, and fought his assailants weaponless and hand to hand, with the defiant bearing and the unwavering courage which he had shown before on many a bloody field. Billy Trebonius and Caius Legarius struck him with their daggers and fell, as their brother-conspirators before them had fallen. But at last, when Caesar saw his old friend Brutus step forward armed with a murderous knife, it is said he seemed utterly overpowered with grief and amazement, and, dropping his invincible left arm by his side, he hid his face in the folds of his mantle and received the treacherous blow without an effort to stay the hand that gave it. He only said, "Et tu, Brute?" and fell lifeless on the marble pavement.

We learn that the coat deceased had on when he was killed was the same one he wore in his tent on the afternoon of the day he overcame the Nervii, and that when it was removed from the corpse it was found to be cut and gashed in no less than seven different places. There was nothing in the pockets. It will be exhibited at the coroner's inquest, and will be damning proof of the fact of the killing. These latter facts may be relied on, as we get them from Mark Antony, whose position enables him to learn every item of news connected with the one subject of absorbing interest of-to-day.

LATER:—While the coroner was summoning a jury, Mark Antony and other friends of the late Caesar got hold of the body, and lugged it off to the Forum, and at last accounts Antony and Brutus were making speeches over it and raising such a row among the people that, as we go to press, the chief of police is satisfied there is going to be a riot, and is taking measures accordingly.

THE WIDOW'S PROTEST

One of the saddest things that ever came under my notice (said the banker's clerk) was there in Corning during the war. Dan Murphy enlisted as a private, and fought very bravely. The boys all liked him, and when a wound by and by weakened him down till carrying a musket was too heavy work for him, they clubbed together and fixed him up as a sutler. He made money then, and sent it always to his wife to bank for him. She was a washer and ironer, and knew enough by hard experience to keep money when she got it. She didn't waste a penny.

On the contrary, she began to get miserly as her bank-account grew. She grieved to part with a cent, poor creature, for twice in her hard-working life she had known what it was to be hungry, cold, friendless, sick, and without a dollar in the world, and she had a haunting dread of suffering so again. Well, at last Dan died; and the boys, in testimony of their esteem and respect for him, telegraphed to Mrs. Murphy to know if she would like to have him embalmed and sent home, when you know the usual custom was to dump a poor devil like him into a shallow hole, and then inform his friends what had become of him. Mrs. Murphy jumped to the conclusion that it would only cost two or three dollars to embalm her dead husband, and so she telegraphed "Yes." It was at the "wake" that the bill for embalming arrived and was presented to the widow.

She uttered a wild, sad wail that pierced every heart, and said, "Sivinty-foive dollars for stooffin' Dan, blister their sowls! Did thim divils suppose I was goin' to stairt a Museim, that I'd be dalin' in such expinsive curiassities!"

The banker's clerk said there was not a dry eye in the house.

THE SCRIPTURAL PANORAMIST

[Written about 1866.]

"There was a fellow traveling around in that country," said Mr. Nickerson, "with a moral-religious show—a sort of scriptural panorama—and he hired a wooden-headed old slab to play the piano for him. After the first night's performance the showman says:

"'My friend, you seem to know pretty much all the tunes there are, and you worry along first rate. But then, didn't you notice that sometimes last night the piece you happened to be playing was a little rough on the proprieties, so to speak—didn't seem to jibe with the general gait of the picture that was passing at the time, as it were—was a little foreign to the subject, you know—as if you didn't either trump or follow suit, you understand?'

"'Well, no,' the fellow said; 'he hadn't noticed, but it might be; he had played along just as it came handy.'

"So they put it up that the simple old dummy was to keep his eye on the panorama after that, and as soon as a stunning picture was reeled out he was to fit it to a dot with a piece of music that would help the audience to get the idea of the subject, and warm them up like a camp-meeting revival. That sort of thing would corral their sympathies, the showman said.

"There was a big audience that night—mostly middle-aged and old people who belong to the church, and took a strong interest in Bible matters, and the balance were pretty much young bucks and heifers—they always come out strong on panoramas, you know, because it gives them a chance to taste one another's complexions in the dark.

"Well, the showman began to swell himself up for his lecture, and the old mud-jobber tackled the piano and ran his fingers up and down once or twice to see that she was all right, and the fellows behind the curtain commenced to grind out the panorama. The showman balanced his weight on his right foot, and propped his hands over his hips, and flung his eyes over his shoulder at the scenery, and said:

"'Ladies and gentlemen, the painting now before you illustrates the beautiful and touching parable of the Prodigal Son. Observe the happy expression just breaking over the features of the poor, suffering youth—so worn and weary with his long march; note also the ecstasy beaming from the uplifted countenance of the aged father, and the joy that sparkles in the eyes of the excited group of youths and maidens, and seems ready to burst into the welcoming chorus from their lips. The lesson, my friends, is as solemn and instructive as the story is tender and beautiful.'

"The mud-jobber was all ready, and when the second speech was finished, struck up:

> "Oh, we'll all get blind drunk
> When Johnny comes marching home!

"Some of the people giggled, and some groaned a little. The showman couldn't say a word; he looked at the pianist sharp, but he was all lovely and serene—he didn't know there was anything out of gear.

"The panorama moved on, and the showman drummed up his grit and started in fresh.

"'Ladies and gentlemen, the fine picture now unfolding itself to your gaze exhibits one of the most notable events in Bible history—our Saviour and His disciples upon the Sea of Galilee. How grand, how awe-inspiring are the reflections which the subject invokes! What sublimity of faith is revealed to us in this lesson from the sacred writings! The Saviour rebukes the angry waves, and walks securely upon the bosom of the deep!'

"All around the house they were whispering, 'Oh, how lovely, how beautiful!' and the orchestra let himself out again:

> "A life on the ocean wave,
> And a home on the rolling deep!

"There was a good deal of honest snickering turned on this time, and considerable groaning, and one or two old deacons got up and went out. The showman grated his teeth, and cursed the piano man to himself; but the fellow sat there like a knot on a log, and seemed to think he was doing first-rate.

"After things got quiet the showman thought he would make one more stagger at it, anyway, though his confidence was beginning to get mighty shaky. The supes started the panorama grinding along again, and he says:

"'Ladies and gentlemen, this exquisite painting represents the raising of Lazarus from the dead by our Saviour. The subject has been handled with marvelous skill by the artist, and such touching sweetness and tenderness of expression has he thrown into it that I have known peculiarly sensitive persons to be even affected to tears by looking at it. Observe the half-confused, half-inquiring look upon the countenance of the awakened Lazarus. Observe, also, the attitude and expression of the Saviour, who takes him gently by the sleeve of his shroud with one hand, while He points with the other toward the distant city.'

"Before anybody could get off an opinion in the case the innocent old ass at the piano struck up:

> "Come rise up, William Ri-i-ley,
> And go along with me!

"Whe-ew! All the solemn old flats got up in a huff to go, and everybody else laughed till the windows rattled.

"The showman went down and grabbed the orchestra and shook him up and says:

"'That lets you out, you know, you chowder-headed old clam. Go to the doorkeeper and get your money, and cut your stick—vamose the ranch! Ladies and gentlemen, circumstances over which I have no control compel me prematurely to dismiss the house.'"

CURING A COLD

[Written about 1864]

It is a good thing, perhaps, to write for the amusement of the public, but it is a far higher and nobler thing to write for their instruction, their profit, their actual and tangible benefit. The latter is the sole object of this article. If it prove the means of restoring to health one solitary sufferer among my race, of lighting up once more the fire of hope and joy in his faded eyes, of bringing back to his dead heart again the quick, generous impulses of other days, I shall be amply rewarded for my labor; my soul will be permeated with the sacred delight a Christian feels when he has done a good, unselfish deed.

Having led a pure and blameless life, I am justified in believing that no man who knows me will reject the suggestions I am about to make, out of fear that I am trying to deceive him. Let the public do itself the honor to read my experience in doctoring a cold, as herein set forth, and then follow in my footsteps.

When the White House was burned in Virginia City, I lost my home, my happiness, my constitution, and my trunk. The loss of the two first named articles was a matter of no great consequence, since a home without a mother, or a sister, or a distant young female relative in it, to remind you, by putting your soiled linen out of sight and taking your boots down off the mantelpiece, that there are those who think about you and care for you, is easily obtained. And I cared nothing for the loss of my happiness, because, not being a poet, it could not be possible that melancholy would abide with me long. But to lose a good constitution and a better trunk were serious misfortunes. On the day of the fire my constitution succumbed to a severe cold, caused by undue exertion in getting ready to do something. I suffered to no purpose, too, because the plan I was figuring at for the extinguishing of the fire was so elaborate that I never got it completed until the middle of the following week.

The first time I began to sneeze, a friend told me to go and bathe my feet in hot water and go to bed. I did so. Shortly afterwards, another friend advised me to get up and take a cold shower-bath. I did that also. Within the hour, another friend assured me that it was policy to "feed a cold and starve a fever." I had both. So I thought it best to fill myself up for the cold, and then keep dark and let the fever starve awhile.

In a case of this kind, I seldom do things by halves; I ate pretty heartily; I conferred my custom upon a stranger who had just opened his restaurant that morning; he waited near me in respectful silence until I had finished feeding my cold, when he inquired if the people about Virginia City were much afflicted with colds? I told him I thought they were. He then went out and took in his sign.

I started down toward the office, and on the way encountered another bosom friend, who told me that a quart of salt-water, taken warm, would come as near curing a cold as anything in the world. I hardly thought I had room for it, but I tried it anyhow. The result was surprising. I believed I had thrown up my immortal soul.

Now, as I am giving my experience only for the benefit of those who are troubled with the distemper I am writing about, I feel that they will see the propriety of my cautioning them against following such portions of it as proved inefficient with me, and acting upon this conviction, I warn them against warm salt-water. It may be a good enough remedy, but I think it is too severe. If I had another cold in the head, and there were no course left me but to take either an earthquake or a quart of warm saltwater, I would take my chances on the earthquake.

After the storm which had been raging in my stomach had subsided, and no more good Samaritans happening along, I went on borrowing handkerchiefs again and blowing them to atoms, as had been my custom in the early stages of my cold, until I came across a lady who had just arrived from over the plains, and who said she had lived in a part of the country where doctors were scarce, and had from necessity acquired considerable skill in the treatment of simple "family complaints." I knew she must have had much experience, for she appeared to be a hundred and fifty years old.

She mixed a decoction composed of molasses, aquafortis, turpentine, and various other drugs, and instructed me to take a wine-glass full of it every fifteen minutes. I never took but one dose; that was enough; it robbed me of all moral principle, and awoke every unworthy impulse of my nature. Under its malign influence my brain conceived miracles of meanness, but my hands were too feeble to execute them; at that time, had it not been that my strength had surrendered to a succession of assaults from infallible remedies for my cold, I am satisfied that I would have tried to rob the graveyard. Like most other people, I often feel mean, and act accordingly; but until I took that medicine I had never reveled in such supernatural depravity, and felt proud of it. At the end of two days I was ready to go to doctoring again. I took a few more unfailing remedies, and finally drove my cold from my head to my lungs.

I got to coughing incessantly, and my voice fell below zero; I conversed in a thundering bass, two octaves below my natural tone; I could only compass my regular nightly repose by coughing myself down to a state of utter exhaustion, and then the moment I began to talk in my sleep, my discordant voice woke me up again.

My case grew more and more serious every day. A plain gin was recommended; I took it. Then gin and molasses; I took that also. Then gin and onions; I added the onions, and took all three. I detected no particular result, however, except that I had acquired a breath like a buzzard's.

I found I had to travel for my health. I went to Lake Bigler with my reportorial comrade, Wilson. It is gratifying to me to reflect that we traveled in considerable style; we went in the Pioneer coach, and my friend took all his baggage with him, consisting of two excellent silk handkerchiefs and a daguerreotype of his grandmother. We sailed and hunted and fished and danced all day, and I doctored my cough all night. By managing in this way, I made out to improve every hour in the twenty-four. But my disease continued to grow worse.

A sheet-bath was recommended. I had never refused a remedy yet, and it seemed poor policy to commence then; therefore I determined to take a sheet-bath, notwithstanding I had no idea what sort of arrangement it was. It was administered at midnight, and the weather was very frosty. My breast and back were bared, and a sheet (there appeared to be a thousand yards of it) soaked in ice-water, was wound around me until I resembled a swab for a Columbiad.

It is a cruel expedient. When the chilly rag touches one's warm flesh, it makes him start with sudden violence, and gasp for breath just as men do in the death-agony. It froze the marrow in my bones and stopped the beating of my heart. I thought my time had come.

Young Wilson said the circumstance reminded him of an anecdote about a negro who was being baptized, and who slipped from the parson's grasp, and came near being drowned. He floundered around, though, and finally rose up out of the water considerably strangled and furiously angry, and started ashore at once, spouting water like a whale, and remarking, with great asperity, that "one o' dese days some gen'l'man's nigger gwyne to get killed wid jis' such damn foolishness as dis!"

Never take a sheet-bath—never. Next to meeting a lady acquaintance who, for reasons best known to herself, don't see you when she looks at you, and don't know you when she does see you, it is the most uncomfortable thing in the world.

But, as I was saying, when the sheet-bath failed to cure my cough, a lady friend recommended the application of a mustard plaster to my breast. I believe that would have cured me effectually, if it had not been for young Wilson. When I went to bed, I put my mustard plaster—which was a very gorgeous one, eighteen inches square—where I could reach it when I was ready for it. But young Wilson got hungry in the night, and— here is food for the imagination.

After sojourning a week at Lake Bigler, I went to Steamboat Springs, and, besides the steam-baths, I took a lot of the vilest medicines that were ever concocted. They would have cured me, but I had to go back to Virginia City, where, notwithstanding the variety of new remedies I absorbed every day, I managed to aggravate my disease by carelessness and undue exposure.

I finally concluded to visit San Francisco, and the first day I got there a lady at the hotel told me to drink a quart of whisky every twenty-four hours, and a friend up-town recommended precisely the same course. Each advised me to take a quart; that made half a gallon. I did it, and still live.

Now, with the kindest motives in the world, I offer for the consideration of consumptive patients the variegated course of treatment I have lately gone through. Let them try it; if it don't cure, it can't more than kill them.

A CURIOUS PLEASURE EXCURSION

[Published at the time of the "Comet Scare" in the summer of 1874]

[We have received the following advertisement, but, inasmuch as it concerns a matter of deep and general interest, we feel fully justified in inserting it in our reading-columns. We are confident that our conduct in this regard needs only explanation, not apology.—Ed., N. Y. Herald.]

ADVERTISEMENT

This is to inform the public that in connection with Mr. Barnum I have leased the comet for a term of years; and I desire also to solicit the public patronage in favor of a beneficial enterprise which we have in view.

We propose to fit up comfortable, and even luxurious, accommodations in the comet for as many persons as will honor us with their patronage, and make an extended excursion among the heavenly bodies. We shall prepare 1,000,000 state-rooms in the tail of the comet (with hot and cold water, gas, looking-glass, parachute, umbrella, etc., in each), and shall construct more if we meet with a sufficiently generous encouragement. We shall have billiard-rooms, card-rooms, music-rooms, bowling-alleys and many spacious theaters and free libraries; and on the main deck we propose to have a driving park, with upward of 100,000 miles of roadway in it. We shall publish daily newspapers also.

DEPARTURE OF THE COMET

The comet will leave New York at 10 P.M. on the 20th inst., and therefore it will be desirable that the passengers be on board by eight at the latest, to avoid confusion in getting under way. It is not known whether passports will be necessary or not, but it is deemed best that passengers provide them, and so guard against all contingencies. No dogs will be allowed on board. This rule has been made in deference to the existing state of feeling regarding these animals, and will be strictly adhered to. The safety of the passengers will in all ways be jealously looked to. A substantial iron railing will be put up all around the comet, and no one will be allowed to go to the edge and look over unless accompanied by either my partner or myself.

THE POSTAL SERVICE

will be of the completest character. Of course the telegraph, and the telegraph only, will be employed; consequently friends occupying state-rooms 20,000,000 and even 30,000,000 miles apart will be able to send a message and receive a reply inside of eleven days. Night messages will be half-rate. The whole of this vast postal system will be under the personal superintendence of Mr. Hale of Maine. Meals served at all hours. Meals served in staterooms charged extra.

Hostility is not apprehended from any great planet, but we have thought it best to err on the safe side, and therefore have provided a proper number of mortars, siege-guns, and boarding-pikes. History shows that small, isolated communities, such as the people of remote islands, are prone to be hostile to strangers, and so the same may be the case with

THE INHABITANTS OF STARS

of the tenth or twentieth magnitude. We shall in no case wantonly offend the people of any star, but shall treat all alike with urbanity and kindliness, never conducting ourselves toward an asteroid after a fashion which we could not venture to assume toward Jupiter or Saturn. I repeat that we shall not wantonly offend any star; but at the same time we shall promptly resent any injury that may be done us, or any insolence offered us, by parties or governments residing in any star in the firmament. Although averse to the shedding of blood, we shall still hold this course rigidly and fearlessly, not only toward single stars, but toward constellations. We shall hope to leave a good impression of America behind us in every nation we visit, from Venus to Uranus. And, at all events, if we cannot inspire love we shall at least compel respect for our country wherever we go. We shall take with us, free of charge,

A GREAT FORCE OF MISSIONARIES,

and shed the true light upon all the celestial orbs which, physically aglow, are yet morally in darkness. Sunday-schools will be established wherever practicable. Compulsory education will also be introduced.

The comet will visit Mars first, and proceed to Mercury, Jupiter, Venus, and Saturn. Parties connected with the government of the District of Columbia and with the former city government of New York, who may desire to inspect the rings, will be allowed time and every facility. Every star of prominent magnitude will be visited, and time allowed for excursions to points of interest inland.

THE DOG STAR

has been stricken from the program. Much time will be spent in the Great Bear, and, indeed, in every constellation of importance. So, also, with the Sun and Moon and the Milky Way, otherwise the Gulf Stream of the Skies. Clothing suitable for wear in the sun should be provided. Our program has been so arranged that we shall seldom go more than 100,000,000 of miles at a time without stopping at some star. This will necessarily make the stoppages frequent and preserve the interest of the tourist. Baggage checked through to any point on the route. Parties desiring to make only a part of the proposed tour, and thus save expense, may stop over at any star they choose and wait for the return voyage.

After visiting all the most celebrated stars and constellations in our system and personally inspecting the remotest sparks that even the most powerful telescope can now detect in the firmament, we shall proceed with good heart upon

A STUPENDOUS VOYAGE

of discovery among the countless whirling worlds that make turmoil in the mighty wastes of space that stretch their solemn solitudes, their unimaginable vastness billions upon billions of miles away beyond the farthest verge of telescopic vision, till by comparison the little sparkling vault we used to gaze at on Earth shall seem like a remembered phosphorescent flash of spangles which some tropical voyager's prow stirred into life for a single instant, and which ten thousand miles of phosphorescent seas and tedious lapse of time had since diminished to an incident utterly trivial in his recollection. Children occupying seats at the first table will be charged full fare.

FIRST-CLASS FARE

from the Earth to Uranus, including visits to the Sun and Moon and all the principal planets on the route, will be charged at the low rate of $2 for every 50,000,000 miles of actual travel. A great reduction will be made where parties wish to make the round trip. This comet is new and in thorough repair and is now on her first voyage. She is confessedly the fastest on the line. She makes 20,000,000 miles a day, with her present facilities; but, with a picked American crew and good weather, we are confident we can get 40,000,000 out of her. Still, we shall never push her to a dangerous speed, and we shall rigidly prohibit racing with other comets. Passengers desiring to diverge at any point or return will be transferred to other comets. We make close connections at all principal points with all reliable lines. Safety can be depended upon. It is not to be denied that the heavens are infested with

OLD RAMSHACKLE COMETS

that have not been inspected or overhauled in 10,000 years, and which ought long ago to have been destroyed or turned into hail-barges, but with these we have no connection whatever. Steerage passengers not allowed abaft the main hatch.

Complimentary round-trip tickets have been tendered to General Butler, Mr. Shepherd, Mr. Richardson, and other eminent gentlemen, whose public services have entitled them to the rest and relaxation of a voyage of this kind. Parties desiring to make the round trip will have extra accommodation. The entire voyage will be completed, and the passengers landed in New York again, on the 14th of December, 1991. This is, at least, forty years quicker than any other comet can do it in. Nearly all the back-pay members contemplate making the round trip with us in case their constituents will allow them a holiday. Every harmless amusement will be allowed on board, but no pools permitted on the run of the comet—no gambling of any kind. All fixed stars will be respected by us, but such stars as seem to need fixing we shall fix. If it makes trouble, we shall be sorry, but firm.

Mr. Coggia having leased his comet to us, she will no longer be called by his name, but by my partner's. N. B.—Passengers by paying double fare will be entitled to a share in all the new stars, suns, moons, comets, meteors, and magazines of thunder and lightning we may discover. Patent-medicine people will take notice that

WE CARRY BULLETIN-BOARDS

and a paint-brush along for use in the constellations, and are open to terms. Cremationists are reminded that we are going straight to—some hot places—and are open to terms. To other parties our enterprise is a pleasure excursion, but individually we mean business. We shall fly our comet for all it is worth.

FOR FURTHER PARTICULARS,

or for freight or passage, apply on board, or to my partner, but not to me, since I do not take charge of the comet until she is under way. It is necessary, at a time like this, that my mind should not be burdened with small business details.

MARK TWAIN.

RUNNING FOR GOVERNOR

[Written about 1870.]

A few months ago I was nominated for Governor of the great state of New York, to run against Mr. John T. Smith and Mr. Blank J. Blank on an independent ticket. I somehow felt that I had one prominent advantage over these gentlemen, and that was—good character. It was easy to see by the newspapers that if ever they had known what it was to bear a good name, that time had gone by. It was plain that in these latter years they had become familiar with all manner of shameful crimes. But at the very moment that I was exalting my advantage and joying in it in secret, there was a muddy undercurrent of discomfort "riling" the deeps of my happiness, and that was—the having to hear my name bandied about in familiar connection with those of such people. I grew more and more disturbed. Finally I wrote my grandmother about it. Her answer came quick and sharp. She said:

> You have never done one single thing in all your life to be ashamed of—not one. Look at the newspapers—look at them and comprehend what sort of characters Messrs. Smith and Blank are, and then see if you are willing to lower yourself to their level and enter a public canvass with them.

It was my very thought! I did not sleep a single moment that night. But, after all, I could not recede.

I was fully committed, and must go on with the fight. As I was looking listlessly over the papers at breakfast I came across this paragraph, and I may truly say I never was so confounded before.

> PERJURY.—Perhaps, now that Mr. Mark Twain is before the people as a candidate for Governor, he will condescend to explain how he came to be convicted of perjury by thirty-four witnesses in Wakawak, Cochin China, in 1863, the intent of which perjury being to rob a poor native widow and her helpless family of a meager plantain-patch, their only stay and support in their bereavement and desolation. Mr. Twain owes it to himself, as well as to the great people whose suffrages he asks, to clear this matter up. Will he do it?

I thought I should burst with amazement! Such a cruel, heartless charge! I never had seen Cochin China! I never had heard of Wakawak! I didn't know a plantain-patch from a kangaroo! I did not know what to do. I was crazed and helpless. I let the day slip away without doing anything at all. The next morning the same paper had this—nothing more:

> SIGNIFICANT.—Mr. Twain, it will be observed, is suggestively silent about the Cochin China perjury.

[Mem.—During the rest of the campaign this paper never referred to me in any other way than as "the infamous perjurer Twain."]

Next came the Gazette, with this:

> WANTED TO KNOW.—Will the new candidate for Governor deign to
> explain to certain of his fellow-citizens (who are suffering to vote for him!)
> the little circumstance of his cabin-mates in Montana losing small
> valuables from time to time, until at last, these things having been
> invariably found on Mr. Twain's person or in his "trunk" (newspaper he
> rolled his traps in), they felt compelled to give him a friendly admonition
> for his own good, and so tarred and feathered him, and rode him on a rail;
> and then advised him to leave a permanent vacuum in the place he
> usually occupied in the camp. Will he do this?

Could anything be more deliberately malicious than that? For I never was in Montana in
my life.

[After this, this journal customarily spoke of me as, "Twain, the Montana Thief."]

I got to picking up papers apprehensively—much as one would lift a desired blanket
which he had some idea might have a rattlesnake under it. One day this met my eye:

> THE LIE NAILED.—By the sworn affidavits of Michael O'Flanagan, Esq.,
> of the Five Points, and Mr. Snub Rafferty and Mr. Catty Mulligan, of Water
> Street, it is established that Mr. Mark Twain's vile statement that the
> lamented grandfather of our noble standard-bearer, Blank J. Blank, was
> hanged for highway robbery, is a brutal and gratuitous LIE, without a
> shadow of foundation in fact. It is disheartening to virtuous men to see
> such shameful means resorted to to achieve political success as the
> attacking of the dead in their graves, and defiling their honored names
> with slander. When we think of the anguish this miserable falsehood must
> cause the innocent relatives and friends of the deceased, we are almost
> driven to incite an outraged and insulted public to summary and unlawful
> vengeance upon the traducer. But no! let us leave him to the agony of a
> lacerated conscience (though if passion should get the better of the
> public, and in its blind fury they should do the traducer bodily injury, it is
> but too obvious that no jury could convict and no court punish the
> perpetrators of the deed).

The ingenious closing sentence had the effect of moving me out of bed with despatch
that night, and out at the back door also, while the "outraged and insulted public" surged
in the front way, breaking furniture and windows in their righteous indignation as they
came, and taking off such property as they could carry when they went. And yet I can lay
my hand upon the Book and say that I never slandered Mr. Blank's grandfather. More: I
had never even heard of him or mentioned him up to that day and date.

[I will state, in passing, that the journal above quoted from always referred to me
afterward as "Twain, the Body-Snatcher."]

The next newspaper article that attracted my attention was the following:

> A SWEET CANDIDATE.—Mr. Mark Twain, who was to make such a
> blighting speech at the mass-meeting of the Independents last night,
> didn't come to time! A telegram from his physician stated that he had
> been knocked down by a runaway team, and his leg broken in two
> places—sufferer lying in great agony, and so forth, and so forth, and a lot
> more bosh of the same sort. And the Independents tried hard to swallow
> the wretched subterfuge, and pretend that they did not know what was
> the real reason of the absence of the abandoned creature whom they
> denominate their standard-bearer. A certain man was seen to reel into
> Mr. Twain's hotel last night in a state of beastly intoxication. It is the
> imperative duty of the Independents to prove that this besotted brute was
> not Mark Twain himself. We have them at last! This is a case that admits
> of no shirking. The voice of the people demands in thunder tones, "WHO
> WAS THAT MAN?"

It was incredible, absolutely incredible, for a moment, that it was really my name that
was coupled with this disgraceful suspicion. Three long years had passed over my head
since I had tasted ale, beer, wine or liquor of any kind.

[It shows what effect the times were having on me when I say that I saw myself,
confidently dubbed "Mr. Delirium Tremens Twain" in the next issue of that journal without
a pang—notwithstanding I knew that with monotonous fidelity the paper would go on
calling me so to the very end.]

By this time anonymous letters were getting to be an important part of my mail matter.
This form was common:

> How about that old woman you kiked of your premises which was beging.
> POL. PRY.

And this:

> There is things which you have done which is unbeknowens to anybody
> but me. You better trot out a few dots, to yours truly, or you'll hear through
> the papers from
> HANDY ANDY.

This is about the idea. I could continue them till the reader was surfeited, if desirable.

Shortly the principal Republican journal "convicted" me of wholesale bribery, and the
leading Democratic paper "nailed" an aggravated case of blackmailing to me.

[In this way I acquired two additional names: "Twain the Filthy Corruptionist" and "Twain
the Loathsome Embracer."]

By this time there had grown to be such a clamor for an "answer" to all the dreadful
charges that were laid to me that the editors and leaders of my party said it would be
political ruin for me to remain silent any longer. As if to make their appeal the more
imperative, the following appeared in one of the papers the very next day:

BEHOLD THE MAN!—The independent candidate still maintains silence. Because he dare not speak. Every accusation against him has been amply proved, and they have been indorsed and reindorsed by his own eloquent silence, till at this day he stands forever convicted. Look upon your candidate, Independents! Look upon the Infamous Perjurer! the Montana Thief! the Body-Snatcher! Contemplate your incarnate Delirium Tremens! your Filthy Corruptionist! your Loathsome Embracer! Gaze upon him—ponder him well—and then say if you can give your honest votes to a creature who has earned this dismal array of titles by his hideous crimes, and dares not open his mouth in denial of any one of them!

There was no possible way of getting out of it, and so, in deep humiliation, I set about preparing to "answer" a mass of baseless charges and mean and wicked falsehoods. But I never finished the task, for the very next morning a paper came out with a new horror, a fresh malignity, and seriously charged me with burning a lunatic asylum with all its inmates, because it obstructed the view from my house. This threw me into a sort of panic. Then came the charge of poisoning my uncle to get his property, with an imperative demand that the grave should be opened. This drove me to the verge of distraction. On top of this I was accused of employing toothless and incompetent old relatives to prepare the food for the foundling hospital when I warden. I was wavering—wavering. And at last, as a due and fitting climax to the shameless persecution that party rancor had inflicted upon me, nine little toddling children, of all shades of color and degrees of raggedness, were taught to rush onto the platform at a public meeting, and clasp me around the legs and call me PA!

I gave it up. I hauled down my colors and surrendered. I was not equal to the requirements of a Gubernatorial campaign in the state of New York, and so I sent in my withdrawal from the candidacy, and in bitterness of spirit signed it, "Truly yours, once a decent man, but now

"MARK TWAIN, LLP., M.T., B.S., D.T., F.C., and L.E."

A MYSTERIOUS VISIT

The first notice that was taken of me when I "settled down" recently was by a gentleman who said he was an assessor, and connected with the U. S. Internal Revenue Department. I said I had never heard of his branch of business before, but I was very glad to see him all the same. Would he sit down? He sat down. I did not know anything particular to say, and yet I felt that people who have arrived at the dignity of keeping house must be conversational, must be easy and sociable in company. So, in default of anything else to say, I asked him if he was opening his shop in our neighborhood.

He said he was. [I did not wish to appear ignorant, but I had hoped he would mention what he had for sale.]

I ventured to ask him "How was trade?" And he said "So-so."

I then said we would drop in, and if we liked his house as well as any other, we would give him our custom.

He said he thought we would like his establishment well enough to confine ourselves to it—said he never saw anybody who would go off and hunt up another man in his line after trading with him once.

That sounded pretty complacent, but barring that natural expression of villainy which we all have, the man looked honest enough.

I do not know how it came about exactly, but gradually we appeared to melt down and run together, conversationally speaking, and then everything went along as comfortably as clockwork.

We talked, and talked, and talked—at least I did; and we laughed, and laughed, and laughed—at least he did. But all the time I had my presence of mind about me—I had my native shrewdness turned on "full head," as the engineers say. I was determined to find out all about his business in spite of his obscure answers—and I was determined I would have it out of him without his suspecting what I was at. I meant to trap him with a deep, deep ruse. I would tell him all about my own business, and he would naturally so warm to me during this seductive burst of confidence that he would forget himself, and tell me all about his affairs before he suspected what I was about. I thought to myself, My son, you little know what an old fox you are dealing with. I said:

"Now you never would guess what I made lecturing this winter and last spring?"

"No—don't believe I could, to save me. Let me see—let me see. About two thousand dollars, maybe? But no; no, sir, I know you couldn't have made that much. Say seventeen hundred, maybe?"

"Ha! ha! I knew you couldn't. My lecturing receipts for last spring and this winter were fourteen thousand seven hundred and fifty dollars. What do you think of that?"

"Why, it is amazing-perfectly amazing. I will make a note of it. And you say even this wasn't all?"

"All! Why bless you, there was my income from the Daily Warwhoop for four months—about—about—well, what should you say to about eight thousand dollars, for instance?"

"Say! Why, I should say I should like to see myself rolling in just such another ocean of affluence. Eight thousand! I'll make a note of it. Why man!—and on top of all this am I to understand that you had still more income?"

"Ha! ha! ha! Why, you're only in the suburbs of it, so to speak. There's my book, The Innocents Abroad—price $3.50 to $5, according to the binding. Listen to me. Look me in the eye. During the last four months and a half, saying nothing of sales before that, but just simply during the four months and a half, we've sold ninety-five thousand copies of that book. Ninety-five thousand! Think of it. Average four dollars a copy, say. It's nearly four hundred thousand dollars, my son. I get half."

"The suffering Moses! I'll set that down. Fourteen-seven—fifty-eight—two hundred. Total, say—well, upon my word, the grand total is about two hundred and thirteen or fourteen thousand dollars! Is that possible?"

"Possible! If there's any mistake it's the other way. Two hundred and fourteen thousand, cash, is my income for this year if I know how to cipher."

Then the gentleman got up to go. It came over me most uncomfortably that maybe I had made my revelations for nothing, besides being flattered into stretching them considerably by the stranger's astonished exclamations. But no; at the last moment the gentleman handed me a large envelope, and said it contained his advertisement; and that I would find out all about his business in it; and that he would be happy to have my custom—would, in fact, be proud to have the custom of a man of such prodigious income; and that he used to think there were several wealthy men in the city, but when they came to trade with him he discovered that they barely had enough to live on; and that, in truth, it had been such a weary, weary age since he had seen a rich man face to face, and talked to him, and touched him with his hands, that he could hardly refrain from embracing me—in fact, would esteem it a great favor if I would let him embrace me.

This so pleased me that I did not try to resist, but allowed this simple-hearted stranger to throw his arms about me and weep a few tranquilizing tears down the back of my neck. Then he went his way.

As soon as he was gone I opened his advertisement. I studied it attentively for four minutes. I then called up the cook, and said:

"Hold me while I faint! Let Marie turn the griddle-cakes."

By and by, when I came to, I sent down to the rum-mill on the corner and hired an artist by the week to sit up nights and curse that stranger, and give me a lift occasionally in the daytime when I came to a hard place.

Ah, what a miscreant he was! His "advertisement" was nothing in the world but a wicked tax-return—a string of impertinent questions about my private affairs, occupying the best part of four fools-cap pages of fine print—questions, I may remark, gotten up with such marvelous ingenuity that the oldest man in the world couldn't understand what the most of them were driving at—questions, too, that were calculated to make a man report about four times his actual income to keep from swearing to a falsehood. I looked for a loophole, but there did not appear to be any. Inquiry No. 1 covered my case as generously and as amply as an umbrella could cover an ant-hill:

> What were your profits, during the past year, from any trade, business, or vocation, wherever carried on?

And that inquiry was backed up by thirteen others of an equally searching nature, the most modest of which required information as to whether I had committed any burglary or highway robbery, or by any arson or other secret source of emolument had acquired property which was not enumerated in my statement of income as set opposite to inquiry No. 1.

It was plain that that stranger had enabled me to make a goose of myself. It was very, very plain; and so I went out and hired another artist. By working on my vanity, the stranger had seduced me into declaring an income of two hundred and fourteen thousand dollars. By law, one thousand dollars of this was exempt from income tax—the only relief I could see, and it was only a drop in the ocean. At the legal five per cent., I must pay to the government the sum of ten thousand six hundred and fifty dollars, income tax!

[I may remark, in this place, that I did not do it.]

I am acquainted with a very opulent man, whose house is a palace, whose table is regal, whose outlays are enormous, yet a man who has no income, as I have often noticed by the revenue returns; and to him I went for advice in my distress. He took my dreadful exhibition of receipts, he put on his glasses, he took his pen, and presto!—I was a pauper! It was the neatest thing that ever was. He did it simply by deftly manipulating the bill of "DEDUCTIONS." He set down my "State, national, and municipal taxes" at so much; my "losses by shipwreck; fire, etc.," at so much; my "losses on sales of real estate"—on "live stock sold"—on "payments for rent of homestead"—on "repairs, improvements, interest"—on "previously taxed salary as an officer of the United States army, navy, revenue service," and other things. He got astonishing "deductions" out of each and every one of these matters—each and every one of them. And when he was done he handed me the paper, and I saw at a glance that during the year my income, in the way of profits, had been one thousand two hundred and fifty dollars and forty cents.

"Now," said he, "the thousand dollars is exempt by law. What you want to do is to go and swear this document in and pay tax on the two hundred and fifty dollars."

[While he was making this speech his little boy Willie lifted a two-dollar greenback out of his vest pocket and vanished with it, and I would wager anything that if my stranger were to call on that little boy to-morrow he would make a false return of his income.]

"Do you," said I, "do you always work up the 'deductions' after this fashion in your own case, sir?"

"Well, I should say so! If it weren't for those eleven saving clauses under the head of 'Deductions' I should be beggared every year to support this hateful and wicked, this extortionate and tyrannical government."

This gentleman stands away up among the very best of the solid men of the city—the men of moral weight, of commercial integrity, of unimpeachable social spotlessness—and so I bowed to his example. I went down to the revenue office, and under the accusing eyes of my old visitor I stood up and swore to lie after lie, fraud after fraud, villainy after villainy, till my soul was coated inches and inches thick with perjury, and my self-respect gone for ever and ever.

But what of it? It is nothing more than thousands of the richest and proudest, and most respected, honored, and courted men in America do every year. And so I don't care. I am not ashamed. I shall simply, for the present, talk little and eschew fire-proof gloves, lest I fall into certain dreadful habits irrevocably.